A Death Dwellers MC Novel

Bridge Book

By

Kathryn C. Kelly

Reckless
A Death Dwellers MC Novel
By Kathryn C. Kelly
Ebook ISBN: 978-0692-28091-1
Paperback ISBN: 979-8-88630-007-9

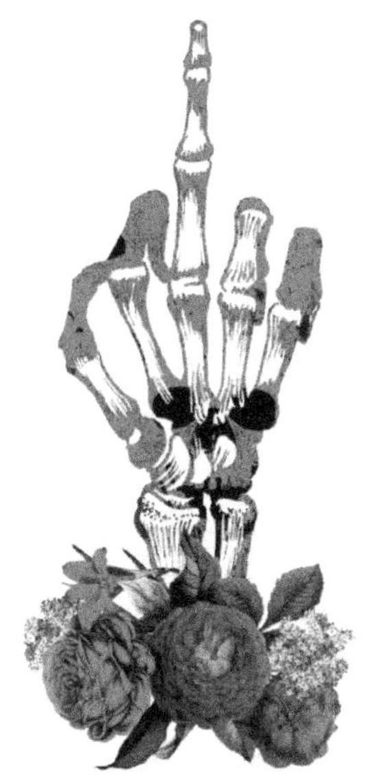

Dedication

Chapter Fifteen is dedicated to Kate. She knows why.

I also dedicate this book to CJ's fans. Thank you.

Blurb

Being the son of a legend isn't easy...

And though CJ Caldwell idolizes his father, Outlaw, he's not sure he'll ever live up to the Caldwell reputation. Worse, he's not sure he'll get the chance. CJ must finish high school and attend college before he will even be considered as a prospect for the Death Dwellers.

To Outlaw, he wants the possibility of a different life for CJ. Whether his boy joins the MC isn't a requirement of his and Meggie's love and support. There's only one thing CJ wants more than his father's approval, the only girl for him, Harley Banks.

But when he asks her to go steady, she shoots him down cold, breaking his heart. Now CJ faces becoming a man, coping with heartache, and saving his cousin, Ryan, from the wrong crowd.

Death Dweller Families

OG Death Dweller Families

Donovan
Logan
Elmira - wife
Simon - son
Patricia - daughter
Tess - daughter

Caldwell
Sebastian "Cee Cee"
Kimber - sister
Bash - son
Celia - daughter
Patricia - Outlaw's mother
Outlaw - son
Tess - Johnnie's mother
Johnnie -son
Several other sons and daughters

Banks
Sharper
Vivian - wife
Mortician - Son
Digger- Son
Charlemagne - 2nd Wife

Bart
Wallace "Rack"
Willard - son

Andrews
Kaleb Paul "K-P"
Roxanne - girlfriend
Bailey - daughter

Foy
Joseph "Big Joe"
Kimber - girlfriend
Joey - son with Kimber
Dinah - girlfriend
Megan - Big Joe's daughter with Dinah
Randolph (Big Joe's grandson)

Current Death Dweller Families

Caldwell
Christopher "Outlaw"
Megan - wife
Christopher Joseph Foy "CJ" - son
Patrick (son, didn't survive birth)
Rebel - (Fraternal twin daughter)
Rule - (Fraternal twin son)
Ryder - son
Axel -son
Gunner - son
Diesel - (adopted son)

Donovan
Johne "Johnnie"
Kendall - wife
Rory -son
Matilda - daughter
JJ - son
Blade - son

Taylor
Matthew "Val"
Zoann - wife
Ryan - son
Devon - son

L Banks
Lucas "Mortician"
Bailey - wife
Harley - daughter
Lou - son
Kaleb - son
Tyler (son from previous relationship with Charlemagne, killed at sixteen)

M Banks
Marcus "Digger"
Albany "Bunny" - wife
Mark JB - son
Ephraim - son
Steele - son
Link - son
Cove - son

McCall/King
Cash "Ghost" McCall - husband
Louis "Stretch" King - husband
Ophelia - girlfriend
Jasper - son
Wynona - daughter
Kade - son
Tarmac - son

Harrington
Knox
Roxanne - wife
Grant (Knox's son from first marriage)

Death Dweller Family Friends

Mason
Shane
Georgiana "Georgie" - wife
Brynn - daughter
Son
Son

Baptiste
Cameron
Jordan "Doc Will" - wife
Ava - daughter
Cam, Jr -son

Redding
Brooks
Charlotte - wife

Hamilton
Walt
Virginia - wife
Albany - daughter
Gabe - son

Family Ties

Big Joe and Dinah are Meggie's parents. He is also Outlaw's mentor and Snake's father.
Cee Cee is Outlaw and Johnnie's father.
Christopher's sisters are Zoanne, Ophelia, Nia (deceased), Avery (deceased) and Bev (deceased).
Christopher and Johnnie are first cousins and half brothers, sharing the same father with two sisters as their mothers.
Cash is Georgie's older brother.
Doc Will is Meggie's obstetrician, Roxanne's good friend and married to Knox's best bud
Walt Hamilton has club ties and his daughter is married to Digger Banks
Brooks is the club's lead attorney and is a father figure to Kendall Donovan

OG Ladies
Elmira Donovan - Logan's wife
Patricia Donovan - Christopher's mother
Tess Donovan - Johnnie's mother
Marie Miller - Kendall's mother
Dinah Nicholls - Big Joe's woman
Roxanne Doucette - K-P's woman
Vivian Banks - Sharper's wife
Charlemagne Banks - Sharper's 2nd wife
Mandy "Hopper" Stevens - Snake's ol' lady

Free Birds
Logan Donovan
Sharper Banks
Sebastian "Cee Cee" Caldwell
Big Joe "Boss" Foy
Joey Foy
Simon Donovan
Kaleb "K-P" Andrews
Wallace "Rack" Bart

OG Parents
Cee Cee Caldwell and Patricia Donovan - Christopher
Cee Cee Caldwell and Tess Donovan - Johnnie
Big Joe Foy and Dinah Brister - Meggie
K-P Andrews and Roxanne Doucette - Bailey
Sharper and Vivan Banks - Mortician and Digger
Mortician and Charlemagne - Tyler
Snake and Hopper - Randolph
Knox and Callie - Grant

Notes

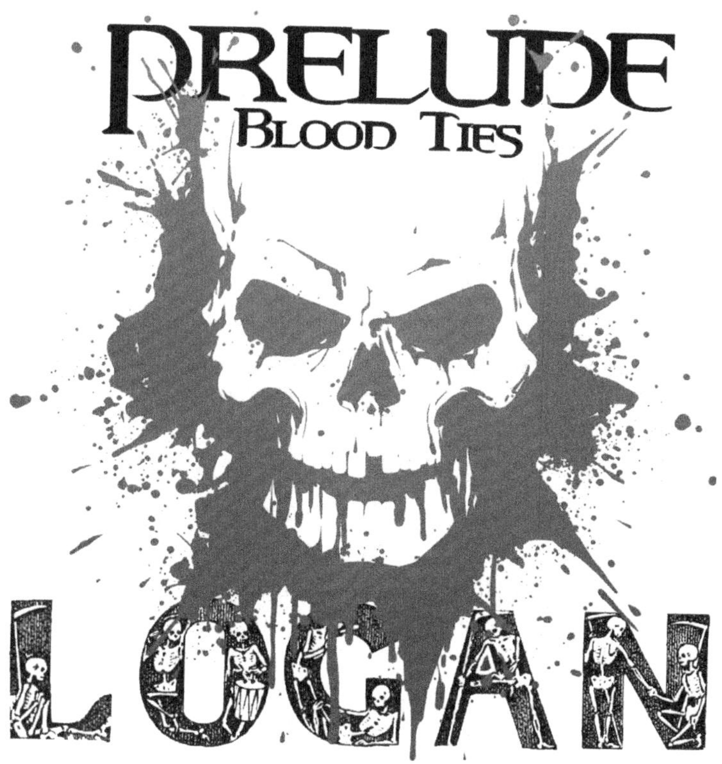

Logan Donovan didn't give a damn how many corpses he'd leave.

One day, he'd be Heaven and Hell. A harbinger of death or a man of mercy. The Alpha and the Omega. Men would fear him and women would follow him.

Today wasn't that time.

Today, he sat *in* Hell—metaphorically—power still elusive.

He swallowed tequila, then wiped his mouth and set the bottle aside, ignoring Cee Cee's gun to study Sharper Banks while he focused on his theology textbook. Tall and lean, the beautiful man's skin veered between medium brown to dark, depending on the time he spent in the sun.

Sebastian Caldwell, aka Cee Cee, drew on his cigarette and the cherry glowed bright red. "I need my cock sucked," he said, flicking ashes onto the broken concrete floor. His startingly green eyes were frightening, his black hair recalling a Devil's spawn.

Smoke and mustiness hung in the air. Not to mention *musk*. Cee Cee reeked of sweat, sex, motor oil, weed, and alcohol.

"Maybe, I should have sweet Patricia again."

Cee Cee's gun deterred Logan from lunging at the animal. He'd violated Logan's precious Pattie and she was now four months pregnant with Sebastian Caldwell's demon. He detested that unborn beast almost as much as he despised its father. "You've done enough," he snapped. "Leave my baby girl alone."

Cee Cee polished off the rum, then smoked his cigarette again. "You have another bitch. Send her to me."

While Tess, his other daughter, was more expendable—she wasn't Pattie—Logan loathed Cee Cee taking the upper hand again. To get Pattie away from Cee Cee, he'd had to send his wife to the man. Elmira hadn't wanted to go, but, as much as it pained him, he'd beaten her into submission. She was a good woman and had stolen his heart the moment he met her. He cherished Pattie so much because she was almost a carbon copy of her mother with her brown hair and brown eyes.

"Where the fuck are your boys, Logan? If I don't get a cunt to take the edge off while I'm waiting for my fucking money, I'll lose my shit. You'll never have a proper fucking club. You know nothing. You're supposed to have bitches to keep visitors happy."

Sharper raised his head and lifted a brow at Cee Cee, who flushed and looked away. Logan met Sharper at Cee Cee's strip club on his very first visit two years ago.

Often, he pondered if Cee Cee and Sharper were lovers. Sharper liked dick as much as pussy. However, Cee Cee loved quim so much he just took it if he wanted to fuck and found no willing females.

Cee Cee threw his used-up cigarette on the floor and stomped it. "Contact me when Patricia goes into labor."

Logan wanted his girl to abort the lunatic's monster, but she'd begged to keep it. She'd suffered enough, so Logan capitulated. Pattie giving birth would allow him to take care of the loathsome bastard himself, reclaim the dignity he'd lost when Cee Cee violated his daughter and filled her belly with his devil seed.

"You heard me?" Cee Cee stroked his gun. His .44 Magnum rested next to his almost empty bottle of rum. The barrel pointed toward Logan, by accident or design. But knowing Cee Cee, that fucking gun lay in Logan's direction on purpose. "If it's a son, I'll claim it just as I have all the others."

"How many children do you have?" Logan asked, curious despite himself.

Cee Cee shrugged. "Eight I'm aware of, but it might be more. Who cares? I can't worry about the motherfuckers I don't know." Picking up the weapon, he offered Logan a half-smile. "I know my kid's dropping out of Pattie's pussy because *you* told me I knocked her up."

Chilling madness sharpened the planes and angles of Cee Cee's features. His eyes were cold and flat. The eyes of death.

"Why'd you tell me about her pregnancy again?" Cee Cee rubbed his chin. "Hoping to gain leverage? Wanting me to feel guilty? What, motherfucker? I'm clueless why you informed me I knocked her up. You don't want my name on the birth certificate. You don't want the kid, but I draw the line at harming babies and children. If I were you, I'd erase any motherfucking thought of harming my kid. Or *else*."

Logan didn't like 'or else'. Nor did he want to piss off Cee Cee.

To someday wield the same power in his young club as Cee Cee did as founder and president of the American Scorpions, he needed the man. Logan's own club, the Death Dwellers, floundered after only a year in existence. He'd turned Sharper's brainchild into a reality. For all intents and purposes, the MC was *Logan's*. On the surface, Sharper wasn't involved with the club. Couldn't have a man of God fraternizing with criminals.

"Does it matter why I told you, Cee Cee?"

What a fucking miscalculation he'd made. He regretted not listening to Sharper, who'd warned him not to inform Cee Cee of Pattie's pregnancy. Logan hadn't appreciated the likes of Sharper issuing orders. Another mistake. "I didn't expect your pride over my daughter's pregnancy."

"Why the fuck not? My children are my legacy."

"That's why you're so involved in their lives," Sharper inserted with sarcasm, not bothering to lift his gaze from his textbook.

Slamming his gun on the table, Cee Cee glared at Sharper's bent head. "Fuck off. I didn't ask for your fucking input."

"Tough shit," Sharper said. "I gave it anyway."

"Motherfuck you, asshole," Cee Cee growled.

Sharper snapped the thick book shut. His teeth flashed white against his brown skin, his smile transforming his entire countenance. He transcended beauty to a magnificence Logan couldn't describe.

No fucking way he'd ever reveal *he* had fallen in love with...*Fuck*...Not only with a man, but a *Black*. Logan hated anyone not his own kind. Sometimes, he hated

Sharper for being so well-spoken and fascinating. He hated his brilliance that deviated between spiritual, philosophical, maniacal, and criminal.

"You still haven't told me you'll follow my orders, Donovan."

Motherfucking Cee Cee was getting out of hand.

"My girl isn't keeping your fucking monster. She's been through enough, so I'll let her carry your garbage, but then I intend to throw away that fucking spawn."

Shock darkened Cee Cee's eyes. Satisfaction eased Logan's stung pride and he swallowed more tequila.

The door to the small building blew open and Joe Foy sauntered in, Kaleb Andrews hot on his heels. Where one went, the other followed. Cee Cee grinned in Joe's direction. He was tall and muscled, with true blue eyes complementing his golden hair. Logan had made a play for the young gun, but he'd backed off at Joe's sound rebuff.

Reaching their table, Joe glowered at Cee Cee.

"Hello, Joe," Cee Cee greeted, the light of insanity surrounding him, like an aura from hell.

Joe nodded, unafraid and unaffected. "Motherfucker."

Sharper and Kaleb glared at each other, as little love lost between them as between Joe and Cee Cee.

The door opened again, bringing in Wally Bart. Black-haired and pig-eyed, he was one mean motherfucker and had a penchant for Medieval torture methods. If he ever patched in, Logan already had his road name: *Rack*.

Cee Cee smirked. "If this isn't a nice little family gathering."

"Fuck off," Joe growled, turning to the crudely constructed bar, another source of Logan's humiliation. The entire situation shamed him. Without *family*, he never would've gotten any members for the club Sharper wanted so badly.

The penniless Death Dwellers consisted of six members, with a metal storage shed for a clubhouse that was set up on overgrown land backing onto the forest for a clubhouse. He'd thought about having their meeting place on his dilapidated farm. Though Cee Cee's fixation on Pattie came in handy, it also changed Logan's mind about the location. Besides, having the clubhouse several miles from where he lived allowed him time alone with Sharper.

Joe sipped from a bottle of tequila; Kaleb Paul swigged hot beer; Wally positioned himself on the other side of Joe, the center of the universe, a radiant being amongst lowly men who pulled everyone into his orbit.

If only Logan had been lucky enough to *have* fathered Joe. Or if *he'd* taken an interest in Patricia. But at twenty-one or twenty-two, he had a conscience. Pattie was fifteen, a child in Joe's eyes. Untouchable.

He'd only seen her from afar. If they met formally, Joe would want her. Yet, the kid refused all invitations Logan extended to visit the farm for dinner.

Joe tipped his bottle toward him. Licking his lips, Logan nodded.

Underneath the table, Sharper kicked his shin. Pain streaked up Logan's leg, the point on Sharper's Derby shoes an effective weapon. "I told you to stop looking at that motherfucker like the sun rises and shines in him. I think you want to fuck him, too."

Leaning back, Cee Cee assumed a negligent pose in the uncomfortable wooden chair. "Too?"

Logan wouldn't tempt fate and confront Cee Cee a second time. Instead, he faced Sharper. "Watch your fucking mouth."

"Suck my fucking cock." Sharper grinned. "Or maybe not. Withholding dick is a better punishment."

Cee Cee's wild laughter captured Joe, Kaleb, and Wally's attention. Hot shame roared through Logan.

"As entertaining as you and your suck boy are, Sharper, *where* the fuck are his motherfuckers with my bitch? I'm here for *her*. Her pussy is my moneymaker and I think Logan and his boys are fucking me over. Our deal was five bitches. This is the third slut and every time, there's a fucking problem. At least *they* arrived. This time..." His voice trailed off and he glared at Logan. "It's *my* fucking money who's fronting this shitty hole you call a club. I lose her, I lose dollars. I also lose fucking face. I already have a buyer for this bitch. I fronted your portion because of your fucking begging, Logan. Now, where the fuck is she?"

Sweat beading his brow, Logan glanced at the door. He'd sent his motherfuckers out hours ago to do a job and they needed to return *now* before Cee Cee lost his temper. Or overheard anymore damning information.

Resting his forearms on the table, Sharper grunted. "You have a fucking problem on your hands, Donovan."

Logan glared at Sharper. A kernel of detestation planted in his gut. "Back off, boy," he growled, still smarting from Sharper's kick.

"You're fucking with the wrong motherfucker," Sharper sneered, hurt quickly morphing into anger. "*You* back the fuck off before you're sorry."

Logan snapped his mouth shut. Sharper, the holy man, was also a killer.

"You disappoint me, Banks." Cee Cee grinned. "I've never known you to tolerate disrespect of this magnitude."

Logan imagined gouging Cee Cee's eyes out and wiping away that damnable enjoyment. Joe's blue gaze caught and held Sharper's dark one, his thoughts closed off.

The door flew open, and the five members of his club trooped in. Krag, Webster, Pete, Talbot, and Boyce rushed to the table. Blood and mud stained their denim cuts and torn jeans. Scratches marred their faces. Broken fingernails topped dirty hands.

The small, cramped shed couldn't comfortably house the club's minute brotherhood and their four guests.

Another nugget of hatred toward Sharper crystallized.

Logan had done all of this for Sharper—become a laughingstock, a weak motherfucker with a stagnant club. The Death Dwellers were just six fuckheads, too unorganized to be taken seriously.

"That whore attacked us. We had to chase her down," Boyce growled, wiping sweat from his brow. "Left us no choice but to fucking bury her."

Cee Cee roared to his feet and grabbed his .44. "*What*?"

Sharper rose too, while Joe, Kaleb, and Wally left their seats. The other four—Krag, Talbot, Webster, and Pete—shoved their hands in their pockets and shifted.

"Prez." Boyce's eyes implored Logan. "We didn't mean—"

The report of the gun halted the words. Blood and brain spattered them, making mincemeat of half of Boyce's face. His body dropped to the ground.

Krag pissed himself.

Cee Cee's maniacal laughter rose up. "The rounds I got in the chamber can drop a fucking bear." His humor dying, he shoved the gun against Logan's temple. "I shouldn't have ever trusted a fuckup like you to run bitches."

"Drop that fucking gun, Cee Cee," Sharper ordered.

"Fuck you." Cee Cee's hand shook. "You have the money to reimburse me for my lost bitch?"

"We'll get more bitches," Sharper promised, a hint of desperation creeping into his tone, as if he cared about what happened.

The fucking liar. He didn't give a fuck about Logan's well-being.

"That's not fucking answering my question," Cee Cee snarled. "I'm not a fucking bank. Defaulting on what you owe me is to your great detriment."

"Fuck off, you sick motherfucker." Joe stalked forward, stepping over Boyce's body, unperturbed by the gore. He threw a wad of cash against Cee Cee's chest.

Bills fluttered everywhere; Joe smirked.

"Take your fucking money and get the fuck away from me," Logan ordered, appreciating Joe's toughness. He'd put his money where his mouth was when no one else would.

Cee Cee dug the barrel deeper into Logan's skin. "One of these days, I swear to fuck I'll fuck you up, Joe."

Joe ignored the impotent anger in Cee Cee's promise. "Back the fuck away from Logan."

At the hammer cocking, Logan closed his eyes, willing himself not to piss his pants like Krag.

"Money's repaid," Cee Cee started, mad dog furious and almost foaming at the mouth. "Balls still full of cum. Dick need a bitch."

"Sounds like a fucking *you* problem, Sebastian," Kaleb pointed out.

"Who asked you, Kaleb Paul?" Cee Cee questioned.

Dislike twisted Kaleb's smile. "I'm all for blowing this dirty fuckhead away. But then, you and this motherfucker would still be around," he said, pointing to Sharper.

"Fuck off." Somehow, Cee Cee had enough focus to not pull the trigger. "One of these fucking days, you and Joe saving my fucking life won't be enough for me not to cut your fucking heads off."

"One of these days, I'll stop kicking myself in the fucking cock for saving *your* fucking ass." Joe reached inside his jacket, pulled a .357 and aimed it at Cee Cee. “Maybe, I’ll remedy my mistake tonight.”

“Your panties still in a twist because I fucked Patricia, Joe?”

Joe glared at him. “She’s a fucking child and you violated her, motherfucker.”

“Kaleb Paul’s self-righteousness is rubbing off on you.” Disgust sharpened each of Sharper’s words. “But, like him, you aren’t a cold-blooded killer. You can’t pull the trigger.”

“Well, Bible Bastard, at least we know you suffer no such problems,” Kaleb Paul said dryly.

Flipping the bird to Kaleb Paul, Sharper focused on Cee Cee. “Put the fucking gun down before you accidentally kill Logan, asshole.”

“Make me.” He smirked at Joe. “You can’t shoot me. You still have good in you and we made a pact. But I swear to Christ, if this motherfucker lives, you’ll all fucking pay. Logan Donovan is a fucking psychopath and he’ll destroy you all one by one.”

“Logan’s a good man, Cee Cee,” Wally countered.

“And you’re a stupid motherfucker, Wally. Donovan is insane.”

“If he’s insane, what the fuck are you?” Kaleb Paul demanded.

“Aww, shucks, you big softy. Fuck it. You’re right. Kill me.” Before Joe could react, Cee Cee pulled the trigger. The gun clicked. “I wonder if the next chamber is loaded.”

“Motherfuck you, Cee Cee,” Joe stormed, lowering his gun.

Piss streamed down Logan’s legs. “I’ll call you when Pattie gives birth to your brat,” he promised, his voice trembling. “And you can have Tess. Fuck her until she can’t walk. I don’t care. Just let me live.”

Fearing his own death more than anything, Logan ignored Joe's horror.

"You disapprove of the offer, Joe? Then let me get rid of this motherfucker. You see good in people when there's evil in everybody."

"The world is what you make it, Sebastian," Joe said quietly. "As long as we're alive we have hope for another day."

"You and Kaleb Paul maybe. Me, Sharper, and Wally? *This* motherfucker?" Cee Cee jiggled his gun against Logan's temple. "Never."

Joe's jaw clenched. "Let the fucking money be enough. Leave his daughter alone. You've already fucked one of them."

"And I intend to fuck the other one and fill her with my cum."

"You're such a fucking pig," Kaleb said with derision as Joe scrubbed a hand over his face and shoved his weapon away.

"What will it be, Joseph?" Cee Cee demanded. "I'm not taking his fucking offer unless I get my fucking money, too."

Swallowing, Joe glanced between Cee Cee and Logan, stark pain on his face. He looked young and vulnerable.

Cee Cee scowled. "You don't want me to kill this motherfucker. You've gotten it in your head he's a father figure. As much as I've tried to teach you, you're still a weak, pathetic motherfucker."

Joe's face darkened. "I don't want a fucking father who sells their own daughters."

"Then you're safe, fuckhead. He didn't sell Patricia."

Cee Cee's lie shocked Logan, but it served his own purpose so he remained silent.

"Logan gave her to me."

"Drop the fucking gun or kill the motherfucker," Kaleb snapped, much to Logan's fury. He'd remember those words. “Who the fuck are you trying to torture? Sharper or Joe?”

“Never liked talking and torture,” Cee Cee drawled. “But there’s beauty in it. Watching a motherfucker piss himself in fear.”

“Did I ever tell you you’re a fucking asshole?” Kaleb asked.

“Many times,” Sharper responded, then sighed. “Drop the gun, Cee Cee.”

“Nope. I want to see if there’s a bullet in the chamber the next time I pull the trigger.” Cee Cee stepped closer to Logan. “How’s it feel, Donovan? Most motherfuckers fear you or pity you.”

Fear him? As far as he knew, only his wife and daughters were afraid of him and they didn’t count. A cunt never did.

“The five of us have a lifelong allegiance nothing can break,” Cee Cee finished. “Kaleb?”

“Whatcha got?”

“You vote for Donovan’s execution?”

“I would,” he said without hesitation. “If it didn’t hurt Joe.”

“In the long run I’ll help Joe.”

“You know something I don’t?” Joe demanded.

Cee Cee snickered. “A fucking lot, puppy.”

Joe squinted at Cee Cee.

“Fuck, fine. As far as I know, Donovan has never spoke against you, Joe,” he admitted. “I just know men like him. He reminds you of your shithead old man? Well, this motherfucker does the same for me. Only I don’t wish to have him as a paternal stand-in. I got more fucking sense. Logan willingly sacrifices his wife and daughters. My old man sacrificed me to whomever and used me however he pleased. He said he loved me. That cunt that gave birth to me said she loved me too but turned a blind fucking eye to whatever happened to me.

She'd say how much she hated him then fuck him and get her pussy off—"

"Shut the fuck up, Cee Cee," Sharper ordered. "I don't want to hear that story another fucking time."

"Fuck you, Sharper. None of that shit happened to you, motherfucker, so choke on my fucking cock."

"Isn't your arm fucking tired by now?" Kaleb Paul asked with disgust.

"No!" Cee Cee screamed, wild-eyed. "They made me hang from bars for fucking hours. That slut didn't care when he played Russian Roulette with me."

"When who—"

"Don't fucking ask, Wally," Joe said, "otherwise we'll be here all fucking night."

Cee Cee's hand shook so violently Logan feared he'd pull the trigger by accident.

"You're just like him, Donovan." Cee Cee's voice dropped to a low, chilling whisper. "They don't see it, but I do. I checked you out. You had a decent life. You don't have a reason to hate bitches and mistrust motherfuckers. You're just a fucking animal who'd sacrifice all of us to save yourself. But I swear to you if you walk out of here with your brain in your fucking head, stay away from Sharper, Joe, Kaleb, and Wally. They are *all* like family to me. If you ever harm one of them, you're a dead man. Am I clear?"

"Yes," Logan croaked, his feet aching from standing in one place for so long.

"Cee Cee, fuck!" Joe huffed. "Fine. You're right. I saw Logan as a father figure but what I remember of *my* old man was someone who'd sacrifice himself instead of one of us." He shook his head and looked at Logan. "Your actions with your daughters disappoint me. I don't know if I'll ever look at you the same. On the occasions I spoke to your son, he praised you and said how much his sisters and mother adore you. I don't know how Pattie feels about you, but I remember how my mother suffered after my father left. I fool myself by saying I want to spare you for their sakes, but I'd be less than a man to tell that lie. No matter how disgusted I am by you, I still see good in you. A man misguided by a need for power." The pain, confusion and sadness in those blue-blue eyes touched Logan. "I don't want you to die even if I don't want you to live."

Later, Logan would calculate how to twist Joe's need for a father to his own benefit. Now, he adopted humbleness. "Son, I promise if you help me tonight, I'll never turn my back on you."

Cee Cee slapped the side of Logan's head. "You're a fucking liar. Joseph, I've told you time and fucking again, *don't* leave yourself vulnerable. Fuck, I should kill this motherfucker just for that. Since I hold you in such high esteem, what's your decision?"

"Let him live, Joe," Sharper said, before Joe responded. "For me."

Heaving in deep breaths, Joe glared at Sharper.

"We pledged our lifelong commitment to each other years ago," Sharper continued, pinning a look between Joe, Kaleb, Wally, and Cee Cee. "As boys struggling in that fucking foster system. We're brothers."

"Fuck you," Joe snapped, glowering at each of them. "I only have one fucking brother in here."

"One blood brother," Sharper corrected. "Now I'm asking you again, let Cee Cee keep the money and take Logan up on his offer for me."

His blue eyes blazing, Joe waved his hand. Cee Cee lowered the gun, while Sharper grabbed Logan's collar and turned him. Without shame, he covered Logan's mouth with his and settled a big hand on Logan's hip.

The scent of body fluids, his piss especially, rose in his nostrils, sharp and pungent. Thanks to his emptied bladder, his underwear plastered to his skin. He wanted to change and have a celebratory drink he was still breathing. More than anything, however, he wanted to wash his mouth and skin, relieve himself of the shame of Sharper's touch.

The moment his lover released him, Logan turned to Joe. "Thank you, son."

Joe stiffened. "I didn't do it for you."

"Yes," Logan said with a nod. "But I'd like you to be a part of my club."

"This isn't a fucking social club where invitations are issued. It's a fucking MC. There are rules and requirements. Initiations. Probationary periods."

"I don't know how to do it, Joe," Logan admitted.

"Did you hear?" Wally inserted, awed. "It takes a mighty fine man to admit he's in over his head. Sir, Mr. Donovan, I'd like to join."

Cee Cee glared at Wally. "How the fuck can you join the Death Dwellers, fuckhead?"

"You're here, Sebastian," Wally snapped.

Undercurrents of resentment flowed between the two men. Uncertain, Logan glanced at Wally.

Joe rolled his eyes. "You want to join, motherfucker?" he demanded. "Get rid of this dead motherfucker and clean this fucking gore."

A muscle ticked in Cee Cee's jaw, but he nodded.

At the go-ahead, Wally stripped off his shirt and jacket, grabbed Boyce's feet and began dragging him away.

"You four," Joe said, indicating Krag, Webster, Pete, and Talbot. "Get the fuck out. Tonight's happening stays in this motherfucker if you want your brains in your heads. Understand?"

They didn't need to be told twice. Slipping in Krag's piss and Boyce's blood, they scrambled the short distance to the door and left.

Cee Cee slid his gun into his side holster. “I have a bitch to fuck,” he said, heading toward the door.

“Cee Cee?” Joe’s voice fell like shards of ice in the small space. “When you walk away, the girl better be alive.”

After Cee Cee left the shed, Joe glanced from Logan to Sharper. “You’re fucking him,” he said, thrusting a chin in Logan’s direction. “What about Vivian?”

“Vivian?” Logan echoed.

“His fiancée,” Kaleb supplied absently, ignoring Logan’s sharp intake of breath.

“What about her?” Sharper demanded. “I still intend to marry her. Do you know how far in life I’ll go—we’ll *all* go—with the wealth and connections her family has?”

Joe turned and started for the door, Kaleb following behind.

“Wait, son,” Logan called, oddly hurt at discovering Sharper’s engagement.

“Fuck off, Logan,” Joe blazed, swinging to him again, though Kaleb left the building. “You’re just a pathetic motherfucker.”

“I—”

“How could you sacrifice your own fucking daughter? *Another* fucking daughter?”

“Joe—”

“Fuck you. I don’t want to hear it.”

Joe’s rejection piled pain onto Logan’s hurt and humiliation. For now, nothing could be done, so he nodded. “I understand. But you saved me, son. You.”

“I did it for him,” Joe reminded him, pointing to Sharper.

“It doesn’t matter,” Logan said thickly. “I am forever indebted to you.”

Growling in frustration, Joe yanked open the door, storming out without another word.

"Don't worry," Sharper soothed, a hand on Logan's shoulder. "He'll come around. He's not down with hurting bitches. He's kicked Cee Cee's ass more than once for trafficking broads. The way he defends those fucking sluts, you'd think they were high-born ladies."

"Why'd he come tonight?"

Logan had been unaware of Joe and Kaleb's return to Hortensia. Or, maybe they were back in town for school, where they'd enrolled at the local community college for certification as mechanics. They'd come down from Seattle to Hortensia and somehow met Cee Cee, who'd given them positions as bouncers at his Portland strip club. Meanwhile, Wally hovered in the background, never quite accepted by the golden boy and his sidekick.

"Cee Cee's been running off at the fucking mouth about Tess. I think Joe came to make sure nothing happened to her. His pride's hurting you offered her up as your sacrificial lamb."

Sharper sighed. "That didn't matter to Cee Cee," Logan said quietly. "If Joe hadn't allowed him to keep the money..." His voice trailed off. "I need him as president."

"He'll come around eventually."

Betrayal

TESS

"*Uno*!"

"No fair, Pattie. You're a cheat."

"*You're* the cheat, Simon," Pattie said with a little sniff.

"I'm twenty, girl," Simon snapped. "I know a cheat when I see one."

"Enough! Your bickering is giving me a headache. Your father expects peace when he comes home. Your defiance has stressed him out enough, missy."

"Keeping my baby isn't defiance, Mama," Pattie retorted tiredly.

"Hush your dreadful mouth."

Simon snickered at Mama's rebuke.

Leaning back on the sofa, Tess Donovan closed her eyes. Pattie announcing her pregnancy lent additional misery to their lives. Daddy shouted at every little infraction. He stayed away longer. He punched and kicked Mama and Simon more. In turn, Mama grew meaner. Extra gray streaked her brown tresses. She no longer bothered dyeing her hair. The wrinkles in her face supported the gray better than the color of her youth, anyway.

Mama wasn't old. She was just Daddy's wife and it showed in her posture, her attitude, and her features.

Tess intended to escape her family the day she turned eighteen. If she stayed, she'd end up with a man of Daddy's choice. Little by little, her soul would die, and she'd end up just like Mama.

Hopeless and helpless, living at her husband's whims in a house badly needing repairs.

Pattie threw her lone game card on the coffee table and stood from the floor. "I don't want to play anymore." She dusted the back of her jeans, then squeezed next to Tess on the faded floral-print sofa. She laid her head on Tess's shoulder.

She caressed Pattie's brown hair. "Are you tired?"

"I stay tired," Pattie responded.

"You're a pathetic weakling," Simon mocked. Though he had Mama's brown eyes, he resembled Daddy with his blond hair and hawkish features, but Simon's blind loyalty made *him* pathetic and weak.

"Indeed, she is, son," Mama agreed in the self-righteous tone Tess hated.

But she hated a lot about her family. The abuse. The coldness. The rigidity.

Daddy.

She even hated her name, bestowed upon her thanks to one Mr. Thomas Hardy and Daddy's love of the book *Tess of the d'Urbervilles*. Instead of sympathizing, Daddy felt the character got her just desserts.

Tess *Donovan* disagreed. Knowing she'd been named after such a tragic heroine taunted her. She lived a dreadful existence as Logan Donovan's youngest child. As his child, period. Simon, the eldest, served as Daddy's verbal and physical punching bag. Pattie had been his favorite, until she turned up pregnant. The more she begged to keep her baby, the more he turned against her.

He finally agreed to her wish, though Tess doubted Daddy's sincerity. The first chance he got after its birth, he'd hurt Pattie, her baby, or both.

Recently, Daddy turned his attention to her. She was the good, obedient one. His new perfect child. Tess didn't like it. She didn't like *him*. No, she feared him. He obsessed over those he deemed *perfect*. He objectified perfection.

Pattie had been perfect, so he hadn't wanted her to work outside of the home. He didn't want her mind polluted with filth. She couldn't laugh too loud or look him in the eye or answer him. When she'd been stolen, Daddy went out of his mind with grief and anger. He'd taken out his fury on Simon and beat him to a bloody pulp. Then, he beat Mama and made her go and get Pattie back, leaving Tess alone to fend for herself and nurse Simon, even though the scent of spilled blood turned her stomach and the sight of it made her throw up.

She'd never seen Daddy drink as much or cuss or cry. He'd almost seemed human. For three days, she'd cooked all his meals, kept laundry, mopped and vacuumed, triaged Simon, and went to the babysitting job Daddy allowed her to have. Then Mama returned, looking so much worse than when she'd left all beaten and bruised. Pattie, assaulted and terrorized, was with her.

At the opening and closing of the front door, Pattie lifted her head. Tension settled into Tess. Daddy was back. She regretted not excusing herself earlier and escaping to her room.

A jingle accompanied each footstep down the hallway toward the family room. Hands flying to her mouth, Pattie stood. Horror twisted Mama's wrinkly features a moment before Simon's confused, "Mother?"

"What are you doing here?" she gasped.

Next to Tess, Pattie trembled.

Tess laid her hand on her sister's knee and looked toward the door. A tall, scary man stood there. Dressed in denim, he had black hair, green eyes, and a cruel mouth.

"Cee Cee," Simon managed. He'd gone ashen, his usual viciousness evaporating. "Wh-what are you doing here? Daddy's at a meeting. I-I-I can guide you there."

Cee Cee folded his arms and leaned against the doorframe. "I just left your old man."

Simon turned beet red but went silent.

"Logan knows you're here?" Mama asked faintly.

"He sent me," Cee Cee replied. His nonchalant manner frightened Tess. He looked at Pattie, walked closer. "What's up, girl?" he asked, holding out his hand.

Fear stopped Tess from snatching Pattie and running. But she wasn't brave so she watched as her sister stood and went to Cee Cee, hesitating a moment before she took his hand. She didn't protest his pulling her toward the hall.

"Wait, please!" Mama called.

"Shut your fucking mouth," Cee Cee ordered, not breaking his stride.

"Go to your room, Tess," Mama said briskly, once it was only the three of them.

"What about Pattie, Mama?"

"Do you want me to slap her, Mama?" Simon's eyes gleamed with the same malice Daddy exhibited.

"There'll be time enough later," Mama responded, then nodded toward the door. "Go, Tess."

"Y-yes, ma'am," Tess said, unease settling into her. Mama and Daddy didn't allow her to move furniture in her room without permission. Tonight, she'd quietly drag her small desk in front of her door. Not much of a deterrent, but enough so she'd hear someone trying to get in. Hopefully, it would afford her enough time to sneak out of her window and hide.

She didn't want to be stolen like Pattie.

Stumbling away, she crept past the living room. Hearing voices, she paused once she cleared the doorway.

"I mean it," Cee Cee was saying. "I might not be available immediately, but I'll get your message. Understand?"

"You've seen Daddy and he told you—"

"Don't worry, Pattie. I reached an understanding with Logan."

Good for Cee Cee. To Tess, Daddy was beyond comprehension and never kept any of his promises.

At the sound of kissing, Tess hurried down the hallway to her bedroom. Inside, she closed her door and turned on her bedside lamp, puzzled by her sister's behavior. Pattie had seemed frightened when Cee Cee first showed himself. Yet, they almost sounded like secret lovers.

Not wanting to run into anyone, Tess didn't shower. She stripped out of her sundress, bra, and panties, and changed into a yellow nightgown. Floor-length, pretty and frilly, it cost $2.00 at the thrift shop. Mama said it washed out her milky skin and made her monochrome with her yellow hair blending into the material. Of course, neither of her parents ever focused on positives, so the criticism didn't surprise Tess.

Yawning, she climbed into bed and pulled the covers to her chin. At some point she fell asleep.

She didn't hear Cee Cee enter her room until he jammed his gun against her head and ordered her up.

Part One

Growing Pains

Chapter One

CHRISTOPHER

Forty-nine fucking years old. Almost *fifty*.

Thirty years ago, if anyone had told Christopher "Outlaw" Caldwell he'd live to see this milestone, he would've laughed in their fucking faces. No one in his acquaintance believed in such luck. Evading Hoof-foot for so long shocked the fuck out of everyfuckingbody, especially his fucking ass.

"Happy birthday, Outlaw," one of his brothers yelled.

"Thanks, motherfucker," Outlaw responded, lifting his bottle and grinning at the cheers rising in the clubhouse.

Several years ago, the floors in the building had been replaced. It was a massive undertaking thanks to all the different rooms, located on the hallways. The main room, his office, the board room, the kitchens, and the bathrooms were finished first. They'd gotten a new HVAC system, upgraded plumbing, and new appliances.

Megan, his sweet angel, pressed her lips against his. She sat in her favorite spot—his lap. "Happy birthday, Christopher," she whispered.

His wife was as lovely now as she had been when he'd first laid his gaze upon her. Then, she'd been frightened and in need of her father. Sometimes, he couldn't believe if he'd met her a month before, she would've been underaged.

Fuck, if he'd fucking met her the fucking *day* before.

What-the-fuck-ever. That shit hadn't happened, so he didn't even need to fucking go there.

What *had* happened was Megan captivated him from the moment they met and she continued to do so, all these years later.

She was still gorgeous with her golden hair and too-blue eyes that turned her into an earth angel. Eye color and hair length didn't fucking matter, either. A few fucking years ago, she'd gotten a pixie haircut.

He'd fucking hated it; she'd looked sixfuckingteen. But she'd still had that face and the inner goodness that made her beautiful even if she'd looked like Miss Fucking Piggy. When her hair grew out again, it relieved him so fucking much.

Thank all the motherfuckers in heaven.

She frowned. "Christopher?"

"Just thinkin' about your fuckin' hair, baby." For a time, after the pixie cut grew out, she'd kept her hair bone-straight and shoulder-length. "How you gone from lookin' like a girl Peter fuckin' Pan back to a fuckin' fairytale princess with your long fuckin' hair."

She laughed and stole another kiss. "Are you enjoying your party?"

He nodded. "Alfuckinways."

And like always, evidence of Christmas decorated the club. Even the Christmas tree was still up since his birthday was January 4th and Twelfth Night happened on the 6th. Thirty years ago, such observances wouldn't have mattered either. But it was a combination of his woman and his best friend's mother-in-law, who hailed from New Orleans that precipitated the change.

Sometimes, he wished his birthday fell in warmer months. Then, they could've held his party outside. Every year, the celebration grew more crowded.

"Outlaw, we have a surprise for you," his sister-in-law, Kendall Donovan, called.

"The Mardi Gras ball's called off and we don't need no tuxt need no tux?" the club's sergeant-at-arms, Marcus "Digger" Banks, asked with hope.

"Yeah, Red, that would be a fucking gift for all us," Lucas "Mortician" Banks, club enforcer and Christopher's best friend, said.

"Boy, shut the fuck up," Roxanne Harrington, Mort's ma-in-law, said in exasperation.

Megan sniffed. "Yeah, Digger. We put a lot of effort into the ball every year to raise money for the kids."

"Fine for you, Meggie girl," Mort said woefully. "Fucked up for us."

"This the fourth year we been doing this—" Digger started.

Her body tensing, Megan threw Christopher an evil glare, still smarting over that first fucking ball and his assfuckery. Before she locked her fucking pussy from residual anger, Christopher shut shit down.

"Shut the fuck up," he warned as she got to her feet and jerked her hair into a messy bun, allowing everyone to see the words *Property of Outlaw* embroidered on the back of her cut.

Kendall and the other women at his table stood too, all old ladies of his officers. Two were his sisters, but all were family. Two presidents from his support clubs and the old ladies as well as a superstar musician and his wife were also seated with him. As Megan, Kendall, and the nine other women headed toward the DJ, the standing room only crowd parted and silence rolled in. At the railed pool table area where the disc jockey was set up, the women crowded around the motherfucker.

Low conversations resumed, while everyone waited for Megan and her friends now joined by his girl, Rebel, Mort's girl, Harley, and the club's VP's girl, Matilda.

"Ever thought this'd be our lives, Prez?" Mort asked, watching his woman tug their girl closer and wrap her arms around Harley's waist.

"Nope," Christopher answered, drinking more tequila.

CJ, his second eldest, inserted himself next to Harley, although the rest of the boys, including his five other sons remained seated at various tables. Diesel, his oldest boy, surrounded himself with women, the only motherfucker amongst five bitches.

Kendall crooked her finger at her eldest, Rory. Grinning, the little motherfucker rushed to his ma. Ryan, another of Christopher's nephews, ignored the summons.

"Ryan lucky it's your birthday, Outlaw," Matthew 'Val' Taylor, his road captain and brother-in-law, said. "Otherwise, Puff would fuck him up."

Over the past few months, Christopher marked a change in Ryan. He was becoming a disrespectful assfuck. However, he'd turn sixteen in May, so Christopher chalked it up to teenage rebellion.

CJ headed to the bathroom designated *Dicks* on the door sign while Rory and the other three boys sat on stools against the wall where a chalkboard, cue rack, and TV hung.

Dweller brothers corralled the crowd, forcing Christopher and his boys to their feet. He nodded, then headed to the pool tables where all his sons and nephews now were to give more room to the other motherfuckers.

"Fuck, Outlaw, I'm glad to be in your inner circle," Derby, Burning Hounds president, grumbled as they reached the wall of boys. "Otherwise, I'd be stuffed in like a sardine can too while our broads danced."

CJ walked out of the bathroom, dressed in a blue blazer and dark sunglasses. "Hey, 'Law," he called, grinning from ear-to-ear and waving, though he didn't stop. He headed to his ma.

"What the fuck—"

The music starting interrupted Christopher's question.

Megan and the other girls filed down the two steps onto the small area his brothers managed to clear. As *Gentleman* played, CJ danced in the middle of his ma and the women, just as Psy had in his video.

Now Christopher understood why they'd watched the fucking video to this song for fucking weeks. He *had* been sick to fucking death of it, but his woman's enjoyment and his boy's showmanship, reinvigorated his appreciation and he regretted the end of the song. He would've followed Megan, but once the women disappeared into the crowd, Ellie, Mattie, and Harley joined their brothers on the floor, line-dancing to *Achy Breaky Heart,* the *Electric Boogie*, and the *Cupid Shuffle*.

By the end of the little motherfuckers dancing, boredom threatened to derail the fucking party. Howfuckinever, no one wanted to offend the children and thus piss off their fathers.

When the kids trooped away, sweaty, red-faced, and giggling, Christopher shifted his weight. "Herb and Al callin' my fuckin' name," he said. "We goin' outside and visit them."

"Say no more," John 'Johnnie' Donovan said with a smile. He dug into his cut and pulled out a baggie stuffed with Herb, handing it to Val. "Would you do the honors, Valentine? Roll one for each of us. My treat."

"You trying to kill us?" Boy, president of the Night Flyers, asked. "If that's Outlaw's Cfc, one or two hits will fuck us up."

"I'm finding Georgie," Sloane Mason said. After decades in the limelight, his star hadn't faded. As a recovered addict, however, he didn't tempt himself with even a small suck on Herb.

As he started to walk away, Megan led the women back onto the dancefloor. Skimpy dresses with fringes and stilettos replaced their cuts, jeans, T-shirts, and motorcycle boots.

Megan's hair was free and her makeup freshened. The red outfit clung to her curves. Still short in six-inch heels, the crystal-embellished sandals drew attention to her toned legs and thighs.

His cock jumped to attention.

She tossed her hair, licked her lips, and winked at him.

Wobble by V.I.C. began, and Christopher forgot his intentions to go outside and say hi to Herb and Al. He dismissed his mild annoyance that his clubhouse resembled a dance studio during a recital. The other girls dancing, twisting, swaying, and bouncing barely registered in Christopher's brain.

Hair swirling and fringes wiggling, his woman shook and crouched to the beat. Only her hot moves and blazing gaze on him mattered.

Four minutes into the song, CJ joined his ma and aunts, loving to dance as much as Megan. Male shouts and roars of approval drowned out the song's end. The women and CJ moved to the side, revealing the Bobs, special Dweller girls possessing exception oral skills, and brought out for big celebrations. They wore beaded thongs and red pumps.

"Did Megan coordinate with them?" Johnnie asked in amusement.

Christopher doubted it, although their pumps almost matched Megan's and her friends.

"Where's Roxanne?" Knox Harrington, Roxanne's husband, asked. "And Jordan?" he added, referring to her best friend and Megan's gynecologist.

As the Bobs fanned around him and his motherfuckers, Knox received his answer. Roxanne and Doc Will rolled a huge cake toward him.

"Fuck, if this is your 49th birthday party, what the fuck going on for your 50th?" Derby asked, cupping the pussy of the Bob closest to him. Although the pool table blocked his old lady from clearly seeing him, it wouldn't have mattered if she stood right there. His hand went to his belt. "Suck my cock."

"Fuck off," Christopher snapped. "Our lil' motherfuckers here. Wait 'til they leave."

Scowling, Derby complied. "Don't go far," he told the girl.

She smiled at him.

"Uncle Chris." Diesel's voice resonated through the speakers as he pushed in front of two Bobs, holding a microphone. "First, I want to wish you a happy birthday. You deserve the best. On your special day, I also want to thank you. You and Aunt Meggie raised me as your own, never distinguishing me from your biological children. Being your son is an honor and a privilege. On your 45th birthday, I patched in and was given the terribly difficult task of overseeing the Bobs."

Christopher snickered, joining everybody else's laughter.

"Today, Potter is retaking the position."

The bombshell killed Christopher's amusement. Diesel had begged to be in charge of those bitches. Christopher expected a bit of fucking courtesy since he'd given into Diesel's whiny fucking pleas. This wasn't the fucking time or place to confront his kid, so Christopher didn't stop Diesel from handing the microphone to a tall, strawberry blonde and stepping aside.

"Floor's yours, Chastity," Diesel said.

"Chastity?" Derby whooped.

"Outlaw," the girl cooed when the chuckles died down. "Somehow, our plans to give you lap dances were discovered."

"Lap fuckin' what?" he demanded, snapping his brows together.

Licking her lips, she lowered her lashes. "We're here to please you and the brothers," she went on, like a clueless cunt. "We vetoed *Meggie*'s idea, although she overrode us, so I want to apologize—"

"Not accepted," Christopher snapped, losing his fucking patience and his temper. He couldn't see his Megan because of all the bitches around him, but that didn't matter. His hand went to his nine.

Kendall shoved Chastity away, glared at her, and snatched the microphone. "Move," she ordered, sure of herself and her place. "Thank me later for saving your fucking life later."

Dismissing the Bob, she smiled at Christopher. All the Bobs, except the one Derby wanted, headed into the crowd.

Kendall cleared her throat. "Outlaw, we've had ups and downs through the years, but in the end, you welcomed me back with open arms as your sister-in-law, cousin-in-law, and the vice-president's old lady. Happy birthday," she said with heartfelt sincerity. "I wish you many more years of happiness and prosperity." Smiling, she leaned in and kissed his cheek.

"Thank you, Kendall," he said, kissing her back, then releasing her to Johnnie.

"Let's go to our old room and fuck, gorgeous," Johnnie said, leering at her exposed skin and the swell of her tits.

She giggled. "I'll send the kids home. Ella is there with Blade and Gunner," she said, referring to her nanny, who was watching over Christopher's nephew and son, "so they'll have supervision."

"John Boy, you got the right fucking idea," Mortician said, giving Bailey the once-over as she helped her ma and Doc Will light the candles on Christopher's cake.

"'Law," CJ said, mic in hand. He'd removed the blazer and sunglasses and was back in his cut with the words *Son of Outlaw* on the back. "You're the best dad any kid could want. Thank you for all your love and support. You're more than my dad. You're my idol and my hero. I love you so much and happy birthday."

The lil' motherfucker embraced Christopher.

"I love you too, boy," he said gruffly, returning his son's hug.

Megan sashayed to them. Immediately, CJ turned and hugged her, then kissed her cheek, handed her the microphone, and stepped away.

Her eyes soft and her cheeks flushed, she gave Christopher a tender look. "My love. My Christopher. My everything. Happy birthday! I look forward to celebrating many more with you. I love you so much."

"And I love you, baby."

She tipped her chin up and he bent and kissed her lips.

"Let's sing happy birthday, everyone, so my children and me can clear out and—"

"The fucking can start!" someone boomed from the crowd.

Smiling, she nodded. "Yes, that."

After cutting the cake, they stayed another hour before heading to their house so his brothers could enjoy the clubhouse debauchery and Christopher could enjoy his wife's private shamelessness.

Chapter Two

Five Months Later

"Is lying ever acceptable?"

Christopher Joseph Foy Caldwell frowned at the question his English teacher posed. Mr. Lumbly was a massive pain in CJ's ass. His stupidly styled balding gray hair worked well with his stupidly oversized glasses.

CJ was so fucking glad the school year was ending. If he could, he'd tell Lumbly to fuck off, forget school, and hang with 'Law all day.

Being the son of a legend wasn't easy.

CJ worshipped his father, but he doubted he'd ever live up to 'Law's reputation. Worse, his dad wouldn't easily give CJ the chance to follow in his footsteps. Fuck, sometimes, it seemed 'Law didn't want CJ to become a biker. Before he'd even be allowed to prospect, CJ had to finish high school *and* go to college.

“The real question is when is lying *unacceptable*?” Willard Byrd blared with a smirk.

Ryan Taylor, CJ’s cousin, laughed. “Never!”

Mr. Lumbly drew himself up, his lips tight, as if he’d sucked on something sour. “Neither one of your answers will be recognized, gentlemen, since you didn’t follow my rules of engagement.”

“I don’t like your rules of engagement,” Willard said flatly, irking the fuck out of CJ.

An easy achievement from that dickhead. *He* irked the fuck out of CJ. Motherfucker didn’t look like a wild pig for nothing. Beady black eyes. Black hair. Snout for a fucking nose. He reminded CJ of Uncle Val’s potbellied pig, Hogzilla.

“Shut up, Willy,” CJ ordered. “I don’t want extra homework or a detention because of your stupid ass.”

“*Mister Caldwell*!” Mr. Lumbly gritted as Willard flipped CJ off and said, “fuck you.”

A panel of back windows allowed the sunshine to stream in. The spacious room easily accommodated the other nineteen students in class with CJ. He sat in the front row, in the line of desks and chairs closest to the door. In the classroom’s grid pattern, his seemed the best spot. Until he had to address Willard on the last row.

Leaning around and staring at Willard, CJ said, “I’ll let that comment slide, so—”

A hand landed on his shoulder. Facing forward, CJ found Mr. Lumbly’s rancid brown gaze on him. “Just what you *didn’t* want to happen has. You have detention and extra homework.” Smug, the teacher backed away, into the open space at the front of the classroom, near the chalkboard. “What do you think, Mr. Caldwell?”

Fuck all because it *wasn’t* happening.

“I can’t do detention today,” CJ announced, as polite as possible. Twatwad held the fate of the next year of

CJ's life in his grimy little hands. However, he'd prefer to face his father's wrath and being kicked off the team before he allowed blatant unfairness. "And I think you forgot to include Byrd in the punishment."

Mr. Lumbly lifted a thin brow, while Willard's laughter filled the classroom, and drowned out Ryan's snickers, the only other amused fuckhead out of twenty-five students. "You don't have the authority to decide when you serve detention. That's my call. As for Mister Byrd—" the teacher glanced in the big oaf's direction, his sucked-lemon face, sphincter-lip pucker increasing—"he did nothing wrong."

"Yeah, Caldwell," Willard taunted. "I just passed my opinion. You bullied me."

"Not yet," CJ snapped, his patience at an end, "but if you keep fucking with me I will." Not for the first time he wondered why Lumbly hated him. "I'll do extra homework for the next month, sir. I'll come to detention on Saturdays. Whatever it takes. Just, please, let me leave today."

Lumbly peered over the rim of his glasses. "Do you have an important engagement, young man?"

CJ nodded. "With my dad."

"Ahh, father-son bonding is so special," Willard called.

Balling his fists, CJ didn't answer the asshole. When the Byrds moved to town and Riley, the club's PI, and Brooks Redding, their long-time attorney, performed background checks, CJ wished they'd been flagged. He wouldn't have two motherfuckers to deal with on a daily fucking basis. Even worse, Ryan gravitated to Willy. An asshole following another asshole led to worse assholery. Not only had they checked out, Willy and his brother, Wallace, were also orphans, living with an aunt and uncle who'd taken them in after the death of their parents in a car accident.

"As loathe as I am to come between, er, *father-son bonding*, you've left me no other choice," Mr. Lumbly said with mock regret. "Stay for your detention today or face suspension. You know what that means."

Coach Yancy possibly kicking him off the football team *and* Dad grounding him for the summer. Confinement to club grounds and his moped confiscated would suck. Missing practice and watching Byrd, his backup, promoted to starting quarterback would piss him the fuck off. But the possibility of not spending time with Harley Banks for the duration of school break, CJ weighed his options.

It would be his third suspension, all courtesy of the little fuckbag strolling to his desk. Even if suspensions weren't dogging his ass, his low grade in this class would. Coach Yancy allowed him to stay on the team after CJ promised to bring his grade from the depths of hell to an acceptable 'C'. No matter what he did though, Lumbly kept CJ's grade between a sixty-eight—in other words fucking failing—and a seventy-one. Just a notch or two on the other side of failure.

CJ should've just told 'Law when it first began. Or his mom. Or Diesel, his adopted brother. Or any of his uncles. Or, even better, Lolly, Harley's grandmother.

Instead, he'd chosen to remain silent about Lumbly's fuckery. Any of the aforementioned people would've dropped everything to visit the fuckbag. Yet, CJ ranked this in the category of bullshit between the cousins. Parents need not get involved. Except, now, if he *didn't* alert his father, CJ would miss a very important meeting 'Law was allowing him to attend with the Scorched Devils MC, arranged by Derby, president of the Burning Hounds, a long-time Dweller support club.

CJ *could* just leave. To conceal his suspensions, he hung out at the creek or rode his moped in the opposite direction of his father. He wasn't Outlaw's son for nothing. A shitload of deviousness hid a lot.

Failing grades with summer break days away? Fucking impossible to hide. All CJ's hard work of thumbing his nose at the dumb shit and keeping the antics of the little asshole to himself, would be for nothing.

If he got kicked off the team, then there'd be no summer camp, so his game would be up when 'Law discovered the other suspensions. Bad enough lying to him but CJ lied to his mother. And *that shit there...*

Goddamn.

The ringing school bell heralded the end of the day.

CJ scrubbed a hand over his face, then smoothed the hair at his nape and rubbed his neck.

"C'mon, Ryan." Willard slid one strap of his backpack onto his shoulder and grinned at CJ like a fucking idiot, "your old man is waiting to take you to that important meeting you told me about."

What?

Shooting to his feet, CJ grabbed the collar of Ryan's starched white shirt—part of their required uniform—and spun him around. "What the fuck's wrong with you?"

Ryan pushed against CJ's chest, his eyes suddenly burning. "Fuck you."

CJ hooked a finger in the part of Ryan's tie circling his neck and yanked him forward. "No, asshole, fuck you. You aren't supposed to discuss club shit with outside motherfuckers, motherfucker."

"*Mister Caldwell*!" Mr. Lumbly yelled.

Willard's balled fist propelled toward CJ's jaw. Ignoring Ryan's purpling face and ducking out of the way of the oncoming fist, CJ elbowed Willard hard enough to send him sprawling—right into Harley as she walked into the room. She squeaked, but Willard couldn't stop his forward motion. They reeled to the floor, arms and legs flailing, and Harley's books tumbling out of her knapsack.

HARLEY

"Get off," Harley gasped.

Willard didn't move his body from her. His beady, black eyes gleamed. "Make me," he said, low.

"Ouch, asshole!" Ryan yelped.

Panting for air—Willard was *heavy*—she yanked away one of her hands trapped between them and dug her nails into his cheek. Before she raked his skin off, CJ jerked him away, then raised his booted foot, literally kicking Willard's ass into the hallway.

Scrambling to her knees, Harley accepted CJ's hand, standing just as Willard loomed in the doorway and Ryan scooted past him.

"I owe you, stupid bitch," Willard snarled.

CJ growled, but Harley pulled him back and glared at Willard from head to foot. "I wish you would," she spat. "If you value what's between your legs, piss off, before I kick it out of existence."

Willard reached for her. "*Cunt.*"

Shoving her behind him, CJ shielded her with his body.

"Miss Banks, I'll thank you to gather your belongings and leave my classroom," Mr. Lumbly ordered.

Harley huffed out a breath, not understanding how such an evil little troll got a position at Ridge Moore.

Daddy and her uncles, especially Uncle Christopher, funded a large portion of the school's budget. She lacked full disclosure on the monetary disbursement, but staff salaries should be under their control so they'd have a say in new hires.

"Mister Caldwell has detention. He stays."

Harley scowled at Lumbly's haughty announcement.

"Aww, Harls," Willard said with mock regret. "I'll just wait for you outside."

Harley placed her hands on CJ's arms, his ever-burgeoning muscles taut enough to pop.

Once Willard walked away, CJ turned to her. "Get your things, Harley. I'm bringing you home."

"Leave my classroom and you'll be suspended," Mr. Lumbly said in triumph.

"I have no idea what you have against me, Mr. Lumbly," CJ snarled, Uncle Chris's doppelganger in looks and mannerisms. "You allowed motherfucking Willard Byrd to get away with more shit today than I've done this entire year, so fuck you, you fucking asshole. Suspend me, but Harley is *not* walking alone today with that motherfucker circling."

Lumbly was an idiot, but he was a vindictive idiot, hell-bent on destroying her best friend. Not happening if she had anything to say about it. She smiled at CJ. "I won't be alone. Rebel and Mattie are waiting for me. Cheer practice, remember?"

Clenching his jaw, CJ nodded and glanced away. Part of the reason she'd become a cheerleader was because CJ made the football team.

He glared at Mr. Lumbly. "I'm still not staying."

He should've told Uncle Christopher about Lumbly's dislike. "I'll be fine," she swore, determined to protect CJ.

"Yeah, you will be, because I'll be with you." He stepped closer, his body brushing hers. "Lumbly's a temporary dilemma, bae."

Lumbly served as more than a 'dilemma'. He'd become an unsolvable problem. Summer break started in three weeks. In that small amount of time, the teacher could destroy CJ's plans.

An idea hitting her, she turned, walked to where one of her books landed near the teacher's desk, and picked it up. She held it close to her chest and looked at Mr. Lumbly.

"Mommie and Daddy have a parent/teacher conference tomorrow at the elementary school." In other words, next door. "It's for my little brother, Kaleb," she added for authenticity. "I'll ask them to stop in so they can relay a message to Uncle Chris and Aunt Meggie." She rocked on her heels. "Your notices of disciplinary issues with CJ aren't reaching them." As if he'd sent any. "I suppose my parents will also have to talk to you about Willy's threats." Lumbly's alarm tickled her. Her eyes widened and she placed a finger on her cheek. "Wait! Are they coming...? Hmmm. It might be Lolly."

He choked, grabbed a stack of neat papers, and unnecessarily tapped the pages on the desk.

Turning, she winked at CJ, and he grinned, taking the book she'd gotten and adding it to the other two he'd collected, then shoving them in her knapsack.

"Oh, my goodness, Mr. Lumbly," she cried, whirling to face the evil troll again. "I overheard Daddy talking. Although I'm not positive to who; it might've been Uncle Chris. Anyway," she said, waving her hand, dismissing the 'speculation', "do you know Daddy said about seventy-five percent of the school's funding comes from the Death Dwellers?"

Lumbly turned ten shades of red.

"Is your salary included?" she asked with innocence, then shrugged, though she really wanted an answer. "Probably not. It's probably from tuition charged to the student body, *including* the children of the club who keeps the lower, middle and upper schools operating."

Jaw clenched, Mr. Lumbly faced forward and clasped his hands together. "Your point is taken, Miss Banks."

"Lovely. CJ *is* free to go without ramifications, yes?"

Baring his teeth at her, he nodded.

"Thank you, Mr. Lumbly," she said meekly, gave CJ a satisfied smirk then marched past him and out the door.

Rebel Caldwell, CJ's sister, and Matilda Donovan, his cousin, rushed over from the opposite end of the hallway where they'd been waiting at their lockers.

Mattie was blessed with Aunt Kendall's red hair, brown eyes, and long legs. She was a very pretty girl and knew it.

Blowing a bubble from the gum she chewed, then popping it, Rebel grinned. To say she looked like Aunt Meggie was an understatement. She had the same golden hair and too-blue eyes.

Even though guys fell all over themselves upon seeing Aunt Meggie, she was so laid-back about her beauty. But Rebel mirrored Mattie. From a young age, she knew she was gorgeous, and used it to her advantage. As much as she liked motorcycles and working on them, she was feminine to the core.

"Did you do it, Harls?" she asked.

"Yep," Harley said proudly as CJ walked out of the classroom and closed the door behind him. She grabbed her knapsack from him. "Are you okay?"

He scowled. "Uncle Mort and Aunt Bailey don't have to come here tomorrow, do they?"

"Nope, but that can change."

Rebel slid the scrunchie out of her blonde hair. The thick mass fluttered around her shoulders and back.

"Yeah, dummy, if you just *said* you were telling Daddy, fuckwad would back off." She blew another bubble and popped it again. "I do it all the time."

"That's different," CJ muttered. "You're a girl. But 'Law expects me to be a fucking man."

"Yeah, dickhead," Mattie offered, frowning, "when you *are* one. You're fifteen, so you're *not* a fucking man. Besides, if you really *were* a man, you wouldn't call your father *'Law*. That's so fucking stupid."

"Yo, Mattie, shut the fuck up," CJ ordered. "I can call my old man whatever the fuck I wish. He's *my* old man, which means *you* don't have shit to say." He cocked his head to the side. "How'd you three know what happening, anyway?"

"Ryan and me were texting when Lumbly started his bullshit," Mattie said.

"No shit? He told you?" CJ's beautiful green eyes widened. "He still left with Willy. What kind of shit is that?"

"Fuck him, brother," Rebel ordered. "He was dropped on his head at birth. He gets all the feels for the wrong fucking shit. Dumbass."

"Stop, Reb," Harley ordered. "Leave Ryan alone. Give him a chance to figure it out."

Mattie snorted. "Oh my God, Harley, please don't go all Aunt Bailey on us. She is way too calm."

Harley smiled at the compliment. "Aunt Bunny, Aunt Meggie, and Mommie are the calmest."

"Ha!" Mattie rolled her eyes. "Aunt Meggie killed a man to save Uncle Chris. How is that calm?"

"Momma doesn't even like guns, stupid." Rebel's eyes darkened in fury. "I don't know where you heard that, but it isn't true! If you like your teeth in your head, you'll never spout that fucking lie again."

Mattie smirked. "I never said she used a gun, Reb."

Before CJ said something he regretted, Harley intervened. “Walk me to the athletic center, so you can leave. You don’t want to be late for the meeting.”

Chapter Three

No way had MegAnn killed a motherfucker.

CJ didn't care about Mattie's certainty, it *hadn't* fucking happened. Still, her words bothered him and he didn't know why. Once he escorted the girls to the athletic center, he used his student ID to purchase a bag of chips and a bottled water from one of the campus vending machines, then went to the front breezeway to enjoy his snacks and a smoke before heading to the Scorched Devils clubhouse where his dad and uncles were.

Lumbly, Willard, and Ryan's fuckfaces distracted him on the ride over, leaving CJ uncertain of his next move. He didn't trust neither of those three motherfuckers, refusing to give Ryan a pass for not opening his fucking mouth about CJ's two prior suspensions. A favor for a favor. He never told how often his jackass cousin cut class.

A wood and brick building housed the Scorched Devils' MC, located in a little town on the Washington-Oregon border. The club skirted the law but didn't flip it off Dweller-style, therefore they didn't have many, if any, enemies. Instead of electric gates with guards and soaring privacy fences that hid a compound, the Scorched Devils' high chain link fence had a simple gate that gaped open. The chain wrapped near the latch hinted at precautionary measures but nothing too elaborate. No one to grill an unknown motherfucker. No probates with sawed-offs kept watch over the bikes in the gravel parking lot. Nothing resembling Medieval siege-warfare that brought to mind hot tar and boiling oil lobbed at stupid fuckheads attempting to breach their grounds.

Intermittent sunbursts broke through the cool, cloudy day. One moment, light gleamed against fat, cottony clouds, and the next a flat gray dulled the sky. Trickling water broke the silent surroundings, a faint sound brushing the ears and revealing the nearby river. Tangy air surrounded the Devils' clubhouse, not scented by dirt and trees and leaves of the forest in Hortensia.

Inside, a bar ringed by high-backed stools stood on one side of the surprisingly large space. The smell of cigarette smoke lingered in the air, so potent you could taste it. Several circular booths separated the area from a dozen and a half four-seat tables. Torn red leather padded the booths, the material rough to the touch. A big red devil with black horns, mustache, and goatee, immaculate white teeth sparkling against full, smirking lips, and a golden nose ring decorated the white wall behind two pool tables in an area carved between the men's and women's bathrooms. If not for Lucifer's sooty, smoking butt, the artwork resembled most cartoonish devils.

'Law and CJ's uncles were grouped around four tables, shoved together to make a bigger one. Suddenly, the stress of dealing with twatwad slid away. School was necessary for the greater goal, but *this* was everything.

Fuck Lumbly.

Because he rode his moped to the meeting, CJ couldn't have a beer and watched his father partake, wishing for his own. Even Ryan had a brew. CJ and Rory were the only ones drinking sodas.

"Fuck, no, Outlaw," one of the Scorched Devil's said, "I never wanted to be president. My boy got what it takes, though."

"Rory does as well," Uncle Johnnie piped in, nodding to Rory with pride.

"I'm a little kid," Rory mumbled, flushing in embarrassment.

"You're a fine young man," Uncle Johnnie countered.

Swallowing, Rory looked at CJ, his gray eyes miserable.

"Ro, you're a bad little motherfucker," CJ said, wanting to ease his cousin's misery. "You'll catch up to me soon enough, so stop worrying. Uncle Johnnie and Aunt Kendall are tall. Mom's the size of an elf and look at me. Her genes didn't stunt my growth," he added, ignoring his father's and uncles' snickers.

"Megan's an anomaly," Uncle Johnnie said. "Dinah wasn't tall, but she wasn't—"

"Smurfette size," Uncle Mortician interrupted.

"Listen to CJ, son," Uncle Johnnie said.

"It's hard, Dad," Rory admitted. "I want to be on the football team with CJ."

Uncle Johnnie settled his hand on Rory's shoulder. "Give yourself a chance."

Easier said than done. Even CJ's suggestions wouldn't be simple to follow with Rory feeling so left behind.

"Even if you don't grow another inch, you'd still make an extraordinary club president," Uncle Johnnie continued.

The words buoyed Rory and he puffed out his skinny chest, glancing at CJ with unease.

"If you're a leader, you don't have to look at CJ for approval for everything." Ryan glanced at Uncle Val. "Pops, what about me? Do...do you think I can be Prez of the Dwellers?"

"You can be anything you want to, boy," Uncle Val said gruffly, "but your main job will be to support whoever *is* Prez."

"Listen to your old man, Ryan," Dez, the Scorched Devil's president, advised. He nodded to CJ. "We got high hopes for him. Val's a good dude and knows his shit. There's nothing wrong with being RC like he is."

"Exactly, son," Uncle Val said. As with CJ and Rory with their fathers, Ryan looked uncannily like his with turquoise eyes, dark brown hair, and the stockiness of an elite welterweight. "You have to be a special motherfucker to be president."

Ryan glared at CJ.

Folding his arms, CJ lifted a brow. He wished everyone fucking stopped relegating their *possible* future club positions. That bullshit drove Ryan's resentment toward CJ. They were too young to patch in and who knew if they all intended to follow in their fathers' footsteps.

"Fuck the fuck off," 'Law growled. "You motherfuckers ain't puttin' that fuckin' pressure on my kid. If he ain't wantin' to be Prez, he ain't bein' Prez, but the shit his choice. Ain't mine or no other fuckin' motherfucker." He leaned closer to CJ. "You got to head off motherfuckers' bullshit before it get outta fuckin control, boy. Don't ever forget that. Hear me?"

"Yeah, 'Law." If he hadn't arrived late to the meeting, CJ would've mentioned Mattie's stupid accusations, thus heading off any bullshit she might cause.

"Nope," his father said to someone else, having the extraordinary ability to hold conversations with different people at once and follow each one without missing a beat. "Fuck off. Fuck no. Fuck you."

The men laughed.

Uncle Johnnie tasted his beer. "The kids don't need interference from us every step of the way."

"We won't be around all the time," Uncle Val put in.

"Yeah, bruh," Uncle Digger said. "We know we don't have to worry about anything when we not around because Outlaw mini-me got shit handled."

After lighting a cigarette and taking some drags, Uncle Mort said, "Full patch members go on our runs. But CJ got our complete confidence."

"What about me, Uncle Mort?" Rory piped in. "I know how to protect our women."

Grinning, Uncle Johnnie head-locked Rory and ruffled his hair.

"You, too," Uncle Mort said.

'Law placed a hand on CJ's shoulder. "There ain't nothin' I ain't trustin' my boy to oversee. The lil' motherfucker know when to fuckin' call in backup."

Uncle Johnnie released Rory after sharing quiet words with him. "All the kids look up to CJ and Harley. They're the responsible ones."

CJ steepled his hands, wincing at the fleeting hurt morphing into anger on Ryan's face.

"No, they're the leaders," Rory inserted happily, adding loads of crap on top of the ever-growing shitstorm.

Uncle Mort leaned forward and addressed Rory. "I'm proud of Harley, but there's only so much she can do."

“The fuck you say, Mort,” Uncle Digger disagreed. “She got Bailey brain and your aim, so—”

“So my motherfuckin’ ass.” ‘Law released plumes of smoke from his mouth and nose. Somewhere along the way, he’d lit a cigarette too. “CJ *and* Harley fuckin’ kids. At a certain fuckin’ point, grown motherfuckers required to step the fuck in, so fuck off. CJ know what the fuck I mean.”

“You either trusting him to handle shit when we not around or he a kid,” Uncle Val said. “It can’t be both.”

“Shut up, Val,” Uncle Johnnie ordered. “We have club business to oversee. Christopher means CJ knows how to manage anything unless it is fucking dire. Now drop the fucking subject so we can get to our priorities.”

“Wait a fuckin’ minute,” ‘Law said. “You makin’ it sound like club business more important than my woman and our lil’ motherfuckers.”

“Oh, perish the thought anything is more important than Meggie,” another Scorched Devil said around laughter.

Snapping his brows together, Outlaw got to his feet. Not hesitating, CJ and his uncles did the same, while Ryan and Rory remained seated.

Members of the Scorched Devils MC also shoved out of their chairs.

Staring at the stupid ass who’d talked about his mother, CJ clenched his jaw. His father studied every detail of fuckhead’s features, not speaking, barely moving.

“We don’t want trouble, Outlaw,” Dez said on a swallow.

“Too fuckin’ late. That motherfucker mine.”

Dez shifted. “Cole is just a young pup. Recently patched in.”

“He could be a fuckin’ midget from Mercury, what the fuck he *ain’t* doin’ is disrespectin’ my woman.”

"What did you fucks do?" Derby called as he strolled into view.

"Let's talk business, then we can settle the problem here," Derby suggested. "Ignore Cole."

All eyes turned to Outlaw. The moment he nodded, everyone returned to their seats.

"Where the fuck your kid?" Outlaw narrowed his eyes as Derby seated himself at the table. "Ain't you the motherfucker that said this might be a good fuckin' experience for our fuckin' lil' motherfuckers?" He nodded to CJ. "There my fuckin' boy." He pointed to Rory. "Johnnie kid." Next, he indicated Ryan. "Val son. Where *yours*?"

Derby shrugged. "Gypsy didn't want him to come. Last kid by me that she pushed out her pussy and she's very protective of him. Overly so. You can't fault her, Outlaw. Look at that pitiful pussyped your kid rides."

CJ grinned at the laughter. "What did you call my moped, Derby?"

"What the fuck we all call it, CJ," Uncle Val said, laughing."

"A pussyped," the men chorused.

"Better than moped," CJ agreed.

"My bitch would have my ass if she knew how often I allowed him to fuck," Derby sniggered when the moment passed.

Frowning, 'Law leaned back and glared at Derby. "That shit between you and *your* fuckin' bitch. *My* lil' pain-in-the-ass motherfucker expect better from my motherfuckin' ass."

"Diesel was fucking and Meggie didn't know," Derby pointed out.

"That shit the fuckin' point, Derby. *Diesel was fuckin'* befuckinfore I found the lil' motherfucker. Once a cock dip in wet pussy, you ain't able to reel that shit in, so fuck you. Ain't wantin' my boy to sneak the fuck around.

That's the quickest way for his shit to rot the fuck off or end up with dozens of lil' hims runnin' the fuck around. Deep down, Megan knew what the fuck was up with Diesel."

"And deep fucking down she knows what the fuck is up with CJ," Derby insisted. "He has a cock, too. Most of all, the little motherfucker is *your* kid. Bitches throw themselves at him, the way they've always thrown themselves at you, Outlaw."

"CJ is right here." Uncle Johnnie drained his beer. He dug in the galvanized tub, one of two that sat on each end of the table, and grabbed another bottle. "He might have something to say about what he wants to do with his cock." Grinning, he guzzled half the beer, then focused on CJ and pointed the bottle at him. "What do you say about the chains Outlaw has placed on your cock to appease Megan, nephew?"

Uncle Johnnie's mocking tone irked CJ.

"Watch your fuckin' tone when you fuckin' talkin' about my fuckin' woman," 'Law warned.

"Yeah, because all our broads bitches," Cole said, "*except* Meggie. Do you fucking know how annoying that shit is, motherfucker?"

Everyone shifted in their seats because nobody wanted to look at 'Law and see anger freezing his green eyes.

"Now, Prez," Uncle Mort said, "we all fucking understand Cole want to become Corpse but..." He glanced at CJ with meaning. "Besides, Outlaw, we don't have a fucking cage to transport a motherfucker."

Visibly shaking in fury, 'Law nodded. "Let's get this the fuck over with, Derby."

"I've been having a dry spell lately," Uncle Johnnie said casually. "We can always get this Cole motherfucker later."

"Bring him to the meatshack?" Rory blurted, almost breathless. He looked at CJ. "It's so cool in there. Have you ever been inside?"

"No," CJ answered, curious at the mixture of revulsion and elation on his cousin's face.

"What you know about the fucking meatshack, little bro?" Uncle Digger asked Rory. "That place not for kids."

"Rory doesn't know a goddamn thing about it," Uncle Johnnie cut in. His glare shrank Rory's enthusiasm.

"Ima tell you this shit *one more fuckin' time*. My ass better not fuckin' find out you bringin' Rory in that fuckin' place, Johnnie. Underfuckinstand?"

Clenching his jaw, Uncle Johnnie glanced away and nodded.

"Fuck, Outlaw," Derby said with disgust. "A day I never fucking expected has arrived. You're raising Dweller sons like fucking bitches. You're having more growing pains than these fucking young guns."

"Derby, asshole, shut the fuck up," Uncle Johnnie barked. "I wouldn't want your clubhouse to run into any problems. It might accidentally go boom-boom-pow with you inside."

"CJ," 'Law said in hushed tones, so only he heard. "These motherfuckers workin' my last goddamn nerve. Derby got one fuckin' foot over that line where I gotta fuck him up. Unfuckinlike that walkin' fuckin' dead man, Cole, Derby and his brothers good motherfuckers to the Dwellers, so somefuckintimes you gotta *try* to make stupid fuckin' assfucks see the fuckin' light befuckinfore you blow them motherfuckers away. Big Joe and Kaleb Paul ain't took no disrespect. *Howfuckinever*, they taught my fuckin' ass to use fuckin' brawn when fuckin' necessary and fuckin' brains when the situation fuckin' called for. This one of them times. Later, me and you talkin' about shit. Hear, son?"

"Yeah, 'Law," CJ whispered.

His father grinned at him and clapped him on the back, then cleared his throat and looked at Derby. "Ima say this fuckin' shit one fuckin' time to you, assfuck. *You* fuckin' know about a lot of this bullshit, so my ass *should* break your fuckin' face. My boy here." He glowered at Derby, who flushed. "Dez? Motherfuckers?" He called. "Listen up, too. Scorched Devils a small fuckin' club that ain't been 'round too long. Derby and Dez came to the Dwellers and got fuckin' permission to have a fuckin' chapter in our territory. You fucks still ain't too fuckin' familiar with my ass, my history, or my club, so this your fuckin' public service announcement. You fuck up *after* my fuckin' PSA and you fucked up. Got me?"

Grumbles and mumbles of concurrence.

"I ain't here to fuckin' bring up the past or what the fuck my woman went through. We here for business. Not a fuckin' tell-all. And not fucking therapy."

"Perhaps, you don't want to bring up Megan because of everything you put her through those first few months," Uncle Johnnie said blandly.

"If I shoot the fuck outta—"

"I want to hear, Outlaw," CJ interrupted before the argument took a dark turn, purposely using his road name. Perhaps talking about MegAnn would ease his father's anger and smooth over the rising tension.

"Meggie needed to fucking leave," Cole called. "Self-preservation happens to be a wonderful thing."

The irony! The motherfucker should take his own fucking advice.

"Cole, shut the fuck up," Dez ordered at Outlaw's growl. "I'm sorry, Outlaw. Cole likes to stir up shit."

"Control that motherfucker, Dez," Outlaw instructed, "or Ima stir his fuckin' brains. Underfuckinstand?"

Uncle Digger shoved his chair back and got to his feet. "My fucking ass don't feel like doing fucking brain detail." He grabbed a bottle of beer from the tub on his end. "Besides, if a motherfucker stupid enough to continually fuck with Outlaw, he might be suicidal enough to pull his piece."

After opening his bottle and drinking deeply, Uncle Digger pounded on his chest, belched, pulled his .44 and began walking amongst the tables, pausing next to Cole. "You got *one* more fucking time to fuck with Prez before I escort you the fuck out."

Cole curled his lip. "Outlaw not my Prez, Dez is, so only he can order me out."

"*We* can order you dead," Uncle Digger retorted. He used the barrel of his gun to tick off his reasons. "First," he said, pressing the .44 against his index finger, "you outnumbered, motherfucker." Next finger. "Second, Scorched Devils in Dweller territory. You fucking here by the grace of Outlaw." Ring finger, where the barrel brushed against his wedding band. "Third, *Dez* as expendable as your motherfucking ass. If that motherfucker give us problems because you a stupid motherfucker and we need to fuck you up because you can't keep your fucking mouth shut...guess what? *He* getting his ass fucked up, too."

"Cole, please shut the fuck up," Derby said. "My ass is on the line, as well. I brought the Devils to Outlaw. *You* fuck up means *I've* fucked up."

Uncle Digger pressed his gun against his pinky. "Finally, Cole, we have some of our lil' bros with us. You disrespectful as a motherfucker. If I have to fuck you up, it's just fucking better if my body a partition between their gazes and your blood."

"Outlaw," Dez said in a shaky voice, "please continue. I'm interested in what you were saying. We all are. I'm trying to clean Cole up, so give him a chance. He had a good woman who he fucked over."

"Fuck," Derby interrupted before Outlaw resumed his story. "He didn't beat on the bitch." He drew in a deep breath. "If he interrupts again, I'll fucking shoot him myself. I'd like to hear your story, too." He glanced away. "It might help me with my bitch."

Outlaw drummed his fingers on the table.

CJ stood, leaned over and got another beer for Outlaw. Once he opened it, he held it out to him. "I want to hear, too, Dad." Another opportunity to study the *president* of the Death Dwellers in action.

Outlaw accepted the bottle from CJ, took a swig, then nodded. "Okay, boy."

Once CJ sat he resumed his story.

"Comments like that motherfucker made one fuckin' reason I protect my woman so fuckin' much," Outlaw started with annoyance. "Ain't able to make no motherfucker like her. Took me fuckin' years to realize Megan responsible for that part. The respect part, though? If one fuckin' assfuck or chick get the fuck away with callin' her a bitch or a cunt or *any* fuckin' thing outta her name, a goddamn domino effect startin'. Befuckinfore long, her name ain't Megan no more, but bitch, cunt, whore, or slut."

"You learned how to refer to women from Big Joe, Dad. You told me he always talked to you about Mom with reverence. Maybe, in your subconscious, you know he'd go ballistic if she's disrespected. Aside from her being your sweet angel, you don't want her called out of her name on his behalf."

Cocking his head to the side, his father considered CJ's speculation. "Maybe, boy," he conceded. He looked at his watch. "Before my fuckin' club move forward with anyfuckinthing about the Devils, you gotta know the fuckin' history of the most important fuckin' thing in my fuckin' life, so you don't accifuckindentally get fucked the fuck up. If motherfuckers ain't able to fuckin' deal with what the fuck my ass sayin', then we ain't even gotta continue the fuckin' meetin'."

"We hear you loud and clear," Dez said, glancing uneasily at Derby.

He shrugged. "I'm fucking curious to know about how you treat your sons."

"Listen up, Derby," Outlaw answered, "my kids havin' the childhood I ain't ever fuckin' had. You wanna treat your fuckin' kid like a fuckin' Silverback livin' on Mount Kilimanjaro, that shit up to you. All our lil' motherfuckers know how the fuck to shoot guns and wield blades. Ain't hidin' fuckin' from them. I know my boy, you know yours. CJ ain't ready to fuck and he ain't ready to go in the fuckin' meat shack. Case fuckin' closed."

Derby grinned. "Why don't we ask him?" He glanced at CJ. "What do you say, boy? Your old man bitching you, your brothers, and cousins out or what?"

"Don't put my fuckin' kid on the spot."

"It's fine, Dad. I can answer."

At CJ's words, all gazes turned to him, but Ryan's smirk annoyed him the most.

"Dad...'Law..." He scratched his itchy jaw. "*Outlaw* is right. I'm not interested in the meatshack right now. Those aren't images I'm ready to live with. It doesn't mean he's bitchin' me out. It just means he's allowing me to be young, wild, and free in a different way than he was." He glanced at Rory, caught between the innocence of childhood, the savagery in the Donovan blood, and the meaning of club life. "You're too young to see that stuff, Ro."

Shame slid into Rory's face while Uncle Johnnie glared at CJ.

Unfazed by his anger, CJ lifted a brow at Uncle Johnnie. "As for girls..."

His feelings about girls and sex were more complicated. Sometimes, CJ's dirty thoughts and complex feelings for Harley made him uncomfortable in Uncle Mort's presence. Fuck, sometimes it was hard to look at *her*.

He focused on a spot over Uncle Mort's shoulder. "There's someone...I want to know what I'm doing with her."

Swallowing, CJ met Uncle Mort's gaze, then wished he hadn't. His look chilled CJ. Motherfuckers who faced him on the wrong end of his goodwill probably keeled the fuck over in fear before he fucked them up.

Well, fuck. In for a dime, in for a dollar. He'd opened this can of worms.

Heat suffused his face at the absolute silence surrounding him. "A part of me—a *big* part of me—wants us to experience everything together. That means waiting. It also means I won't know what the fuck I'm doing." The more CJ spoke, the darker Uncle Mort's look became. Everyone knew who he meant. "And, well..." He sighed, confused and miserable. "She might just see me as a friend. She's never once looked at me as anything other than her best bro. So when...when I, um, *think* about going with one of the club girls, I stop because of her and because if Mom finds out she'll be disappointed in me and pissed at Dad. Until my cock starts thinking for me, I'm not ready for sex." He blew out a breath. "It's a big fucking responsibility. You have to keep yourself safe and clean. You have to keep girls safe and clean. Even if you don't want a relationship with them, you can't be a dickhead and hurt their feelings." He rubbed the nape of his neck. "Girls are fucking *trouble*. Mix in sex with that and fuck, man, everything gets all hazy."

His father placed a hand on his shoulder. "Listen up, boy, my ass ain't knowin' how a motherfuckin' meetin' about fuckin' clubs turned into fuckin' true confuckinfession time, but lemme explain some shit to you. First? You workin' on my last fuckin' nerve sayin' sex."

CJ smiled at the snickers.

"Say sex 'round your ma. Not the fuck between us." He twirled his index finger in the air. "Second, bitches got the fuckin' power to make us motherfuckers miserable. They make us wanna tear our hair the fuck out and cut our cocks off."

"Or knock the fuck out of them," Derby added.

"If you ever fuckin' lay a hand on a fuckin' woman in front of my ass, Derby, it's the last fuckin' thing your fuckin' ass'll do," Outlaw spat. He glared at CJ as if *he'd* spoken those fucked up words. "Don't hit a girl, CJ. Ever."

"I know, Dad. Is there any time when I can pretend Rebel got a cock? She should've been born with one."

"Fuck no, you ain't able to act like your sister got a cock. She a girl. Case fuckin' closed. Just fuckin' take the ass whippin' she give you like a man."

Derby snorted, but wisely kept his mouth shut.

"Mort, you okay? 'Cuz you tryna laser my boy to fuckin' smithereens with your fuckin' looks."

"Prez, I don't want to say something I shouldn't, so I'm not saying anything. CJ your son and a good kid. I love his fucking ass like he my fucking blood. But Harley my baby girl."

"Don't stop us from hanging out, Uncle Mort. She doesn't even know...She doesn't look at me as anything other than her best friend."

"Bitches and motherfuckers can't be friends," Derby protested.

"That's my motherfuckin' cue to halt this deep shit." Outlaw waved Uncle Digger back to his seat. "We gotta get to fuckin' business so we can get the fuck gone."

"I'm not stopping you from spending time with Harley, CJ," Uncle Mort reassured him. "Simply because she *don't* see you no different than she always has."

"Don't look so sad, kid." Derby rested an ankle on a knee. "Focus on the meeting and learn from your old man." He grinned. "Who knows? Might even see some action."

"What the fuck does that mean?" Uncle Johnnie demanded.

Derby put his hands behind his head and leaned back. "Nothing, John Boy."

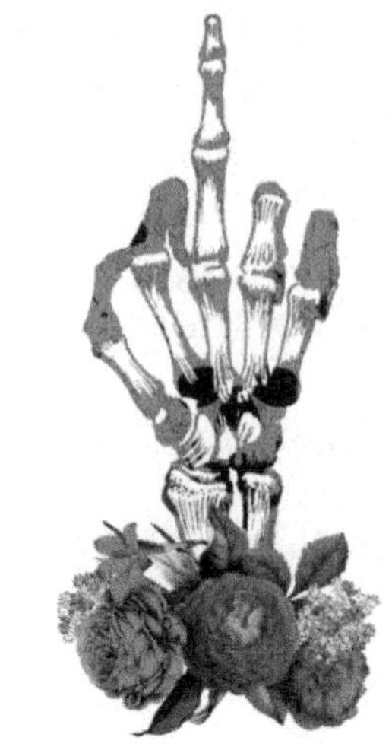

Chapter Four

REBEL

“Psssttt, Rebel.”

Glancing over her shoulder at Molly Harris’s call, Rebel Caldwell lowered her body out of her bridge pose and stood. As usual, their substitute coach hadn’t made an appearance yet. That bitch worked on Rebel’s finest nerve.

Crossing her legs underneath her, she smiled at Molly, a sophomore like CJ and Ryan. Molly was tall and pretty with long brown hair and deceptively intelligent blue-gray eyes. Ordinarily, Rebel wouldn’t torture herself by conversing with Molly, but her scheming to see Diesel had worked, lifting her spirits.

“Hiya,” she greeted, glancing around the athletic facility, built with her mother’s money, Dweller funds, bonds, and local taxes, and backed by her daddy’s vision.

The huge building had centers within centers, to offer students a variety of physical ed, electives, and afterschool activities. Half the space had two levels. A cantilevered third level loomed over a section of the stadium seats where parents crowded during a smorgasbord of games and tournaments. Almost whatever their heart desired.

Literally. *Their* heart's desire. Rebel and Harley liked cheer, gymnastics, yoga, swimming, and volleyball. Mattie as well, but she also liked horseback riding. Because, yeah...*Mattie*. Rebel's twin, Rule, loved art and religion. The boy was born five centuries too late and in the wrong fucking family, but whatever. CJ loved football. Daddy loved CJ. The school's outside stadium should bear her brother's name.

For that matter, Ridge Moore Charter School should be named the Death Dweller School for Offspring and Cronies. To be fair, not every kid was affiliated with the Dwellers. Ridge Moore had an application process with exorbitant fees, rigorous testing, and competitive selection for everyone else.

"Reb?" Molly's prompt reminded Rebel of her presence.

Wondering how Molly scored high enough on the entrance exam to earn a spot at Ridge Moore, Rebel frowned.

"Reb?" Molly called, louder.

Rebel searched for rescue from the girl, but found her friends preoccupied.

Harley and Matilda were doing side planks. Jaleena Davis practiced handstands, while the other dozen girls on the team used Coach's lack of attention to complete circuits on the floor, still outlaid for the track meet that happened Saturday. Inside, because of inclement weather. Running was okay, however their cheer team didn't need the skills for a relay race. Fuck, not even a sprint. Their team was centered around gymnastics and pyramids.

She uncrossed her legs, planting her feet firmly on the ground. Bracing her arms, she lifted herself and bent her body into another bridge. "What's up?"

"Oh, um, okay." Molly scrambled into the same position, so close to Rebel their chins nearly touched. "I have a question for you."

"I'm listening, dude." Holding her position and kicking out one leg, Rebel grunted. Slowly, she lowered the leg, then lifted the other one, wishing for Coach Ericks. They'd be practicing, instead of doing their own thing.

"Here's my problem," Molly said, unaware of Rebel's growing annoyance with their substitute. "I had to retake the second semester of biology *again* because I failed it *again*. Well, I'm failing *again* and if they make me retake it in the fall, that'll be the third time." She untangled herself from the pose and sat.

With a sigh, Rebel did the same. Noticing Harley and Matilda glancing her way, she beckoned them over. Bursting into high-pitched, annoying ass laughter, Mattie flipped Rebel off. Harley rolled her eyes, grabbed Mattie's wrist, and yanked her forward.

Rebel glanced at the huge digital scoreboard that included a clock on the far end, high above the doors leading to the girl's locker rooms and the coach's office. Until Coach Erick's maternity leave, she'd always enjoyed practice. Between the substitute's jack shit behavior and Rebel's anticipation to see Diesel, dusting practice couldn't come fast enough. Since he'd moved into his own place, he seldom visited.

"Hey, Harley," Molly greeted. "Hi, Mattie."

"Repeat what you told me," Rebel ordered Molly when her two best friends joined them, relieved to focus on something other than missing her old coach and her anxiety over seeing Diesel.

Mattie snapped her strawberry-blonde brows together once Molly finished her explanation. "What does you being a stupid bitch have to do with us?"

"Yeah," Rebel agreed. "What she said, Molly."

"You need our help, right?" Harley asked, always the diplomat.

"Still not *our* problem, Harley." Rebel gnawed on her pinky nail. "Stop being so nice."

"People will think you're boring, Harley," Mattie said with a nod of her head as Rebel spat out the remnants of her chewed nail before starting on another.

"Hellloooo." Wrinkling her nose, Molly snapped her fingers to recapture attention. "This is about me, not Harley. She's perfect just the way she is." She smiled. "That's why CJ's so devoted to her."

Brown eyes gleaming, Mattie plopped between Rebel and Molly. "Bros before hoes, Moll."

Scrunching up her face in confusion, Molly studied Harley, eyes widening. "You have a dick like him?" she gasped.

Spitting her newest chomped off nail in Molly's direction appealed to Rebel but she changed her mind at Harley's small head shake.

"B-but where?" Molly went on, clueless Rebel contemplated lobbing a loogie her way instead of just a torn, spitty nail. Otherwise, she would've shut the fuck up. "How small is it? Is that why you don't have tits yet?"

"No, Molly," Harley growled, her pretty eyes flashing with indignation as she, too, sat on the other side of Rebel. "You've seen me in the shower after gym *and* practice. Where would I hide a penis?"

Mattie crawled to Harley and settled next to her. "See? Boring. No adults are around. You don't have to say penis, Harley."

"I know," she admitted, chewing on her lower lip. "I practice saying curse words in my bedroom mirror."

"And you pronounce them just the way I wrote them out phonetically?" Rebel asked to be certain. Harley needed every assistance.

"Oh, I want a guide to cuss phonetically to make me a bad ass," Molly chirped. "My cussing is definitely too politically correct."

Rebel made a *huh, bitch?* face at her. "What an oxymoron. What the fuck is politically correct cursing, dumb ass? Last I heard, saying motherfucker isn't appropriate in any situation."

"Well, I always pronounce my ings and ers. Moth-ER fuck-ER. Fuck-ING. I sound so dorky."

"Ooookkkkaaayyyy," Rebel chanted. "Let's get back to biology. I'm not a fucking profanity professor."

"What do you need from us?" Harley asked.

"I turned in the first draft of my final paper." Molly switched topics with ease. Shocking, with her lentil-sized brain. "And got another 'F'. Mrs. Campo doesn't teach correctly. She should go back to school. I provided firm proof a platypus is actually a frog."

Uncertainty swept into Harley's face and she pressed down on her lips. Meanwhile, Mattie seemed a breath away from beating Molly's ass.

"Get the fuck out of my face," Rebel ordered. "I don't have time for your fucking games, Molly."

"What games?"

"The one where you're pretending to be a stupid airhead," Mattie supplied.

Molly blinked. "I'm not pretending anything and I'm definitely not an airhead. You two are jealous of me and Mrs. Campo is threatened by my brilliance."

"Yeah...uh, *no*." Rebel shook her head in disgust. "There's not a fucking thing *we* can do. Ignorance is solvable. Fucking stupid isn't."

"I'm not stupid, Rebel," Molly argued, unaffected by Rebel's outburst. "I speak the truth. Platypussases lay eggs. Other frogs do too. In water. Boy platypussases AKA dude frogs are poison. And—"

Growling, Rebel jumped to her feet, glaring at Mattie and her annoying cackles. "Those animals aren't in the same classification."

"They aren't animals, Rebel," Molly sneered, rolling her eyes. "They're reptiles."

Harley giggled before she clapped a hand over her mouth.

"First?" Rebel snarled. "If you like your fucking eyes in your head, *don't* roll them at me." One of Daddy's tenets for respect. "Second, a frog is a fucking amphibian and a platypus is a mammal."

"No—"

"I don't know much about a fucking platypus," Rebel interrupted before Molly finished her protest, "other than they are stupid looking motherfuckers."

Rebel looked in Harley's direction, and Molly followed suit.

"Don't look at me." No longer amused, Harley rose to her feet. "I know nothing about them."

"You're the quiet good girl. You're supposed to be the smart one, too."

"Unlike us loud bitches, right, Molly?" Mattie stood to better glare at the brown-haired girl, whose head really did no fucking good on her shoulders, filled with fucking air as it was.

"Exactly, Mattie," Molly said brightly.

"Molly, piss off," Harley ordered. "Stop stereotyping me."

"By the way, dumb ass, plural for platypus is platypuses," Mattie announced. "*Platypi* is also correct, but people pushed it aside. If we followed the rules of the Greek language, it's *platypodes*. Most frogs aren't venomous, stupid bitch. Except poison from one golden frog can kill eight motherfuckers and I do believe it is both the males and females. Like Rebel said, frogs are amphibians. The platypus is a mammal."

"Nuh-uh," Molly protested. "'Cause I think humans are mammals and we don't lay eggs. We don't even have eggs in us, unless we eat them."

"Molly!"

If Harley hadn't slapped her hand over Rebel's mouth, she'd have torn Molly a new asshole.

"Molly, don't ever have children, 'kay?" Mattie advised. "You'd be hit with a criminal charge the moment you gave birth. Understand?"

As Harley removed her hand from Rebel's mouth and did her best to hold in her giggle, Molly's blue-gray eyes rounded. "For real?"

Rebel nodded. "Yeah, boo," she said gravely. "Even Einstein's sperm couldn't raise their IQ."

"Oh." Molly thought for a moment. "Right. They found his brain and brought him back to life when they put it back in his head?"

Another burst of laughter escaped Harley before she shifted her weight and looked away. Harley's struggle to contain herself sent Rebel into fits of giggles.

"We want in on the joke." Already smiling, Jaleena Davis guided her besties over. "What's so funny?"

Shaking her head, Rebel said, "Don't worry about it, Leen. I'll clue you in later."

"Hey, Harls." Jaleena waved at Mattie and nodded to Molly. The eight of them spoke amongst each other for a few minutes before Jaleena led her three friends away.

"She's soooo beautiful," Mattie whispered dreamily, watching Jaleena talk quietly to the three girls she always hung around. "Her skin looks so soft. Like black satin. And...*fuck*...her fucking face. Gorgeous."

"She doesn't have any hair," Molly pointed out, wrinkling her nose. "Furthermore, you sound like a dude the way you talk about her."

Flushing, Matilda glanced away.

Molly wasn't malicious. However, being dumb as a fucking brick made her ten times worse.

"Hey, Molly, Rebel." Harley's call pulled Molly's attention away from Matilda. "Mommie got this new lip gloss for me and you need to try it." She placed an arm around Mattie. "It makes my lips so plump."

"You don't need plumper lips. What are you talking about?" Molly demanded.

"Okay, so look, Molly." Harley released Mattie. "We ignored your messed up comment about Jaleena's hair. Don't test my patience, dude. Please keep your ignorance to yourself."

Molly scowled. "I'm not ignorant," she said with a sniff. "If anyone is, it's you, Harley. You have a friend called Rebel."

"What?"

"Helloooo.....*Rebels....Civil War*," Molly said with exasperation. "My God, don't you know history? Her name is Rebel, so she must be related to a Civil War dude from the south."

"If anyone's related to a southern Civil War dude, it's me," Harley said. "My mother, grandmother, great-grandmother...well, generations back, are all from New Orleans."

"I've never met anyone from New Orleans," Molly chirped. "I've always wondered something about that place. Maybe, you can answer."

Indecision tore across Harley's face, but she sighed and nodded. "What do you want to know?"

"Where's Old Orleans?"

Harley frowned.

"You don't know either, do you?" Molly persisted. "If there's a new something, then there must be an old one, right?"

"Sure, Molls," Rebel said, tired of going round and round with her. If they kept it up, Molly's stupid would rub off on them, and then they were all fucked.

"Now, about being friends with her—" Molly nodded in Rebel's direction— "She was named after the Stars and Bars."

"What the fuck?" Mattie exclaimed, eyes wide. "You don't know basic biology, but you know a few things about the goddamn Civil War? And according to your first dumb motherfuckery, Rebel got her name from a Civil War dude, *not* the battle flag."

"It doesn't matter, does it?" Molly tossed her shiny hair. "You're still named after—"

"A flag or a Civil War dude has nothing to do with Rebel's name," Harley said with impatience. "It's for Uncle Chris. Okay?"

"No," Molly insisted. "Chris starts with a 'c'. Rebel's name doesn't, so see you're the stupid one, like I said."

"I'm done," Harley yelled, turning on her heel. "I can't take it anymore. Where is Coach anyway?"

"Wait, Harley!" Mattie cried. "Don't leave me here!"

"Harls, c'mon," Rebel coaxed, "finish telling me about the lip gloss Aunt Bailey bought you."

"Well, I'm not interested in hearing," Molly said breezily, waving her hand in dismissal. "We don't even have the same coloring."

"I know a color that'll look good on you," Rebel said with an innocent smile.

"Depends on the shade," Molly protested. "Or the name. Good lip gloss also has cool names."

"The color has a really cool name," Rebel promised.

"What?" Molly asked with suspicion.

"Color is Bleeding Lip," Rebel said with a glower. "Designer is Beat a Bitch to the Ground."

"Isn't it Fuck a Bitch Up?" Mattie put in, studying her manicured nails. "By the way, doofus, the name of the color is usually the name of the gloss, unless you're talking about who puts out the line."

"Ladies!" Coach barreled down one of the concrete staircases and blew her whistle. "Practice is over. You're dismissed."

"Coach, we barely warmed up," Harley blurted. "We haven't gone through one routine."

Coach smiled. "Sorry, Harley. You're welcome to practice on your own. I know you miss Coach Ericks. Her maternity leave ends in July, so she'll be back in time for your August cheer camp." She turned back in the direction she'd come. "See you ladies tomorrow evening," she said over her shoulder as if future practices under her direction would be any better than today's.

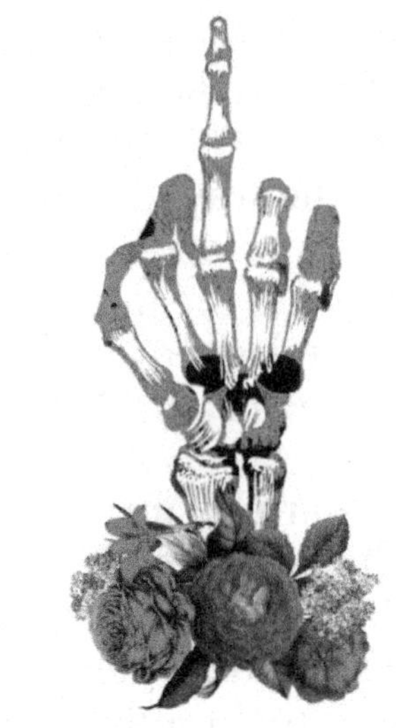

Chapter Five

In the wake of CJ's revelations, no one looked down on his feelings for Harley forever. Not even Uncle Mort, despite the death stares he gave CJ.

As for the inconsequential and unimportant Lumbly, 'Law didn't need to know about the fuckhead. CJ would find a way to handle him.

His uncles and father engaged in a deep conversation with Dez and Derby, so CJ doubted they noticed as Cole stood from his seat and headed to the bar. No one tracked his movements or saw him taking out his cellphone.

But, then, 'Law stiffened and glanced at Cole, who was laughing and busily texting. From that point on, Outlaw kept one eye on the motherfucker at the bar and another on Derby.

An odd feeling settled into CJ. An expectation the bogeyman would jump out.

Cole grinned and nodded, still texting. A glance in his father's direction showed him once again fully engaged in the discussion.

Cole slid off the bar stool and headed toward the back door. Opening it, he peeped around it.

"...put it to the fuckin' vote, Derby..." Outlaw's voice trailed off. "Ain't promisin'..."

Once more, the conversation slipped from CJ as Cole looked over his shoulder. Throwing CJ a taunting look, he fashioned a finger gun, raised it to his head, and pumped his thumb.

Without warning, his dad jumped to his feet, his .9mm drawn and aimed at the asshole at the door so fast it took a moment for anyone to register the actions. When they did, the Dwellers got to their feet and drew their own weapons.

"Hands the fuck up," Outlaw ordered. "One of you motherfuckers make a fuckin' move and you fucked. Ain't takin' no fuckin' chances with my boy and my nephews here."

"It's nothing bad, Outlaw." Dez stood and raised his hands. "We want to entertain you and your boys. Tell him, Derby."

"Told the stupid motherfuckers don't do this, Outlaw," Derby said instead, glaring at Dez.

"Fuck you, motherfucker," Outlaw snapped. "You knew what the fuck motherfuckers was doin' cuz you fuckin' mentioned entertainment."

Derby paled. "Outlaw—"

"Shut the fuck up," Outlaw commanded.

"D-don't shoot," Cole wheedled, still next to the half-open door. "I promise it isn't bad—"

"According to you," Derby said on a snort, then nodded toward Outlaw. "This motherfucker will see it differently. I guarantee."

"You say that now!" Cole said with irritation.

"Shut the fuck up," Derby ordered, anger and unease in his face. "If you don't want a fucking bullet in your piehole, remember your fucking place."

"My ass outta fuckin' patience." Unafraid standing head and shoulders above everyone and a perfect target, Outlaw stalked to Cole and shoved the gun against his temple.

"Don't shoot," Derby pleaded. "The Dwellers not bitch killers."

"Cole look like a fuckin' bitch to you?" Outlaw asked.

"And bitches fuck up motherfuckers, too," Uncle Digger grouched.

"I swear—" Derby started.

"You workin' my last goddamn nerve, Derby," Outlaw snarled, then addressed Cole. "If I ain't likin' what the fuck on the other fuckin' side of this fuckin' door, you the first motherfucker missin' a fuckin' brain."

"Get behind me, son," Uncle Johnnie instructed Rory.

"CJ, I got a spare piece on my holster on the other side of me," Uncle Mort told him. "Get it and train it the same way we got ours."

"Okay." CJ cleared his throat, surprised at shaky tone. He'd been handling guns for years. Except he'd never aimed with the potential to fire at a person.

"Rory, take my second weapon from my side."

Uncle Johnnie's amended instructions reached CJ through a fog. Fearing the possibility of shooting someone stole his focus.

"Ryan, fella, I have another gun inside my cut," Uncle Val said.

"Open the motherfucker," Outlaw instructed once CJ, Ryan, and Rory held guns.

CJ buzzed with both anticipation and dread at the slow opening door. Who was on the other side?

Another inch.

His stomach twisted. Any minute he'd vomit.

If he wasn't fast enough, his father, cousins, or uncles could be wounded or killed. Fuck, *he* could be, too. His hand trembled.

"Steady, lil' dude," Uncle Digger said. "Steady."

"You got this, CJ," Uncle Mort said.

"Focus, nephew," Uncle Johnnie soothed. "Keep calm."

Sweat dripped down CJ's back and neck. The gun felt enormous. In his imagination, it weighed a ton. His hand wavered. Goddamn, he hadn't signed up for this shit.

Finally, the door opened fully and...

And...

He blinked, his arm falling to his side, his mouth damn near dropping to the floor.

A line of girls, wearing only stiletto sandals, strutted in. Each girl headed to one of them. *His* chick had the biggest breasts he'd ever seen and a narrow waist. Her pussy hair was dyed neon orange and sprinkled with glitter.

"I'm Peaches," she said in a soft, throaty voice.

At the gun jerking from his hand, CJ couldn't bother to see who took it.

His father's woman was tall and voluptuous with dirty blonde hair and a mole on her cheek. Outlaw allowing her to whisper in his ear shocked CJ.

The partition opened to a stage running the width of the room. Four girls dressed in glittery costumes sashayed out. *Honkytonk Badonkadunk* suddenly blasted through unseen speakers. Two of the girls amongst the bikers wrapped themselves around one another, crashing their lips together. On stage, the girls moved their bodies in time to the beat of the music, their clothes flying away piece by piece.

Peaches grabbed CJ's cock and he jerked. Nervous and uncertain, he glanced toward his father. Both him and the girl were gone.

Harley and his mother flitted through CJ's mind. Then Peaches unbuckled his belt and he bit his lip, torn between anticipation and despair. Harley was anxious to know about club meetings; Mom was *MegAnn*, 'Law's sweet angel and the backbone of their family.

She trusted Dad.

Anger and betrayal surged into CJ, yet Peaches didn't notice. She stuck her hand in his boxer briefs and wrapped it around his dick. He gasped, his brain clouding...

The sound of a gunshot cut through the noise. Everything screeched to a halt.

Peaches squealed in terror and jumped back. His uncles, Rory, and Ryan sat at their table alone, watching the goings-on with clenched jaws. However, his father...stormed back through the door, dragging the woman with him by the collar on the shirt she now wore.

Cole's shirt. She must've put it on while outside with his dad after...

When Outlaw arrived at the table, the other men got to their feet. Derby and Dez set their women aside before rising too.

"Take this cunt before I fuckin' kill her," Outlaw snarled, shoving her away with bloody hands.

She stumbled and swiped at blood-stained cheek. "You killed Cole," she screamed around pitiful sobs. "I begged you not to kill my little brother! You don't even care that his blood is on my face and your hand. You killed him!"

"Ima kill *you* if you ain't gettin' the fuck outta my fuckin' face."

Derby rushed to her. “Serina, listen to the man.”

“Why?” she snapped. “I followed him outside to explain you keep *your* stupid cunt and still fuck me.”

Narrowing his eyes, Outlaw stared at Serina. “You callin’ my woman a stupid cunt?”

“If the shoe—”

Derby clapped his hand over her mouth. “Outlaw, don’t kill her. She might be expecting my kid. Or my grandkid. Or...she’s expecting, okay?”

Rory and CJ glanced at each other. They seemed to be the only motherfuckers shocked a girl wouldn’t know whose baby she carried.

“I ain’t givin’ a good fuck if she expecting Daffy Duck fuckin’ kid,” Outlaw roared, red-faced. “Clue that cunt in. I walked my fuckin’ ass away from her octofuckinpussy hands to fuck up Cole. *She* followed *my* ass. I gave her a fuckin’ pass, blew Cole the fuck away *and* let that bitch wear his shirt. And she still fuckin’ with me? Fuckin’ with my woman? Not only disrespectin’ my girl by tryna gimme pussy but callin’ her a fuckin’ cunt?”

Peaches squeaked and sidled closer, wrapping her arms around CJ.

Dad turned his furious gaze to them. If CJ’s guilt at believing his father betrayed MegAnn hadn’t wilted his cock, Outlaw’s mad-dog look would’ve. He’d never been afraid of his father, but he’d never seen him so livid either.

“Get the fuck away from my kid.”

Every woman except Serina ran to the stage and crowded there.

Outlaw glowered at CJ. “Zip your fuckin’ pants, boy.”

Shame swept through CJ. Outlaw didn’t have to fucking bellow the order and humiliate him. Worse, Uncle Mort’s dirty glare ratcheted up CJ’s embarrassment.

"You wouldn't know what to do with your fucking cock anyway," Ryan taunted.

"Shut your fucking mouth, Ryan," Uncle Val ordered.

"You know what to do with your cock, Ryan?" Rory asked, his eyes wide.

Gritting his teeth, CJ put himself to rights, wanting to beat Ryan to the fucking ground and cursing Outlaw for disgracing him. If club meetings were like this, he never wanted to attend another one of these motherfuckers. When he became Prez, he'd see shit done differently.

Outlaw's unexpected whistle startled CJ and he frowned.

"Listen up, motherfuckers and bitches." Outlaw made a three hundred sixty degree turn. "Battin' your fuckin' cunt from the fuckin' Eiffel Tower up to you. I ain't got a motherfuckin' thing to say. Your pussy. Your decision." He held up his hand and wiggled the finger with his wedding band. "Fuck with this, fuck with your life. Disrespect my fuckin' woman, you endin' up in fuckin' pieces all the fuck round this motherfucker. Ain't *nothin'* more fuckin' important to me than my wife." He walked closer to Derby, who'd wrapped his arm around Serina. "You got motherfuckin' jokes, huh, motherfucker? Ain't no fuckin' reason Dez and his motherfuckers shoulda brought these bitches out. *You* vouchin' for them so that mean *you* clue them the fuck in."

Swallowing, Derby nodded. "It was all—"

"I adfuckinvise you keep your fuckin' mouth shut," Outlaw warned. "Hearin' your fuckin' voice might tip me the fuck over the edge. Hear me?"

"Yeah, Outlaw."

"Bitches wanna strip," Outlaw continued as if Derby hadn't spoken, "my ass can fuckin' look the other fuckin' way. Naked bitches hangin' the fuck on my fuckin' ass on a different fuckin' level."

"Son, you the fucking reason Meggie girl can't stand your dumb ass," Uncle Mort pointed out, addressing Derby, looking less than pleased. "Always fucking over Gypsy. No matter how many times she leave you, you always get her back. *You* got Roaming Cock Syndrome. *We* don't."

"You been pulling this bullshit for years, Derby," Uncle Val scoffed. "Trying to get us to fuck over our bitches—"

Outlaw lifted a brow and CJ stifled a laugh at Uncle Val's panic.

"And Meggie," he added.

"This fucking sneak attack was uncalled for," Uncle Digger said with disgust. "And with some of our lil' dudes here too. Bruhhhhhhhhh."

"Fuck, fine." Derby scowled. "Gypsy fucking left me again when I told her this cunt might be carrying my kid," he said, nodding to Serina. "I figured why the fuck should I be miserable on my own. I love my bitch but she keeps walking out. All Meggie do is hate me and tell my bitch to leave me because I know what to do with my cock. Watching you stick your cock in another bitch would vindicate me."

"You'd fuck up my parents' marriage?" CJ asked in disbelief, sounding more like a disappointed kid than an angry man. "You've known Mom for years."

"I wouldn't tell Meggie," Derby snapped. "But I could look at her, knowing Outlaw was no better than me."

"Now, Prez," Uncle Mort started.

"Dad?" CJ called, his father's concerning trembling removing CJ's annoyance and humiliation.

"Fuck, Outlaw! I didn't mean anything," Derby blurted, sweat beading his brow.

"Think about our wives, Christopher," Uncle Johnnie said slowly. "Our lives. How good things have been for us. We prefer peaceful negotiations than bloody wars that might risk our families."

"Digger, Mort, roll the fuck out," Outlaw said. "You got fuckin' disposal duties."

Rory's eyes lit up with an anticipation lacking when the naked girls had been roaming. "Can I help?"

"No!" Uncle Johnnie barked, a guilty flush creeping up his neck.

Outlaw studied Derby again. The motherfucker looked ready to piss himself.

"Please, don't hurt Derby," Serina begged. "Cole started calling your wife names but..." She blinked away the tears filling her eyes.

Unmoved, Outlaw captured Derby's gaze and held it. Just as he lifted his weapon to fire, his phone rang. Hearing *When A Man Loves A Woman* stopped Dad.

Derby closed his eyes. "Fuck, thank you, Meggie."

That wildness swept over Dad's features, somehow making the ringtone more urgent and insistent. Dad wanted to pull the trigger and yet killing Derby would upset Mom, despite what the stupid motherfucker did.

The ringing stopped. Dad twitched, aimed the gun. Derby raised his hands, opened his mouth. To beg. To apologize.

Serina sobbed.

Ryan didn't shrug away Uncle Val's hand on his shoulder, when, normally, he would've.

Mom's ringtone blared again.

Growling in frustration, Dad lowered his weapon, yanked his cellphone from his cut, and answered, walking out the front door and into the parking lot where the bikes were.

Derby dropped heavily into a chair.

Uncle Digger blew out a noisy breath and rubbed his brow. "Mort, you was right to advise me to keep my kid home."

Sitting across from Derby, Uncle Mort folded his arms and stared at the motherfucker.

"What, Mort?" he finally asked.

"What the fuck you mean *what*, son? What? You a stupid motherfucker? What? You a deathwishy motherfucker?"

"What? You a hypocritical motherfucker?" Uncle Digger added. "Wanting Outlaw to fuck over Meggie then thanking her for interrupting your rightful fucking up?"

"Derby, fuckhead, you a lucky fuckhead," Uncle Val acknowledged. "Make no mistake Outlaw would've blown you the fuck away and found a way not to let Meggie know he buried you."

"That's what I mean!" he said, grabbing onto Uncle Val's words. "He lies to her about other shit. He could lie to her about getting pussy from other bitches."

"*Wrong*, bruh," Uncle Digger said in exasperation. "His fucking trigger finger and mad dog fury the only part of Outlaw not belonging to Meggie."

"If you not knowing Outlaw a fucking wild psycho over Meggie after all these fucking years, you deserve any fucking thing he do you," Uncle Val scoffed. "This shit was unnecessary. I feel like telling Puff so *she* could kick your fucking nuts in."

Derby stiffened. "I wish that bitch, *any bitch*, would."

"If your cunt lay a hand on my man, I'll fuck her up," Serina spat.

"First, bitch, *you* shut the fuck up. My woman'll drain your fucking blood without blinking an eye."

"She sure would," Uncle Johnnie said proudly. "She's my cousin and Christopher's sister."

"Second," Uncle Val continued coldly, his full attention on Derby, "you ever touch my woman, that'll be the last motherfucking thing you fucking do."

"Well, Bailey..."

Uncle Mort lifted a brow and Derby snapped his mouth shut.

"I'm a little annoyed, Derby brother," Uncle Johnnie remarked, seating himself and lighting a cigarette. He nodded to Dez. "With you, too."

"Me?" Dez asked, swallowing. He sat in his earlier spot, while his club members took everything in from their tables. "Wh-what I do, Johnnie?"

"It's what the fuck you didn't do," Uncle Mort responded with disgust.

Uncle Val took up the conversation, as if they shared a brain. "Give us a solid reason for today's urgency."

Uncle Johnnie pointed to Derby. "*You're* the motherfucker who called for this meeting, fuckhead."

"We got offtrack," Derby said quickly.

"I don't think so." Uncle Johnnie bared his teeth. "You called this meeting to fuck with Megan."

Derby jumped to his feet. "I didn't! I swear! I wanted to fuck with her, but the meeting wasn't only for that. Outlaw isn't fucking me up over that fucking lie."

"You got another fucking lie he need to fuck you up over?" Uncle Mort asked.

"*What*? No, fuck! Mort, I'd never fuck over Outlaw. If I got to die by the sword, I want it quick. Getting on the wrong side of you fucks might subject me to Johnnie and I've seen what he does. I just miss Gypsy."

Uncle Digger raised his hand. "I got a idea."

"Speak, Mr. Digger," Uncle Val said, sounding like a professor offering a student permission.

"Stop fucking over your bitch and she might stay with your fucking ass," Digger growled.

"I can't stop being a man." Derby returned to his seat, grabbed a napkin from the table and patted his forehead. "Gypsy not always in the mood to fuck. She only suck dick when she want something. *And* she's menopausal. It's a lot of work to get her pussy wet."

Serina parked herself on Derby's lap and kissed his mouth. "My snatch is hot and juicy," she murmured.

At the words, CJ's balls tingled and his cock sprung to life. Diesel kept him supplied with a porn stash, so Serina's words brought very vivid images to CJ's mind.

"Get the fuck away from me," Derby ordered, shoving Serina to the floor.

CJ jumped to his feet, intending to lend his assistance to the sobbing woman. She'd disrespected his mother but she didn't deserve Derby's abuse.

Shaking his head, Uncle Mort's nod indicated CJ return to his seat, though he went to Serina and helped her to her feet.

"You a cold motherfucker," Uncle Val spat.

"I need a cock suck, Serina," one of the Devils called.

"Earn your fucking keep, cunt," Derby snapped, waving her toward the tables.

Her lower lip trembling, she sniffled and tripped away.

"Why's she crying, Dad?" Rory asked.

Because Derby was a fucking asshole. CJ wished he could say that, but his father expected CJ to respect adults, even the fuckheads who didn't deserve it. His father believed it taught him the value of hierarchy and authority.

Serina sobbed as the Devil led her outside, using the same back door that Cole had.

"Dad?"

"I'll tell you later, son," Uncle Johnnie promised.

"Johnnie, we really wanted to meet about doing more runs for the Dwellers," Dez explained. "We've proven ourselves loyal. We're much smaller than Derby's club. Or even the Gnomes, but we can handle increased payloads."

Uncle Johnnie shrugged. "Talk to Christopher."

"He won't listen as long as he wants to blow my fucking ass off," Derby said.

"That's a fucking *you* problem," Uncle Mort declared. "You shouldn't have fucked with Meggie."

"In all these fucking years, Outlaw hasn't *once* fucked another bitch?" Derby asked in disbelief.

"No," his uncles chorused without hesitation.

"Not *once*," Uncle Mort stressed. "I never fucked over Bailey. Val, Johnnie, and Digger faithful to their women too. What the fuck don't you understand about that, son?"

"He got stunted fucking growth, Mort," Uncle Digger declared.

"A useless brain," Uncle Val said.

"Then why the fuck is it still in his head?" Uncle Johnnie considered Derby. "Luckily, I prefer peace over payback nowadays."

"Part of the reason we're with the Dwellers is for protection," Dez admitted, his eyes wide with sudden fear. "Sometimes, peace don't cut it."

"*You* might like peace, Johnnie," Derby said, "but Outlaw does things his way."

"Yeah, bro," a Devil called, "he's a fucking legend."

"A fucking legend with a fucking family," Uncle Johnnie amended. "His family comes first. Like mine. *Ours*."

Dez frowned. "I'm not following."

"My wife and children are everything to me," Uncle Johnnie said. "Kendall has stood by my side and believed in me through good and bad. She is a wonderful mother to my children."

She was also a good aunt. CJ had firsthand experience of Aunt Kendall reading Shakespeare to them. She also played games, and even danced, with them. She'd advocated for Diesel to join the law firm she partnered with Brooks.

"Mom's a riot," Rory piped in dryly. "She can't cook good food, though. That shit her and Mattie whips up..." He shivered dramatically.

Yeah, cuz that shit was on another fucking level.

"Shhhh," Uncle Johnnie chuckled, placing a finger over his lips. "That's a secret amongst us men, Rory."

"I wish *them* women gave Kendall fucking cooking lessons for *us* motherfuckers," Uncle Digger grumbled.

Uncle Johnnie laughed along with everyone else. "Our love for our wives and kids, as deep as it is, doesn't compare to what Christopher feels for Megan. In his eyes, you've disrespected her on more than one front. You had women here to fuck us. You *wanted* him to fuck over Megan to vindicate her rightfully telling Gypsy to leave you. And you insisted we bring our boys. *CJ. Megan's fucking pride and joy.* Now, Christopher has to tell his wife that *her son* got a fucking hand job from one of your whores."

Oh, fuck.

Jesus.

Goddamn.

CJ's cock would never harden again. He'd never look his mother in the eye again. He'd be ten times more embarrassed than he'd been at his father ordering him to zip his pants and she'd be so disappointed in him.

"Meggie probably telling Bailey all about it," Uncle Mort announced, his gaze lasering CJ.

Nausea hit CJ. Suddenly, he wished he was holding a gun on a motherfucker. *Any* motherfucker. That experience couldn't compare to his current panic. Even if Aunt Bailey didn't tell Harley what went on, *she'd* know and might look at him differently. Maybe, even believe he wasn't right for Harley.

"There are times when Christopher is *Outlaw*. Like this evening with Cole," Uncle Johnnie said quietly. "Outlaw has no mercy, forgiveness, or understanding.

He wants death and destruction." His eyes glazed. "Blood. Dismemberment. Gore."

"Sometimes that shit required, motherfucker," Uncle Mort said tightly, snapping Uncle Johnnie out of his trance.

"I need Christopher, Megan's husband, who doesn't want to put her in danger and risk her. I need Christopher to protect *my* wife, so I keep peace by reminding the club president of what the family man might lose if he declares war."

It almost sounded as if Uncle Johnnie was manipulating situations to his advantage, disregarding what was best for the club.

"Your bitch ass reaping what the fuck you sow," Uncle Mort spat.

"You just fucking lucky shit been relatively peaceful," Uncle Digger said with disapproval. "But you wrong, Johnnie. You so fucking wrong, sometimes casually bringing up when Mystic kidnapped Meggie and left her in that fucking hole to die. You know what the fuck you doing."

"No matter how we try to talk to him when you do that bullshit he can't think of nothing but almost losing his woman," Uncle Val said, eyeing Uncle Johnnie. "We not in no social club. A day coming when we need *Outlaw*—"

"And not just to fuck up stupid motherfuckers like Cole and Derby," Uncle Mort said.

"And *Outlaw*, the *real Outlaw*, won't be around," Uncle Val finished.

"Johnnie, even I wouldn't bring that up to Outlaw," Derby said, emotion filling his eyes. "That's so fucking low. They took her and just abandoned CJ. He could've wandered in the fucking street and been hit by a car. Fuck, one of those motherfuckers could've rolled over him! Meggie was lucky not to be raped, but she would've died if Outlaw hadn't found her when he did."

CJ had vague recollections of his mother's kidnapping. Mostly, he'd been too young to remember and the rest he pushed away.

"Boys?" Uncle Johnnie's gaze swept from CJ to Ryan to Rory. "This is club business. We expect you not to discuss the conversation you've just heard with *anyone*. If they aren't present to participate, then it isn't required they know."

"Uncle Christopher is Prez, Dad. Shouldn't he know?"

"No!" Uncle Johnnie barked.

Nostrils flaring, CJ glared at his uncle. Unless he sewed CJ's fucking mouth shut, no way would he *not* tell his father.

"As much as I want you to tell Outlaw, CJ, it'll just cause unnecessary drama," Uncle Val said. "Since we not facing no threats, I'm asking you to keep this to yourself. One, Johnnie should keep his fucking mouth shut in front of other motherfuckers, even support clubs. He can face disciplinary actions."

Rory gasped. "Please don't say anything, CJ," he begged.

CJ hated his predicament, but Uncle Val was right. Ongoing peace meant his father didn't have to know. "I'm doing it for *you*, Ro."

Low murmurs from the stage drew Ryan's attention and he craned his neck to see the women there.

"Dad, can the girls on stage finish stripping?"

Pulling a small flask from inside his cut, Uncle Val shrugged. "After Outlaw leave. If you want to watch those bitches, I'll wait for you outside." He drank again. "When bitches onstage stripping while we at a meeting, I can't do anything. But I'm not actively disrespecting your mama, boy."

The entrance door opened and Outlaw headed to them. He was calm, even relaxed, with his piece out of sight and a small smile curving his lips, as if he hadn't almost shot Derby's fucking ass off.

"Mort, Digger, get to fuckin' steppin'." Outlaw lit a cigarette before continuing. "Derby, motherfucker, you fuckin' live another fuckin' day. CJ, let's ride the fuck out."

Orders issued, his father offered the room one last glower, pinned Derby with the promise of vengeance, and sauntered back to the parking lot.

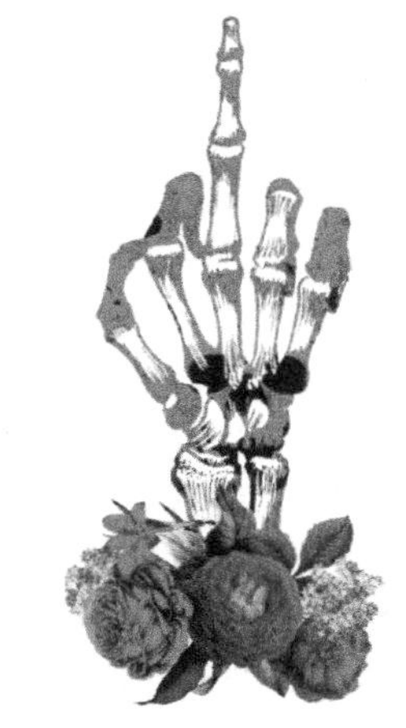

Chapter Six

REBEL

Rebel hid herself in the shadow of Clark Hall until Aunt Kendall drove off after picking up Harley and Mattie. Riding home in comfort was a big perk of afterschool activities when *seventeen* motherfuckers went to school. No, wait! Her cousin Kade was five now, old enough to attend school. Next year, Cove would be added into the mix.

Fuck all these motherfuckers. Over the next several years, three more kids—one her littlest brother—would be enrolled. Goddamn, but the babies needed to fucking stop coming. Unfortunately, her momma loved those annoying little crybags. It wouldn't matter to Rebel if her parents guaranteed she'd remain their only daughter. After fourteen years as the Caldwell princess, she didn't want her position usurped.

A glance at her watch revealed five minutes had passed, so she shifted her bookbag from her left shoulder to her right, marched over the lawn to the covered breezeway and sat on a stone bench.

Peacefulness settled into Rebel at the quiet, early evening surroundings, unlike the hustle and bustle of mornings. Although she wasn't a fan of school, since she had to go, the beautiful campus pleased her. The red-bricked buildings featured imposing architecture sat on manicured grounds and ultramodern security and technology. Away from the clubhouse, she was any other rich girl with a love for shopping, makeup, cooking, and her comic book collection. Yet, if she had her way, she'd work on bikes all day. She'd hone her shooting skills and knife-throwing abilities. She'd practice hacking. *Those* things interested her.

Solving 5(-3x-2)-(x-3)=-4(4x+5)+13 or simplifying 2(a-3)+4b-2(a-b-3)+5 was ghastly futility. It didn't even make sense. Mathematics was the science of numbers and counting. Whoever decided *alphabets* qualified as a reasonable inclusion needed fucking up. Letters and numbers were like cats and fucking dogs. The two *didn't* mix well.

A breeze fluttered her hair. Maybe, she'd call Momma to ask about Mattie's claims.

However...

If Megan Foy Caldwell had killed a stupid motherfucker to save Daddy, he'd still be talking about it. If a stick bug got in the fucking house, Momma rescued it and brought it outside. The only reason she fucked-up bees and wasps was because Rebel was allergic to them. She'd been stung once and almost died. Nowadays, her pediatrician claimed she might've outgrown the reaction, so she no longer had EpiPens at home.

It was *possible* Momma fucked up someone to save Daddy. It just wasn't *probable*.

Fuck Mattie and her lies. Rebel wouldn't bother herself or her mother with the bullshit.

Sighing, she took her purse out of her bookbag, then dug to retrieve her phone and a stick of gum. After chewing for a few minutes, she shifted on the seat, restless.

Not far away, an SUV turned onto school property. Rebel froze, her heart galloping a mile a minute.

Had Mattie and Harley ratted her out...? Aunt Kendall believed Rebel left with one of the girls on the squad to hang out.

The SUV drew closer; it didn't belong to anyone she knew.

For the next few minutes passed, she snapped selfies. Usually, she'd upload her best pictures to the 'Gram, but *that* would be dumb motherfuckery, revealing she wasn't where she claimed.

Leaning forward, she attempted to focus on a game. It didn't work. She opened the phone's camera app again. Not to take photos but to assess her third outfit of the day.

This morning, she'd arrived at school in her uniform. For cheer, she'd changed into a T-shirt, yoga pants, and sneakers. Summer was upon them, so her nearly empty bookbag came in handy today, allowing her to sneak with her jeans, a pair of motorcycle boots, and another T-shirt—her current outfit. Even if her bookbag had been stuffed, she would've found a way to bring another change of clothes with her. Uniform equaled school. And school equaled age. In her case, *underage*.

She glanced toward the road. Nope. Nothing. Despair hit her and she fought back tears.

Diesel had been acting so strange. Daddy hadn't been pleased at Diesel's announcement at the birthday party.

After all his stupid begging and sex jokes, he'd suddenly decided to give up managing the Bobs. Days later, he'd moved and barely visited nowadays.

Rebel wasn't sure what happened at the closed-door meetings between Daddy and Diesel, but his absence hurt her deeply. She missed him terribly.

The bond with her twin had severed years ago. Maybe, they'd never really had one. He'd always been gentle, too sensitive for Ryan's taunts. She and CJ protected Rule as best they could, until, one day, he stopped participating with their brothers and cousins. He preferred his own company and rejected Rebel's invitations to spend time together. She'd even offered to learn to draw so they could reconnect, but Rule declined, saying it would be unfair to her.

Momma found a way for Rebel and Rule and all their brothers to enjoy each other's company every Wednesday evening. It was exclusively Caldwell family time—with exceptions for Harley and Rory. If they didn't eat in the 50s-style diner in the basement, they always ended up there after dinner to bowl, play arcade games, watch a movie, or dance. No matter the activity, Momma, Daddy, Rebel, her brothers, *and* her twin loved that sacred time together. Otherwise, Rule ignored her. He'd even insisted on different class schedules.

She'd lost Rule, but she wouldn't lose Diesel. He was hers. When he still lived under the same roof, he dined with them at least once a week and attended most of the weekly get togethers. Nowadays, she considered it a miracle if she saw him once a month.

Had Diesel forgotten her? What the hell would she do then? Call home and confess and face grounding for the rest of her fucking life?

Daddy didn't appreciate being played. And the fact that Rebel had also played Momma...oh, Jesus.

Diesel *had* to come. About the only person she could call who *might* come to her rescue was Ryan. And, frankly, he could be the biggest dick on earth. Fuckhead would probably blackmail her, too.

What had she done?

Fuck.

Hopefully, she'd covered all her bases since she'd had to plan a way to see Diesel on a dime. Until late yesterday evening, she hadn't known CJ and Daddy were attending a meeting. She'd stayed up half the night, plotting. Finally, at breakfast, a plan solidified in her mind. Daddy wasn't easy to outwit. He just knew *everything* and...

The sound of motorcycle pipes captured her attention, and cold sweat popped out on her. How had Daddy...?

The bike rode into view, gliding to a stop at the edge of the walkway. Rebel chewed her gum faster, butterflies twirling in her stomach.

Not Daddy. *Diesel.* He went helmetless, leaving his brown hair vulnerable to the wind. Broad-shouldered and tall, he waited as she gathered her purse, phone, and bookbag. Other than to make sure it was her, he was texting, not paying Rebel a bit of attention.

"Hey," she greeted over the idle of the bike, opening one of his saddlebags to stuff her belongings into.

"Hey, Monkey Butt."

"Don't call me that stupid name, Diesel."

He glanced over his shoulder, his smile distracted. "Sorry I'm late, honey. Meeting ran over." He nodded to the seat behind him and stuffed his phone into the pocket of his leather jacket. "Hop on, Monkey Butt. You're probably tired and need a nap, so I'll have you home in a flash."

She glared at him, inches away from his dreamy face. "I don't need a nap, stupid. I'm not a baby anymore. And stop calling me Monkey Butt!"

He drew his brows together. They were not overly thick, where he'd look like caterpillars were stuck to his forehead. "Right. Yeah, sweetheart. Twelve isn't a baby."

His statement added injury to insult. "Dumb ass," she growled. "I'll be *fifteen* in about eleven months."

Amusement lit his gray eyes. While Rory and Uncle Johnnie had more silver in their eyes, Diesel's were a beautiful, soft color, ringed by thick lashes. "Definitely not a baby," he said gravely.

At his condescension, she clamped her jaw before she called him a worse name.

His lips, full and dreamy and...and *perfect* curved into a grin. "Get on," he told her.

Her scheming and lies got her only a few sentences showing Diesel barely thought of her and a ride home? Nothing else? No...*I miss you.* Or...*I'll call you more often to check on you...hold a conversation with you...*

None of that?

His phone rang and he glanced at it. Rebel craned her neck to read the name on the screen, but he shoved it back into his pocket before she could.

"I have to get going, darlin'," he drawled.

Inside her sneakers, her toes curled. She absolutely loved the way he dropped the 'g' from darling. The word wrapped around her insides and filled her with all types of feels.

She gazed at him through the fringes of her lashes. "I'm hungry, Dee. Can we stop at Burger Palace?"

"I don't have a helmet for you. It's bad enough you're riding to the house without one. I'm pushing my fucking luck with a pitstop."

"You've never eaten concrete before. You won't do it now. I'm really, really hungry. I probably won't make it home. I'll faint and fall off the back of your bike."

He burst into laughter, so contagious and carefree she smiled. "Fine, brat. Get on."

Half an hour later, Rebel sat at a booth in the Burger Palace, a mountain of French Fries before her. She'd eaten half her burger, enjoying the combination of flavors—BBQ sauce, jalapenos, onions, mustard, tomatoes, lettuce, pickles, bacon, and cheddar cheese. Bread was pretty fucking soggy, but whatever.

Diesel's burger sat in front of the seat opposite her, untouched. After paying for their meal and following her to the corner booth, his phone rang again. He'd excused himself and, from the window next to her, she watched him pace, yank his hair, and throw his hands up in frustration.

Obviously, he was arguing. Every now and then, he'd remember to nod at her before returning to his conversation. Suddenly, he stormed through the doors and back to their booth.

"Rebel—"

She grabbed a French fry. "Can I have a milkshake? We didn't order drinks."

He opened his mouth, then nodded and stalked away to place the order. Since it was a weekday, the Burger Palace wasn't busy, therefore, he returned within a couple minutes.

He stuffed his bank card back into his wallet, then shoved it into his leather jacket before sliding in on his side of the booth and tearing into his burger.

Rebel sipped her shake, shoring up her courage, assembling the words in her head that she practiced in her room at night. She always swore if she ever got the chance, she'd tell Diesel how much she loved him and that he better wait to marry her.

Or else.

She never made up her mind about what the "or else" consisted of, but the threat sounded ominous, so she'd work with what she had.

"I've thought of becoming a lawyer," she said to kickstart the conversation, since he seemed perfectly happy to chomp his burger like a newly hatched crocodile.

"It's a lot of work and years of studying," he said after he swallowed, then glanced at her shake and an empty spot near his food perfect for his own drink.

She slid her cup to him. "Have some."

He nodded, then removed the lid and drank deeply. Afterwards, he re-secured the lid and set it back in the space she'd had it. "Thanks. Tell Aunt Meggie I'll swing by this weekend to unclog the drain in the hallway bathroom on the second floor."

Nervous laughter escaped Rebel. "I heard Dad telling her that's on his honey-do list for Saturday."

"Damn. I hope he isn't mad at me. Never mind, sweetheart. I'll call him. Maybe, I can help him."

So not good. He was distracted, so he *might* forget. Or not. She couldn't risk it. Until she came up with a way to deter him, she changed the conversation. "I've been so worried Momma will announce another pregnancy."

Diesel's pearly white grin dazzled Rebel. She almost melted into a puddle.

"Aunt Meggie loves babies, Reb, but I see how that might irritate you. Babies are noisy and demanding."

"You don't want kids?" She did. At least four. But if Diesel didn't want them, what did that mean for her?

"I don't feel one way or the other about children of my own. If I meet the right woman and she wants a baby, then I'll become a father."

Rebel sighed dreamily.

"Has Aunt Meggie been ill?" Diesel asked, his deep voice turning her insides to mush.

"No. And it isn't about babies," Rebel said quickly. She didn't want him questioning her mothering skills. "It's about baby *girls*. Mom can have as many babies as she wishes as long as they're boys."

"I understand, baby. It'd be hard to share your title of family princess when we've all put you on that pedestal for your entire life."

He called her a princess. Shifting in her seat, she licked her lips and combed her fingers through her hair. She lowered her lashes and smiled at him. "I'm so glad you made it," she drawled, her pulse thumping. "Daddy had a club meeting. You're a Death Dweller, so I'm surprised you weren't required to attend."

"I'm a working man, sweetheart," he said. "I had a meeting already scheduled and knew I would arrive at the Scorched Devil's clubhouse late, if at all. If not, I would've been at Uncle Chris's side."

"Then, it worked out perfectly. If not for your meeting, I wouldn't have gotten to see you."

He winked at her. "And I wouldn't have known you fear a little usurper is on the horizon."

She giggled. "I can't imagine Momma and Daddy having another girl and that baby bitch stealing them from me."

Diesel barked a laugh. "Rest assured, Monkey Butt. Our parents love you."

She frowned.

"Even if Aunt Meggie ever had another girl, it won't change how we feel about you. You'd still be my beautiful little sister and the reigning princess."

Her happiness evaporating, Rebel sniffed and changed the subject again. "Maybe, Daddy will let me become an enforcer."

That caught Diesel's attention. He grabbed two fries, bit into them, and chewed, contemplating her the entire time. "Of the Death Dwellers?"

She nodded. "Where else?"

"What do you think a club enforcer does, Rebel?"

Her patience was wearing thin. "Fuck, Diesel. Enforce shit. What the fuck else *would* a club enforcer do?"

"Stop cussing. You sound like a fucking sailor."

"Fuck you. Daddy doesn't say anything, so *you* have fuck-all to say."

He scowled. "Enforcing isn't for you," he declared, obeying her order. "Besides, unless the charter is changed, women can't join."

She stared at him, almost swooning with love and happiness. "You called me a woman."

"Oh, my fucking God," he snapped. "*Girls*, then. *Girls* aren't allowed to join."

"You're such a fuckhead," she said crossly. The meeting with Diesel wasn't going as she'd believed it would. He acted pressed for time and not particularly happy to see her. Worse, *he* thought he was her brother. The big fucking dummy. "Before I called you earlier today, I hadn't heard from you in days. You can't call me to say 'hi'. You barely answer my texts."

"Rebel," he said on a sigh. "Stop reminding me of what a horrible big brother I am. I'll try to do better."

She glowered at him, but he either ignored her look or worse, didn't notice it at all.

"Since enforcer is out and you're not sure about being a lawyer, what else have you considered for a future career?" he asked, biting into his burger.

"Building custom rides," she answered sullenly, refusing him the satisfaction of a long answer.

He didn't say anything else until he'd finished chewing.

"No shit?" He sounded impressed. "You and Harley know as much about bikes as the boys do."

"And handling guns. Throwing blades. And whatever else."

He stuffed the last piece of burger into his mouth. "Can I have another swallow?" he asked a moment later, pointing to her shake.

"Sure."

Once her cup was back in its place, he looked at her half-eaten burger and mountain of remaining fries. "You didn't eat. I thought you were hungry, Monkey Butt." Heaving in a breath, he leaned across the table and *tweaked her nose* like she was five. "Another bad brother move—"

"You're *not* my brother, Diesel," she almost snarled, at the end of her patience. He was so busy with his life away from the house, he no longer paid attention to her. She was invisible. To him especially. Every time he referred to himself as her brother, she died inside. "You have never been my brother, and never will be in my eyes. I don't care if Momma and Daddy adopted you. You're not my family, dickhead."

Not until he married her. She'd never love anyone the way she loved him. But if she didn't end his idea he was her big brother, he'd never see her as anything other than a little child.

"I'm not a part of your family, Rebel?"

"No!" she yelled. "And I'll bet you never considered Momma and Daddy your parents. God, you're six years younger than my mom. How *could* you see her as a mother figure?"

His friendliness and humor evaporated, turning him into a stranger, not the Diesel she knew and loved.

"*You* might not see me as your family, but everyone else does. They've all accepted and embraced me. Now that I know how you feel, I'll be sure to stay clear of you."

Shocked at how the conversation spun out of control, Rebel couldn't think of a response.

He got to his feet and gathered the food wrappers. "I'm ready to ride out. Do you want a to-go bag?"

She shook her head.

Jaw clenched, he nodded, then removed the mess from her side, too. After discarding everything, he returned to the booth and indicated she slide out. Usually, she didn't give two fucks about the people she hurt. This was the first time she'd ever wounded someone close to her in such a way. But he had made her so angry, wearing her patience thin.

Fuck the dumb shit was her daddy's creed, and one she embraced.

"I didn't mean what I said. At least not the way you're taking it."

"Is there any other way I can take what you said, Rebel?"

She couldn't understand why he was making the situation so hard. He loved girls. That's why he'd wanted to manage the Bobs. Through the years, Rebel studied Diesel's every move. She watched him interact with the opposite sex. Strangers in the mall. Club girls. Foreigners on their trips. Her aunts. Lolly. Harley. Mattie. Momma.

Her.

Diesel understood the female population. He had to know what she meant.

But as she stared into his gray eyes, she saw no comprehension. Only annoyance.

"I don't *want* you to be my brother. I want you to be to me what Daddy is to Momma." The urge to cry hit her but she gritted her teeth and lifted her chin. "Go ahead. Tease me."

For the first time since he picked her up, he looked at her. *Really* looked at her, taking the time to study her eyes, her nose, her cheeks. Her mouth. His look softened and he gave her a gentle smile.

Clearing his throat, Diesel nodded to the space next to her. Once she slid over and he sat, he took her hand in his. "Rebel, sweetheart, I—" He stopped, hesitating. "I'm honored," he said finally. "But..." He shoved his free hand through his hair. "Even if you were a *grown* woman, there's a few reasons why I could never be with you. By law, I'm your *brother*."

"You're treating me as if I'm stupid. Just because Momma and Daddy has a legal claim to you, doesn't mean fuck all to me or the law, asshole. You're my *adopted* brother, unrelated by blood. That makes all the difference in the world."

He glared at her. "To *me*, you're still my sibling. My little sister. *Monkey Butt*. I've known you since you were in fucking diapers, Rebel. What kind of fucking pervert do you take me for? Anything other than brotherly feelings would be low and unforgivable, a fucking betrayal of all the trust you've placed in me since you were *two fucking years old*."

Rebel processed Diesel's angry words. "Let me get this straight. If you met me on the street, each of us strangers to the other, you wouldn't be opposed to having me?"

Diesel's eyes darkened, disgusted fury snatching away his staid anger. "Were you dropped on your head as a fucking baby? You're a goddamn child. Stranger, relative, or friend, I don't see you as anything but a little girl. If it makes you feel better, I think you're a very pretty child."

"Fuck you," she spat, low. "I already know how beautiful I am. Daddy says all the time that I look like Momma."

"You do. Uncle Chris isn't the only one who says that."

"Momma's gorgeous. If I look like her, then I am too, so shove your pissy compliment up your ass. I don't need it."

Hurt, anger, and humiliation ripped through her. She clenched her jaw and glared at him.

"Jesus Christ," Diesel said with unamused laughter. "Why the fuck are we even having this conversation?" Before she could respond, he caught her gaze and stared at her. "What *if* you were older? And what *if* I saw you as more than a little sister? What then? I wouldn't live long enough for us to be together for any length of time. Uncle Chris would kill me slowly and painfully."

"He wouldn't. I wouldn't let him. Neither would Momma. Besides, it's *my* life. *He* wouldn't be your lover. *I* would."

Diesel choked and released her hand as if it suddenly burned him. "God. You're not supposed to talk about *lovers*. You're too young to even think that. And..." He glanced around, pale and wide-eyed. Maybe, expecting Daddy to jump from the shadows. "Do not *ever*, fucking *ever*, *ever*, *never*...Jesus. Do not put my name with yours *ever* when you use the word lover." He squeezed the bridge of his nose. "Quickest way to get my cock hacked off," he mumbled, though she still heard him, and she flushed, then giggled, embarrassed and intrigued.

"Reb, darlin'," he started again. "You're a beautiful young lady. Whoever you end up with will be lucky to have you. Rebel...never mind," he said on a sigh.

"Say it. Whatever it is." She was her father's daughter, and she wouldn't hide from anyone's words. Ever.

"I will never see you as anything more than a sister. A *younger* sister."

Somehow, Rebel kept Diesel in her company for another hour. No matter what argument she presented to him, he wouldn't capitulate.

"*Enough*!" he finally said. "I'm done trying to get through to you, Rebel."

Her lower lip trembled, her heart breaking.

Diesel kissed her cheek, then brushed away an escaping tear. "I'm sorry, sweetheart."

He slid out of the booth and waited for her to do the same. She didn't say much to him until she remembered the trouble she'd be in if Daddy discovered her shenanigans.

"Don't take me home. Go through the back entrance and drop me off by the cave."

"Why?"

It was nighttime and she had been out with him much longer than expected. No, strike that. She shouldn't have been out with him at all. She'd risked so much. Only for him to spurn the future she dreamed of having with him.

"Answer me, Rebel."

"Only Mattie and Harley know I'm with you. I told everyone else I would be hanging out with a friend."

"Fuck! Fuck! Fuck!"

He threw an angry glare at her and jerked his head in the direction of the seat, indicating she mount up.

She annoyed the hell out of CJ and, more than once, Rory complained about Mattie. Apparently, younger sisters were the bane of the world.

Especially to older brothers.

Chapter Seven

HARLEY

Shifting in her seat at the clubhouse table reserved for herself, Mattie, and Rebel, Harley glanced toward the entrance for the thousandth time. She'd sent Rebel several texts but received no response. Now, she awaited both Rebel and CJ's return.

Unlike Daddy, CJ would spill all the tea.

"Hey, sugar."

Harley forced her gaze away from the door at her grandmother's greeting. She seated herself and Harley squirmed, crossing her fingers Rebel walked in before questions arose.

"You look soooo pretty tonight, Lolly."

She lifted her brows.

Harley lowered her gaze and rubbed her finger on the scarred wood table. She hadn't lied. Roxanne Doucette Johnson Jones Rousseau Harrington was a gorgeous woman with fine bone structure, brown eyes, and a layered haircut with both definition and body. The barest hint of lipstick, rouge, and eyeshadow painted her face.

"Spill it, baby. What's on your mind?"

Harley glanced toward the entrance again just as her mother sat at the table's one remaining chair. Dr. Bailey Banks amazing eyes were more green than brown. Silky, dark hair along with her skin tone that fell somewhere between marshmallow and buttery brown hinted at her mom's biracial heritage.

"Daddy's on the way," Mommie announced.

"CJ too?" Harley asked with hope.

Mommie smiled. "Yes, hunny bunny."

"Finally," Harley muttered.

"You right, baby," Lolly agreed. "That was a long fucking meeting. Outlaw wasn't even home for dinner." She nodded in the direction of where Aunt Meggie sat with Aunt Kendall, Aunt Bunny, and Aunt Zoann. They were laughing amongst themselves.

"Is everything okay, Bailey?" Lolly pressed. "It's fucking rare Outlaw not here to break bread with his family."

Mommie sighed. "Lucas and Digger are going back out. He didn't say why. Just that stupid fuckheads will forever be stupid fuckheads."

"I'll ask CJ," Harley promised, excitement rising in her. "When he tells me what happened, I'll let you know."

Clasping her hands and resting them on the table, Mommie leaned forward. "Don't ask him what goes on at club meetings, Harley. If he doesn't volunteer, he either can't or won't talk about it."

"We tell each other everything," Harley reminded her mother. "There's no reason why I can't ask him, since I want to know so bad."

"There is," Mommie insisted. "You'll put him on the spot, and risk coming between him and his club."

Harley scowled. “He’s not even *in* the club.”

“No, he isn’t,” she agreed. “But he *is* on club business tonight. I’ll ask your daddy how his day went. It is the simplest question to show both interest on his behalf and curiosity on my own.”

“But you and Daddy discuss the club. I’ve heard you.”

“Harley, sweetheart, you aren’t old enough to understand. The situation requires finesse, especially in the beginning. CJ’s your best friend, but he’s wetting his feet in club life. Girls aren’t allowed to patch in, so eventually your lives will go in different directions.”

Harley glared at her mom.

“All right, young lady,” Mommie said crisply, “drop the attitude. The last thing I want to do is upset you, but I’ve never lied to you, and I won’t start now.”

Lowering her lashes, Harley fought her irritation, but her nerves were on edge. Uncle Chris had never taken him to an official club meeting before and she was anxious to know the details.

“Harley, baby,” Lolly started, “Bailey forgot to add that it don’t matter what CJ is willing to share with you about the club, it stays between the two of you. First rule is he isn’t supposed to say anything, so if he trusts you with that information, keep his confidence.”

“Momma’s right, Harley. That’s a vital part of your daddy’s faith in me. He knows what he shares with me won’t go any further.” Mommie reached across the table and grabbed Harley’s hands. “None of us know much of what happens on a day-to-day basis. It’s against club rules and it could prove dangerous for us. If we ever fall into the hands of the enemy, we can honestly say we don’t know anything.”

“They might not believe us,” Harley said.

“No *might* in it, sugar,” Lolly said. “A motherfucker being a motherfucker think everybody is a fucking liar. But, if you know shit and claim you don’t, all it take is a fucking flinch, a stutter, a fucking slipup, for a motherfucker to realize you know a lot more than what you're admitting to. Then, you beyond fucked."

Harley heaved in a sigh. "How do you figure it all out, Mommie?"

"I take it one step at a time," she answered as her gaze strayed toward the entrance and her face lit up. "Your daddy's back," she announced, getting to her feet and hurrying in his direction.

Mommie stepped into Daddy's embrace, tipped her head up and brushed her lips across his. He whispered to her and she laughed.

Uncle Chris walked in. Unable to stop herself, Harley swiveled her head in Aunt Meggie's direction. She was still talking to Harley's other aunts, but her demeanor changed. She knew her husband was heading toward her. When he reached her, he bent, kissed her mouth, then spoke close to her ear.

"Harley," Lolly said, recapturing her attention, "you and CJ besties. If he want to stay your friend as club life draws him in, then he'll help you adjust." Her phone rang and she took it out of her pocket. "That's Knox. Hold on, baby." Grinning, she answered her husband's call. "Hey, sugar. On your way home?" She listened a moment, then laughed. "Boy, you a fool. I'm talking to my princess." She had a lot of babies, but only one princess. "I'll see your dirty ass when you get home. Yeah," she agreed. "I love you, too." Hanging up, she got to her feet and shoved the phone in her pocket. "Pop said hi."

"I'll text him later," Harley said morosely.

CJ still hadn't come in.

"Where's Rebel and Matilda?"

Suddenly, Harley understood her grandmother's meaning about knowing information that could lead to trouble. "Matilda is home. Rebel went to a friend's house."

Hands on hips, Lolly stared at her for so long, heat rushed up Harley's neck and into her face. She couldn't meet her grandmother's eyes because she'd see her lie.

"Where is she, Harley?"

"I don't know, Lolly," she mumbled, the truth. "I-I don't know the a-address of her friend's house."

Lolly pulled a chair next to her, sat, and crossed her legs. Her zippered denim dress with strappy shoulders showed both her skin and her figure.

"Your legs are very pretty. What lotion do you use? Those sandals look so comfortable."

"Hush, baby," Lolly snapped. "I was a young bitch once, Harley. We do stupid shit and only tell one or two trustworthy confidantes. Now, I'm asking you again. Where is Rebel and who is the boy she's meeting?"

Harley's gaze flew to her grandmother's. "She's not meeting a boy, Lolly." Technically, Diesel *was* a boy. He'd just leaped into man territory. "I swear."

"She's not in any danger?"

"No." Not physically, but the meeting wouldn't turn out as Rebel expected. Diesel would burst Rebel's dreams when he turned her down. But she was so stubborn. Harley just couldn't reason with her. "She isn't in any danger."

Her grandmother nodded. "You don't lie, sugar, so I believe you."

"Thank you." Twinges of guilt hit Harley, although she hadn't exactly lied. She just hadn't given full disclosure.

"Hey, baby girl," her father said, walking up to the table with his arm around her mother's waist. In his other hand, he carried a bottle of vodka.

Glancing toward the door and seeing no sign of CJ, she sighed. "Hey, Daddy."

"Well, fuck, Harley, show a little more enthusiasm." Daddy tasted the vodka. "CJ outside."

Relief flowing through her, Harley smiled. "Oh," she said, antsy to see him but not wanting to blow off her daddy. "Uh, Mommie says you're leaving again."

Daddy laughed. "Baby girl, you don't give a fuck if my ass about to fly to the fucking moon," he teased. "It's cool. Go talk to your *best bro*." He took another gulp of vodka. "That's how you see the little motherfucker, right?"

"Of course," she answered, surprised. "How else would I see him?"

Dropping his arm from around Mommie's waist and setting his bottle on the table, he got a cigarette from the pack in his cut and lit it. "As long as you got a cock like him or he got a pussy like you in your head, shit cool."

"Oh my god, Lucas," Mommie said around laughter. She looked at Harley. "Go ahead, hunny bunny."

Anxious to see CJ, Harley hurried toward the entrance, barely remembering to respond to the greetings thrown her way.

Outside, tall halogen stadium lamps dotted the parking lot, dulling the stars in the clear skies. Probates armed with sawed-offs guarded the club grounds and manned the gate, but no CJ. Maybe, he'd walked home.

Gates and fences separated the private access road and pathway to the houses. She had the required codes. But it was scary dark in the forest. The first minute or two swallowed her whole when people were with her. Alone, she'd go into screaming fits.

"CJ?" she called. Waiting for a response, she fired off another quick text to Rebel and slid her phone back into her pocket. The cool night breeze swept over her and she shivered; she regretted leaving her jacket. "CJ?"

Two tall men wearing bandannas and tattoos up to their necks glanced in her direction. The one with the white bandanna shifted the shotgun from one shoulder to the next. She didn't recognize either of them, so they must be new and didn't know her daddy was a club officer.

A moderate number of motorcycles filled the parking lot. A line of kickass bikes stood close to the door. Uncle Chris's. Uncle Johnnie's. Uncle Digger's. Uncle Stretch's. Uncle Val's. Daddy's. Uncle Cash's.

The next available space belonged to CJ. Seeing his moped told Harley he was back.

Drooping, Harley decided to go back inside. The two, new men gave her the creeps. Since they'd spotted her, they'd barely looked anywhere else.

"Harley?" CJ rounded the corner close to his parked moped and headed over.

"Hey, dude," she greeted.

Grabbing the cigarette behind his ear, he dug into his pocket and pulled out a lighter. He still wore his school uniform, although he'd discarded the required necktie and his white shirttails were untucked.

"I've been dying to talk to you," she confessed. "How was it? What happened?"

Smoke poured from his nostrils and mouth. "Too much. A lot of which I can't talk about."

Shoving away her disappointment, she'd heed Lolly's advice and not press the issue. "Oh, yeah. Um, right. So, um, Lumbly is an asshole, isn't he?"

CJ's body relaxed and his frown line cleared. Stuffing his cigarette in the corner of his mouth, he grabbed her hand and guided her in the direction he'd come, activating the motion-sensor halogen light.

He dropped into the lone chair and pulled her onto his lap. After hitting his cigarette a couple times, he held it between his fingers, turned his head and released the smoke.

They'd once shared chairs all the time. As small kids, he'd sat on her lap. She'd sat on his lap. It hadn't been a big deal. She couldn't understand why her pulse raced and she...he...his...she shifted her weight, embarrassed. She *should* stand up, but she didn't want to. She liked being in his lap.

She shifted again and he...*it*...jumped.

They stared at each other, and he caressed her cheek, offering her a smile, the kind she'd never seen on his face before. But she wanted it from him again and she wanted to be the only one he ever smiled at in such a manner.

Taking one more drag on his cigarette, he flicked it to the ground and stomped it underneath his boot. His movements bounced her around and brought her a little closer. When he began unbraiding her single plait, she faced forward and allowed him to glide his fingers through her hair.

"So many girls were at the meeting, Harley," CJ said, still stroking her scalp. "It's no wonder my mom can't stand motherfucking Derby. He brought all those women so my dad, *your* dad, our uncles would cheat."

She gasped.

He dropped his hand from her hair. "It didn't end well. My dad had to fuck up a motherfucker. He didn't do it in front of me. I didn't even see the body. But I didn't give a fuck. Asshole deserved it for trying to fuck with my mom." He laid his hand on her shoulder. "Shouldn't I feel sorrow? Remorse? Fear? *Anything* other than vindication and satisfaction."

"They shouldn't have disrespected Aunt Meggie, a killing offense in Uncle Christopher's eyes."

He laughed, a real, true CJ laugh Harley understood. "You didn't even mention Uncle Mort."

She giggled. "Daddy was probably angry. Uncle Chris was murderous."

"I think the Dwellers are absorbing that other club. Dad says he'll put it to the vote."

She'd wanted to hear about the meeting, but she wasn't sure how to respond, so she raised her gaze to the night sky. A patchwork of stars glistened against the obsidian backdrop. The halogen light had flickered off, blanketing the club's western side in frightening darkness. Except for a small parking garage, it was more or less deserted over here. It was also the most visible part of the club from the street and backed onto the woods.

"What are you thinking?"

Harley sighed, sadness rising in her. CJ's voice crept into grownup territory and he'd started shaving a couple months ago. She didn't even have breasts yet.

"Harley?"

"I was so anxious to hear about everything, but I don't know what to say about what you've shared."

He caressed her cheek again, and the light flared on, bathing them in a spotlight. "You just listening helps." He rested his head on the back of the chair. "One of those women started giving me a hand job. Her name was Peaches."

His meaning dawned on her, and her mouth fell open. They were best dudes and he'd never *not* shared something with her.

She pursed her lips. "Soooo what stopped her?" she asked, sharper than intended, not like one of the guys at all.

"Fuck. *Dad.* First, the fucking sound of his gunfire then by him dragging Sabrina or Serina or whatever the fuck her name is, in with the blood of Cole on him and her—"

"Who's Cole?"

"The stupid motherfucker who got on the wrong side of my dad." He situated some of her hair over her shoulder. "When Peaches started stroking my dick again, Dad made her move away."

Harley forced a breezy laugh to cover her annoyance. She had to listen to whatever he talked about without judgment. Loads of hot jealousy and a heap of irritation surged into Harley at CJ discussing someone touching *it*. She scowled. "I'm sure you were disappointed Uncle Chris interrupted her."

He gave her another intense look. "I was, but I was also relieved."

She turned the confession over in her head. "I understand. It makes weird sense."

They broke into peals of laughter.

"What a fucking day, Harley," CJ said when their giggles stopped. "I wish you could've been with me. Club dynamics are so interesting and my dad...fuck, dude...my dad is everything. He's just fucking amazing. If I can be just half the man he is, I'll be so happy."

She slid to her feet and turned to CJ, his closeness overwhelming. Everything about him felt new to her, *looked* new. The emerald eyes that mirrored Uncle Chris's, but without the hardened edge. Swaths of inky hair fell onto his forehead and brushed his ears because he needed a haircut. A GQ jawline carved away the babyish roundness, while muscles chiseled his lankiness.

But she needed to call Rebel. She should've been home and real, true worry settled into Harley.

CJ stood, too.

"You're so tall now," she told him, awed.

He smirked at her. "Somebody has a crush," he chortled.

Yes, as a matter of fact she did. "Shouldn't you have all your girl organs working to have crushes and notice the opposite sex?"

"Fuck, Harley, I don't know. Can't little, little girls have crushes on singers and movie stars and shit? Besides, I don't even know what the fuck you're talking about since I don't know what girl organs you're referring to."

Embarrassment flamed her cheeks. She'd never tell her miserable secret, though she expected CJ to share everything with her. "Never mind."

He hugged her and tangled his fingers in her hair, backing her away from the halogen light and into the darkness.

"That scalp massage feels so good," she admitted. "Whenever I have a spa day with Mommie and Lolly, I also request that service."

"Spoiled," he teased, not stopping the movement of his fingers.

"Harley!"

The unexpected sound of Daddy's voice startled her out of CJ's embrace. Thank goodness the darkness swallowed them. Otherwise, Daddy would've seen how close she stood to CJ before the lights flicked on. It was a place she'd been a thousand times before, for as long as she could remember. This time, though, felt different. Special.

Forbidden.

CJ sat. "Hey, Uncle Mort," he greeted as Daddy walked up.

Daddy glared between them, but his angry gaze lasered CJ.

"H-hey, Daddy," she said as casually as possible. She and CJ hadn't done anything wrong.

"Hey, boy," Uncle Chris said from somewhere behind her father.

"Mort, we got to roll," Uncle Digger added. He placed a hand on his shoulder and whispered something that made her father elbow him. "You a cold motherfucker, Mortician."

Uncle Christopher stood next to CJ. "Me and you talking, boy."

The same guilt Harley felt dropped into CJ's face.

"You got that all wrong, Outlaw," Uncle Digger chided. "You need to talk to Harley, and Mort need to talk to CJ."

Daddy and Uncle Christopher exchanged glances.

"I kinda like that fuckin' idea, Digger," he admitted.

"Me, too," Daddy said, surprised.

"Fuck, Mortician, your ass don't have to look so fucking shocked," Uncle Digger complained. "I do got a fucking brain in my head."

CJ snickered.

"Aww, you too, lil dude?" Uncle Digger said.

"Yeah, ashfuck," CJ retorted, teasing him with an old nickname.

"I got to leave, baby girl." Daddy pulled her into his arms and kissed her cheek. "How about we do some target practice soon?"

"For real?" she asked with excitement.

He nodded. "It's a school night, so I'll drop you off before I head out," he said, a little more himself. "Your brothers already left with Roxanne since your momma waiting here for me."

"Okay." She hurried to CJ and hugged him, before bumping fists. She smiled. "Have a goodnight, my dude."

"You too, Harls," CJ responded.

Giving Uncle Christopher a quick hug, she stepped next to her father. He placed an arm around her neck and guided her to his bike.

"Get the van, Digger, and meet me here in ten minutes."

Uncle Digger saluted. "Aye aye, Captain."

Snickering, Daddy mounted his motorcycle. Once she hopped behind him and he started off, it didn't take long to reach their house. As the sound of his pipes faded into the distance, Rebel's ringtone finally came through.

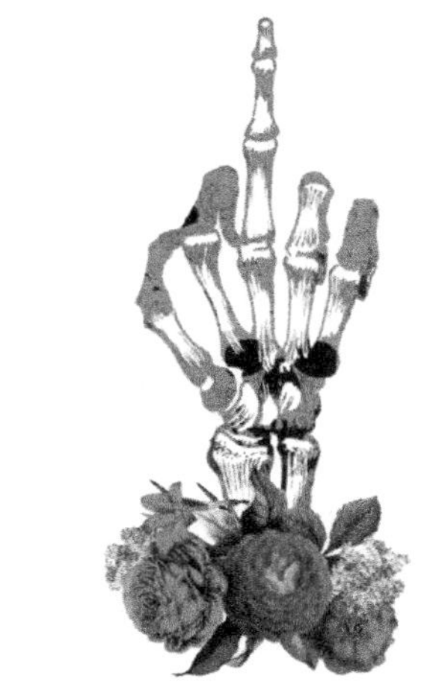

Chapter Eight

Rory

The noise of the reciprocating saw stopped with the same abruptness it began five minutes ago.

"A sharp blade makes the cut quick and clean." Dad sat the saw next to the body on the autopsy table.

Suspicions about the body's identity welled in Rory. The Scorched Devil meeting was yesterday, yet without a head and no clothes, he wasn't certain who the pieces belonged to. "Is that, um, *Cole*?"

Dad placed a just-severed arm on the counter behind him and nodded.

Over twenty-four hours later and the body showed no signs of rotting. Rory always believed decomposition began immediately after death.

"How's the..." Vestiges of nausea rose inside of him. He couldn't say corpse while staring at one. No, *pieces* of one. "How's he so fresh?"

"Refrigeration drawer." Dad pointed to the middle of the room and the huge counter with drawers of all sizes and several doors, close to the special autopsy table outfitted with shackles and chains. Meat market hooks hung from the ceiling and a chair with restraints stood on the opposite side. Several years ago, the club's old meatshack was demolished. Uncle Mort funded the new, kickass one. The building had several floor drains, windows to see outside though no one could see in, and sterile white walls and floors.

"Nowadays, dismemberment is only for special cases." His father smiled at him. "It's been a while since I've used the woodchipper."

Excited curiosity about what happened to a body in such a machine washed away Rory's revulsion.

Removing his plastic gloves and throwing them in a trashcan, Dad walked to Rory, then took his face between his hands. Dad's hands, cold as a corpse's, made Rory tremble.

In July, his father would be forty-nine, though he didn't look it, even with the distinguished façade of a seasoned executive. He preferred suits to cuts but wore both well. Strands of gray flecked his blond hair. Mom kept Dad on a strict skincare regimen, minimizing any wrinkles other men his age had.

"Son. If this is too much for you, tell me. You can't talk to CJ about your visits here. This is *our* secret. I'll never admit how often you've come here, no matter if it's today or two years from now, and you've been with me two hundred times. But tell me if you really *like* coming here?"

The first couple of visits to the meatshack was a real life horror show and Rory had nightmares for weeks. Mom always rushed to his room to comfort him. He never betrayed Dad, even when she asked about his bad dreams. Rory loved horror novels, so he blamed them.

It was the same excuse he gave CJ during his nightmares at sleepovers. They accepted his explanation and backed off.

"Your mother hasn't gone to your room to calm you in months," Dad continued at Rory's silence. "She told me you'd read a particularly scary book and thought it best I don't bring it up to you."

At Rory's nod, Dad dropped his hands, but the deathly cold lingered on his skin.

"Are you sure, son?"

Rory now looked forward to time inside this death house. The wild, forbidden excursion was their secret. Still, he'd seen Cole alive, being a jackass. *Breathing.* Now, *that* man was *these* pieces.

His stomach turned again and tears filled his eyes. "I keep seeing him as a person, Dad. Not just a body."

Dad wrapped his arms around him in a tight hug. "I'm so sorry. You boys are growing up so fast. Before I know it, new blood will lead the club. I'll advocate for fairness in the election process from now until then. Between you and me? Heading up the club is hard. When I do it for an extended period, I fucking hate it. You must have the stomach for it, son. If Christopher insists on CJ becoming president, he'll need strong officers to be effective."

Rory tightened his hold on his father for the briefest second before stepping back. Sniffling, he wiped his nose on his hand, then grinned. Mom would have a fit. From the twinkle in Dad's eyes, he was thinking the same thing.

He held up his fist. Grinning, Rory balled his hand and bumped it against his father's. "Woof," they chorused, signaling their bro code.

"It'll be years before we're members, Dad," Rory said. "Don't we have to prospect first?"

"Probate," Dad corrected, then nodded toward the door. "Why don't you go home? I'll be there in a bit."

Rory lowered his eyelids and stared at the floor. "I want to be the strong backup CJ needs. Mostly, I want you to be proud of me."

Dad guided him to the torture chair. Rory's name for it, but knowing what he did of the meatshack, the hand, feet, and abdomen restraints could only be to hold someone down and inflict pain.

"I *am* proud of you, Rory," he started, crouching down. "Nothing will ever change that. I was overzealous in what I wanted to teach you. I should never have allowed you here. Derby said Christopher is having growing pains. It seems like I am, too. In the meantime, you boys are taking our behavior in stride."

"Maybe, we're all having growing pains, huh? You and Uncle Chris because you can't decide what's right for us, and me and CJ, because we can't decide what's right for us either."

"I think you're right, son," he agreed as he got to his feet.

"Do you think I'll grow to be as tall as you? Mattie's younger than me and already taller."

"Without a doubt, you'll catch up, Rory," Dad said with confidence. "Mark my words, a growth spurt will shoot you up."

Rory trusted his father, so he didn't doubt his words. He shoved his hands in his pockets. "C-can I stay?"

"It's hard on your soul when you take a man's life." Dad shrugged. "Until it isn't. Somewhere, along the way, there's a shift and you don't give a fuck. This motherfucker behind me...?" He jerked his head in the motherfucker's direction. "He was a stupid assfuck and taunted your uncle. He disrespected him. There's a time and a place for leniency and even clemency. This fucker used both. If a man wants respect, he gives it. Cole didn't, and Christopher acted. One less asshole in the world that, down the road, might've ended up causing trouble. Respect everyone. Fear *no one*. That's our creed, son."

Rory peeped around his father. "What would've happened if...if he came in like he is, but a breathing person would've been here?"

"If another fuckhead's on our wrong side, then the dismemberment would've been slower." He tapped his finger against his temple. "Psychological torture for the live fuckhead. There's absolutely nothing in this world like watching a man piss himself and hearing him beg for mercy because he knows what's coming and he fucking wishes he could go back in time and unfuck himself."

Rory allowed the words to sink in as his father turned back to the body. Or what remained on the table—the torso.

"Where's the rest of him?"

"Head's face down in the big sink. His legs, cock, and balls are in the refrigeration drawer."

One day, Rory would be as nonchalant as his father.

"When disrespect isn't blatant, how do you decide who to bring here?" He frowned at the table. "Why didn't he bleed? The other one..." That dissection made a gory, stinky mess. With each of his father's cuts, blood had pooled on the table, fascinating and disturbing Rory.

Dad lit a cigarette before answering. "Trust me, son. You'll know. But I'll give you a tip. If a motherfucker or *motherfuckers* committed an offense against the club, that's an automatic death sentence. If he disrespects your colors, he dies. If he fucks with your woman, he's dead. As for why the lack of blood? Arterial blood flow is pulsatile. No heartbeat, no blood. If you crave a motherfucker's blood, make the first incision while his heart's still beating. Otherwise, there's coagulation and staining."

His father's knowledge impressed Rory, even as the terminology confused him. But he needed answers to a more basic question. "You keep saying *he*. What if it's a girl?"

"Don't hurt a woman, Rory. Revere and respect them."

He thought of his sister. "Some girls are meaner than dudes, Dad."

"If a woman commits any type of crime against the club..." His voice trailed off and he dragged on his cigarette, clueless about the real Mattie. No, willfully blind to her behavior. "It depends on what she's done. Never torture a woman. If she must die, shoot her in the head and get it over with."

Rory looked at the torso again, the gray pall of death coloring the skin. "How would we get rid of her?"

"Take her to the funeral home and put her in the incinerator."

"That doesn't sound enjoyable. Where's the fun in that?" Rory mumbled, almost embarrassed by his morbid ideas.

"Say that again, please?"

Shame sizzled through Rory, and he shook his head. "Forget it."

"Don't back down from your beliefs," Dad chastised. "Always stand by your words."

"Yes, sir."

Dad finished his cigarette and discarded it in the ashtray. "Well?"

"I said where's the fun in that. A stupid thing to say and—"

Pride shone in Dad's eyes. "Nothing about those words is stupid. It shows an understanding in our work. Not everyone is cut out for this. Take your Uncle

Christopher, not wanting CJ in here. If you boys take over one day, you need disclosure. Exposure. Not only riding lessons, target practice, runs and parties."

"CJ wouldn't be afraid in here." He wouldn't have been a pussy and woke up screaming like a baby.

The truth would've made Dad disappointed in Rory and himself. He'd really thought visiting the meatshack was a good tenth birthday present.

Rory *could've* told one of his uncles.

Nah.

Uncle Chris would've knocked Dad out. Uncle Mort would've knocked Dad out. Uncle Val would've told Aunt Zoann and she would've knocked Dad out.

He could've told Aunt Meggie. She would've confronted Dad...then again, he couldn't tell her because things would spiral out of control and Uncle Chris would've still ended up knocking Dad out.

What it all meant was one thing: Rory had had no one to turn to. Not even CJ.

Because...

Uncle Christopher. Enough said.

Dad pulled Rory into a hug, and he smiled, happy he'd made him proud.

"You're not CJ," Dad said gruffly. "You're *you* and I'm so lucky to have you as my son. I love you, Rory."

"I'm lucky you're my father, Dad." He returned his father's hug, then pulled back, bowed his head and shoved his hands into his pockets. "I-I enjoy coming here with you."

"Don't be ashamed if you like this part of the job. And don't be ashamed if you aren't ready for it. Either way, this is what we do. Who we are. You must be tough, strong, *lethal*. You must be a leader. Leaders stand up for their beliefs. Take in the scents and sights. Revel in our art," he stressed. "I could've taken this motherfucker to the funeral home, but this is a teaching moment. You never know what you will need to get what you want. When asking nicely doesn't work, you must find another way."

"The smells can get disgusting."

"Fair enough, but imagine how you'd feel if you found yourself in this type of situation and had never experienced the meat shack?"

"I still wish CJ could come with me sometimes."

"Your cousin is a strong young man, but CJ won't handle this place well."

Rory opened his mouth to disagree, but Dad raised his hands and stopped him.

"Before you defend him, listen to what I have to say. Everyone assumes how things will go when your uncles and me step aside. They believe CJ will lead, and you will be second-in-command. Think about the way your cousin reacted at the Devils' clubhouse. He froze and couldn't fire the fucking gun, son. I have no doubt you would've rose to the occasion."

"Firing a gun at a real person is different than shooting at inanimate objects, Dad." He couldn't keep the annoyance out of his voice.

Dad's eyebrows snapped together. "You've never shot at a motherfucker."

"Neither has he. Besides, he might've thought about upsetting Aunt Meggie."

"Megan consistently has misplaced anger and fits of theatrics," Dad said. "Her behavior affects her children, so when I think deeper on the matter, CJ is not cut out to be the leader *you* are meant to be."

"If CJ can't run the club, then neither will I be able to."

"You sell yourself short, Rory. You're a fine young man."

Short, skinny, and pimply. He was just fucking awesome. Rory scowled.

"Or as CJ said, a bad little motherfucker," Dad remarked, changing tactics. "You have what it takes to run this club, Rory. CJ doesn't. Fuck, Rebel is more suited to run the club than CJ will ever be. That young child runs wild with her cussing and smoking."

"You're talking about Aunt Meggie being dramatic and Rebel being uncivilized, when you're forgetting about Mattie and Mom."

"There's absolutely no comparison between your mother and sister, and your aunt and cousin. Kendall is involved in all types of charities. Matilda is a perfect young lady. Rebel is steps away from juvie. She drinks. She smokes. She cusses. Megan puts up a perfunctory argument, while Christopher encourages that child's bad behavior. God only knows what other illicit activity Rebel's engaged in. Kendall has told me she has it on good authority that that little girl is no longer pure."

Rory blinked. "You mean Reb's not a virgin?" he asked, to be certain of his father's meaning.

Dad glared at him. "She's still a little girl, so please don't use that kind of language in front of me when you're discussing her."

"But Uncle Christopher—"

"I'm not Uncle Christopher!" Dad blared. "He censures me for bringing you, my son, in a place for men." He made an arc of his hand. "I'd prefer to think of *you* fucking than my baby girl."

"Don't, Dad!" Rory snapped, outraged. "Girls are scary."

"Christopher doesn't care one way or the other," Dad continued, not remarking on Rory's observation. "He doesn't censor his conversation around Rebel. No wonder she's running wild."

"Where are you getting your information from, Dad?" Either his father was being purposely obtuse about

Mattie's rowdy behavior, or his sister was more of a champion liar than Rory credited.

"Your mother tells me," Dad answered. "And she gets it directly from Matilda."

Rory hooted with laughter. His father believing two of the most unreliable narrators in the world shocked him. If nothing else, his mother and sister were teaching Rory that most women's honesty were worth shit. He loved them, but they were cutthroat and devious, so unlike both Rebel and Aunt Meggie his father's blindness mystified him.

Rory tried to take cues from his aunt and cousin. Yet, Mom's shenanigans were pervasive, affecting him to his soul.

As Lolly would say, what gris-gris was at work here? What spell had his mother cast over his dad for the man to be so...so...so fucking *stupid* where she was concerned?

Rory snorted.

"I won't tolerate disrespect from you, Rory Donovan."

"Yes, sir," Rory said morosely, shoving his hands into his pockets.

"How did we get on this topic anyway?"

"We were discussing CJ and—"

"That's right. CJ. The sun does not rise and set in him, son. He's fallible, like the rest of us. Stop looking at him as if he knows everything."

"He knows a lot."

"Head home, son," Dad said, instead of responding. "I'm bagging this sorry motherfucker and bringing him to the incinerator. I've wasted enough time on this fuckhead. Fuck him."

"See you at home, Dad."

Rory's brisk walk along the forest path got him home within ten minutes.

Inside, the scent of lavender filled the toasty warmth. Voices floated from the kitchen, so Rory headed there.

"Add the whey protein, then the chia seeds, Matilda darling," Mom said as Rory walked into the kitchen.

His mother and sister stood with their backs to him, in front of a blender, defiling unknown ingredients with organic disgustingness. Their smoothies usually included a combination of fruits, vegetables, activated charcoal, edible clay, protein powder, seeds, and nuts. Completely horrific.

"Should we add more Acai seeds?" Matilda shoved some of her flaming red hair behind an ear, revealing the diamond earrings she got for her tenth birthday. "Maman?"

Rory sighed at how Mattie referred to their mother. Mom glanced over her shoulder.

"You're just in time, Ro," she said. "You need this to grow into a big, strong, healthy, young man."

"Uh, that's a no, Mom." It didn't matter how Rory craved for clear skin, height and muscles. He would buy fucking stilts, padding, and foundation before he consumed the homemade putridness bubbling in the blender. "I don't like your smoothies. Give me fruit and ice cream. A nice, juicy steak. Salty fries, dripping ketchup."

"Oh my god, so unhealthy," Mattie complained. "Tell him, Maman. We want you to live a long life. We choose only healthy ingredients, so—"

"So, nothing," Rory huffed.

His sister and mom enjoyed that gross shit. Like CJ and Dad, Rory ate what the hell he wanted to and damned the consequences. Long ago, Uncle Chris banned mom's attempt to serve nutrition in a glass when she brought the meals for their family get togethers.

Rory glared at the smoothie. “Just let me die if I have to drink that to stay alive.”

Drawing in a sharp breath, Mom faced Rory. “Son, please, don’t discuss your death. It would completely crush me. You’re my firstborn and I adore you. You’re such a perfect young man.”

Matilda snorted. When Rory lifted a brow at her, she flushed and glanced away.

“You’ll live a long, fruitful life and make your dad and I so proud.” Mom smiled at him. “You’ll lead the club for years to come.”

“Not if CJ has anything to say about it,” Matilda chirped, licking thick maroon-gray glop from a spoon.

“Let the members decide,” Mom said firmly. “It’s time for new leadership. The Donovan era with new rules is rising. We’ll bring elegant music, upgraded food, and superior gatherings meant for only a select few. Caldwells will be second fiddle.” She placed one hand on her hip. “I’m not promoting a rivalry. I would never do that.”

“You just did.”

Mom ignored Mattie. “I’m facilitating a changing of the guard. Your father dreams of you following in his footsteps in the club. That means we must prepare you.”

“Yes, ma’am,” Rory said meekly, not pointing out Dad had never been president, nor had he ever wanted the position.

His father was teaching him to be a killer who dismembered and incinerated their targets, while his mother wanted him to run a social club.

“How was school, son?”

“Boring,” Rory responded. “It’s the end of the year. There’s not much to do.”

Dad picked him up early today, without Mom’s knowledge, since no one could know about Rory’s visits to the meatshack. As long as Mom's world was perfect, she didn't investigate particulars.

They all coped in their own ways. As long as Mom was safe, *stable,* life was good.

"Where's your dad?" Mom turned back to the smoothie, grabbed a bag of macadamia nuts and handed them to his sister. Mattie promptly poured the contents into the sludge they intended to consume.

"Dad had to take care of some business at the club, Mom," Rory explained. "He'll be home soon. I'm heading upstairs for a quick shower. Change for dinner," he added, knowing his mother would be pleased.

"Of course, darling. Do you want to know tonight's menu?"

Matilda smirked at him. "I think you know what we're starting with."

"Stuff it, Mattie," Rory said, laughing. "Dad won't go for that."

His father's word was law. On the surface, at least.

Chapter Nine

HARLEY

"Hold it steady. Focus on the target, baby girl. And remember, in a real-life situation, motherfuckers not waiting for you to get in position."

Anticipation made Harley twitchy. Daddy would allow her to fire his Rossi 12. Whenever he brought the prized shotgun pistol out for practice, she always left annoyed. He never hesitated to allow CJ, Lou, and Rory to pull the trigger. Today, she'd finally have her chance.

"Relax."

She loosened her pose and pointed the barrel toward the ground, still clutching the grip. Her mind ran a million miles a minute. Yesterday's intensity kept her awake until the early morning hours, thinking about CJ and Rebel.

"Okay, baby girl," Daddy said. "Ready."

Bracing her legs apart, Harley shoved aside her worry and fatigue.

"Aim."

Her heart pounded. She was moments away from firing the Rossi 12.

Only, he never said, "*Fire!*" Instead, he held out his hand. "I'm proud of you. You did good."

"I have a steady hand and a good eye." She handed over the gun, muzzle down. "You've been teasing me with the prospect of shooting that gun for days."

Jamming his nearly finished cigarette in the corner of his mouth, he narrowed his gaze at the smoke curling from the tip. He raised the gun and fired, the recoil jerking his hand back, although he didn't lose his grasp.

They were in a clearing near the emergency entrance (or exit, depending on the situation) of club grounds. Permanent targets stood at various distances, the farthest three hundred yards away.

Uncle Cash, former military, was the only one with the skill to hit targets from such a vast expanse. Not even Daddy...not even Uncle Chris...could make those shots, and they were two of the best marksmen ever.

Daddy returned the Rossi 12 to its holster at his shoulder, then shoved his cut aside and pulled out the Desert Eagle .44 Magnum. It was 24k gold with a full Picatinny rail to mount a scope. She loved that gun. The day she turned eighteen, she'd buy herself one.

He handed her the gun and nodded toward the field. The metal stands equipped with assorted targets were positioned in a staggered pattern.

Aiming for the smallest plate, Harley got into her shooter's stance. She squeezed the trigger four times, digging her heels in and holding her hands tight to counteract the recoil. The Eagle's kick was outstanding. If she wasn't familiar with the gun, the muzzle's flip would've caught her off-guard and she might've lost control.

Yet, none of her bullets hit its target. Whenever they practiced at Uncle Chris's in a room he'd turned into a small range, Harley always hit dead center.

"Baby girl?"

She turned, gun still poised to fire, her finger on the trigger. Glaring at her, Daddy stepped aside, then pushed her arms down before grabbing the Eagle from her.

"Where your mind at, Harley?"

On things.

He was strict about his gun rules. "You could've shot my fucking ass off."

After staying with Rebel until almost two this morning, Harley got to school five minutes before first bell. Exhaustion pressed her. She'd gotten two hours of sleep.

Unfortunately, she couldn't reveal that to her father. She was supposed to have been in bed, not working on a bike with Rebel.

At some point, she'd told Harley that Daddy was back to the club. Minutes later, she also warned Harley that Uncle Chris, Aunt Meggie, and CJ were on their way home. That meant her parents were leaving the club, too.

She snuck away from the garage through the small side door installed for easier access to the bathroom from the garden. She and Rebel tapped into the security system and erased all evidence of their adventure.

As she ran through the forest, cursing the darkness and her fear, she worried her parents discovering her lie. Uncle Chris received alerts in real time, so he must've at least known of she'd spent the evening with Rebel and informed her parents.

Arriving home two minutes before her parents, Harley ran to her bedroom. Since neither Mommie or

Daddy confronted her, they didn't know about her late night adventure.

Daddy's hand landed on her shoulder and she jumped. The Eagle was nowhere in sight and his cigarette was gone, too. Folding his arms, he stared at her and waited.

She wrinkled her brow. Maybe, she could share a little since she was acting so weird. "Suppose a problem needs handling? Someone...The person in trouble might not have the power to change stuff and yet they don't want to tell anyone who does. What, uh, what should they do?"

"Why wouldn't they go to a higher up?"

Harley scratched her head. "They don't want to lose respect."

Part of the reason she hadn't been able to sleep was because of CJ's problem with Lumbly. Her threats would only go so far.

"Respect from who? If a motherfucker abusing his authority, then the targeted motherfucker already lost fucking respect. If they ever fucking had it."

Lumbly completely disliked CJ. Yet, he let Willy Byrd do and say anything.

"Daddy, they don't want *people* to think they're weak. I don't know when a confidence should be broken," she added glumly.

"Harley, when you betray the trust somebody puts in you, it's harder than a motherfucker to get it back. However, if that person life on the line or their freedom at stake, then you got to do whatever you must to save them from the threat."

Pursing her lips, she nodded.

"Now, talk to me," he encouraged, taking her hand in his and guiding her in the direction of their house. "Why you so distracted? And who in trouble? You or CJ?"

Both, if she were being honest. But she wasn't. *And* Rebel also needed guidance.

Her dad halted, leaving her no choice but to do the same, since he still held her hand. "Me and Outlaw got to bust some fucking heads, baby?"

"Daddy, isn't there an unspoken rule that what happens between the brothers stays between you all?" She looked away from her father's steady regard. "The kids have been told whatever issues come up between us to handle amongst us."

"Harley, that rule in place for simple shit. Disagreements and misunderstandings. Not anything to fuck up your life."

"That should've been clarified years ago," she snapped.

Daddy narrowed his eyes. "What the fuck going on, Harley? Tell me *now*."

His annoyance cooled her temper immediately.

"Um...I..." Confiding in Daddy about CJ's problem was a betrayal. Mentioning Willy risked Daddy seeking his own type of justice. Asking him to talk to Rebel about her devastation over Diesel would be disloyal to Rebel and possibly detrimental to Diesel. Even if he'd rejected Rebel in no uncertain terms, he'd still assisted her schemes when he'd picked her up from school. "C-can I get back to you?"

"Nope, baby girl. I want to know what's happening right now."

She tugged her hand away and shifted from foot-to-foot. "Will you promise not to tell anyone else?"

He lit another cigarette. "Until I know what it is, I can't make that promise, Harley. If it involve CJ, I have to tell Outlaw."

"Our lives aren't at stake. And I think I took care of it, but I'm not sure."

Through a blanket of smoke, Daddy narrowed his eyes. "What the fuck you talking about?"

"It has to do with a teacher. I might've told him you and Mommie had a conference at the lower school—after school today—with Kaleb's teacher and, if the person in question didn't back off, you'd take it up with him." She wrung her hands together. "Actually, I said it would be you or Lolly."

"And CJ not telling Outlaw because the little motherfucker thinks Prez would see him as weak."

"Yeah, Daddy."

"And you don't want me to tell Outlaw 'cause then CJ would feel betrayed by you." Cigarette trapped between his fingers, he regarded her. "You tell me about the situation with CJ and—"

"Mr. Lumbly," she supplied.

"Okay, that motherfucker. The minute he get on CJ ass again, I'm telling Outlaw."

"No, Daddy!" she cried, her heart pounding as she imagined the fallout from that scenario. "CJ would know I ratted. You've always said a snitch is the lowest of the low."

"You not a fucking snitch, Harley. You a child. Snitches grown and roll on motherfuckers to save their own fucking asses. That don't fucking describe you since your biggest concern passing to the next fucking grade."

CJ's inclusion in a club meeting signaled his introduction into *certain activities*. If CJ was involved, *Harley* was too, whether her father liked it or not. "CJ would never confide in me again," she pointed out, ignoring Daddy's view on snitches.

"What the fuck business he got that he need to confide in somebody?"

"It isn't business *business*, Daddy. It's friend stuff. Dude stuff. We're each other's favorite bros."

Instead of appeasing him, his annoyance grew. "I did dude stuff with motherfuckers before, and if CJ doing any of that with you, I'm beating his ass. What type of *dude shit* you two do?"

"I can't tell you."

"Me and him talking," her father said, then turned on his heel and headed toward the house.

She ran to catch up to him, but his long legs ate up the distance. "Daddy," she said, grabbing his wrist to halt him. "Don't say anything to CJ, please. It isn't anything bad, I swear. Trust me."

"I trust *you*, Harley. *He* the motherfucker I don't."

"CJ has always taken care of me," she said, a little indignant on his behalf. "What has he ever done for you to believe he'd harm me in anyway?"

"Got to be a fucking teenage boy," Daddy snapped. "He changing and so are you."

"I don't care how much he changes, he'll never hurt me."

"Not intentionally, but he a fucking dude and dude shit not just fucking listening to music and watching movies and whatever the fuck else you talk him into doing. As a matter of fact, what you two do together more bitch shit than dude shit."

She opened her mouth to refute Daddy's words, but he flicked his cigarette away and raised his hand. "Back to Fumbly."

"Lumbly," she muttered.

"Motherfucker Fumbly to me. If the stupid fuckhead still fuck around with CJ, I'll pay him *one* fucking visit. After that, if he do it again, tell me. I'll let you decide if you want me to talk to CJ, or we talk to him together to give him a chance to tell Outlaw himself. If he decline, *I'm* informing Prez. Got me?"

"Yes, Daddy."

"Good." He drew her into his embrace. "I love you, baby."

Laying her cheek against his cut, she smiled. "I love you, too, Daddy."

Chapter Ten

MATILDA

Shifting her weight, Matilda Donovan leaned against the wall right outside Fuckhead Lumbly's classroom. She should be in her own class, but she wouldn't get into trouble. Unlike CJ, Mattie apprised her father of the happenings at school. She'd gotten detention *twice* for tardiness. The first time Maman was running late, so it hadn't been Mattie's fault. Her teacher hadn't listened. The second time was in the very class she was brushing off right now. She'd said she needed to pee. Her teacher hadn't believed her. Even when she said her daddy wouldn't be happy, Mrs. LeBan gave her detention.

Mrs. Wallace, the instructor who'd dared to fault Mattie for *Maman's* tardiness no longer taught at Ridge Moore. Mrs. LeBan was on probation. If that bitch fucked with Mattie again, she was gone.

"Can someone tell me the name of the first play Shakespeare wrote?"

Lumbly's whiny, little-man voice threw out the question as if it was the first month of the school year, instead of the last.

Grimacing, Mattie studied her nails. She needed a fill. If Maman wasn't working on a case this weekend, they could go to the salon.

"Mr. Caldwell, please answer the question."

"I didn't raise my hand, Mr. Lumbly."

Her cousin sounded bored, not stupid. He *was* a fucking doofus, though. Instead of taking full advantage of his resources at hand—namely Uncle Christopher—he wanted to handle Lumbly on his own. He was thumbing his fucking nose at how the stars aligned to make him a Caldwell. Not just any Caldwell either, but *Outlaw's* son.

"Miss Banks is unavailable today," Lumbly said into the silence, "so I suggest you answer the question or else."

Glancing at her watch, Mattie yawned. Could Lumbly spout a more pedestrian threat? Expanding upon it would add weight.

"Scholars aren't certain which play Shakespeare wrote first," CJ said.

"That's a dumb motherfucker answer," Ryan jeered.

It took a dumb motherfucker to know. Mattie rolled her eyes. Maman loved reading Shakespeare to her, her brothers, and all her cousins. CJ *and* Ryan were well-versed on the Bard.

"Yeah, Taylor, you're right." Piggy face Willard snickered. "Caldwell's bitching out. Fucking cuck."

"No, dick face, I'm not," CJ snapped. "And your brother's a fucking cuck."

A cuck? Wallace? He was plain fucking evil. And Ryan was a fuckface, suck-up, sellout, pandering to Willard and pretending to know jack shit about Shakespeare.

"*Mister Caldwell*," Lumbly squealed, "if you don't wish to have a thirty-day suspension, you will not use foul language in my classroom."

Yeah. *No*. With a few days left until the end of school, the suspension would affect the beginning of CJ's junior year.

Scowling, Mattie pulled out her phone, opened her recording app, and pressed record.

"Unless you want a 'F' for today's lesson, you will tell me the name of The Bard's first play."

"Do *you* know it?" CJ huffed. "My guess is *no*. There's controversy in the Shakespearean community because by the time the plays were published in the 1590s, they'd been in theaters for several years. Shakespeare also collaborated with other playwrights. Christopher Marlowe, Thomas Nashe, and John Fletcher, amongst others. A lot of them contributed significant parts to each other's works. Shakespeare's plays were owned by theater companies. Four plays have been debated as being the first he wrote. *Titus Adronicus*, *Henry VI, Part 2*, and *Comedy of Errors*. *Arden of Faversham*, the fourth, is a tragedy whose author of record is anonymous, but many scholars believe Shakespeare wrote it. I can't answer what his first play is because no one knows."

"Give him an 'F', Mr. Lumbly," Willard ordered. "How could a part two come before part one?"

"Mr. Caldwell, since you purport to know more than me, a man from a family of educators, tell me five popular Shakespearean phrases he invented."

"Vanish into thin air," CJ started. "In a pickle. As dead as a doornail. Mum's the word. Setting my teeth on edge."

"It's set *your* teeth on edge," Mr. Lumbly snarled. "And you failed to give me the plays in which they are from." Tiny little feet resounded. Assmite was marching between the desks. "Give me five expressions from Shakespeare."

"*Thou whoreson, senseless villain, The Comedy of Errors. The tartness of his face sours ripe grapes, Coriolanus. He is white livered and red face* from *Henry V. You are a tedious fool, Measure for Measure. Thou lump of foul deformity*. That's from *Richard III.*"

The ensuing silence tickled Mattie. She couldn't wait for Rebel and Harley to hear of how CJ told off the miserable little man on the sly. If she could, she'd tell Maman and Aunt Meggie, but neither could know for two different reasons.

Maman would say Mattie's behavior wasn't ladylike because...well, Mattie wasn't sure. But her parents classified almost *everything* as unladylike. Aunt Meggie would enjoy the story. She just wouldn't like the reason. Since she knew nothing about the issues, Mattie wouldn't open that can of worms. Maybe, she wouldn't tell Harley and Rebel either.

Rebel would judge CJ and Harley would worry. Though Mattie didn't like her cousin's passive aggression, she understood. She used the same tactics with her parents.

"I suppose you think you have the brain to outsmart *me*," Lumbly finally sneered. "You don't. You should do us all a favor and drop out to start your life of crime."

Jealous little bitch.

"I don't know what you mean, sir," CJ said calmly.

"Outlaw's your old man," Willard called.

"You've failed today's lessons, Mr. Caldwell," Lumbly interrupted. "It's *Arden of Favers*. Thomas Kyd and Christopher Marlowe are documented as the authors. I don't know where you got your information from, but Mr. Byrd is right. *Henry VI, Part 1* was written before part two. *The Oxford Shakespeare*'s chronology puts *The Comedy of Errors* as ninth in The Bard's canon."

Off with that little twerp's head!

Mattie rummaged through her purse for bubblegum, then she sailed into the classroom. Lumbly stood over CJ, barking bullshit at him. Blowing a bubble, she popped it as the nasty little troll turned and faced her.

"Yes, Miss Donovan?"

Another bubble. Another pop.

Disgust swept over Lumbly's face.

She tossed her hair and grinned. "It's *Arden of* Feversham, and it's part of the Shakespeare Apocrypha, works whose original author or authors are questioned for whatever reason. Maman is big into opera and Shakespeare." She popped her gum again. "Should I tell Daddy you're questioning my mother's intelligence?" She stopped the recording and pressed play.

Offering a small smile, Lumbly strolled to his desk and sat. She turned off the playback.

"Your point is made, Miss Donovan," he said mildly. "I'm as familiar with your parents as I am with Miss Banks' grandmother. Unlike *her*, Mr. and Mrs. Donovan are cultured and civilized, and hold their *little princess* to the highest standards. We had a lovely conversation about you during my end-of-year conference with them for your brother. I wonder how they'd feel about you loitering outside my door instead of attending your own class."

Unlike the other two times, Mattie wouldn't have much recourse to argue on her own behalf. Her parents saw her not only as a princess, but a small girl. Especially her father. He expected her to be above reproach, flawless, and virtuous. She couldn't drink or smoke or curse. Yet, at the club, everything she was forbidden to even think about, was front and center.

"Mattie, come on," CJ said, tugging her hand. "Let me walk you to your class." He leaned closer. "Don't let that dickhead see you cry."

She hadn't realized her eyes were watering. "He's being so unfair to you," she whispered. "I wanted to help."

He grinned. "You wanted to cut class."

"Not cut, just miss the first half." Less time around Willard's bovine brother.

"Sit down, Mr. Caldwell," Lumbly ordered.

CJ glanced over his shoulder, but Mattie squeezed his hand. "Don't. You'll end up missing practice."

Although Ryan was a couple months older, CJ took his responsibility as their protector with frightening ferocity.

"I'm just going to class," she swore, and she'd keep her word. He had enough to deal with as Lumbly's student.

"Mr. Lumbly," another student called. "I need help with a definition."

Lumbly scowled between CJ and Mattie, then glared at the student at the back row. "Fine," he huffed, stomping off.

Mattie started toward the door. "I'll be fine."

"Mattie, don't tell anyone about this."

"I knew you'd say that," she sighed, blowing a bubble then sucking the gum back into her mouth.

"Lumbly'll fail me no matter what. I can't go to my dad for stupid shit like this."

Marching to her misguided cousin, Mattie jabbed CJ in the chest. "This isn't "stupid shit". It's a teacher abusing his power and that's serious. Uncle Chris expects you to respect adults. He *has* to deal with Lumbly, CJ."

He was stupid or stubborn or both because he shook his head. "No, I have to handle Lumbly. How will my dad ever believe I can work shit out for myself?"

"I'm so glad I have a pussy," she whispered. "What you just said is strictly testosterone-infused, dick-measuring talk. In other words, stupidity. Lumbly's out of control. He needs to be dealt with. Preferably with cement poured down his miserable throat and his body thrown into the fucking ocean."

"You have detention, Mr. Caldwell. Get to your class, young lady," Mr. Lumbly growled as he strolled to his desk and sat. "*NOW!*"

Mattie turned to the teacher, popped her gum, and narrowed her eyes. "Did you just raise your voice to me?"

Lumbly snapped his mouth shut. He knew he'd fucked up. Mattie bit the inside of her cheek, drawing blood. Pain streaked through her and tears rushed to her eyes. She sniffled.

"Daddy never raises his voice to me," she wailed. "You did, and in front of the entire class, Mr. Lumbly!" Carefully, she pressed her teeth into her tongue. Tears leaked down her cheeks. "I'm telling on you."

"That won't be necessary!" Lumbly exclaimed, jumping to his feet and hurrying to her. "Mr. Caldwell, please escort Miss Donovan to her class. You're dismissed for the day to see to her well-being. Your failing grade stands."

As much as she tried, she couldn't come up with a way to change that.

Lumbly drew himself up. "Please don't tell Mr. Donovan, Matilda. I need my job. Your father's medical laboratory donates a lot of money to Ridge Moore."

Either he didn't know how much Aunt Meggie and Uncle Chris donated or the fuckhead didn't care.

"Your father told me himself," Lumbly went on.

Mattie shook her shoulders and sniffled again. Fake crying hurt her fucking head, adding to the pain from her bitten cheeks and tongue. She swiped at her wet face. "I-I'll tr-try t-to c-c-c-compose myself."

"Mr. Caldwell, please see to your young cousin."

CJ shoved his notebook into his rucksack and nodded toward the door.

Outside in the hallway, Mattie halted and dug in her purse again, this time for a compact to check her appearance. Her nose was red and her cheeks pink, but the lingering tears brightened her brown eyes. She looked positively tragic. After applying lip gloss, she snapped a selfie and texted the photo to Daddy with the message, *I'm having an awful day.*

"Come on, Mattie," CJ said with impatience. "You have twenty minutes left to your class."

Shopping will cheer you up, princess.

Mattie grinned. *I couldn't, Daddy. Maman just bought me a watch from Tiffany's.*

How about I buy you a pair of earrings?

Uh-uh. Not what Mattie wanted.

You're the best, Daddy! Earrings are so expensive. Can I send a link to a Louis Vuitton handbag?

Certainly, princess.

Before Mattie found the link, CJ grabbed her by the elbow and dragged her toward Columbia Hall, the building housing the middle school. This was Rory, Devon, Rebel and Harley's last year in Columbia Hall, then they'd leave Mattie for the upper school, spread across several buildings on the huge campus. She hated to think about the coming separation.

She needed a hit to remove the sudden sadness and regret enveloping her. If she hadn't shown herself by strutting into Lumbly's classroom, the choice of attending geography class would be hers.

The buildings for the upperclassmen didn't seem as gothicly oppressive as Columbia Hall. As CJ held up his key card to register his leaving Douglass Hall, Mattie's insides shook. She didn't feel like sitting in class being the perfect princess to make her perfect parents proud.

Nicotine wouldn't help calm her as much as a joint, but something was better than nothing. "Let's go to the Quad for a smoke."

"Fuck no."

Jerking away from CJ's grip, Mattie snorted. "I wasn't asking you."

"Don't give a fuck. I'm *telling* you *fuck no*. You need to get to class."

"To do what? School's about to close. We've already turned in our books."

"School has three weeks left. We're still wrapping up. My final history essay is due next week."

"Oh God," Mattie groaned, tipping her head back. "Can I just drop out? Like seriously. School bores the fuck out of me."

"I'm sure it does. Your pretty head's too fucking crammed with conniving."

She giggled, panic rising as they skirted Williams Hall and headed toward the middle school. But CJ was as hard to deceive as Uncle Chris. *They* paid attention to her. "Scheming makes the world go 'round."

"Thank you for trying to help, but don't get into Lumbly's crosshairs."

"Fuck him. He swept in on the same hot air as the Byrd brothers three years ago. They all need burying."

"Keep your fucking voice down," CJ whispered, as if their surroundings possessed ears. "Besides, their enrollment isn't connected to Lumbly's hiring."

"To me it is because I hate all three fuckheads."

CJ opened one of the huge wooden doors and held it until she walked into the main hallway. Columbia Hall was the original building for Ridge Moore. In the beginning, it had only a few students whose wealthy parents demanded exclusivity.

The staircase to the second floor had a deep red runner down the center and a huge chandelier that added to the offensive misery. The expensive piece of shit supplied little light but wafted of money. At the second-floor landing, Mattie almost turned around, then changed her mind. CJ would drag her to class.

As he started up the final flight of stairs, she glared at his back. "Why don't you put the same fucking energy into Lumbly?"

"What energy is that?"

"Your unbreakable will where we're concerned. You boss the fuck out of us."

"Lumbly's a teacher, Mattie. I have to do what he says or he will fail me."

"Exactly why you should clue in Uncle Chris, jackass. And, might I remind you, Lumbly's *already* failing you." She stomped next to him on the third-floor landing, wanting to smack the smile off his face. "Uncle Chris doesn't expect you to be perfect. He accepts you, Rebel, and your brothers just as you are."

"Dad wants me to go to college before I can even prospect. That's non-negotiable," he said flatly. "That's four years of my fucking life wasted when I could use that time to patch in. If I have any hope of finding a way around that rule, it'll be shot to hell if I run to him about stupid shit. Dad won't look at me the way everyone looks at him."

Mattie blinked, then roared in laughter. "You're a fucking dumbass," she said, abruptly cutting her chuckles. "No one will ever look at you like him because you aren't him, stupid. You're *you*, and frankly if I had Uncle Chris and Aunt Meggie as parents, I wouldn't hesitate to sing like a fucking canary on that evil little fuckhead."

"You'd do it anyway," he said with humor.

"I would," Mattie agreed without apology. "I don't have to suffer idiots, so I won't. Daddy would think that's harsh because I'm a young lady, so I'd tell him I can't deal. But you? Rebel? Your brothers? You *could* say Lumbly's a fucking idiot and a mean little bastard, in those exact words, and Uncle Chris would take care of it. He wouldn't make you feel lesser. He wouldn't make Rebel feel unfeminine or like she's disappointed him."

CJ glanced at the floor, but he couldn't reprove her because she was right. "You have ten minutes until the end of class, then cheer practice." He started walking again, opening the door to the third-floor hallway. "Coach Yancy texted and said to meet on the field behind the center because the team's working out with the cheer squad today," he said once they were headed to her geography class.

"I guess our substitute coach flaked out." The bitch wasn't worth her paycheck. She canceled half their scheduled practices. "I'll be so glad when Coach Ericks returns."

"Reb will be, too."

At the door to her class, Mattie tugged the sleeve of CJ's blazer. "Did you ask anyone about Aunt Meggie shooting someone?" she asked when he turned to her.

"Nope, because I don't believe you," he whispered. "If Mom shot a motherfucker, that shit would have a special wall of fame."

"I overheard my parents talking one evening."

CJ shrugged. "Did you hear the entire conversation?"

"No," she admitted. "Just Daddy saying Aunt Meggie shot a guy named Traveler using Uncle Christopher's gun."

"Mom hates guns, so there's no fucking way she'd have access to Dad's guns to shoot anyone."

"You have a point," she conceded.

Before she could stop him, he turned and opened the door.

"Why are you on my turf, big brother?" Ryder called as Mrs. LeBan said, "good afternoon, Mr. Caldwell, how can I help you?"

"I didn't want Mattie to get in trouble on my behalf, ma'am," CJ responded, stepping aside to reveal her. "She had a book for me and brought it to my class, but when she arrived we were in the middle of a quiz."

The décor in the class was as miserable as the rest of the building. Maps and whiteboards hung on each side of the room. A black chalkboard dominated the front wall. Wood paneling the same shade as the wooden floor made her dizzy. It was almost impossible to discern where the walls ended and the floorboards began.

"Hey, Mattie," Wallace Byrd called. He nodded to the empty seat next to him. "I saved a spot for you."

Memories of his gross, clammy hands and his wet mouth swept through her and she shivered. She still regretted asking Wally for a hit of his bud when they'd crossed paths, cutting school and hiding out at the same spot. It wasn't that he'd expected compensation. Everyone did. It was that he hadn't given her the choice of how she'd repay him.

"She's my partner in geography," Lou piped in, cutting his eyes at Wally.

"It's fine, cousin," she swore.

Lou scowled but didn't press the issue.

She trudged to Wallace and sat, shoving hair behind her ear and smiling. If ever she needed her father, it was now, but she couldn't bear his disapproval and disappointment. She'd gotten herself into this situation because she smoked pot.

Perfect princesses weren't weed heads.

CJ skirted the desks and walked to the study lab.

"You may wait with your cousin until the bell rings, Miss Donovan," Mrs. LeBan chirped. Her horn-rimmed glasses and severe bun turned her into a caricature of a mean, judgmental teacher. She loved A-line skirts, high-necked blouses, and Mary Janes.

With those statistics, Mattie would be a fucking bitch, too.

"Come to the exploration table," CJ called.

"Stay with me," Wallace whispered. "My brother'll beat Rory to death if you don't."

Nausea hit Mattie. Rory was a small kid. He tried to be tough, but he didn't have the size for it. He wouldn't stand a chance against the monstruous Willard. But she couldn't tell her parents about the Byrd brothers either. Daddy would find a way to accuse her unladylike behavior for all her problems with the boys. And, if Rory was caught in the crosshairs of her miserable conduct, they'd never forgive her.

"Tell him," Wallace instructed.

"Tell me *what*?" CJ demanded, right beside them suddenly.

Wallace jerked in surprise.

"Sit down, Mr. Caldwell!" Mrs. LeBan ordered.

"I told you this is *my* turf, CJ," Ryder said.

CJ flipped Ryder off, then smiled at the teacher. "Sorry, Mrs. LeBan. I'm not trying to disrupt the class."

She pursed her lips and nodded. "Bell's about to ring," she said primly, patting her bun and blushing at CJ's smirk. "You and Miss Donovan head to practice."

"Come on, Mattie," CJ instructed, glaring at Wallace. "Let's jet before I have to beat Ryder's ass."

Wallace slid down in his seat, trying to disappear underneath the desk. He seemed so innocuous and soft-spoken.

CJ didn't speak until they were downstairs, heading back to Douglass Hall to meet Rebel and Harley and make their way to the athletic center.

"Do I have to sic Ryder on that motherfucker?"

"No," she fibbed without batting an eye. Her entire life felt like a big lie. "Wallace just has a crush on me."

"Let me know if you need assistance. Ryder'll be happy to put a bug in his ear."

A real one, no doubt. The Caldwell boys were terrors. Well, except Rule, the anomaly. Not that it mattered. Uncle Christopher and Aunt Meggie didn't demand they change to fit a certain ideal.

Meanwhile, CJ mimicked the strict codes of his father where women and children were protected. In this case, the older kids didn't jump the younger ones. CJ wouldn't touch a middle schooler, but he could beat an upperclassman to a bloody pulp.

How she wished Wallace qualified.

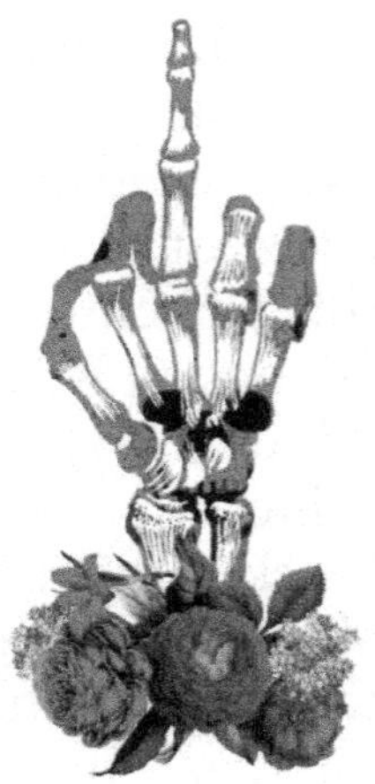

Chapter Eleven

"Your legs are soooo long," Molly Harris complained half hour later, standing straight before completing another walking lunge and twist. "We're practicing together, so we should keep pace with each other."

CJ grinned over his shoulder. Three yards separated him from the pretty, brown-haired girl. She had wide, blue-gray eyes and a generous mouth, not to mention a body that would make bank on Only Fans.

"Wait for me," she pouted.

"I can't stop, bae. Coach'll have my ass. Extend your legs out more and I'll shorten my lunges, so we can even up. Deal?"

She giggled. "Yeah, CJ. Whatever you want."

Ignoring the insinuation, he amended his steps, allowing her to catch up. Two days had passed since the scene in the Scorched Devils clubhouse. Two days since Harley sat on CJ's lap and...

Coach Yancy blew his whistle, in that short, sharp way revealing his displeasure. The cheer squad and CJ's fellow teammates halted. "Caldwell!"

Fuck. CJ knew what he'd be called out on. To be sure... "Sir?"

"What the hell do you mean? *Sir*?" Coach Yancy growled, barreling to him. "You're the quarterback. You lead by example. I don't expect to see one of my best players slacking during warmup. You have one chance to explain yourself. If I don't like what I hear, you're giving me one hundred pushups." He pointed to Molly. "Or she is, if you did it for her."

"No, Coach Yancy, you can't make me!" Molly blared. "The most pushups I can do is thirty-two. I refuse to go any higher. My birthday is in February, and it's the only month with thirty-two days. It's special."

CJ frowned. She was fucking joking. His outrage prevented his enjoyment of Yancy's ashen shock.

"Coach!" Roger Marksum called, standing near the gated entrance of the practice field. He was the head of athletics, a former pro wrestler and a cool dude.

"I'll deal with you when I return, CJ," Coach Yancy vowed and hurried off.

"Dumb ass," Rebel growled, hurrying over the moment Yancy and Marksum disappeared into the athletic center. "There's twenty-eight days in February. Twenty-nine if it's a leap year."

"No, Reb," Molly denied. "I was born on the 29th of February, and I have a birthday every year. Otherwise, I would only be four years old, instead of sixteen. Besides, my momma said there are thirty-two days in February and my mother would never lie to me."

"Nope, she'd just be a stupid bitch like you," Mattie inserted. His cousin had left her spot entirely, where she'd been working out with Wallace, the younger Byrd brother.

"Mattie, get the fuck back where you belong," CJ snapped.

Unlike earlier when she'd walked to Wallace like he was her executioner, she'd regained full control of herself. CJ would have Ryder keep watch over Mattie. She just wouldn't know about it.

"Make me," she ordered.

Growling, CJ lifted his cousin off her feet, threw her over his shoulder, and ran to Wallace Byrd.

She pounded on CJ's back. "Put me down, asshole."

"Gladly," CJ said, bending so she wouldn't drop too far then letting her go. His unexpected release caught her off-guard and she teetered. Unable to gain her footing, she plopped on her ass.

Immediately recovering, she got to her feet and balled her fist. The first punch grazed his chin. Before she landed the second one, he caught her wrist.

"Don't fucking hit me again, Matilda," he ordered as if she'd listen. She was as hardheaded as his little sister.

"Fuck you," she retorted, struggling to free herself. "You had no business dropping me. I could've hurt myself really bad." She stomped his foot.

Yelping in pain and releasing his cousin, he gritted his teeth, refusing to hop around like a jackass.

Hands on hips, Mattie rocked on her heels and smiled. "You can't hit me, so what will you do now?"

"He can't, Mattie," Rebel said before CJ answered. "But I can." She punched Mattie's jaw and sent her reeling back.

Recovering quickly, she lunged for Rebel.

Fuck these two. They couldn't scratch and kick and 'if' at each other. No, they threw fucking punches like pro boxers. Coach Yancy would hold him responsible for this lack of control.

"Enough!" Harley almost snarled, coming up on them.

Rebel and Mattie broke apart and stared at each other. His sister's eyes gleamed, though. Before they threw hands again, he stepped forward and grabbed a handful of Rebel's T-shirt, dragging her back and ignoring her struggles.

Harley hurried to Mattie, crouched next to her, and whispered in her ear before helping her to her feet.

"I resent you asking me to apologize, Harley," Mattie spat, the moment Harley guided her over.

"I didn't ask you to do anything," Harley retorted. "I *told* you."

"Oh, shut up," Mattie said, "whining like a fucking baby because Molly paired with CJ. You should do us all a favor and fuck him already."

CJ had only a moment to register those words and his body's response before Harley bristled.

"You're wrong, Mattie. I want to screw *you. UP*," she added viciously. "Don't make me lose my temper."

"Miss Banks, Miss Caldwell, and Miss Donovan, leave the field." Coach Yancy's voice rose into the silence.

The motherfucker *would* reappear before the bullshit ended.

"Young ladies, report to the principal's office first thing in the morning," Marksum added.

Mattie glared between the two men. "Harley didn't do anything."

"Yeah, she broke us up," Rebel added. "Leave her out of our battles."

Harley folded her arms and tossed her hair over her shoulder. "We're in this together. If you two go to the principal's office, then so do I. We all disrupted practice."

"Harls, no!" Rebel said. "Uncle Mort and Aunt Bailey would be so upset. You've never gotten a disciplinary action."

Neither had Mattie. She took care with her behavior. While Uncle Mort and Aunt Bailey would be upset over Harley, Uncle Johnnie and Aunt Kendall would be livid.

"Coach, the argument between my sister and our cousins started at home," CJ said. "Can you give them a little slack and—"

"Enough!" Coach Yancy boomed. "Escort these two away," he said, pointing to Rebel and Mattie.

Marksum nodded toward the athletic center.

Not backing down, Harley walked away with them, pissing the coach off by leaving after he'd given her a reprieve.

CJ started to protest Rebel and Matilda being marched away like criminals.

"I wouldn't if I were you, Caldwell," Coach Yancy warned, then blew his whistle. "Practice is over. Exit the field. Except you and you." He pointed to Molly and CJ.

Molly sidled closer, pressing her body against his. "What will he do to us?"

"Drop down and give me one hundred pushups and one hundred sit-ups. It was the two of you who created the chaos."

The tail-end of practice left CJ grimy and sweaty. He'd been wrong to interrupt and adjust his warmups for Molly, but he thought the cheer squad practiced conditioning and strength-training with the football team for guidance. This was the first time, and hopefully the last, he'd ever been paired with Molly, who, unlike Harley, couldn't keep up.

Not being with Harley annoyed him. Worse, she'd teamed with Willard. Coach Yancy made sure she practiced with CJ as often as possible. When she didn't, she sure as fuck wasn't with Willard.

Besides, the thought of her being upset...and the reason for it. She hadn't been upset she *wasn't* with him. It was because Molly was.

He tried not to think about the meaning. His feelings for Harley flipflopped between seeing her as his best bro to noticing her every move.

She didn't have tits and ass yet, or *any* curves like Rebel, Matilda, Molly, and many of the other girls he knew. Yet, her boyish body didn't matter. CJ still thought about her almost every waking moment. He—

"CJ!" Molly whispered. "You really should wear your hearing device. Coach has been talking to you and you haven't heard anything. You don't have to be embarrassed you're audibly challenged."

Drawing in a breath, CJ scrubbed a hand over his face. "I'm not," he said, still distracted. "I'm just thinking."

"I do that a lot, too. Normally, not when I'm talking, though. Is it only me or does your brain shut off when you're in a conversation?"

"What the fuck do you mean? How the hell can you have a conversation if you're not thinking?"

"Coach Yancy, when you're talking don't you stop thinking, too, to focus on the conversation?"

Lifting his thick brows, the coach opened his mouth, then closed it again and squinted. He put a little distance between them and looked at CJ. "Why did you amend my warmup instructions without my permission?"

"I was tired—" he started.

"No, silly, you did it because I said your legs were too long." Molly rolled her eyes. "Remember? You shouldn't ever try to talk and think. It messes up your memory."

CJ sidled a glare at Molly. "Shut up," he warned, low. "Or Coach'll make you do the same fucking pushups and sit-ups I'm in for."

"But—"

"Fuck, Molly," he whispered. "Don't say another fucking word. I'm trying to protect you."

Eyes rounding, she nodded. "How?"

"Are you sure you want to take the fall for her, CJ?" Coach Yancy said with amusement. He'd heard every word of the conversation.

"Yes, sir. It wasn't Molly's fault."

"If she hadn't complained about your height, you would've minced around like you were part of the Nutcracker performance on your own?"

Molly giggled.

"I didn't shorten my lunges that much, Coach. C'mon," CJ protested.

"You have a bright future ahead of you," Coach told him sternly. "If not at the pro level, then in collegiate football. You must stay focused. The girls weren't due to practice with us for another week. But their substitute coach couldn't stay after school."

"Harley keeps up with me."

Coach sighed. "Miss Banks can do no wrong in your estimation. When you graduate, what will she do then? She will still have two years left. Stop depending on each other! Your lives will go in different directions. By the way, *she* was the one who asked to be paired with Byrd."

"The fuck you say!" CJ blurted, so surprised a fucking pin could've knocked him over. "She can't stand that motherfucker."

"Not from what I saw," Coach Yancy said kindly.

Impossible. Harley hated Willard.

"Coach, can I stay while CJ exercises?" Molly sounded so sweet, not like a fucking super dummy. "He looks really sad now."

Coach Yancy grinned at her. "You can do the countdown." Folding his arms, he studied CJ. "Stay focused, son. You're failing Language Arts. If that happens, you're off the team. You don't want that."

He didn't. If he had to attend college to patch into the Death Dwellers, he'd need to involve himself in what he enjoyed. He loved football and was determined to play at the collegiate level while he bided his time. And, yet, he'd walk away in a minute, if his father told him his probationary period in the club would begin.

Lumbly's...*whatever*...toward him threatened to derail the plans he'd made for himself to satisfy his parents' requirement over CJ's four fucking years in college.

CJ heaved in a breath. "Coach, I don't know why that little asshole has it in for me so much, but—"

"Three days ago," Molly interrupted, "I went to the office to talk to the principal about the inaccurate information in our health textbook. It says girls have eggs and I have never hatched an egg in my life. Neither has Momma. Anyway, Lumbly was in there and he's totally doing the receptionist. Like...yuck. He was telling her how Mr. Caldwell had his cousin Pete Hart fired from a daycare CJ once attended. Lumbly said his cousin was a doctor, so I don't even know how he could teach at a school. Duh...even I know that. Dr. Teacher Pete Hart *disappeared*. Lumbly, the dumb ass, believes Mr. Caldwell did it. I think he ran away to be a doctor again."

Fuuuucccccckkkkkk.

He wasn't sure what was worse—the information Molly provided or the fact he understood everything she said. And, fuck, if she'd had a brain in her head, she would've understood herself, too.

Pressing his lips together, CJ scrubbed his fingers through his sweaty hair. "Dr. Hart had a Ph.D., Molly," he snapped, although he hadn't known it when that asshole was terrorizing him. "And he wasn't a teacher, he was the principal. It wasn't a daycare; it was a fucking school."

"Daycares are schools for babies." Her eyes widened. "Wait! Are you saying Mr. Caldwell really made him disappear?"

"No!" *Fuck*. Maybe, she understood more than she let on. Who the fuck was he kidding? Nobody was as fucking stupid as Molly made herself out to be. Her ignorance was a prank, a foil, a fucking *show*. But why? Exactly what the fuck was her end goal to portray herself as a dumb bitch. Wary, CJ gave her a sharp look. "My father isn't a killer. What's wrong with you?"

He knew his dad had Hart removed from the school, but he *hadn't* known Hart had been separated from *life*.

MC life had made his father the man he was today—made his mother the woman she was—and he couldn't think of better role models. If stupid motherfuckers existed in the world, then oh-fucking-well, *they* precipitated Dad divorcing them from the land of the living.

"Does Lumbly really have a cousin who's a teacher but should be a doctor?"

"I don't know who Lumbly is related to, Molly," CJ barked.

Lumbly's attitude finally made sense. The motherfucker *did* have it in for CJ. Perhaps, justifiably so. Except he hadn't done a fucking thing and 'Law only protected him from a mean fuckhead.

Goddamn. CJ was in over his head on this one. He *should* tell his father. If he did, and stupid assfuck Lumbly disappeared, it might raise suspicions, especially with Molly and her fucking games.

CJ had no choice but to manage the teacher on his own.

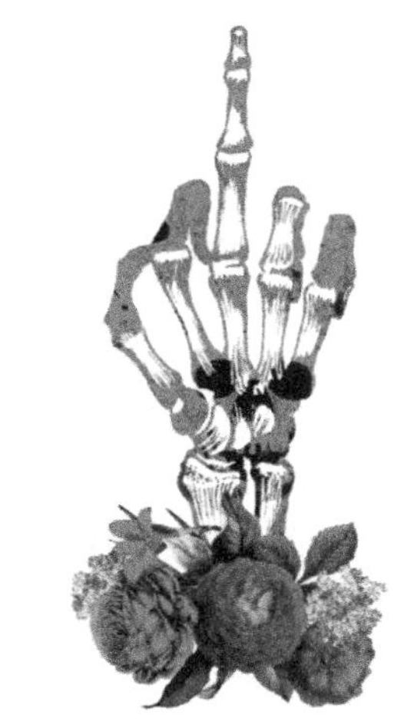

Chapter Twelve

HARLEY

Despite Harley's protests, Mr. Marksum insisted she go to the locker room, while instructing her friends to follow him. She waited a bit, hoping they wouldn't be far behind. After ten minutes, she gave up because outside practice left Harley sweaty and gross. She took a quick shower, wrapped a towel around herself and her hair, then headed to her locker, where she'd stashed her bookbag and clothes. Summer break was days away, so she'd already cleared her locker. The emptiness allowed her to haphazardly throw her school uniform in earlier. Now, she grabbed the shirt, skirt, and blazer, folding each piece neatly and stuffing the items into her bookbag. Underneath the uniform lay the outfit she intended to wear home. Once she dried herself and applied deodorant, she put on her jeans and crop top before grabbing her sneakers.

Mattie and Reb stomped in, both bruised with various little wounds and dried blood.

Harley glared at them and finished dressing. Once she detangled her hair and fashioned it into one, long braid, she put her earrings and watch on, then applied lip gloss and mascara.

"She started it," Mattie finally said, pointing at Rebel.

"Did I?" Rebel asked coldly. *Like father, like daughter*. "How about I finish it?"

Before Rebel moved, Harley inserted herself in her pathway. "What's up with you two? Don't let her push your buttons." She glanced over her shoulder, annoyed at Mattie's smirk. "And stop being so confrontational with CJ. You know Rebel would beat Jesus down to the ground for him."

"He can take care of himself, Harley. Rebel doesn't always have to jump in."

"You don't always have to screw with him," Harley countered.

"To be fair, I haven't fought Reb in days. And if it was anyone else, she would've been on my side. You both know I was right. What stupid asshole tells a stupider asshole there's *thirty-two* fucking days in February? The only reason *CJ* spoke on Molly's behalf is because he gets a hard cock around her."

Harley scowled.

"It's true," Mattie insisted. "You're not putting out, so he has to get off *somewhere*."

"And all you do *is* put out," Rebel retorted.

Once more Lolly's warning beat in Harley's head. Not listening meant she could legitimately claim she knew nothing of Mattie's activities. The burden of confessing to her parents wasn't hers to bear. Besides, she really didn't want to think about Mattie having sex. And, yet, if she *didn't* tell, she had to make sure Mattie used protection.

Harley sighed. "I hope you're at least using condoms."

"I'm not a fucking dummy!" Mattie snapped. "I only started doing it three months ago." She lowered her lashes, high color rising in her cheeks. "Mostly when I don't have money for my bud."

"Mattie..." Harley started.

"Shut up!" she ordered. "If we don't talk about it, you bare no responsibility."

"What if you turn up pregnant?" Rebel asked, her annoyance gone. "What then?"

"Don't tell on me," Mattie pleaded, ignoring the question. "Maman and Daddy would be so disappointed."

Rebel's blue eyes widened in confusion. "Who the fuck is Maman?"

"My mother."

Sniffing, Rebel folded her arms. "You're stupid."

"Because I know French? Fuck off. Maman likes it, so shut up." Mattie ran her fingers through her red hair. "If she doesn't have anything to say about it, neither do you."

"Yep," Rebel drawled, raising her hands in surrender.

"Anyway, they couldn't handle my behavior."

"Uncle Johnnie could, Mattie," Rebel said with reassurance. "He'd help Aunt Kendall to accept it."

"They need to know," Harley insisted. "*Especially* if you're paying for marijuana with sex. Your dealer is, uh..." A grown ass man. The knowledge left a sinking feeling in her belly. "Yeah, so, this isn't—"

"If I promise not to do it again," Mattie wheedled, "will you agree not to say anything?"

"I didn't tell about the meeting between Rebel and Diesel but this is different."

"It isn't." Mattie looked at Rebel. "Make her understand what sex is like."

Rebel narrowed her eyes. "I'm a virgin, dickhead. I'm saving myself for Diesel. Besides, you're having sex with a pedo—"

"Oh my god!" Mattie and Rebel's delusions placed Harley in the middle of their stupidity. She was out of patience. Mattie was headed for disaster and an authority figure needed to know. Mattie was twice as reckless as Rebel since Diesel was a good, honorable man. "Enough, both of you. We're too young to have sex. We're too young to save ourselves for anyone. Mattie, tell your parents and leave that creep alone. You're a child. You're smart, so you know messing with a grown man is dangerous and illegal. Rebel, girl, Diesel won't ever get with you. He's your adopted brother. He's known you since you were in *diapers*. What kind of snake would he be if he ended up as your lover?"

"My husband," Rebel corrected.

Harley growled. "He could be your garden gnome. The history you two have is of brother and sister."

"Not if I can help it," Rebel declared, then hugged Harley. "Diesel said something similar. Our entire family sees us as siblings. I aim to change that perception."

Harley gripped Rebel's shoulders. "Uncle Chris will castrate Diesel if he touches you."

"Well, yeah, if he did it now. And if he did, frankly, I would be disappointed in him, too. He's not a pedo." Rebel frowned. "I thought you had a higher opinion of Diesel."

"Of course, she does," Mattie said with certainty, wiggling herself underneath Harley's arms.

They repositioned themselves to make a real circle.

"Mattie's right, Rebel," Harley said. "I love Diesel. He's so kind and sweet, but he's a grown ass man."

"I know," Rebel said, her easy acceptance of Harley's words surprising and suspicious.

They leaned in for a group hug, before straightening, although their arms remained linked.

"Can I ask you something, Harley?" Mattie said.

"Sure, girl, what's up?"

"There were a lot of things you said we were too young for. What about you and CJ? It's almost like Aunt Meggie and Aunt Bailey birthed you two just so you'd be together."

"I know, right?" Rebel said with a happy giggle. "You and my brother were made for each other."

As the months progressed and CJ grew taller and more muscular, Harley awaited her own changes. Except they were happening at a snail's pace, while CJ was turning into a man before her very eyes.

"I'm sorry, Harley," Mattie said. "It must get annoying how everybody assumes you two will end up together. You might have different plans for yourself."

"No," she said quietly. "I dream of us marrying one day."

They looked amongst each other and giggled before going in for another hug. When they broke apart, Mattie put her right hand out. "Ride-or-die forever."

"Forever," Harley and Rebel chorused, adding their own hands.

At a faint series of beeps, Rebel broke from their group and headed for her locker. "Momma's outside, Mattie," she said a moment later.

After gathering her belongings, Rebel paused and glanced at Harley. "You're sure you'll be okay waiting for CJ?"

"Certain," Harley swore.

Usually when CJ had to stay longer than she did, she left with the girls. However, every now and then, she opted to wait, so today's behavior wouldn't seem out of the ordinary.

Besides, Harley was the good girl...the *boring* girl. No one would ever think her capable of scheming. While her friends...CJ...was growing up and becoming exciting. As his best bro, his dude, his pal, his—

She heaved in a breath.

He'd need someone as strong as him in a girlfriend.

"What the fuck do you want with me?"

Harley jumped at the sound of Willard's voice. "Idiot!" she snarled, her heart racing at his unexpected intrusion. "This is the girl's locker room. I told you to text me."

He looked her up and down. "And I take orders from you since *when*?"

He didn't currently, but he would, and Harley would see to that. "Meet me at one of the walkway benches."

He opened his mouth to argue.

"*Please.*"

"A bitch finally knows her place," he sneered and walked away.

Willard had threatened her, but he'd never gotten to the point where he'd hit her. Modern sensibilities were divided on whether boys had the right to hit a girl, especially if she crossed a line and punched the living hell out of him for being a stupid ass.

She groaned and squeezed the bridge of her nose. What was she doing? She had no business confronting Willard without anyone knowing and she had no business making a pact with Mattie.

"Hey, Harls, what are you doing in here?" Molly greeted, breezing into the locker room. Her cheeks were flushed, her blue-gray eyes were clear and bright, and sweat plastered her brown hair to her head. "Waiting for CJ, right? It'll be a while. The coach took him to review some stupid footage. He wasn't happy at all. He told me the film will run an entire hour."

"CJ told you that? You had to do reps, too?"

"No, silly. CJ took up for me, so I stayed on the field to help him through the exercises. One hundred sit-ups and one hundred pushups."

The delay afforded Harley time to confront Willard without CJ's interference. As to Molly helping CJ, Harley had only herself to blame. She'd been the genius who requested to partner with Willard, then hadn't gotten the chance to talk to him.

Molly lifted her t-shirt and pulled it over her head. "He's so mean and CJ is just...*dreamy*." She released a soft sigh and removed her bra, revealing high, round tits. "I can't wait until we become an item."

"A-an item?" Harley echoed, unable not to feel self-conscious as Molly unashamedly peeled the rest of her clothes away. "C-CJ wants to date you?"

Widening her legs, Molly grabbed the string that Harley had just noticed peeping out of her and yanked. She held up a bloody tampon.

Bleh, yuck, *gross*! Huffing, Harley turned her back.

"Harls, can you take this for me and throw away? I'm closer to the shower than the trash can."

"Fuck off," Harley snapped. "Do it yourself."

"You're so mean." Molly stomped passed Harley, tampon still dangling in the air. "Do you know how glad I was when I got my period? The alternative was..." She shivered delicately, then tossed the tampon in the trashcan.

"A baby?"

Giggling, Molly nodded and faced her. "Yeah...duh. I need to teach you about the birds and the bees. How are you even related to Rebel and Matilda? They know about sex. You don't even know how babies are made and you act all embarrassed when anyone mentions it." Unashamed in her nakedness, she cocked her head to the side. "How are the three of you related? Aren't you like, Black, or something?" Her eyes rounded and she slapped her forehead. “Oh my god! Of course! *Rebel. Antebellum*. You are part of her legitimate family’s secret relatives. You—”

“Stop, Molly! Just stop. Okay? We’re not really related. Well, Mattie and Reb are, but my parents are very close to theirs. We’re all one big, happy family.”

“If you say so,” she said in dismissal, then spun around. “Do you think CJ will like what he sees? He called me bae!” She squealed, then jumped up and down, her bouncing breasts reminding Harley how woefully lacking she was.

Harley was CJ’s *dude*. Whatever *she* had felt between them a few days ago, whatever she thought she’d seen in his face, hadn’t been real.

“Did you tell your mom when you started having sex?” Harley asked. “H-how old were you?”

“Why would I? About thirteen or fourteen.”

Gaze flying to Molly’s, Harley gasped. “Th-that’s so young—”

“Do you know girls used to marry at that age? I mean Snow White was like, um, like...ten or eleven and she found her prince. Juliet was...was...was...I don’t know...younger than that, I think, and she killed herself over love. Sex is no big deal, Harley.”

“Lolly used to read the fairytales to me,” Harley said, a little sad, remembering when times were so much simpler.

“Who is *Lolly*?”

“My grandmother.”

Molly’s giggles turned into peals of laughter. “Oh my god, that is the stupidest name I’ve ever heard. Sounds like you’re talking about a lollipop.”

“Her husband is *Pop* to me and my brothers. Some grandfathers are *Pops*. That’s why we call her Lolly.”

Molly's laughter abruptly stopped, and her eyes rounded. "Do you mean you really did break the word *lollipop* in half to refer to your grandparents?"

Willard stormed back into the locker room. "Harley, bitch, what the fuck do you have me waiting for?"

Harley rushed in front of Molly to cover her nudity from the jerk.

"Get out!" Harley snarled.

Neither her order nor Molly's indignant screech fazed the bozo.

"I'm talking to Molly. I'll be there."

He stopped, craning his neck to see around her. When he couldn't, he turned and left. Maybe, he had some decency after all.

"I need to get to the shower, Harls," Molly said as if the past several minutes hadn't happened. "Missing tampons can make for messy thighs, ya know?"

Nope, she sure didn't.

In silence, she gathered her things. She still had about forty-five minutes before whatever footage CJ was watching ended.

"Harls!" Molly called just as Harley reached the door.

She glanced over her shoulder. "What's up?"

"Can you talk to CJ? I tried to give him my phone number and he wouldn't take it. Even worse, he refused all my social media contact info." Molly gasped. "Does he already have a girlfriend?"

"Not as far as I know," she answered, desperately wanting that title herself.

Molly's face brightened and she placed a hand on her chest, her sag of relief overly dramatic. "Then you'll do me a solid and put a bug in his ear?"

She couldn't assist Molly in winning over CJ. "I don't have any control over who he keeps in contact with. Sorry." *Not.*

"We should totally connect on our socials. I'm *Pillar of...*" Molly thought for a moment. "*Pillar of Salt.*" She frowned. "I think."

"That's an interesting user ID."

"My mama told me only special women are salt pillars. She cited Gomorrah."

"Say what?" Harley snapped her brows together. If Molly's mother told her that... "Gomorrah was turned into salt because she looked backward when she should've kept moving forward."

"No."

"Yes!"

"No, Gomorrah received her due."

"She was *destroyed*, Molly. She was punished, not rewarded."

"No, Gomorrah was a Woman of the Bible, just like Molly."

She'd never heard of a Molly from the bible but refused to point that out.

"Momma told me I will get mine, too."

"Like Gomorrah?" Harley asked with unease. She wouldn't talk against Molly's mother, but something didn't seem right.

"It doesn't matter, Harls. Just look for my friend requests from my social. *Pillar* of *something*."

"Fine," Harley grumbled.

As she walked from the athletic center and pondered her conversation with Molly, she realized she'd forgotten to ask Rebel and Mattie what happened with Mr. Marksum. She'd hear about it later. Besides, it couldn't have been that bad if neither of them mentioned it.

A few minutes later, she reached the Quad, bookended by Williams Hall, the cafeteria for the lower and middle schools, and Lewis Hall, the cafeteria for the upperclassmen.

Upperclassman cafeteria was a loose definition, since all the younger siblings in her extended family were allowed to eat with them. Harley never considered how the other students viewed such favoritism. Perhaps, the special privileges of the Death Dweller kids was why Willard hated CJ so passionately.

Clark Hall loomed ahead. It was the administration building and the quickest route to the breezeway, but she detoured to Lewis Hall and headed to the vending machine just outside the cafeteria for a bottled water. It would have to do as a weapon.

She found Willard sitting on the bench closest to the student drop off location. Legs spread, he leaned back, one arm sprawled out. His other arm was bent with his hand fisted. Each time he shook it, she heard clanging.

As she sat next to him, he paused his fist and sidled a glance at her.

"What do you want?"

"*Test the waters, Harley. Assess your opponent.*"

Her father's voice rose in her head so clearly, it was as if he stood next to her. She sat her knapsack on the ground. Willard commenced shaking his fist, the clanking beating in her head.

"Marbles?" she asked, nodding toward his hand.

He paused his fist, stared at her, and then nodded. "Besides skeet shooting and target practice, I collect marbles and comic books."

"Bet," Harley said, torn between real curiosity and vague interest. She settled the bottle of water between her legs, wincing at the cool perspiration against her skin. "My little brother, Kaleb, loves to collect the old horror and suspense comics."

"For real?" Willard started shaking the marbles again. "That's..." His voice trailed off and he looked away, his hand moving faster.

"Can I see your marbles?" she pressed, not liking how his body tensed.

He clenched his jaw, the muscle spasming. Finally, he glanced down at her and held his hand open. From a rough estimate, he held ten or fifteen marbles.

"You have a Bennington taw!" she said, impressed.

He snapped his hand closed and yanked it away, then stood and shoved the marbles into his trouser pocket. "What do *you* fucking know about marbles?"

"Rebel collects them," she said. "She's purchased several rare and valuable ones. But *we*—me, Reb, and Mattie—play marbles. Not as much as we once did." Because nothing was the same anymore. The moment she crossed over from the single-digit age to double numbers, things changed. She just hadn't figured out if it was internal or external. "Uh, yeah, anyway, Benningtons are easy to spot because they are shaped differently. Not round-round like other marbles. As the biggest out of the bunch, I recognized it as the shooter. Your taw."

"Do you know *why* Benningtons are irregularly shaped?"

Rebel had explained the reason, but Harley didn't remember.

Willard pushed his face closer to hers, and she scooted toward the edge of the bench. Grinning, he straightened, satisfied he'd intimidated her.

"Enough with the fucking small talk, Harley. What. Do. You. Want? If I discover you've wasted my time..."

"I want you to leave CJ alone." That's why she'd requested him as a practice partner. She'd expected to be able to talk to him on the field, but the asshole set a relentless pace, and she'd had to concentrate all her energy on their drills. "You mess with him and he'll get into a lot of trouble. Before that happens, *you* back off."

His sudden laughter abruptly stopped. "Are you sucking my cock for my cooperation? Letting me fuck you in the ass?" Once more, he offered her an insulting perusal. "My dick is too good to stick in your pussy."

Harley refused to dignify that comment with a response.

Willard grabbed her throat and pulled her closer. "I didn't think so," he whispered, low.

"Let go of me," she managed, yanking the bottled water from between her thighs. "And, I'm not doing any disgusting stuff your narrow mind cooks up, Willard, but *you* are backing away from CJ. You're leaving me alone and you're leaving Ryan alone. You're not ruining CJ with your stupid games."

"If he allows me to yank his chains, who's the stupid one, Harley?" Willard demanded, his fingers still around her throat.

"Your dumb ass is," she said, not ready to use her only line of defense. "CJ will beat you to a pulp, then stomp what's left of you."

Shaking his head, he shoved her away. "I forgot how fucking stupid you people are. Mouthing off to me when I have the power of life and death in my hands."

"We both know you wouldn't severely injure me. You like living, fuckbag. I die, you do, too. Gruesomely."

"They'd have to know it was me."

"You're the only fuckface I have a problem with. They'd immediately know it was you."

"*Not*. If your old man thought I was giving you a problem, he would've taken issue with me long ago."

Her daddy wouldn't hurt a kid. "My father might not know, but my classmates do. If you hurt me, *you* won't be a problem anymore, because *you* won't be anymore. If you don't back away from CJ, I'm telling Uncle Chris." She studied her nails. "You're turning eighteen in three or four months." Yeah, and brick-for-brains was in the same grade as CJ. "An adult in the eyes of the club."

The smugness dropped from his face, and Harley smirked at him. Rage transformed his countenance, suffusing his skin red and darkening his eyes to flat black pools.

Yanking her ponytail, he stood and dragged her to her feet. She gasped. With all her might, she swung her water bottle and walloped him on the side of his head. The bottle burst open, sending water onto their hair and their clothes.

Momentarily stunned from the impact, Willard released her. She ran as fast as she could.

Halfway down the breezeway, he caught her and wrenched her backwards. Before she screamed, he clapped his other hand over her mouth, lifted her off her feet and carried her to a small cutoff between William and Clark Halls, shoving her into the brick and pressing into her.

"You want me to hurt you, yeah?" he breathed close to her ear. "You forget I have a little brother. Wally's younger than CJ and is years from turning eighteen. I can get him to snap your fucking neck after I do whatever I want to you. You're fucking trash, Harley. Beneath CJ. You and your fucking family shouldn't mingle with them." He whispered a harsh word to her. "The Dwellers don't fuck up children and they don't fuck up women. My little brother would gladly do my bidding." Still clutching her hair, he spun her around and pinned her against the wall so fast, she didn't have time to defend herself. He yanked her ponytail, snapping her head back.

Hatred burned in his gaze.

Same here, fuckhead.

His slap across her face brought tears to her eyes.

"I'll do you a favor and back off CJ. I don't want to start a war. If you promise me you'll never tell Outlaw and Mortician about today." For the briefest moments, he let his guard down and loosened his hold.

Seizing the opportunity, she shoved him with all her might. His shock gave her time to escape.

Meeting with him alone had been dicey. Yet, she took that risk, and now ran for safety with an aching cheek.

She ran as fast as she could, but his legs were longer. Just as she reached the grassy knoll separating Clark Hall and the breezeway, he tackled her and knocked the wind out of her. She blinked at the blue skies overhead. Suddenly, he loomed above her and blocked out the brightness of the day. Glaring at her, he hocked a loogie. The wad of spit landed on her cheek.

Disgust rose within her. As she swiped away the saliva with the back of her hand, Willy leaned toward her. Forgetting her spitty cheek, she headbutted him, then kicked him in the crotch and scrambled out of his reach.

He sank to the ground, moaning and cursing, blood sliding from his nose.

Somewhere along the way she'd lost her flipflop. She couldn't take the time to search for it and took off running. She had to get back to the locker room and clean herself up.

Or all hell would break loose.

Chapter Thirteen

CJ

After watching footage with Coach Yancy, CJ didn't bother showering before changing into his street clothes and heading to the breezeway in search of Harley.

He swore he wouldn't ask her why she wanted to pair with Willard. It didn't matter that he'd barely focused on the footage, thinking about Harley *asking* to be that motherfucker's partner. On rare occasions, CJ and Harley teamed with other classmates during joint practice sessions, so it was her prerogative if she didn't want to partner with him.

No matter how fucking much it galled the fuck out of him.

Tired, hungry, and annoyed, he stormed across the Quad and veered off between the administrative building and the cafeteria. The warmth of the day was cooling as the evening sunlight cast long shadows across the concrete.

The closer he got to Harley, the more his temper flared. She'd *asked* to be with Willard!

Fucking *Willard*.

Unfuckingbelievable.

When he reached the breezeway, it was empty. Harley wasn't on any of the benches, waiting for him like usual.

Jealousy roared through him, piling onto his outrage, and his pulse pounded.

Had she left with that motherfucker, too? If it was anyone else, CJ wouldn't have given a fuck. But how could she buddy up to his dead fucking enemy?

Dropping onto one of the benches, he threw his rucksack next to him and glared into the distance. Never in recent memory had a mere three or four hours ruined an otherwise ordinary day.

Lumbly's bullshit kicked off the crap and things went downhill from there. Yet nothing compared to his current misery. If he had any fucking pride, he'd get the fuck.

Except he couldn't leave her without knowing if she was okay.

Sighing, he snatched his phone from his bag and texted her.

Are you still at school?

She responded almost immediately.

Yes. Meet you at your bike.

The short response surprised him. She had no questions about his disciplinary reps and how hard the exercises were. Not one query on why he'd taken so long.

CJ's annoyance deepened. Maybe, while he was paying for Molly's stupidity, Harley cleaned up after Marksum escorted her off the field and she reconnected with Willard. Now, she didn't have time to pepper CJ with questions.

Fuck this. He wanted answers to *his* questions.

You requested Willard as your practice partner. Why?

When it became obvious she wouldn't answer, he stomped to the student parking lot. He got his under-the-seat saddlebag, removed the two open-face half helmets and shoved his rucksack in.

There was still no sign of Harley.

Gritting his teeth, he returned the saddlebag to its place under the seat, got on his pussyped and rode to the end of the breezeway. Since it was a short distance, he placed Harley's helmet on top of his own.

Five minutes later, she finally walked outside, her hair fluttering about her, her sunglasses already on, although she usually put them on after they mounted up. Equally as shocking, she wore her uniform, complete with blue blazer and long socks. After practice, she never redressed in school clothes.

"He's an asshole," she started, by way of greeting, and climbed behind him without standing and talking to him.

Too busy analyzing her voice, it took CJ a moment to remember the text he'd sent her about Willard. "Something you already knew, Harley," he snapped, "so why'd you ask to workout with him?"

"I needed to discuss something with him." She *sounded* mostly normal, but her small tremble put CJ on alert. "It's been resolved."

Something wasn't right. Immediately, CJ imagined the worst. "Did Willard hurt you?"

"Nope," Harley said cheerfully. "Why would you think that?"

"Because he's a fucking bullying asshole who always fucks with me and who threatened *you*."

"He's nothing but hot air."

Jesus Christ, girls were strange. Cool one minute and absolute terrors the next. Take Molly Harris. She'd remained out in the heat with him like another pal, then pitched a fucking fit when he wouldn't take her phone number. She'd flipped from dude-ish to girl-ish without missing a beat.

But Harley had never been that way. Maybe, pinning Harley's behavior as *girlish* came down to his changing perception of her. With each passing day, he forgot their shared love of motorcycles and sports and saw her delicate beauty and feminine mannerisms. He noticed what made her a girl and disregarded what made her his friend.

Peeping over his shoulder and seeing her hair still fluttering around her face, he cleared his throat. "Will you secure your hair in a ponytail?"

"No."

Her sunglasses blocked her pretty eyes. Her flowing hair covered the sides of her face, and her voice held an unfamiliar note.

"You need your helmet," he reminded her, grabbing it from the top of his head and handing it to her.

In silence, she placed it on and secured the strap underneath her chin.

"Are you sure you're okay, bae?"

"I'm fine, CJ," she said quietly.

Harley wasn't a liar, so he took her at her word.

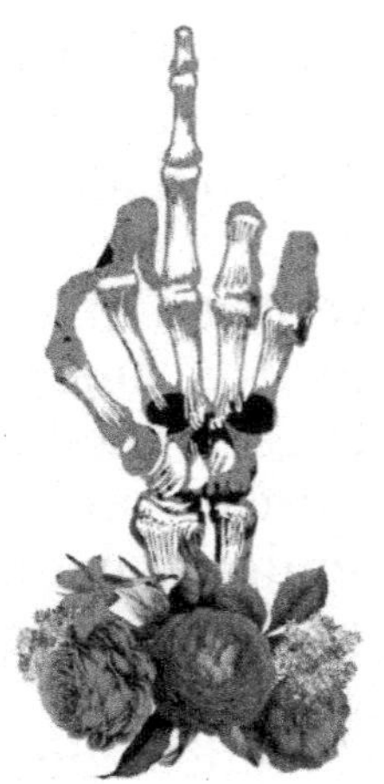

Chapter Fourteen

RORY

"What's up with Harley?" Rory asked Lou.

They were on the pedestrian deck of Turn Creek Bridge, a little used bridge near their school. Lou leaned on the rails and stared down at the river, while Rory had climbed up and sat on one of the steel beams, dangling his legs.

"She's a girl," JJ, Rory's younger brother, complained. He dug into his pocket for another rock he'd gathered as they snuck off the schoolgrounds and hurled it over the railing. "That's a stupid question, bro. You've lived with Mom and Mattie all your life, so you already have your answer."

"Aunt Kendall isn't that bad," Mark JB, Lou's cousin, said with a shake of his head.

"Dude," Ryder said with disapproval. Out of all the Caldwell boys, Ryder was the only blond. He could've passed for one of Rory's brothers, resembling Rory and

JJ more than CJ. "Every time Aunt Kendall cooks, it's attempted murder."

"Yeah," Ransom added, "and she's teaching Mattie all her deadly recipes. They should be arrested."

"Don't eat what she tries to feed you, dumb ass," JJ said. "When Dad's away on business, I make it a point to eat at Aunt Meggie or Lolly's. I can't risk it, man."

Dad hadn't gone away in a while. The club even moved the corporate office of their lab company to Hortensia because the commute cut into Dad's family time.

"What's Mom cooking today, Ran?" Ryder asked, digging into JJ's pocket and taking a rock. His pitch sent it sailing through the air.

Ransom licked his lips as his stomach growled. "Cherry chipotle short ribs and mushroom risotto rice with salad and warm cinnamon applesauce for dessert."

"Hey, Yo, I haven't visited my favorite aunt in *days*," Mark JB said. "I have to right my wrong."

"Man, shut up," Lou ordered. "We were just there three days ago for our weekly dinner."

"Yeah, but Mom cooked, Lou," JJ said woefully, shoving Ryder's hand away when he tried to steal another rock.

"It wasn't that bad," Lou insisted. "My dad tried it, so I did, too. The vegetable lasagna was good, although I didn't care for the sweet almond, grilled pineapple, and caramelized onion tart."

"My dad liked it," Mark JB said. "He farted all the way home. I was worried about Hogzilla. I thought he'd gassed her when we passed Uncle Val and Aunt Zoann's place."

"Man, fuck that pig," Ransom growled. "Whenever she's bored, she runs people and for her to be so fucking big, she's quick."

Ryder climbed next to Rory. Instead of sitting, he stood and stared at the water. They'd dove from the bridge before on really hot days.

"I told Uncle Val he needs to get Hogzilla a boyfriend. Anything to keep that bitch occupied," Ryder said.

"Aunt Zoann said Hogzilla was bacon if she ran her one more time," Lou revealed. "Dad, Kaleb, and me helped Uncle Val and Devon build a stronger pen."

Ransom's stomach growled again. "I'm starving, Ryder, so tell us why you summoned us here, so we can leave."

"Not," Rory said on a snort. "There's two hours until the end of the school day."

"Goddamn," Mark JB grouched, glaring up at Ryder.

The sun haloed him, glinting off his golden hair and swallowing his expression. "It's the end of the school year," Ryder said, jumping to the deck and forcing Ransom to back up, "and it seems like eyes are everywhere. Our only opportunity to leave was after lunch when I set off the fire alarm."

"Why—?"

"If you shut the fuck up, Ran, I'll explain," Ryder snapped. "CJ wants me to watch over Mattie. No, he wants me to monitor Wally."

Rory snapped to attention. Next year, he'd leave his little sister behind and move to the Upper Hall. Even though he couldn't wait because he missed CJ so much, he wouldn't be able to keep an eye on Mattie. Summer break started in a week and Rory intended to work extra hard and bulk up so he could join the football team.

If Dad allowed him. When Rory mentioned his plan to him a few days ago, he didn't seem pleased. Instead of encouragement, he'd told Rory he needed to focus on his future as the Dweller president. A job Rory did *not* want if it pitted him against CJ.

"Mattie seems afraid of Byrd," Mark JB said.

Ryder nodded. "I wasn't sure if I was seeing right. He doesn't force her to sit at his table, though she always does but she doesn't seem happy near him."

"What made CJ want Wally watched?" JJ asked.

"Last week, he walked her to class," Ryder said. "Whatever he saw, he didn't like. I still don't know what it was. Later that night, he told me to watch Wally and make sure Mattie didn't leave my sight when he was around."

"You've known about this an entire week and just clued us in?" Mark JB asked.

"Fuckface, I've been busy with very important business. I was playing Northgard and that Viking settlement kicked my ass. I was so fucking mad. Then, at lunch today, Wally, that overgrown motherfucker, tried to steal my chocolate chip cookie, and I remembered what CJ said."

Usually, Harley and Rebel scooped the younger siblings from the Lower Hall during lunch, but Harley was absent and Rebel was *something*.

"You never told me what's up with Harley," Rory said to Lou.

"I don't know," Lou said. "She's been moping in her room and barely opens her door for anybody."

Ransom thought for a moment. "Girls act weird when it's their periods. Maybe, that's it."

"Ew," JJ said, wrinkling his nose. "That's gross."

Rory grinned at his little brother. "It is," he agreed. "Let's spare you and talk about spilling the blood in Wally's veins and arteries. I bought a Vampire straw and want to test it on something. How many stabs until death? How much blood will it cause?"

"I volunteer Hogzilla."

Rory's senses perked, then deflated. "She's too big. I couldn't handle her on my own."

"Ransom was joking, bro," JJ said, frowning at him.

"Yeah, Ro," Ransom said. "I hate that fucking pig but she's ten and Uncle Val loves her."

"I volunteer Wally," Lou grumbled. "He's a mean fuckhead and he hates me."

"He doesn't like me either, cuz," Mark JB admitted.

"He's such a smug motherfucker," Ryder said.

"Like he knows something we don't," Ransom added.

The boys looked amongst each other. Rory studied each of his cousins, wondering if they suspected how often he'd gone into the meatshack.

Since he'd seen pieces of Cole, something inside Rory shifted. He wasn't sure what, though. Instead of a nightmare, he'd had a dream...a *fantasy*. It had been bloody and gory and he'd awakened in a cold sweat, his heart pounding. He hadn't felt fear or shame. It had been arousal and anticipation.

He'd fallen asleep with dreams of dismembering a body.

"We only have a few days to do anything about Wally," JJ said.

"Or," Ryder said, his eyes gleaming, "we can watch over Mattie for the next week and then take our time over the summer, plotting Wally's downfall."

Chapter Fifteen

“On the fucking nose!” Wallace Byrd sounded as awed as always whenever Ryan hit his target from one hundred yards out.

Which was *always*. Which, in turn, made Byrd a fucking idiot. He should’ve been accustomed to Ryan’s shooting abilities.

“My dad and my uncles are ace shots,” he said, walking to his foldable chair with a netted cupholder sewn into the arm, where his beer sat. Not caring it wasn’t yet ten in the morning, he grabbed the bottle and swigged. “I couldn’t help but have mad skills, bro.”

Pounding his chest, he belched, then drank again.

“You’re so lucky, dude,” Byrd commented. “I want to shoot like that.”

His shooting skills was one of the few good things of being a Dweller son. They had mad aim because of the club’s dedication to target practice.

"Don't give up, kid," Ryan said smugly. "You'll get there one day."

Wallace gave him a sly look. "Maybe, I'll use Mattie for target practice."

"What?" Ryan said, almost strangling on beer. It took him a moment to recover from his coughing fit. When he did, he stared at Wallace. "Leave Mattie alone," he ordered. Other than being spoiled as fuck and placing herself above everyone, he didn't have a problem with her. She never singled him out. Her bad behavior targeted everyone. "And definitely don't use her to fucking practice shooting guns. She could be seriously hurt. Or killed."

"Fuck her," Wallace spat, sounding more like Willard than the awkward asshole with hero worship. "She thinks her fucking money can buy anything. She needs to know her fucking place and I remind her, every chance I get."

Ryan drained his bottle of beer, wishing for another one. But when he'd left the ramshackle house and headed to the backfield of the property owned by Willard's adopted parents, Ryan had been slightly thirsty not overly anxious. "What the fuck does that mean?"

Upon hearing Wallace's explanation, Ryan plopped onto the chair, horror washing through him.

"CJ pretended he knew what the fuck was going on and stood next to me," he added, detailing the day CJ walked Mattie to class.

"Wally, dude, don't underestimate that cocky motherfucker. Uncle Chris is teaching him..." Ryan wasn't sure what, but it was fucking scary. Somehow, his uncle knew *everything* and CJ was learning that skill, too.

"Fuck him, Ry," Wallace said. "He's a kid like us. He don't know shit. And, even if he did know something, he can't prove it and he can't watch her all fucking day. He's in the upper school. What can he do?"

Tell Uncle Christopher. Or, worse, tell Uncle Johnnie. *Or* summon his army of brothers and have them fuck up Wallace. Not Rule. He'd write a poem or a prayer before he raised his fists. But Ryder and Ransom were fucking monsters and Axel was quickly learning.

"Hey, cuck," Ryan's real best bud, Willard, called, walking to where they stood in the back field of the Byrd property. Perfect place for a shooting range without prying eyes.

Perfect spot to unwind during the first weekend of school break.

"Go away, douche." Wallace's voice was so high-pitched he sounded like a girl. "I don't want you here. Ryan came to see me."

Willard extended the invitation to Ryan; Wallace hadn't.

Ryan liked thirteen-year-old Wallace much more than he did his own dickhead brother, but Wallace was still a baby and too strait-laced. His most daring accomplishment was target shooting.

"Hey, Wally, I left my cellphone on your dining room table," Ryan said. "Get it for me. I've probably missed a few calls from my bitches." More like his mom. *Possibly* Molly Harris, Rebel and Mattie, but *never* Harley.

Wallace's eyes lit up. "How many bitches do you have, Ryan?"

"Almost too many to keep track of, kid," he lied. "I'm always running out of condoms."

The increasing awe on Wallace's face tickled Ryan. In mere seconds, the boy elevated him to a legend. If only he hoodwinked Devon so easily.

"I'll be back," Wallace promised, darting away.

"Made your decision?" Willard asked the moment they were alone.

Ryan pointed to his close-cropped hair. "Doesn't this tell you anything?"

"It's more than a haircut, cuck." Willard's beady eyes hardened. "It's beliefs and ideology."

"Don't call me a fucking cuck, cuck," Ryan fired, keeping humor in his voice to hide his annoyance at both Byrd brothers.

"You've got to stop hanging with that melanin-loving beta boy. It's bad enough he cares what a femoid thinks, but CJ is turning his back on his own womankind. At least, Christopher stuck to the script, even if his bitch is a stupid cunt."

Together, Ryan and Willard could bury CJ, Val, and Devon, but Uncle Chris...yeah, that was one battle he didn't want. Especially over Aunt Meggie.

A month ago, Ryan saw the aftermath of those who broke that rule at the Scorched Devils' clubhouse.

At first, Ryan had been so fucking bored, then Uncle Christopher started talking about Aunt Meggie and Ryan kinda, sorta, found himself interested.

And *then...then...*the naked bitches had paraded in.

While Rory and Ryan had swiveled their heads in every direction possible and reveled at any attention the women offered them, their fathers treated the chicks as an afterthought. Even CJ, who monopolized Harley, had been down for some fun.

Later, when Ryan's father had disappeared through the door with Mortician and Digger, Ryan was happy to stay inside with all the free pussy. He wasn't a virgin, but he'd never fucked a grown woman before.

"Don't be left out," Derby had said, nodding toward the door his father went through.

Remembering how CJ not only froze when he'd had the gun, but hightailed his fucking ass out as soon as he could, Ryan accepted Derby's challenge.

Then, immediately wished he hadn't when he'd walked outside. Ryan had never seen a dead man before, especially one subjected to several headshots with hollows. Even now, his stomach turned. He cleared his throat.

"Listen, man. Leave Uncle Chris and Aunt Meggie out of our war. You don't want to stir up that powder keg."

Willard shoved Ryan. "Don't ever fucking gainsay me."

Most of the time, Ryan agreed with Willard. What he didn't agree with, he fucking ignored. However, he wouldn't tolerate the level of disrespect Willard handed out.

Ryan pushed the big motherfucker away. "Don't put your fucking hands on me. *Ever.*"

"I'm the big man in charge, Ryan. You risk your life when you forget and lose the privilege of hanging out with me and my close associates."

"Fuck you," Ryan retorted, unimpressed. "I don't need your fucking company. You sought *me* out. I couldn't give less of a shit about being in your fucking inner circle. I got one of my own." Which wasn't a lie. He had his cousins. His brother.

Something was missing, though. Everyone expected his life to go a certain way without any input from him. His father didn't see a fucking thing wrong with expecting Ryan to serve CJ—the Chosen One.

Right of birth shouldn't guarantee the presidency. He should have as much of a chance at being Prez as CJ.

Ryan tried to work through his anger and jealousy and keep to himself as much as possible. When Willard began sitting at Ryan's table during lunch, CJ advised Ryan to steer clear. The bossy motherfucker pushed Ryan closer to Willard. Ryan enjoyed his and Willard's deep conversations.

Ryan began questioning why he'd been born into such an unfair world. A family of social justice warriors who didn't care that people like Mortician and Digger seemed...they just seemed more respected than Uncle Johnnie, and it wasn't even their club.

"Ryan!" Wally yelled, racing across the field. When he reached them, he stopped so fast, he almost lost his balance. He yanked Ryan's cellphone from his back pocket and held it out.

"Thanks, kid." Ryan snatched the device and clenched his jaw when he read his mother's text about his 16th birthday next weekend. Most of the celebrations would be held at Uncle Chris's The Taylor lot was amongst the smallest. Of course, CJ had to have grown up with half the fucking forest belonging to his family. Perhaps, that's why his mom and dad always celebrated Ryan's birthday at Uncle Chris's place.

Mentally flipping his mom off, he threw the phone to the ground, then nodded to Wally, a little puppy always begging for Ryan's attention. Except, hearing what he did to Mattie, Wally had a vicious layer underneath the awkwardness he displayed.

"You got skills like your old man, huh, Ryan?"

Willard's random question caught Ryan off-guard.

"It depends on what skills you're talking about," Ryan said, irritated his parents thought a stupid log cabin a good place to raise children.

"Technical skills," Willard clarified.

"I was weaned on that shit. Dad thinks that makes him so fucking smart. Any loser could run wires."

"You call him *dad*," Willard snorted. "You must be a fucking loser too, cuck."

"I call him *dad* because that's who he is."

"You sure about that?" Willard demanded with grating laughter. "When I hung out at your place, the femoid that pushed you out her hole bossed that idiot around like *she* had the right. She did the same to you and your little weakling brother."

The memory of his mother bitching out the men in her house humiliated Ryan. He couldn't even remember why she'd been so upset.

"Dad's bitch knows better than to raise her voice to me, Wally, and especially my father," Willard bragged. "It keeps order in the world. Women are meant to cook, fuck, clean, and shut the fuck up until they have permission to speak."

Ryan nodded, mortified at his mother's behavior. She was such a vulgar cunt.

"I have a little project for you, involving spy cams and beta boy's bitch."

"Harley?" Ryan asked in surprise, forgetting his shame.

"We have to weaken CJ before we take him out," Willard explained.

Maybe, Ryan was on the fence about his father, but he loathed CJ.

"What better way to weaken fuckface than to fuck with her?"

Challenging CJ was fine. Using Harley to do it...

He'd never admit to Willy how pretty he found Harley. Or how much Uncle Mort frightened him.

"I knew you were nothing but a fucking cuck!" Willard nodded to his little brother. "This twatface has more balls than you."

"Your mama's a twatface," Wally yelled.

Willard guffawed. "She's your mama, too, stupid, so shut it. I'll deal with you later." He glared at Ryan. "Get the fuck out of my face. You're a beta boy just like that fucking CJ."

"I am not!"

Ignoring Ryan's snarl, Willard glanced at his watch. "We have a long drive ahead of us, so let's grab a bite, then get on the road."

Envy ran through Ryan. Willard had freedom, a real man for a father, *and* his own wheels.

Hours later, Ryan followed Willard into a wood and metal building dropped in the middle of a fucking desert, west of Salt Lake City and surrounded by high fences. At the gate, Willy spoke low, so Ryan couldn't hear what he said for the man to let them in.

Inside, small American flags painted on the walls shared space with scorpions. Although they were painted too, they looked realistic enough to make Ryan lean away. The bar was long with lacquered wood and stools. On the opposite side stood a small stage. The pole in the middle gave it away as a place for strippers.

"What do you think?" Willy asked.

Signs pointed in the direction of bathrooms and the staircase. Seeing the cuts on the men sitting around the bar clued Ryan in that this was a clubhouse.

"Are you fucking crazy?" he demanded on a whisper. "You'll get us killed." Especially *him*. As the son, nephew, and cousin of Death Dweller officers, he didn't know if these bikers were friend or foe of the club. He didn't even know whose MC they stood in. "I'm leaving, Willy."

Before Ryan moved, Willy placed a hand on his shoulder. "Stop being a fucking pussy. You can't call your folks. I don't think they'd be so happy—"

Ryan shoved Willy's hand away. "Fuck off. Mom and Dad would be angry—" They'd beat his ass— "But after they disciplined me, they'd let it go. And I don't care how fucking much I've lied to them, if I need them, all I do is call and they come."

"Fucking baby," Willy taunted.

"Goo goo gaga, then, bitch," Ryan snapped, yanking out his cellphone to call his father and storming toward the door. "I'm out."

"If you leave, I'll be very fucking unhappy, cuck."

Ryan faced Willard, aware he had the attention of the entire club. "Fuck you. I'm not interested in making *you* happy, motherfucker."

Some of the bikers snickered and Willard's face flushed.

"You'd prefer to have me as an enemy rather than a friend?"

Fed up, Ryan glared at Willard from head to heel. "I have better enemies than your bitch ass."

He started off again, waiting for one of the bikers to shoot him or Willard to tackle him and break his neck. The overgrown fuckhead liked obeyance and deference, so his catching up to Ryan and placing a gentle hand on his shoulder before he stepped into the cold desert air surprised him.

Turning, he knocked Willard's hand away.

"My daddy don't respect weak men."

"How the fuck does that relate to me, Willard?"

Pig Face rocked on his heels. "Not you. Your old man. Logan Donovan was your great-grandfather, Ryan. I've heard so many stories about him."

So he kept saying. What Ryan knew of the man he'd heard from Willard. In his house, Logan Donovan was taboo.

"Do you really think he'd respect Val?" Willy pressed. "Your mama needs her ass beat and your old man don't have the balls to do it. Not like my dad or my grandfather."

"I've never met the man who raised you and just heard about your grandfather, so I still don't give a fuck."

"Your folks are a lost cause. You aren't, Ry. You're ten times the man Val, Christopher, and Johnnie could be. They allow those freaks to stay in the club. Cash and Stretch are a disgrace. And don't get me started on that half-breed's father and uncle. If Val loved you, he wouldn't force shit like that on you. He'd protect you. Didn't Val say you'd never be Prez?"

He hadn't said those *exact* words. "What's your fucking point, Byrd?" Ryan growled.

"What's all the racket?" a voice demanded, walking from the direction of where the stairs were supposedly located. Upon seeing Willy, he halted. "What are you doing here?"

"I wanted you to meet my friend," Willy answered with none of the assholery he usually displayed. "Ryan Taylor."

The man snapped his green regard toward Ryan. Something about the biker resembled Uncle Chris, although this man had a bald head and sported a beard. What the facial hair didn't cover revealed scarred and pockmarked skin.

"You're Val's son?"

Suddenly, he was so fucking sorry he'd come to Utah with Willard, lying to his parents because they never would've given him permission for the excursion.

"Are you?" the man demanded.

Ryan shoved his hands in the pockets of his jeans. "Yeah. So?"

The biker studied him, then smiled and held out his hand. "I'm Bash."

Standing taller, Ryan accepted Bash's hand and gave it a firm shake.

Bash nodded toward a table near the jukebox, then beckoned someone at the bar. When he took a seat, Ryan and Willy followed suit. Soon, a tin bucket filled with ice and six beers arrived at their table. Bash handed each of them a bottle, then opened his own.

"Have you ever heard of the American Scorpions?" he asked after they drank in silence for a few minutes.

Ryan shook his head. "Was I supposed to?"

Bash shrugged. "Depends on who you ask."

"My grandfather was a Scorpion," Willy said with pride. "Everybody says I look just like him."

"A pig?" Ryan asked because that's exactly what the fuck Byrd resembled with his black hair and beady eyes.

Willy jumped to his feet, but Bash snickered and said, "Sit the fuck down, boy."

"I'll not forget that insult, Taylor," Willy sneered, back to being a fucking asshole.

"You are and you have," Bash declared in a hard voice. "And your fucking fat grandpa deserted us for..." Voice trailing, he offered Ryan a scowl.

"The Dwellers?" Ryan guessed.

"Did I say that?" Bash asked.

"You didn't have to," Ryan said flatly. "Your look said everything."

Finishing off his first beer and opening a second, Bash turned his attention back to Ryan. "Don't put words in my mouth. That's never a good idea."

What an ominous threat. The deadliest warnings came through unspoken words.

"The American Scorpions fell on bad times," Bash started. "A few years back, we were falsely implicated in a bombing. It almost destroyed our club. But we're back. Stronger than ever."

"What does that have to do with me?"

Bash grinned. "Willy speaks highly of you. He's here often. He wants to patch in when he's older. I wanted to offer you the opportunity to see what we're about."

"Uh...yeah...*No!*" Ryan might despise CJ and dislike his lot in life, but he wasn't a fucking traitor.

"With the Scorpions, you'll have a real chance at rising in the ranks," Bash swore as if it would sway Ryan. "CJ Caldwell is being primed to take Outlaw's place. That's not how *we* operate. And what about those other people?"

"I don't know because I have no clue who the fuck you're talking about."

Bash polished off half the bottle then leaned forward. "Mortician, Digger, that Roxanne bitch, that half breed, Bailey, and her get."

"Harley?" Panic bloomed inside of Ryan. Bash's harsh tone made him uncomfortable. Uncle Mort, Uncle Digger, Lolly, Aunt Bailey, and Harley were his family.

"I owe that cunt," Willy snarled, massaging the side of his face where Harley had scratched him.

The stupid motherfucker deserved what he'd gotten. He'd allowed a *girl* to best him and complained for days. Fuckhead better hope Uncle Mort never found out.

"When I get my hands on her, I'm breaking that bitch in half," Willy blurted.

"You like to fuck with CJ, but I didn't know how badly you wanted to die, bro. Uncle Mort would tear you to pieces. If not him, then Uncle Chris would."

"That's the point," Bash said, recapturing Ryan's attention. "They wouldn't. We have them outmanned and outgunned."

Glancing around the clubhouse, and finding it all but empty, Ryan smirked. "You think?"

"All the members aren't here, stupid," Willy bit out. "They are setting in motion some very important plans."

Before Bash's appearance, he'd been ready to beat Willy to the ground. Now, he couldn't go off half-cocked. He wanted to survive to see another day. "What do you want from me?"

"Nothing but your loyalty."

"And your friendship," Willy added.

"How'd you get into my school if you're affiliated with a Dweller enemy?" He'd sworn he'd overheard his dad and uncles discussing the money they put into the school. Unfortunately, he wasn't sure. Usually, he was so resentful of CJ and Devon, he paid attention to nothing else. "And who the fuck is your father and grandfather?" He glanced at Bash and lifted a brow in question.

"Not I," Bash murmured with another grin, but the *Little Red Hen* reference didn't land. He had a cruel mouth and hard eyes that flattened the green and stole all kindness from his face.

"My granddaddy was Rack," Willy said with pride.

"Still means nothing to me," Ryan admitted.

"Do you know who Rack was?"

"Other than a dead motherfucker with a photo in the Free Bird gallery?" Ryan scoffed, glaring at his friend. "I sure the fuck don't."

Willard's face burned red, but Bash patted his arm and the motherfucker stood down.

"Rack's real name was Wallace Bart, though few people know it or remember it," Bash explained. "Whether or not Outlaw is aware Willy and his little brother are Rack's grandsons is up for debate. But Big Willy, Rack's son, is a Noxious Gnome."

The parents didn't discuss much club business in front of him. Or any of the other kids, so he wasn't sure where the puzzle pieces for Rack, Big Willy, or the Gnomes fit.

"You boys are a bunch of pussies," Bash said in disgust. "They're raising you to be soft twats. You know nothing of Dweller history." He ticked off his grievances on his thick fingers. "You aren't familiar with other MCs. You don't have street cred. Or common sense."

"Wait." Ryan frowned. "Willy isn't an orphan?"

"I'm not even a Byrd. I'm a *Bart*," Willy boasted.

"But—" Hadn't Ryan overheard his parents' discussing background checks for the Byrd brothers? At the time the club targeting kids annoyed the fuck out of him. He'd dismissed it as bullshit to protect Prince CJ.

"Look at the little fucker's blank look, Willy," Bash said, whooping with laughter. "He's as stupid as his old man, destined to be the same type of ass licker."

"You don't know what you're talking about," Ryan spat. He'd *never* brown nose any motherfucker the way Val did Outlaw. He glared between Bash and Willy, feeling as betrayed by his friend as he did when his father exalted CJ and minimized Ryan. "Your folks are alive and you forged your documents to get into Ridge Moore?"

Willy's wide grin revealed the answer. "My brother and me got as much right to attend that fucking school as CJ and the rest of Outlaw's cum squirts."

Ryan wouldn't refute that truth. Fuck, if he wasn't related to those assholes, he might've been in Willy's position, too. However, it placed him in a fucked up predicament. "Why are you telling me this bullshit?"

"My family name isn't bullshit," Willy said stiffly. "Once upon a time, hearing *Bart* meant something. It got results."

"Once upon a time? Fairytales are for toddlers, librarians, and teachers, bitch. If Bart meant something, your grandpa would've kept using it."

"Shut your fucking mouth," Willy yelled.

"Fuck off, asshole. If you hear the name Outlaw, you know who it is. If you hear the name *Christopher Caldwell*, you still fucking know that's Outlaw, so suck my fucking dick. If my uncle finds out I'm fucking with motherfuckers who forged shit, I'm fucked and so are you."

"The Gnomes and the Dwellers have a truce," Willy said on a swallow, while Bash drank, eyeing the two of them in silence.

"And that matters how?" Ryan asked. "A truce means nothing if your old man thought it was a good fucking idea to hide your identity."

"Do you even know about Rack?"

"He's a Free Bird, Willy. I told you his photo is on the memorial wall in the clubhouse."

Free Bird? *Free...Byrd.*

Fuck.

"Do you know how my grandfather died?"

"*Should* I know how his ass croaked?"

Willy narrowed his eyes.

"Tell me what you know about Logan Donovan, Ryan."

"Nothing, Bash," Ryan answered. "He's persona non grata with everyone from my parents to the hangers-on."

"That isn't fair. He was a great man and it's only right that you know of him." Bash signaled the bartender and more beer was brought. "Have you heard of Boss?"

"Big Joe? That's Aunt Meggie's old man. Who hasn't heard of him?"

"What if I told you Boss betrayed your great-grandfather?"

"Boss betrayed everybody," Ryan retorted. "Dude was a fucking drughead."

"Before he became an addict, he was a fucking thief. He fucked over Rack, Logan, and Cee Cee, my father. By extension, *you*."

"He was killed before I was born."

"I have a job for you," Bash said after a moment. "They have to do with Harley and Kendall."

The motherfucker knew a lot about the Dwellers. *However...* "That sounds like two fucking jobs to me,

Bash," Ryan said. "One's a Donovan and the other's a Banks. Separate households."

"I may want you to do something simple like plant a bomb in a vehicle they're both in."

"Fuck no," Ryan said. "I'm not killing Aunt Kendall *or* Harley. No girls. I'll shove a fucking bomb up CJ's cockhole free of charge. I'm not touching a chick."

"You don't have to touch either one of those cunts," Bash snapped. "I was giving you an example. With Harley, just make sure her firewall is down so Willy won't have a problem getting to her on her socials."

Fucking with Harley meant crossing Uncle Mort. He was the last person Ryan wanted to tangle with. Uncle Mort would snap him in two.

"I don't know," he hedged.

"I mentioned it earlier, Ryan," Willy said. "If you want to bring CJ down as badly as you claim, we have to use that half-breed."

Other than liking CJ, Harley hadn't ever mistreated Ryan. "As long as she isn't hurt—"

"We won't hurt her physically," Bash swore.

"If she's hurt and upset, CJ is distracted," Willy said. "Using her is the only way to weaken that incel."

If CJ was celibate, Rory doubted it was involuntary. That motherfucker always had choices. If he wasn't currently fucking or if he was still a virgin, it was because Prince CJ wanted it that way.

Fucking asshole.

"Fine," Ryan bit out. "Fuck Harley. I'm in. I'll do it with Kendall, too." Or he'd try. Mattie would catch suspicious activity quicker than anyone, including Val and Stretch. "Just give me a head's up before you make your move."

"I already have help with Kendall," Bash admitted.

"To do what? You said you wouldn't hurt them."

"I said not physically. Remember?"

Aunt Ken...er...*Kendall* wasn't working with a full deck. The chick loved Shakespeare, Opera, and drinkable sludge. Definitely cray.

"Is she still obsessed with Meggie?" Bash asked. "Does she still want to fuck Outlaw? No, does Johnnie still want pussy from that little blonde slut?"

"Blonde...who the hell are you referring to?"

"Meggie, boy," Bash snapped.

"*Aunt* Meggie? Megan Caldwell, married to my momma's brother?"

"Answer my fucking questions, Ryan. I'm losing my patience."

"I don't know what you mean, jackass. Aunt Kendall and Aunt Meggie are good friends and love their husbands."

"Maybe, but they didn't have the best start, so their happiness will be easy to undermine."

"Uncle Christopher will kill you if you fuck with Aunt Meggie. How many fucking times do I have to repeat that?"

"I'm not concerned with Outlaw and his cunt for the time being. Destabilize Johnnie's bitch and their house of cards start to crumble. Then, I'll move in for Joe's daughter."

Finishing his beer, Bash sulked in silence. Ryan hoped he kept his mouth shut. He had nothing to do with the machinations of Big Joe or any of the other motherfuckers mentioned. Neither did Aunt Meggie, Aunt Kendall, or Harley. He needed to end his association with the Byrds...the Barts and whatever he was involved in. It would be the wisest course.

Except...he couldn't. He hated CJ and he disliked his father more than he cared about what happened to Megan, Kendall, and Harley. If any of them had to choose between CJ and Ryan, he would lose to that smug motherfucker.

"My father's dead," Bash said bitterly. "Five of my brothers are dead."

"How many brothers do you have?" It sounded like there were still a few alive.

"Ten. Fifteen. Twenty. Who knows? What I *do* know is how five were killed."

Someone close to Ryan had never died, so he couldn't identify with Bash's anger and grief. However, he had enough manners to say, "I'm sorry."

"It's all their fault, Ryan. Outlaw. Johnnie. Those filthy dogs, Mortician and Digger. Those abominations, Cash and Stretch. That dickless wonder, Val."

Bash's hostility wore on Ryan. "I get you're enemies of the Dwellers and don't like certain people, but they're all my family."

"No, son." Bash reached for his third beer. "We aren't enemies of the Death Dwellers. We just don't agree with who they allow in and their unfair elections. Don't *you* think it's unfair? Wouldn't you like to have a real chance of being elected president one day?"

Ryan drew in a deep breath and glanced away.

"Will you live your life in the manner your old man has mapped out? If he was happy as Road Captain for all these years, fine for him. But it isn't fair for you to grow up, knowing you were born to be nothing but support for Outlaw's kid."

"You're right," Ryan admitted quietly. "I think about that shit a lot."

"What if I told you Big Joe left a will bequeathing the clubhouse and those vast grounds to your Aunt Meggie and there are bylaws that would give CJ control of the club for the rest of his fucking life?"

"What...? No! That's impossible. Besides, the man has been dead for...*no*!" Ryan stood. "I'm not listening to this nonsense."

"Son," Bash said, standing and rushing to block Ryan's exit. "I've recently come across documents that says otherwise. I wouldn't bullshit you on this. Do you think it's fair that we're not worth the smallest consideration? My old man, your great-grandfather, and Willy's grandfather, sacrificed their fucking lives for the Dwellers and CJ will get it all."

"No." Ryan shook his head in denial. After enduring CJ as the golden child all their fucking lives, no fucking way life sucked so much. He'd grown up in the biggest house with a notorious father and grandfather and a mother that loved being a *mom* as much as she loved to dabble in fucking stocks. That motherfucker couldn't even have fucking acne!

Tears rushed to his eyes and he rested his head on Bash's chest.

"Fuck them all!" Ryan said, sobbing at the unfairness. "I'll help however you want."

"Just keep watch on Johnnie and Kendall's behavior. I'll take care of the rest for you," Bash swore.

"Okay," Ryan sniffled.

Bash hugged him. "C'mon, buddy. Willard borrowed a few of my books to lend to you. Let's talk in my office. Give me a chance to open your eyes to how things *should* be amongst us and answer any questions. Then, maybe, I'll call some bitches in to give us a few lap dances."

Chapter Sixteen

CJ

School break had finally arrived. CJ would've been happy for the summer recess and spending as much time with Harley, his siblings, and his cousins as possible. *Except*...motherfucking Lumbly had failed CJ. He'd expected it, but when it actually happened it broke him up.

That one bad grade threatened everything. As a junior on the football field, scouts would *really* notice him and take his skills into serious consideration.

Somehow, all hadn't been lost. After receiving the potentially life-changing news, Coach Yancy demanded CJ meet him in Mr. Marksum's office. Instead of going home, confessing his suspensions and failure to his parents, he'd gotten an ultimatum. Enroll in summer school to make up the credits or cut his losses with the team and not play in the fall.

Although his mother had been upset and his father suspect, CJ reassured them Shakespeare bested him. No, he'd straight-up fucking lied and said the Bard was boring and hard to understand when everyone knew Aunt Kendall read Shakespeare to the kids so much, they recited that motherfucker in their sleep.

What else could he say? *Lumbly's a fuckhead who wants revenge for a meaner fuckhead?*

For whatever reason, his mother and father accepted his explanation.

The whole situation disgusted the fuck out of CJ. He burned for vengeance. That little motherfucker didn't have the balls to confront 'Law. No, he was taking out his anger on a student.

Unfortunately, the private school was small and elite, with a select student body, small acceptance rate and highly qualified teachers. It was a good fucking chance he'd end up with Lumbly again next semester.

Jesus. How could he survive that fuckbag again?

"Hey, kid, you've been waiting long?" Uncle Mort asked, sliding into the seat on the other side of the booth CJ had chosen.

"I don't think so." He'd been so lost in his thoughts he'd just walked in the place, nodded to Symphony, his favorite waitress, and found a seat in her area.

"Hey, Mort," Symphony greeted, then grinned at CJ with all types of suggestions. "Hey, boo."

She'd started working there almost a year ago. She couldn't have been any older than twenty. Twenty and fucking gorgeous, with long dreads, dark chocolate skin, the best tits *ever*, and legs for days. Every time she was near him, his cock jumped.

"And what can I get for you, sweetie?" she cooed, turning her attention to CJ.

Uncle Mort must've already ordered while CJ salivated over Symphony.

"Uh..." CJ hadn't even looked at the menu.

"Bring him what I'm having, Symphony," Uncle Mort said with a smile.

The moment she walked away, he glared at CJ.

"You've been doing that a lot lately," CJ remarked. "You're not one for all those scowls and growls, Uncle Mort."

Instead of lightening the mood, it dampened it a little more.

"You get a hard cock for my baby girl?" he demanded without warning.

Jesus Christ, what a fucking question.

CJ wanted to answer—lie—but he couldn't. When Uncle Mort told him to meet him at the diner and then Harley mentioned that 'Law wanted to talk to her at the same time on the same day, CJ knew it was Uncle Digger's recommended sex talk.

"Fuck, man," Uncle Mort grumbled at CJ's silence. "She not ready for no relationship with you. And she sure as fuck not ready for...fuck..." He rubbed his eyes. "I can't even say it, talking about Harley."

"Uncle Mort, I would never pressure Harley to do something she wasn't ready for."

He wasn't appeased.

"I'm sorry," CJ blurted, not knowing the right words to say. "I haven't seen Harley in days. I've talked to her." And he'd asked her if Willard Bart had had something to do with her sudden absence. Because that's what CJ felt, and his father always told him to follow his gut. 'Law said that could be the difference between life and death.

"All I'm telling you is she not fucking ready for girl and boy stuff. *Man and woman.* You two not Adam and Eve fucking around with Satan and biting forbidden fucking fruit. Don't try to convince her otherwise. She been sulking in her fucking room for days. She wasn't even feeling well enough for school. Bailey thought it was a good idea to let her stay home, especially because it was the end of the year. Harley summer break started almost two weeks ago."

CJ frowned, suddenly on the alert. "Harley...what do you mean she's been sulking in her room?" She'd barely spoken to him since that day after school when he'd confronted her.

"Just what the fuck I said," Uncle Mort snapped. "Me and her momma thought something happened at school. Roxanne said she hadn't heard of any arguments between Harley, Rebel, and Mattie. Her grades fine and she passed all her classes. That left only *you*, CJ."

At the hostility in Uncle Mort's voice and on his face, CJ raised his hands in supplication. "I'm trying to figure out what's wrong with her, too."

"After some digging," he went on as if CJ hadn't spoken, "Rebel called Bailey and told her about a little chick named Molly Harris. According to Rebel, Molly been after Harley to convince you to take her phone number because she want you."

"How the fuck does she think bringing her bullshit to *Harley* will change my mind?" CJ snarled, so frustrated at this information, he could've gnawed glass. "What the fuck is wrong with that girl?"

"Did you give her any encouragement?" Uncle Mort demanded. "Show an inkling of interest in her?"

Yes and yes.

"Molly is a very pretty girl, but she doesn't have the fucking sense of a rock. I don't know why they even allowed her on the cheer team. She gives cheerleaders everywhere a bad fucking name. It's girls like her that make people believe it isn't a real fucking sport, when it is. Harley puts a lot of goddamn work into being on that team and in her classes. *Molly* is a fucking stereotypical cheerleader, almost a caricature, Uncle Mort. The only thing she has is that body—her tits are amazing—and that beautiful face."

Uncle Mort snorted, his features darkening by the minute at CJ's rant.

Quite the accomplishment, considering how angry he already looked.

Running off at the fucking mouth showed CJ's guilt. It didn't help his case, especially since he hadn't spoken answers to Uncle Mort's questions.

"In other words, you noticed her."

No inquiry. Just a cold, hard fact.

CJ's righteous indignation fled. If he wanted Harley as his girlfriend, he wasn't supposed to notice any other chicks. Nothing about Molly should've mattered. He shouldn't have observed Symphony bouncing around the diner. As best friends, he would've expected Harley to talk to him about Molly. At this point, though, he wasn't sure where their friendship stood. Something wasn't right and hadn't been since she'd partnered with Byrd. Imagining Harley giggling with that motherfucker and sharing secrets with him kept CJ awake. He saw no other reason why she'd so suddenly backed away from him, so it made sense she kept the conversation to herself.

There had to be more to this scenario than what met the eye. Maybe, Byrd *had* injured her in some way. But Harley didn't lie and she didn't suffer fools. If Willard had put his hands on her, she would've told CJ or Uncle Mort or Lolly. Together, the three of them could've jumped Willard and fucked him up completely.

But fucking up wasn't required. Harley *chose* to pursue a friendship with Byrd and knowing that cut deeply. Yet, he missed her so much. Their lack of communication these past weeks was as much his fault as hers. His hurt pride and simmering anger wouldn't allow him to contact her. He'd wanted to see how long *she'd* wait. After the first day, he'd sworn she wouldn't go past the second. It shocked the fuck out of him when she had. Fury made him dig his heels in.

CJ didn't understand how he still wanted Harley so much, in spite of her betrayal with Willard, while noticing other girls, too.

"Noticing them different from wanting them, CJ," Uncle Mort said when CJ opened his big fucking mouth yet again and asked the question.

He heaved in a breath. "I'm sorry, Uncle Mort. I'd never do anything to hurt Harley."

Resting his elbows on the table, he scrubbed a hand across his face. "This not easy, CJ. I remember your little ass when you was a newborn and the first kid to live at the clubhouse. I never thought I'd be a father, and I damn sure didn't think I'd help create a beautiful little girl that stole my heart the moment I saw her. You were just as smitten. Almost from the moment me and Bailey brought her home. We thought it was cute. We even joked you two would end up married."

"What's changed?"

"You. Me. *Her*." Uncle Mort glanced away.

In the silence between them, CJ's attention strayed to Symphony.

"It's no longer fucking cute watching you two whisper to each other and giggle and *cuddle*. Teenage hormones and shit." he grumbled.

"But—"

Uncle Mort held up his hand. "No buts, CJ. Your cock lasering in on Symphony. A dick on a puppy like you a brutal motherfucker. It got no conscience. No fucking aim. It just home in on whatever pussy willing to open for him."

Guilt rushed through CJ and he studied the table. "I won't ever look at another girl when me and Harley get together. I swear."

Uncle Mort's hand landed on CJ's shoulder and he looked up. They were both leaning forward and just missed bumping their heads together.

"That's it right there, CJ. You got fucking eyes. As long as you breathing, if a fine chick cross your path, you looking."

"Dad doesn't. You don't."

He smiled. "We do. We fucking men. Nothing wrong with appreciating a beautiful woman. The issue whether you know your boundaries. Can you keep your hands, and more important, your cock, away from another bitch?"

"I don't *want* another girl."

"*You* don't. Your cock do. Besides, you at a point in your life where you trying to do the right thing and hold out on fucking. Harley don't have...*fucking*...on her radar."

"Did you say Harley don't have *fuck*—"

"Don't you say it!"

"You shouldn't have said it with the way you mumbled it," CJ grouched.

Snickering, Uncle Mort shook his head. "She grew up too fast. Harley not full grown yet, but she not my baby anymore, either. That shit killing me. I fucking blinked and, somehow, we got here."

"Mom says that about me."

"Meggie adore you, CJ. I'm sure this is hard for her, too. Fuck, she didn't give birth to Diesel, and it took her almost until that motherfucker was in college for her to accept he had a cock that he did more than piss with. When you start fucking...fuck, man."

"Dad accepts I'm not a little kid, anymore."

"If your old man nothing else, he a fucking realist. He can't stop you from growing up, but don't think he don't miss the days when you followed him everywhere."

"How can I make them feel better?"

"No way to do that, CJ. We the motherfuckers that got to come to terms with where you all at in life."

"I don't want Mom and Dad to hurt."

"I didn't tell you none of that shit to upset you. I'm trying to get you to understand how hard it is for me to accept the time when Harley ready for a boyfriend. If it's you, she'll be a lucky girl. You a fine young man, CJ. But she not ready *now*. And you not ready to settle down."

"Do you want me to cheat on Harley?"

"You two just friends and you ready to get in pussy. She not allowed to give hers up for years to come."

"I thought you said she wasn't ready."

"Fuck, it's either one. Both. Whatever. Don't get it into your fucking head to seduce her. Don't let your cock brain fuck over you or her."

"I wouldn't even know how to seduce her, Uncle Mort."

"Good, because I'd hate to have to cut your hands off."

CJ scowled at him. "Harley and me are friends. She's my *best* friend. I won't jeopardize that."

"The shit I walked up on when you two were alone on the side of the clubhouse? Don't let that happen again."

"We used to sit on each other's laps. All she was doing this time was standing near me." When they'd been caught. Harley *had* been on his lap minutes before and the feel of her against him...fuck. He wouldn't think about that particular moment while he was talking to Uncle Mort. He cleared his throat. "What's so bad about us being next to each other, while we're on our feet?"

"The fact you got a fucking hard-on, and I almost lost my fucking life by hacking your cock off."

Heat rushed to CJ's face and he groaned. "How do you know I was aroused?"

"Because I been a fucking young motherfucker before, that needed to hide a swollen dick, that's how the fuck I knew what was going on with your ass when you rushed to sit the fuck down."

"I won't hurt Harley."

"We both know where we stand, CJ, and I trust you." Uncle Mort beckoned Symphony over. "We ready for the check."

"We didn't eat anything," CJ protested. "You told her to bring me whatever you were having."

"Yeah. *Nothing*. I ate already."

"I'm starving!"

Uncle Mort pulled out his billfold and pressed two one-hundred-dollar bills into Symphony's hands. He winked at her then looked at CJ. "Your little ass should've ordered."

Symphony giggled.

His stupid oversight was so ridiculous, CJ laughed, too.

"Bring us two halibut sandwiches with fries and asparagus salads," Uncle Mort relented. "I'll have a beer and he'll have...?"

"A cola," CJ said.

Still giggling, Symphony walked away.

"That was low, uncle," CJ said with mock annoyance.

"No, that shit was funny. You should've seen your panic."

Uncle Mort was such a cool dude. CJ forgot he was his uncle and flipped him off.

Instead of anger, Uncle Mort returned the gesture, snickering.

"I lost myself in the moment," CJ admitted after Symphony brought their drinks and he sipped his cola. "I meant no disrespect to you."

"Boy, if I thought you was disrespecting me, I would've beat your ass. As a grasshopper, you got to start spreading your wings and getting a solid footing."

"Dad doesn't feel that way. Sometimes, I think he doesn't want me to patch in." Tasting his cola, CJ thought of Rory and Uncle Johnnie. He didn't seem to put pressure on his younger kids the way he did his two older children. True, Blade wasn't two yet, but JJ was eleven. "Uncle Johnnie is fucking stupid the way he treats Mattie and Ro. At least he wants Rory in the club."

"A cardinal rule is not forgetting your place. Running off at the mouth about a higher-up, in your case an adult *and* a relative, not cool."

CJ flushed.

"*However*, you still my grasshopper today. Let me unpack your concerns. How much you know about Lowman...?" He cleared his throat, drank more beer. "Excuse me, *Logan* Donovan?"

"My great-grandfather?" CJ asked in surprise. "Not much. Just that he was a fuckhead."

"That motherfucker was worse than a fuckhead, CJ. He was a racist, misogynistic, homophobic, insane hypocrite. Johnnie, Zoann, and Outlaw was his targets. His pawns. His possessions. Johnnie and Chester was exalted, until he needed to use them for his own gain. Your daddy was his nemesis. All prez got from Lowman was abuse. Physical. Verbal. Emotional. Johnnie was Lowman golden child. Maybe, he loved John Boy momma more. Or, maybe, he liked blond hair. Or, maybe, 'cause Johnnie had silver-gray eyes like him, he glorified your uncle. My guess is Johnnie treating Mattie and Rory the way Lowman handled him and Chester. According to Lowman, worthy men meant to be tough, smart, wily, and deadly. Respectable bitches chaste, demure, pliable, and refined."

"Aunt Zoann isn't..." CJ wouldn't finish the thought since it bordered on disrespect.

Uncle Mort smiled. "Chester will cut a bitch in a fucking minute."

"Yeah," CJ said, laughing. "That."

Mattie and the day she tried to help him came to mind. Ryder, Ransom, Rory, JJ, Lou, and Mark JB were busy devising a plan to fuck up Wallace the next school year since they hadn't had enough time for recon once CJ ordered them to watch the younger Byrd and his interactions with Mattie. CJ was also in on the plans and he'd recruited Axel and Devon. They'd considered Ryan, but he was too far up Willard's ass for trustworthiness.

"Mattie is—" CJ shrugged, unsure how to define her with all his suspicions running through his mind.

If they discovered anything amiss between Wallace and Mattie, they'd try one time to handle the situation. After, if he kept his bullshit up, they were telling Uncle Johnnie.

"Mattie is—"

"A bad little motherfucker, little dude. Johnnie should foster that, but he too blind to see it."

"Can't anybody talk to him?"

"Nope, 'cause he a stupid motherfucker sometimes, especially toward his daughter. And Rory going to end up a worse fucking *path* than him."

CJ guffawed. "*Path*, unk? Like psycho?"

Uncle Mort nodded. "Rory a sweet, sensitive kid. Kind of like Rule. Only difference is Rory idolize you and Rule adore his twin."

"Rebel and Rule are so different. It's hard to believe they're twins sometimes."

"Your sister look like Meggie girl but act like Outlaw. Rule look like Outlaw but act like Meggie."

CJ nodded. "He wants to be a *priest*. Can you fucking believe that shit? I sure the fuck can't."

"His fucking life. His fucking choice."

"Fuck! How does *Dad's* progeny, *my* brother, *Rebel's* twin, turn...*holy*? Does he want to administer last rites when our death sentences are carried out?"

"Only way you gassed is if you convicted."

"It's not gas. It's lethal injection mostly."

"Death penalty punishment also depends on the state you iced a motherfucker. And the degree you charged with. Our state abolished it years ago. Here in Oregon there's a gubernatorial moratorium. There are so many fucking factors, that shouldn't even cross your fucking mind. Unless you in Texas. The Lone Star State carried out forty fucking times more motherfucker fucking-up than Cali in the last five or six decades, and almost twice as many in the last ninety years."

"How do you know so much about this?"

"I stay up to date on this shit due to my line of work, little dude. If I have a bad day and fuck up, and get fucking caught, I want to be sure I'm alive for my woman and my kids to at least be able to visit me. Can you fucking imagine the double travesty of me being a stupid motherfucker *and* a fucked-up one? But if you got that mentality, maybe this not the life for you."

"No!" CJ said in a panic. "I mean, yes, it is. It's just that..." Death frightened him as much as failure and disappointing his dad. "Wait a minute, Uncle Mort. Do you want Harley with a biker?"

"I want my baby girl with the motherfucker that make her happy. As long as he treat her right and I don't have to widow her, he could be just like me." He leaned closer and whispered, "A fucking killer."

CJ's eyes widened. Uncle Mort, Dad, nor anyone else had ever described themselves so bluntly. The reality of their lives had been brought home at the Scorched Devils' clubhouse. Still, no one discussed it.

"You looking a little green, kid."

Words escaped him, but the daily dangers of club life hit him full force.

"What the fuck you think the club enforcer do?"

"Enforce?"

"And what the fuck *that* mean?"

"Uh—"

"I set motherfuckers on the correct path if they stray from us. And if they fuck over us too bad, they don't get to course correct. They get fucked up."

"Who...who gives the orders?"

A small smile ghosted across Uncle Mort's face. "You not a club member. That's classified information."

"That's fucking bullshit! You've told me this much."

"Watch your fucking tone. *This* one of those ass-beating times because you being disrespectful."

"How am I supposed to know the difference?"

"Either from ass beatings, teeth knocking out, or using your fucking brain and thinking about the context of the conversation. As a club officer, I *said* information classified. You drop the fucking subject or face the fucking consequences."

"But—"

"But nothing. If I'm describing my goddamn job, you fucking immediately know that's club talk. That mean you stand the fuck down and follow *my* lead."

CJ dropped his gaze onto the inlaid booth table to hide his irritation.

"Outlaw want better for his kids," Uncle Mort said a few minutes later, no longer annoyed.

"So he's told me. Unless Mom told him privately she wanted me to graduate from college before I can patch in, his rule seems unfair all things considered."

"Nope, that shit all Prez. Your momma been at his side for years. She know the deal."

"Yeah, but it was her choice," CJ flared.

"At least she got one, CJ. Outlaw didn't want to disappoint Big Joe, just like you don't want to fail *him*. Your granddaddy was entrenched in club life, and he was the only one that made Prez feel like he belonged. He buffered Prez from Lowman bullshit."

"Dad's so strong and independent. It's hard to imagine him not having a choice over his own life."

"Prez didn't fucking hatch a full-grown dude. He was once a little kid, too."

"I understand." The thought of his father as a vulnerable little boy with only one person in the entire world to rely on was sobering. "I'd still like to patch in as soon as I can after I turn eighteen. What value is an education if I won't use it?"

"The right degree could be useful to the club. Not to mention thumbing your nose at the status quo. Look at prez and he's unfairly typecast. Look at Johnnie and he's unfairly typecast. John Boy fucking brilliant, but he the stupidest motherfucker alive. Prez, though? Prez damn near a genius. Give him a puzzle, unsolvable to most motherfuckers, and within an hour, you got the answer. Life taught him what he know, but where the fuck you get a degree for that? Not a goddamn place. I didn't know your daddy when he was your age. You turning sixteen in a few weeks. Prez had already killed a motherfucker or was *close* to killing one. He want you to have what Johnnie had. What *I* had. We got to go to college and just be young motherfuckers looking for parties and pussy. You was born into this life but it don't have to *be* your life. Feel me?"

"Yeah, Uncle Mort." For the first time, thinking of his dad as a sad, frightened child helped CJ see 'Law's point-of-view. "If I just patch in, then it'll seem like my life was predestined to be that way as his son. Whereas if I go to college and then graduate, it'll seem like I chose it of my own free will."

At Uncle Mort's pride, CJ blushed. He was used to getting it from his parents, but he'd never seen such admiration from any of his uncles.

"You Outlaw to the core," he said with a smile, "but always remember you *CJ* first."

Drawing in a deep breath, CJ nodded. "I, um, I...remember all that stuff Uncle Johnnie said at the clubhouse when Dad stepped away to talk to Mom?"

"What about it?"

"I...should I have told Dad? I promised I wouldn't, and I haven't, but Uncle Johnnie sounded..."

"Like a manipulating motherfucker," Uncle Mort finished. "Club allegiance sometimes test family loyalty. That's a tough fucking road and require a lot of fucking finesse."

"None of which Uncle Johnnie displayed. He sounded fucking treasonous, especially since he was talking about how he acted in front of another club." The audacity of that motherfucker. That day changed CJ's perception of his uncle.

The thought sent guilt through CJ and he glanced away.

"Your old man know, CJ, 'cause me, Val, and Digger marched Johnnie ass to Prez office a couple weeks ago and made him confess. You right on all accounts, even calling that motherfucker a motherfucker."

Hot embarrassment rushed to CJ's face. "I didn't—"

"You did, 'cause I saw it on your fucking face, but you handled it the way you supposed to. You kept your cool and your fucking mouth shut."

"Do you mean today or at the meeting?"

"Both times. Never look at a situation as Outlaw son. Look at a situation from the perspective of the lowest of the low, until you know the lay of the land. If you was a regular Tuck Fuck and you was at a meeting where Johnnie running off at the mouth and you run to Prez *after* Johnnie said shut the fuck up, Prez and those loyal to him might appreciate it. On the other hand, even if only Johnnie felt betrayed, you fucked. You went against an officer's direct order and you fucked over Johnnie.

Never ever expect fealty 'cause of who your old man is. Earn it by being a solid motherfucker."

"Dad never mentioned it to me. He must feel I betrayed him."

"Nope. He feel like Johnnie put you in a bad fucking position and he wasn't fucking amused. Even *if* he understand and feel the same way."

"Nahhhhhh. Dad is 'Law. *Outlaw*. He's always the club president."

"At one time. But your daddy Meggie girl husband first. Since Mystic and the Imperials kidnapped her and he took care of the problem, shit been quiet. I fucking pray it stay that way, 'cause kid, if you little motherfuckers spoiled, we spoiled too. My fucking ass almost as soft now as I was the first seventeen years of my life. I barely remember what the fuck roughing it is and you and Harley and all the rest of that fucking tribe we created know nothing about it. Outlaw was madder at Johnnie over you than he was over the other shit. Motherfuckers know if they want to break Prez and bring the club down, get to your momma. Your old man can survive anything except losing her. Just thinking about what she might go through until she died or was killed so they could bring him her body is his worst fucking nightmare."

"Her...her b-body?"

Uncle Mort sighed. "The life we live brutal, filled with revenge and betrayal and retaliation. Love got little place in it, but Prez love like he live. Hard. Or *lived*, 'cause that's not really us no more."

If 'Law had kept private how deep his love for MegAnn went, it might've removed the target from her back. Perhaps, that's what CJ would do with Harley. Adore her behind closed doors and only acknowledge her as his in public.

"Thank you, Uncle Mort. I can't remember Dad ever having this type of conversation with me. He usually shuts me down. That's why I was so happy when he allowed me to come to that meeting."

"Outlaw itching to teach you and have you riding alongside him, but he not changing his mind about what you need to do before you allowed to patch in. Why talk about shit when it'll only feed your determination to patch in and make him long for you to do it? Only shit that'll do is make you both miserable and the one thing Meggie not standing for is seeing her man and her kids unhappy. Before that happen and she end up convincing him that maybe college really not for you, Prez not even broaching the topic. It was your momma that talked him into letting you go to that fucking meeting after Derby called. When she heard what happened, I swore Meggie girl would tell Outlaw to fuck Derby up."

"Fuck, then Mom *has* killed someone?" CJ blurted before he caught himself.

Uncle Mort stiffened, then gave him such a fierce glower, CJ shrank back. "Who the fuck told you that?"

"Uh..." Swallowing, CJ faltered, not wanting to rat out Mattie. "I-I don't remember...it's a rumor—"

"Rumors like that get you fucked up," he snarled. "Tell me the fucking name of the rumormonger so I can set that motherfucker straight."

"I can't. Let's drop—"

"Either you tell me or you can't see Harley for the next month."

"What? No! That's not fucking fair. You can't keep Harley away from me because of that."

"She my daughter. I can keep your fucking ass away from her for the rest of your fucking life. I don't want her with a fucking gossip that can get him and her killed for repeating stupid shit."

CJ weighed his options. Mattie had enough to deal with and he didn't want Uncle Mort mad at her. She visited Harley and Rebel a lot. They allowed her to be herself without judgment. However, as much as he loved Mattie, she wasn't Harley. "Mattie told me, Reb, and Harley that Mom killed someone to save Dad's life."

"Fucking Johnnie, bruh," Uncle Mort growled.

"No, she overheard Aunt Kendall and Uncle Johnnie talking one night about Traveler."

"Okay. Fine. Fucking Johnnie *and* Kendall."

"It's true," CJ guessed, the anger in Uncle Mort's eyes a dead giveaway.

"We got to tell Outlaw you know, but yeah, it's true. There's so much bullshit surrounding what happened, CJ. Prez was cleaning his gun so it was on the table. When he got up and had his back to Traveler, the motherfucker fired at him. Your momma made a split second decision. If she hadn't pulled the fucking trigger at the same time, Outlaw would've been killed. She had a lucky fucking shot and hit him near his heart 'cause she aimed for the biggest target on him. But she was freaking out so Prez shot the motherfucker in the head and told her *he* fucked up Traveler."

Mom was so...so...so... "Fucking badass!" CJ said, grinning and awed and riding a sudden high.

Uncle Mort smiled. "Don't tell her. *Ever.*"

"But she saved Dad."

"Prez insulated Meggie with insane ferocity, kid. If she'd been told the truth when motherfuckers was gunning for us, she would've been upset but she would've moved on quickly. Meggie adore Outlaw. Now, after all these years, thinking she disabled Traveler rather than killed him, she'd feel betrayed by Prez and us. Being years removed from all the danger skewer the intensity of that time. She'd be happy she protected your daddy, but she'd feel just as horrified over the life she took instead of focusing on the one she saved."

"I promise I won't tell Mom, but can we not tell Dad? He'd confront Uncle Johnnie and the fallout for Mattie would be horrendous. Uncle Johnnie would be so mad and that's the last thing she wants." Or needed.

"Another cardinal rule? Don't lie to Outlaw and don't lie to *Christopher*, especially if it's about Meggie."

"We wouldn't be lying. We just wouldn't be giving full disclosure."

Uncle Mort huffed a breath and scowled. "Let me get this straight. You threw Mattie under the bus to not get barred from seeing Harley, but now you trying to protect her from Johnnie?"

"Yeah. That sums it up."

"I'll do it this one time but take her aside and tell her to keep her fucking mouth shut. Make sure you tell her you told me and I verified it's a fucking lie."

"Thank you—"

"Here you are," Symphony interrupted, startling CJ.

He'd been so lost in their conversation, he hadn't even noticed her coming. She smiled at him, promise in her eyes, her fresh coat of purple lipstick drawing attention to her mouth.

"Anything else?" she asked once she'd set their plates, another beer, and a fresh cola on the table.

"We good, baby," Uncle Mort said, smiling at her. "I'll let you know if we want pie."

Symphony licked her lips. "Anything for you and CJ, Mort." She lowered her lashes and handed CJ a slip of paper. "I make the best cream pie you ever want to see. I get off in an hour. I can show you then."

CJ's nostrils flared and he swallowed, his balls throbbing.

"How a cream pie taste more important than how the motherfucker look," Uncle Mort responded, biting into a fry.

Suddenly, CJ didn't know if Symphony was offering to show her pussy with cum leaking out or an actual piece of pie.

"Mine looks and tastes delicious."

After stuffing a handful of fries into his mouth, Uncle Mort shifted and pulled out some cash. He didn't count, he just handed her the roll. "Your tip." She snatched it and he went back to eating.

"You don't have to do this. I'll fuck you and CJ for free."

"Not interested. Not saying you not fine as fuck. But I love Bailey. Remember her? *She* tipped you a fucking grand the last time we came in here. When I told her I was meeting CJ here, she sent that." Glaring at her, he nodded to the money in her hand and bit into his sandwich.

"She's nice and all, but that doesn't get me dick."

"You can't get *her* dick," he snapped. "She just let me carry the motherfucker until she ready for it. If I misuse that privilege, she relieving me of cock duties. If I'm not responsible enough to keep it to myself, then she hacking it the fuck off. Even though it belong to her, I like it attached to *me*."

"You don't have to fuck me, Mort. I'll suck your cock. I've dreamed of tasting your cum."

If she didn't shut the fuck up, CJ *would* come.

"Symphony!" Uncle Mort growled. "Have some goddamn pride. I'm not fucking you. You a pretty chick, cool to talk to and fine to look at, but I don't want you."

She looked at CJ. "My number's on there. You ride a bike, don't you?"

CJ's hand shook as he picked up his fork to dig into his asparagus salad. "A pussyped for now."

"I'll suck you off and let you fuck me in the ass—"

"He fucking jail bait," Uncle Mort snapped in disgust before biting another piece of his sandwich. "Go now before I lose my goddamn patience and take my woman fucking money back."

As she stomped off, CJ laid his fork on the plate and snatched up his soda, drinking deeply. His blood was boiling and his cock was as hard as stone.

"Was she serious?" he squeaked.

"As a motherfucker."

"How can you be so unfazed?"

"How you know I'm unfazed? I'm married, not a fucking monk. But I love Bailey and I'm not fucking over her just to get my nuts off. My vows as sacred to me as my wife and what we have."

Considering their earlier conversation what happened a few minutes ago felt like a setup.

"Think what the fuck you want, little dude," Uncle Mort said when CJ explained his theory. "This just fucking coincidence. Some bitches try for biker dick on the fucking regular. You think I would've brought Symphony money from *Bailey* for a fucking teachable moment?"

"Well, um, no. When you put it like that."

"Just like Meggie wouldn't have talked your daddy into taking you to the meeting with the Devils if she had the *smallest* fucking thought, Derby would invite those bitches."

Mom knowing about the women clicked in CJ's brain, although Uncle Mort mentioned her anger a few minutes ago. Embarrassment swarmed CJ and he fell back, closing his eyes. "God! She knows Peaches was giving me a hand job." Misery cracked his voice. "I won't ever be able to look Mom in her eyes again." He straightened, annoyance overtaking his mortification.

"She knows Derby. Why wouldn't she think he'd be up to some bullshit?"

"Hey, boy, don't blame your momma," Uncle Mort warned. "You should thank her for talking Outlaw into inviting you to the fucking meeting."

"I love Mom, Uncle Mort," CJ said in frustration. "But she's fucking human who has fucking faults. She can be criticized."

"Not if you like living. Outlaw not killing his kids for disrespecting her. I'll say he'll even give you and your brothers a chance or two—"

"Not Rebel?"

"Don't have to include Reb. Your sister adore and admire Meggie. She'll never look down on her. The way you look up to Outlaw is the way Rebel look up to your momma."

Truth, so CJ wouldn't refute Uncle Mort.

"If Outlaw heard you talking about your momma, he'd be hurt on her behalf. If, after a chance or two and you still feel that way, he'd want nothing to do with you."

"Uncle Mort, I love Mom. Aren't you hearing me? But *she* allowed me to go, then got angry with Derby for being Derby. Now, I have to live with Mom knowing I-I..." Fuck, he couldn't even finish the thought.

"Almost lost your fucking mind because a woman had her hand around your cock for the first fucking time. You didn't even notice when I yanked the fucking gun away from you. I could've shot your ass off and you wouldn't have seen it coming."

CJ didn't like the censure on Uncle Mort's face. "Are you blaming me for that?"

"Fuck, yeah! Always be aware of your surroundings, no matter what the fuck going on, unless you behind locked fucking doors in friendly territory."

"I'll do better next time," CJ bit out, still annoyed and ashamed. "But how can I look Mom—"

"Did Meggie confront you?" Uncle Mort interrupted in exasperation.

"No, but—"

"No buts, boy! You know how fucking tired I am of hearing motherfuckers say what Meggie *should* do? What about what the fuck she *do*? How much shit she overlook in the name of peace? Not only for the fucking club but her family, too?"

"Mom can be everybody's punching bag," CJ grouched, not meaning his disrespect because he knew there was so much more to his mother.

Uncle Mort's glare made CJ hunch down in his booth. "If you ever fucking invited to a meeting again, I'll tell Meggie not to bother talking to Outlaw on your behalf. Instead of asking the full fucking story, you blaming her for another motherfucker actions."

More shame poured into CJ, only this time it was for his unfairness and the last of his mortification over Peaches slid away. "I'm sorry," he said honestly. "I don't mean to be unfair to Mom. She *is* our rock. Dad always says she's the most important woman in the club. Mom says it's Lolly."

"Roxanne look after all us, including Meggie, so I understand why she feel that way."

"Lolly keep motherfuckers in their place and doesn't sacrifice herself."

"Your momma don't sacrifice herself, CJ. She work with what she got and one of the best fucking strategists on the fucking planet. I told you to think about Outlaw as a kid. Do the same for Meggie. While you at it, consider *her* momma and how Dinah groomed Meggie to be her protector and caregiver, then threw her under the fucking bus whenever Meggie called the cops. Your momma had to stay one step ahead of her stepdaddy to survive and make sure Dinah survived."

CJ blinked. "What...I don't...Mom and Dad don't have much to say about the past, so my knowledge is vague."

"It was a bunch of bullshit, mostly tied in with the club," Uncle Mort said, his irritation still evident. "None of the kids know a lot, so don't feel bad."

"I don't mean to sound harsh," CJ said defensively. "Mom doesn't deserve my..." *Censure* was such a mean word, but he couldn't think of another.

"Your scorn?"

Well, fuck, that was even meaner. He couldn't bring himself to answer. "What made Mom talk Dad into allowing me to come?"

"At first the motherfucker didn't know about the bitches."

"When did he say that?"

"We had a follow-up meeting with Derby 'cause Outlaw wasn't letting that stunt slide. He told us when Gypsy talked to Meggie and swore there'd be no foolishness, she hadn't left him yet. Then, she found out about Serina carrying a kid that might be Derby's. Your momma encouraged Gypsy to leave Derby. When she left that motherfucker, she also opened her motherfucking mouth and snitched on Meggie girl, pissing Derby the fuck off. Instead of seeing his own worst enemy staring at his dumb ass in a fucking mirror, he targeted your momma. Ironically, *she* was the one that saved his fucking life. Not only the day of the meeting, but when during his burial meeting. Somehow, Gypsy found out and she called Meggie all hysterical."

"Dad intended to kill Derby?" CJ gasped. "A club president? Wouldn't that have started a war?"

Uncle Mort shrugged. "The Dwellers would've absorbed the Hounds. That fucking club stay together 'cause of Derby. He not relationship material but he a kick ass Prez. He knew what the fuck was up. That's why he told Gypsy and left it hanging. He didn't tell her to call your momma. She did that on her own. Derby didn't commit no offense against us. It was personal, so she was able to get Outlaw to stand down."

"I was really unfair to Mom," CJ said quietly. "I've never really thought about the position she finds herself in all the time."

"That's understandable. It's never been required of you. Any of you," he amended. "But you're growing up and you itching to be in the club. You got to look at the bigger picture while still having the ability to understand the intricate details and smaller circumstances. Sometimes, you got to do that shit at rapid speed. It's instinct but it's also a skill honed over time. Leaders always willing to learn. They don't go off halfcocked. Always use your fucking brain. You need brawn, but your mind is your best weapon."

CJ enjoyed history, so he considered what he knew about some of the most famous warmongers. "The deadliest motherfuckers are also brilliant tacticians."

"Exactly."

His uncle's invaluable insight gave CJ a lot to think about, though he regretted not having his father talk to him. He was so fucking ungrateful! Uncle Mort didn't have to take the time to explain things. Instead of feeling sorry for himself, he should've been appreciative.

"CJ, Outlaw showing you the ropes in time."

"What are you talking about, unk?" CJ didn't want to offend his uncle because he hadn't had to share all he had. Explaining how he wished Outlaw saw him as grown enough for such a conversation would be an insult. "You already explain Dad's reasoning."

"Your brain accepting what I told you, but your heart not. You still hurt and want *him*. Even if he said the same thing as me, it's not the same."

"I appreciate—"

"I know, little dude, but I *understand,* so don't think you hurting my feelings by wishing it was Outlaw. You not. No matter what I say, you have to grow up and look back to understand his position. Words meaningless right now. Only time will help you. And when you look back on this day, you'll understand all that Outlaw is sacrificing by not giving in to you. He miss having you dog his steps and challenge his time with Meggie, boy. So don't be so hard on him or yourself."

"I don't mean to be. I miss him, too. I'd leave school behind in a minute if he allowed me to."

"Enjoy the life your momma and daddy built for you and your brothers and sister. You can be anything you want. Harley, Lou, and Kaleb can, too. All you kids. The world at your fucking feet. You want to be a Dweller. Make sure it's for the right fucking reason 'cause Outlaw loving you regardless."

At CJ's silence, Uncle Mort lifted a brow.

"Club life represents freedom and brotherhood. Living by a strict code while still being your own man."

"Respect all. Fear none."

"Damn, that's...that's tight."

"Big Joe's philosophy."

"Mom's old man?" CJ said in awe.

"A biker's creed, but one he strictly adhered to."

CJ grinned. "So did I get it right?"

"No right or wrong, little dude. Only honesty. If you said what you did to please me, then it's definitely wrong."

"I didn't. I swear it's how I feel."

"That's all any of us can ask of our boys. And, I believe you, by the way."

At the dismissal in Uncle Mort's tone, CJ changed the subject. "What happened with the Devils? What was finally decided?" Something else occurred to him. "And where did Cole's body go?"

"Club business."

CJ should've dropped it since Uncle Mort had warned him to do just that in these circumstances. However, this time didn't seem fair. "C'mon, dude! I was invited to the meeting. At least I can have closure and know the outcome."

"You one persistent little motherfucker," Uncle Mort growled.

"Please, ashfuck," CJ coaxed.

Uncle Mort snickered. "That shit don't hit the same now that your voice changing, kid, but I'll relent for old time's sake. We've met with Dez and the Scorched Devils again. At the moment, we in a holding pattern. We can't absorb those motherfuckers without knowing their enemies and shit. They need protection from the Gnomes while we have a peace agreement with them. Absorbing the Devils would impact our treaty. Before we take on that bullshit, we have to see what the Devils bring to the table. How loyal are they to us and each other? What other enemies do they have? If it was Derby and the Burning Hounds, it wouldn't be a question. We'd step in because we have a time-tested partnership with them. For now, the Devils are performing some mid-level runs. We plan to meet again in the fall."

"Can you suggest to my dad that I attend?"

"I'll think about it."

Since it wasn't a flat-out no, CJ accepted the response. "What happened to Cole? Where's he buried?"

"Nowhere. Johnnie dismembered him, then threw the pieces in the incinerator. He probably let the motherfucker fly away after that."

Nausea turned CJ's stomach. All he could say was, "You believe in angels?"

Uncle Mort's laughter was so loud, other diners turned their way. "Fuck, boy. I don't mean that way," he said, wiping his eyes and howling again. His shoulders shaking, he leaned closer. "He let the fucking ashes blow away in the wind or he threw them in some body of water," he whispered, in control again.

"Oh, right," CJ said, chuckling at his dumb assery.

For a few moments, they fell silent, then Uncle Mort spoke again. "I hear you failed English because of Shakespeare."

CJ fingered the rim of his glass. "Yep."

"Ummmhmmm." Uncle Mort drank again. "Shakespeare boring as a motherfucker but you smart enough to understand that shit especially with Red and her readings and mini plays. Your old man know that, too. He so busy getting ready for the yearly vacation, he letting the shit slide right now. We all have to add extra money because of the last minute reservation changes since you in summer school."

"Nooo," CJ protested, picking up his fork again to dig into his salad. "I'll talk to him. Diesel can stay with me. I'm kind of tired of Disney World, anyway."

"I feel you, little dude. After visiting all the fucking Disney properties around the goddamn world, not much fucking else to see. Mickey Mouse don't fucking change. He still and will always be a happy motherfucker. But, fuck, the girls keep having babies, which mean the family stuck with Disney every fucking year."

"I wish the babies would stop, too," CJ confessed. "Because of that mostly. We get to go on cool trips as individual families, but with all of us together? Disney...damn it, man."

They looked at each other, "or Six Flags," they chorused around laughter.

"Meggie want you to go, so just tell Outlaw what you told me. Man-to-man. Okay? The women of the house can't be around because your momma and your sister have him wrapped around their pinkies."

"Same as Aunt Bailey and Harley with you, Uncle Mort."

"Fuck, you got my ass there."

"Even if it is just me and Outlaw, once he tells Mom, she'll influence him."

"You make him understand you don't see a need to spend extra money when you old enough to stay home with Diesel's supervision. When you pass this course, you'll be starting football camp not long after. Once you present all these facts to him, he'll do his part and get your momma to understand."

"Or—"

"I'm not saying she won't be disappointed. She will be. But I agree with you. All this extra money a pain in the fucking ass."

CJ laughed. "I thought you were giving me advice for my benefit. You just don't want to cough up the money."

Uncle Mort threw him the stink eye but didn't deny the accusations.

"We got our plan of action together?" he asked once CJ stopped laughing.

"Yeah."

"All in all, I think we had a very productive meeting."

"Me, too," CJ agreed.

"Good, little dude. Let's finish eating."

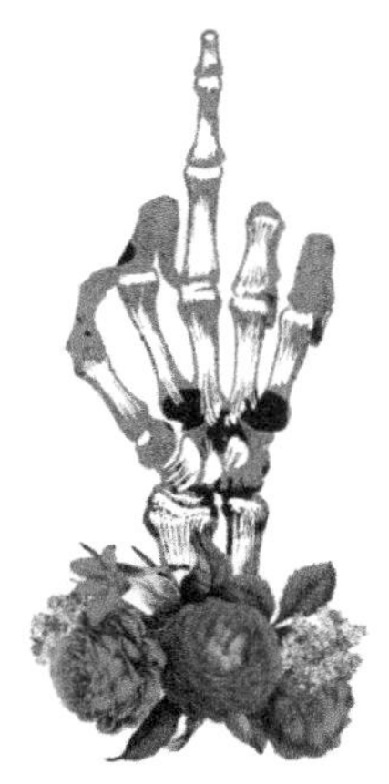

Chapter Seventeen

HARLEY

Because she'd needed her bruises from her run-in with Willard to heal, Harley stayed in her bedroom as much as possible.

For almost two weeks, whenever she heard anyone approach her door, she'd dive into bed and pull the covers up. Mommie and Daddy attempted to draw her out. Lolly had stormed in and tried to yank Harley's comforter and top sheet away. Mattie had bombarded her with questions and Rebel demanded the truth.

The girl was too suspicious for her own good. It was just another secret added to an ever-growing list. Eventually, their pit of deception would explode. They'd heard a few stories about when the club had been in such upheaval ten or fifteen years ago. A lot of it could've been avoided by someone speaking up.

While the boys didn't want to lose the respect of their fathers, the girls, especially herself, didn't want to risk confessing *one* thing and then blabbing *everything*.

Harley already knew the chaos that would create. Rebel would be grounded, and Diesel would die, even if he hadn't arranged the "date" between the two of them *and* he'd done the right thing by trying to let her down gently. He'd still taken Rebel to a restaurant and spent time with her behind their parents' backs. Matilda's extracurricular activities took their deceit to another level. Sex. Drugs. *Grown* ass men. Yeah, Harley didn't need to be a rocket scientist to know a catastrophe in the making. Aunt Kendall would be devastated, and Uncle Johnnie would be infuriated. Finally, she couldn't forget barely escaping Willard.

CJ would go ballistic. And Daddy...yeah, uh, *no*. She refused to allow her father to murder a minor, sure his conscience would suffer for the rest of his life.

Still, she felt like a fraud with all the dishonesty she, Rebel, and Matilda spouted. When Mommie came to her room earlier today and told her Uncle Christopher invited her out, Harley was grateful her bruises were gone.

Uncle Chris engaged her in small talk as he ran errands, then took her to *Build-a-Bear*, where she'd purchased a bear, clothes, and scents, to add to her collection. He waited patiently while her bear was stuffed and she received its birth certificate, before buying pizza in the mall's food court.

Now back in Hortensia, they were at the supermarket, their final stop according to Uncle Chris.

"My ass ain't doin' this shit often," he grumbled, yanking a cart from the bay.

At the sight of her big, bad uncle pushing a shopping cart, Harley giggled. "Daddy doesn't like grocery shopping either."

Uncle Chris pulled out his phone and held it between them. "Where the fuck this shit at, Harley? What the fuck whole millet, caraway seeds, and turmeric?"

Aunt Meggie's long list included pork loin, lentils, rhubarb, leeks, arugula, dried cherries, the items Uncle Chris asked about, and a few other things.

"Turmeric and caraway seeds are spices. They're located on the aisle with the salt and pepper."

He shoved the phone back in the inside pocket of his cut. "My ass always fuckin' thought millet was bird fuckin' food. Whenever I pick up the shit for the annoyin' motherfuckers Megan insist our youngest lil' motherfucker like to feed, the fuckin' shop said millet in the bird fuckin' feed area."

"You can feed birds millet, peanuts, black-oil walnuts. Rebel, Mattie, and me take Gunner out sometimes to feed the birds, so we had to look up what was best to feed them."

"What the fuck wrong with your Aunt Megan? Tryna feed me bird fuckin' food?"

"Aunt Kendall prepared a millet and greens salad the last time we had a girls' day. It was delicious. Aunt Meggie and Mommie was saying how salads were the one healthy thing they could get you and Daddy to eat." Harley shrugged. "Maybe, Aunt Meggie's looking for a new salad recipe."

"Fuck me. You know where the fuck that other shit at?"

She nodded.

"Fuck, fine. We in the fuckin' produce section, so let's just start here."

Harley couldn't stop another giggle at his misery. "Text me Aunt Meggie's list, and I'll do the shopping."

He looked over his shoulder and stepped closer. "Mort get you to fuckin' shop when Bailey send his ass to the fuckin' store, yeah?"

"Yep."

"How much the motherfucker pay your lil' ass to shut the fuck up?"

"A hondo. But you already bought me a bear and fed me, so let's call it even. To be fair, Uncle Chris," she continued, shaking the hand he offered, "I tell Daddy he doesn't have to pay me a hundred bucks. Sometimes, Mommie's in a jam and needs him to shop and he doesn't want to disappoint her."

"Text sent," he told her.

When she received the notification, she unlocked her phone and opened his message.

"And Mort right. But I think your ma know his fuckin' game. I pull the same shit with Reb. Megan called my fuckin' ass out on that shit months afuckingo."

She snapped her brows together. "Really?"

"Fuck yeah. *They* in control. *They* just allow us stupid motherfuckers to pretend we got the fuckin' power. Come on. We gotta get this shit the fuck over with and get the fuck home. CJ just fuckin' texted so I guess your old man ain't fucked him the fuck up."

"What...? Oh my god," she screeched, opening the phone's keypad. "Give me a second. I have to make sure he's okay."

"Mort fine, Harley," Uncle Chris said in exasperation. "What the fuck you think CJ can do to the motherfucker?"

"Not Daddy, Uncle Chris," she cried. "CJ."

Uncle Christopher snatched the phone from her hand and pressed the end button.

"The lil' motherfucker fine, too. I wouldna let my boy go if my ass really thought he was in fuckin' danger."

As her phone started ringing, CJ's name flashed across the screen.

Uncle Chris handed her the phone.

"I'll call you when I get home," she said before CJ said anything when she answered.

"Okay, Harls."

CJ hung up so fast she couldn't gauge his mood.

Uncle Chris rolled the basket to the vegetable case and picked four leeks, two bunches of rhubarb and one of asparagus, a container of arugula, a bag each of sweet and white potatoes, and twelve ears of corn.

"I can push the basket," she volunteered.

He moved aside, silently ceding control. Reading his text again, she realized he'd bypassed the fruit. While she picked out the firmest apples, Uncle Chris wandered to the baked goods before returning to her side and choosing the apples, then adding cherries, strawberries, and blueberries to the basket.

Back in the bakery, he placed two boxes of prepackaged doughnuts in the basket, then moved to the bread, setting packages of dinner rolls on top of his doughnuts, neither of which were on Aunt Meggie's list.

He guided the cart to the meat department. "Megan just gonna have to deal with shit already packaged. That butcher line too fuckin' long."

At least five people awaited a turn behind the current customer.

Uncle Chris turned to her, folded his arms and leaned against the chest brimming with frozen pork.

"Me and Rebel had a long fuckin' talk. Diesel my kid, and I keep a fuckin' bead on all my lil' motherfuckers."

Harley giggled. "Diesel isn't little, Uncle Chris."

"Nope, he ain't, but he my kid. The fuckin' night Rebel was supposed to be at a fuckin' friend house, I found it mighty fuckin' strange her fuckin' phone location showed up the same fuckin' place as Diesel."

Harley's amusement died.

"Later that fuckin' night, the fuckin' feed to my fuckin' garage got fuckin' scrambled somefuckinhow. You know somethin' 'bout that shit?"

Instead of incriminating herself or Rebel, she remained silent.

"See? What the fuck I think happen? Rebel fuckin' schemed her fuckin' way into Diesel company. After he turned the lil' motherfucker down for what-the-fuck-ever she mighta asked him—ain't none of which my ass wanna really fuckin' think about—she was fuckin' crushed so she called you to her workshop. You lil' motherfuckers wasn't supposed to be out and she had been where the fuck she shouldna been, so she scrambled my goddamn feed."

Harley swallowed.

"Your lil' ass got somethin' to fuckin' say?"

"I-I thought you were meeting with me to have the talk that Uncle Digger suggested, since Daddy met with CJ."

"What the fuck I gotta say about that, Harley?"

She almost wished the meeting *had* been about that, instead of topics that might get them all into trouble. *Or*, somehow, lead her to blabbing what happened between her and Willard. *Or*—

Rubbing the nape of his neck, Uncle Chris sighed. "Boys dirty motherfuckers. They ain't meanin' to be but, fuck, our cocks get us into all types of bullshit. Even my boy, who been needin' to see your lil' ass everyfuckinday almost since you was fuckin' born. He got a wonderful fuckin' ma that put her own influence on him and if he ain't respectin' her or no other woman, Ima kick his fuckin' ass. He young and you young. We used to joke and shit that you lil' motherfuckers would end up tofuckingether."

Smiling, she nodded at him.

"But that shit influenced the fuck outta him and you."

"It didn't, Uncle Chris. I swear."

"Baby, you ain't old efuckinnuff to realize that the bullshit you and his lil ass fuckin' heard over the years and been exposed to, somewhere deep the fuck in your psyche. Befuckinsides, CJ a stubborn lil' motherfucker.

He got it the fuck in his head you the girl for him. Case fuckin' closed."

Tears rushed to her eyes. "You don't think we are?"

"Don't cry, Harley," Uncle Chris said gruffly as she sniffled. "In my fuckin' heart, I fuckin' think you both gonna have to appease your curiosity about each other. Whether that lead to somethin' life long, my ass can't look into a fuckin' crystal ball and predict that shit. But you too young *right now*. Fuck, his ass is, too."

"But?" She heard the word in his voice.

"CJ been fuckin' exposed to those fuckin' bitches at the clubhouse, even if they keep their pussy covered 'til you lil' motherfuckers leave. The shit still hyperfuckinsexual. Befuckinsides, it's easier for my ass to think of *him* fuckin' than you," he finished, scowling. "I watched your lil' fuckin' ass grow the fuck up."

"Me and CJ will spend our lives together."

Uncle Chris grunted, then nodded. "That might fuckin' be, Harley, but you fuckin' can't start now. You not ready."

True, but not for the reasons he was thinking.

"You got a good fuckin' head on your shoulders. You both need to grow the fuck up. Date other motherfuckers. Ain't nothin' like openin' your fuckin' eyes one day and realizin' your whole fuckin' life passed you the fuck by and you just with a motherfucker who you woulda been better the fuck off without."

Harley pursed her lips and drew her brows together.

"Like Gypsy, Harley," Uncle Christopher said with irritation. "Rebel gonna tell you about it when her lil' ass unfuckingrounded. Gypsy spent the fuckin' day at my house yesterday, cryin' over Derby, then decidin' she goin' back to his miserable fuckin' ass cuz she ain't knowin' nothin' else."

"You're stopping CJ and me from hanging out together?" She'd been miserable for the past two weeks because of her self-imposed exile.

"We just gotta monitor all you lil' motherfuckers more. It ain't the same now 'cuz not only brains a-fuckin-ware but cocks and pussies, too."

Relieved at his decision, she threw her arms around him. "Thank you, Uncle Christopher."

He grunted and patted her back.

"Now that all that shit out the fuckin' way, we gotta get a fuckin' move on. We been in this fuckin' store for over a fuckin' hour."

She headed to his side as he turned toward the freezer and grabbed a huge pork loin then set it in the basket. "We gotta find the fuckin' lamb and get the fuck. My ass ready to fuckin' roll."

That evening, Harley accepted a friend request from *Pillar of Earth*.

Chapter Eighteen

REBEL

In the silence of the early morning, Rebel circled the crusty, old bike her father had had delivered two nights ago. It would take long hours and a lot of work to get the motorcycle road-worthy, but she was looking forward to the challenge.

Today was Ryan's 16th birthday. Knowing Diesel would show up agitated Rebel. She'd be expected to talk to him.

Swallowing, she yanked her cellphone from the pocket of her overalls and began snapping photos of the bike. Her daddy taught her it was always a good idea to inventory a rusty hulk of metal *before* dismantling, to serve as guidance for reassembly.

For a few minutes, Rebel focused on her task and blocked out what she'd say to Diesel. Knowing her father would be watching the exchange closely only added to her unease. Without a doubt, he suspected...he *knew*...she'd met Diesel. So far, Diesel still breathed and Rebel hadn't been grounded for the rest of her life. *And*, her dad had plunked down money for another bike to practice on. All for her, not a strip and rebuild to teach CJ.

To be fair, the last two, old rusty, crusty heaps had been more for Rebel and Harley, then any of the boys.

Setting her phone on the worktable, she slid onto the stool, grabbed a pen and notepad from the middle of the table, and began cataloguing the bike parts. Usually, in the early morning hours when her parents were still locked in their bedroom doing parent-y things, and her brothers were wherever, Rebel enjoyed me time, assessing what was needed and imagining the finished product.

But she hadn't slept much last night, so she finally gave up about an hour ago and came to the garage, with its lingering scent of motor oil and WD-40. The shiny slatwalls and carbonite-colored garage floors complemented the red and gray cabinetry that contained all types of tools, manuals, spare motorcycle parts, and sports equipment. The room wrapped her in familiarity, good memories, and future goals.

For instance, Dad gifted Momma with a red Corvette Stingray this past Valentine's Day. He worried about Momma's safety, but she'd seen the car at a show, and he'd gotten it for her. Although Momma rarely drove it—preferring her Lexus SUV—she still had the Corvette. Despite his concerns about her well-being, Dad loved Momma enough to give her whatever she wanted.

Goal number one for Rebel: A relationship as loving as her parents'. Goal number two: Driving the Stingray.

Snickering at the thought, she looked at her father's newest black pickup, all sleek lines and mirror-shine chrome. The modified engine was as loud as one of the motorcycles. It, along with Mom's vehicles, took up three of the four car bays on the opposite side of the garage. CJ's moped sat next to their dad's two Harleys.

Rebel envisioned her own bike situated next to her brother's and father's. Except Dad would never allow her to ride.

Diesel would, though. Whenever he babysat Rebel and her brothers, he permitted her to do whatever the boys were doing, even if Dad would never sanction it.

Tears rushed to her eyes at the memory of Diesel's rejection. She stiffened, hating her weakness. For the past weeks, she'd managed to put the day she'd laid her heart bare to him, behind her. But, today...*today*...she'd see him and—

She sniffled, folded her arms on the table, and rested her head against them.

Without warning, the door leading into the house opened. Startled, Rebel jerked up, just as her father sauntered in. Though he wore jeans, he went shirtless, showing the full sleeves on both muscled arms as well as the tattoos on his upper body covering evidence of old gunshot wounds.

Seeing him made her cry harder.

"Fuck, Ellie, your ma ain't ever thought I was such a ugly motherfucker that I made you lil' motherfuckers bust into fuckin' tears when you saw my ass."

"Oh, Daddy!"

Reaching her, he wrapped his arms around her and allowed her to cry with all the hurt and devastation inside of her. He didn't demand explanations or bombard her with questions.

Once she ran out of tears and got herself under control, he kissed her cheek and released her, then pulled the other stool from the corner and sat.

"Your ma makin' coffee. Gunner woke us the fuck up."

Rebel smiled and swiped at her tears, appreciating her father permitting her to open up in her own time. If she couldn't discuss why she cried just then, he'd let her be. "Gunner doesn't like sleep. He needs some type of strong drug, Dad."

Amusement lit his green eyes, and he snickered. "You a vicious lil' bitch, baby. You wanna roofie your own lil' brother, even though the lil' motherfucker ain't even three yet?"

After thinking on her father's question for a moment, she giggled. "Not really, Daddy," she admitted. "He's like the bear who couldn't sleep."

He scowled at her. "Don't fuckin' remind my ass of that fuckin' cartoon. You and Rule watched that fifty fuckin' times a day."

"I was curious about it after it came up in my search when I was looking for the Donald Duck comic book from 1938 to add to my collection."

"Don't give a fuck. My ass almost blew that fuckin' screen the fuck up to keep from hearing that fuckin' bear."

Rebel giggled.

"Ain't funny, Ellie," he complained.

"Well, it didn't happen, and you let us watch the movie as much as we wanted to." She grinned. "I think I'll show it to Gunner. He might like it."

"If you do, lil' girl, Ima lock this garage the fuck up for the next six months."

Brushing off the threat, she shook her head. "If it made me sad, you wouldn't keep it locked up, Dad," she said with certainty.

He grunted. After lighting a cigarette, he studied her in silence before getting another one, lighting that one too, then holding it out to her, butt first.

Her eyes widened. "Uh, I don't—"

"Ain't saw a fuckin' dumbass lookin' back at my motherfuckin' ass in the goddamn mirror."

Sighing, she accepted the cigarette and took a drag. "How did you know?"

Smoke poured through his nostrils. "I'm your old man, Rebel. It's my fuckin' job to know," he answered, standing and going to one of the cabinets for an ashtray. When he returned to the stool, he sat it between them.

"You're not upset?"

"Ain't happy, Ellie," he admitted. "But my ass ain't that fuckin' hypocritical, where I sit down and talk to CJ while that lil' motherfucker smoke with me, but ain't lettin' you do it, too."

They fell silent, enjoying their cigarettes.

"After Rule and you was born, I didn't see your lil' ass again, 'til I went to the fuckin' nursery. You was this small." Smiling, he held his hands apart. "A fuckin' lil' doll." He took another drag on his cigarette, flicked ashes into the ashtray, then glanced away. "I told Rule me and him was gonna have to keep watch over you and keep motherfuckers away." Soft laughter rumbled from him as he glanced at her again and took his cigarette between his forefinger and middle finger, pointing at her. "My ass said somethin' to the efuckinfect of let the dick hackin' commence."

Yep, that sounded like her dad.

Taking another drag on his cigarette, he sat it in the ashtray, then looked at her. "Ain't expect the fuckin' time to go so quick and your lil' ass to grow the fuck up so fuckin' fast."

Not answering, she enjoyed her cigarette for a moment, still amazed that her dad was actually cool enough to let her smoke the way he did with her brother. "When I was little, you were like Superman to me," she said, remembering all the times her father read her bedtime stories, helped Mom to get her and her brothers dressed for the day, fed them, played with them and so many other things. Once or twice, he even allowed Rebel and Harley to polish his fingernails just because it made her happy.

"I'm not grown yet, Daddy."

He smiled at her. "You ain't too sure if you wanna call me *Daddy* like you did when you was lil' or if you wanna call me *Dad* to show you a teenager now."

"True," she said, accepting the ashtray her father handed to her and tamping her cigarette out as he'd done his. "I prefer *Daddy*," she admitted shyly. "But I am a big girl now. I try to be like you. I want you to be proud of me. People look up to you and respect you. You don't take any shit, er, stuff." He might've surprised Rebel and allowed her to smoke, but she doubted he'd sanction her cursing. "That's the image I try to project too. I try to make sure to tell people what I want, so they can be clear. Sometimes, when I think over conversations with my friends, it just seems I'm always angry. Like I'm not nice. I just don't want to show any weakness."

"First, Ellie? I know you curse like a lil' motherfucker, so you ain't gotta pretend you ain't. Second? Ain't nothin' ever gonna make me not be proud of you. You got a sharp fuckin' brain and a beautiful fuckin' face."

"If I was an ugly heiffer you'd be ashamed of me?"

He sniggered, his eyes twinkling, and she giggled.

"No, baby, you know my ass ain't sayin' that."

"Then what—"

"Shut the fuck up," he said, laughing. "You gorgeous and your lil' ass know it, so stop fuckin' fishin' for compliments. Along with everyfuckingthing else, you got a lotta courage and you light up a room. A winnin' fuckin' combination any motherfucker'll be proud of. You still figurin' *you* out. I ain't wantin' you to be me. I wantcha lil' ass to be *you*." He scraped his hand through his hair. "Ain't nothin' wrong with bein' a gentle bitch, like your ma, Ellie."

"Momma is like a fairytale princess. I could never be like her."

"Your ma ain't perfect, Rebel," Daddy said in an unfamiliar tone. "Ain't gonna like it if you fuckin' look down on her."

"Look down on *Momma*?" Even if Mattie had told the truth about Momma killing someone, Rebel wouldn't think badly of her mother. "I love her to pieces! I don't look down on her. I'm just saying, in my eyes, she's incomparable, and I say she's a princess because..."

Daddy lifted a brow in question.

"Because..." She drew in a deep breath as heat rose to her cheeks. "You're her knight in shining armor. *Our* prince. The way you two love each other is like a fairytale to me." She thought of Diesel. With effort, she beat her tears back. "I can go to Momma with anything, and she'll never judge me. She always listens to me, and she always has time for me. More than anything, she champions my right to be given the same leeway you give to my brothers."

He nodded. "Your ma know you smoke?"

"I don't think so, but I'm not sure. It's never come up between us since she doesn't smoke. You let me have a cigarette, though, because of her, right?"

"Yeah, baby." Folding his arms, he studied her before asking, "Your fuckin' tears you was sheddin' when I came in got anyfuckinthing to do with Diesel?"

Irritation surged in her. What didn't her father know? She lowered her lashes.

"When you defuckincide to scheme and pull low motherfucker moves, you gotta cover all your fuckin' bases. If you was gonna put the fuckin' story out that you was with a fuckin' school friend, you shoulda made sure your fuckin' phone was at that fuckin' place."

She groaned, the words catching her off-guard. When Harley told Rebel about the conversation in the store, she'd expected Daddy to confront her the same day. But the closer the time came for Ryan's birthday party and seeing Diesel, her head crammed with other shit and she'd forgotten what Daddy knew. She decided to keep calm and carry on. "I disabled the alerts."

"The alerts, yeah. Not the trackin' on the main panel. When I fuckin' reviewed that night's events, your fuckin' phone and his was at the same fuckin' place." His look turned severe. "What the fuck you fuckin' plotted to have Diesel pick you the fuck up from school?"

She pursed her lips and, before she knew it, the entire story fell from her. "He turned me down, Daddy," she finished on a sob, covering her face with her hands, hot tears pooling in her palms. "He'll only ever see me as his sister."

At her father's silence, she wrestled back her anguish, sucked up her tears and looked at him.

His eyes were narrowed. "At least the motherfucker gonna live to fuckin' see your lil' ass as anyfuckinthing."

"Daddy!"

"Maybe, my fuckin' ass ain't the smartest motherfucker around, but I ain't understandin' what the fuck you expected from meetin' up with the motherfucker, so clue me the fuck in."

Folding her arms, she lifted her chin. "I expected him to tell me he loved me and wanted me to be his. I thought we would talk everything over and he'd promise me that he'd wait until I turned eighteen so we could marry."

"Forfuckinget my fuckin' ass crushing his fuckin' bones then pulling them motherfuckers from his fuckin' body with a tweezer."

A cry escaped her at the gruesome description, and she dropped her arms to her sides, staring at her father in horror.

"If *I* ain't got to his fuckin' ass first, he still woulda went to fuckin' jail. He a grown motherfucker. He ain't able to promise *you*, a lil' fuckin' kid, that he want to spend the rest of his fuckin' life with you."

"But—"

"No buts, Rebel. The assfuck your brother. I brought him the fuck under our roof when you was a fuckin' lil' baby. When you was fuckin' *two*, he was sevenfuckinteen. Motherfucker almost thirty fuckin' years old."

"But you were almost thirty-three and Momma was eighteen."

Grown men trembled at the glare he gave her. "My ass ain't fuckin' watchin' your Ma grow the fuck to that fuckin' age while livin' under the same fuckin' roof as her. What the fuck wrong with you, girl?" Veins popped out at the side of his neck and his temples. "Not only would Diesel be a dirty motherfucker if he took up with you, even if you was eightfuckinteen, he would be a dead fuckhead. I would cut his fuckin' cock off and stuff it the fuck in his fuckin' mouth, then pull his ball sac through his goddamn nostrils. He better never fuckin' touch you. I ain't givin' a fuck if you fuckin' forty. He your fuckin' brother. Case fuckin' closed."

"If I'm eighteen, you can't tell me what to do, Daddy," she challenged on a miserable sob. "If I want to be with him, and he wants me, you can't do anything. It's between us and it's my body if I want him to have it."

At any moment, her father would keel over in a stroke. Or steam would blow from his ears and nostrils. His complexion graduated from red to purple, his eyes black. "You ain't givin' not a motherfuckin' thing to Diesel," he snarled, slamming his fist against the table. "He fuckin' family. Your fuckin' brother."

"He's nothing to me," she yelled, losing her own temper. "He's not *my* family."

"Don't fuckin' *ever* say that bullshit to him, Rebel. The motherfucker got efuckinnuff issues without you spoutin' them fuckin' words at him. He a fuckin' Caldwell. You a fuckin' Caldwell."

"He's not a Caldwell," she spat. "He's a *whoever*. He was old enough to know his last name. He chose not to divulge it *or* use it. Oh, well. That's on him. But he's *not* a Caldwell," she reiterated.

"The fuck he ain't."

"Why is it okay for CJ and Harley to be so close, but it's a problem with me and Diesel?"

"Cuz CJ and Harley ain't fuckin' livin' in the same motherfuckin' house and them two motherfuckers only eightfuckinteen months apart."

"So it *is* his age?"

"It's the entire goddamn situation, Rebel. He your fuckin' brother and been knowin' you since befuckinfore you was fuckin' walkin' and talkin'. You and that motherfucker ain't *ever* bein' together. And if you fuckin' push it, Ima fuckin' bury him."

"No!" Rebel shrieked. "I'll never forgive you if you hurt Diesel."

"Then you just ain't forgivin' my fuckin' ass cuz I'm *gonna* fuck that motherfucker up if he ever fuckin' cross that line."

"I hate you."

"I ain't givin' a good fuck. My ass ain't here to be your fuckin' friend. My ass here to protect you and steer you right."

"The day I turn eighteen, I'm moving. You'll have no sayso over my life."

"Move to the bottom of the fuckin' ocean. If you with a motherfucker that *know* he ain't got no fuckin' business bein' with you, Ima feed him to the fuckin' sharks," he snarled.

The door opened and her mother rushed in. Without hesitation, Rebel slid from the stool and barreled into Momma's open arms. Although Rebel was already taller than her, nothing in the world compared to her quiet strength.

"Momma, talk to Daddy," she begged around hysterical weeping.

"I was coming to tell you and your daddy breakfast is ready, but the moment I walked into the hallway, I heard the shouting."

"Tell him, Momma. Diesel isn't related to me. *Any* of us, and when I'm eighteen, I have every right to choose whoever I want as my boyfriend."

"Rebel," she said softly, taking Rebel's face between her hands. "you're underage, so Diesel couldn't have answered in any way but how he did."

"But tell Daddy—"

"I'm not telling your father anything. Not now when there's no point. We'll talk about it if the need ever arises, but for the time being, there's no point."

"And when the fuckin' time come, *if fuckin' ever,* you ain't gettin' my ass to change my fuckin' mind, Megan.

Rebel flinched at the finality in Daddy's tone.

"Diesel fuck around with Ellie and he fuckin' dead to me *and* plain fuckin' dead. He ain't gonna be anything but a dirty fuckhead. That motherfucker helped Rebel with fuckin' *schoolwork*. He helped her paint a fuckin' bike. Search for exfuckinspensive comics. *Talked* to her about the first lil' motherfucker she ever liked—"

"I never liked anybody but Diesel," Rebel yelled.

"That motherfucker ever take up with you and Ima put him the fuck outta his fuckin' misery. To my fuckin' way of thinkin', he woulda been fuckin' groomin' you to fuck."

"*Christopher*!" Momma yelled in exasperation. "Calm down. Okay? You and I will talk about this in private."

"Ain't not a motherfuckin', goddamn, fuckin' thing you can fuckin' tell me that ever gonna make me change my fuckin' mind."

"Oh, my god, shut up! Not only is Diesel our son, but he's a club member, so no matter how he feels he has to follow your orders."

"How the fuck he feel? What the fuck that mean, Megan. You soundin' like you supportin' our grown motherfuckin' son havin' a relationship with our underage daughter."

"I am not! Calm down before you keel over!"

Daddy opened his mouth to speak and pointed a finger at Momma. "You ain't changin' my fuckin' mind, Megan. *Ever*," he added ominously, then stormed out, slamming the door behind him.

"Momma, you've got to talk to him," Rebel cried.

Her mother guided her to the stool, then went to the garage bathroom, emerging with a wet towel a moment later. She folded the washcloth and dabbed it against Rebel's cheeks and forehead.

"You don't agree with Daddy, do you, Momma?" A ray of hope bloomed in her. "Diesel and me are meant for each other."

Momma hugged her. "You put Diesel in a very bad position," she said, not revealing whose side she was on. "First by going to him with your feelings and now by revealing them to your father."

Panic settled into Rebel. "Will Daddy kill him?"

"No, of course not," her mother said, settling her hands on Rebel's arms. "Diesel's an honorable man. Trustworthy. He proved that during his interaction with you."

"But—"

"Shhh, little love. Today is Ryan's birthday. CJ and Grant are already headed to Val and Zoann's, so they can talk to Ryan about a volleyball game."

"Yeah, um, I think we're playing while the grills are being set up." She tried to bolster enthusiasm, but the thought of dealing with her grouchy cousin annoyed her almost as much as Molly Harris did whenever she said something stupid. Which was on the regular. That reminded Rebel… "Momma," she said, clearing her throat. "Um, why did you and Daddy name me Rebel?"

"I named you," she said with a smile, gliding her fingers through Rebel's hair. "It's a unique and pretty name." She laughed. "It gave your father nightmares. He said the name courted trouble."

"It, uh, it isn't because we're, uh, you know… It isn't because our family fought for the South in the Civil War?"

Pursing her lips, Momma squinted, then wrinkled her nose. "I…I…uh, where did you…umm, no."

Fucking Molly! Rebel sounded as stupid as that dummy. No wonder Momma stammered over her response.

"What made you think that?"

Since Rebel wouldn't see Molly until school opened again and it would be kind of hard to explain the girl to her mom, she said, "the subject came up at school and I was just curious."

Momma nodded, then situated Rebel's hair over one shoulder. "Why don't we go upstairs and style each other's hair?"

Rebel liked that idea. "Can you braid mine since we're playing volleyball before the party?

Linking her arm with Rebel's, Momma guided her toward the door. "Enjoy yourself today, my love. Your heart is hurting and I wish I could take that pain away, but it'll ease. I promise you. Years from now, you'll look back on this day with fondness."

"But I love him," Rebel whispered as they reached the door to the house.

Momma paused. "Love's never easy, Rebel. Don't allow how you feel about Diesel to define your life. We can't predict the future. If you and he are meant to be together, nothing, other than death, can prevent that from happening."

Her mother meant her words as comfort. For some reason, they just left Rebel apprehensive.

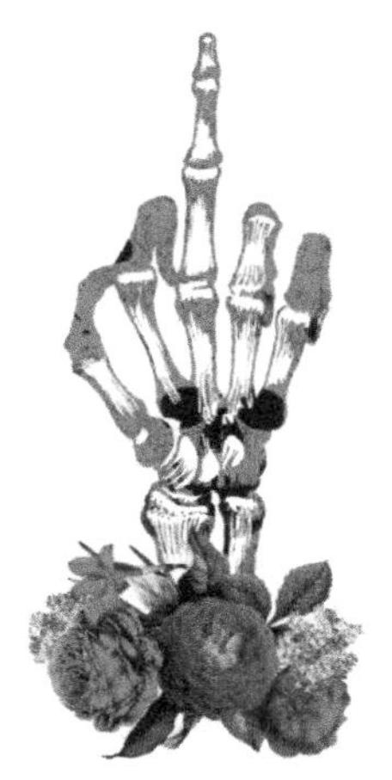

Chapter Nineteen

"Look at Molly's tits bounce." Ryan snickered as she connected with the volleyball for the fourth time. "I'm not calling four hits just so I can watch those puppies."

"Which one's Molly?" Grant Harrington asked. Lolly's stepson was home for the summer but would return to Boston mid-August.

Rebel stomped to Molly and pinched her arm.

"Owwww!" Molly yelped.

"That one," CJ said.

"Why'd you pinch me, Reb?" Molly demanded.

"Because you're a dumb ass and you'll get us called," Mattie inserted.

Molly thought for a moment. "What will we be called?"

"Stupid bi—" Rebel started.

For most of the afternoon, his sister was listless and sad, so CJ was happy to see her spirit returning. Earlier, when he'd found her in her room with Mom, searching for outfits, Rebel hadn't sent him packing, which was the first sign something was wrong with her.

Later, when she'd come downstairs, she hadn't grilled Grant on living in Boston. She hadn't joined in the conversation between Grant, CJ, Mom, and the other guests there for Ryan's birthday.

Then when Outlaw arrived with Diesel, she'd glared at Dad, mumbled something to Diesel, and announced she was heading over to Ryan.

Definitely out-of-character for her since their cousin wasn't her favorite person. CJ was worried about her and intended to talk to her after the party. Now, as she continued arguing with Molly, he decided she was fine.

"Stop!" Harley interrupted, losing her patience. "We're here to win!"

Brynn Mason stepped beside Harley and nodded. "Harley's right. If we start fighting, we'll never beat them."

"How can we beat them?" Molly questioned, her eyes wide. "There's ten of them, Brine, and only seven of us. We need one more to be even."

"My name's Brynn." Brynn was fucking gorgeous with a wealth of black hair and eyes somewhere between the blue of her father and the purple of her mother. "And to be even with the guys we need three more. You know? Seven plus three equals ten?"

"Noooo," Molly disagreed. "Seven is an uneven number. Eight isn't."

"Oh my," Ava Baptiste, the daughter of CJ's mother's gynecologist, said.

Scratching his neck, CJ sighed, understanding that *oh my. Oh my*, how the fuck could a girl be so separated from her brain and survive? *Oh my*, did this girl *have* a fucking brain?

Ava caught CJ's gaze and giggled when he winked at her. At thirteen, she was on the quiet side. Her dad was a former cop and the best friend of Lolly's husband.

"You're the stupid one," Molly huffed, giving Brynn the once over and scowling. "We don't need ten to be even with them. We need *one* more to get to an even number. You know?" she added with sarcasm. "Even plus even equals even."

Wynona McCall, CJ's nine-year-old cousin, stepped in front of Brynn, interrupting whatever she might've said. "Um, I think to be even with the boys we *do* need three more girls, Molly. But eight and ten are even numbers, so you're right too." She turned to Rebel. "Right, Elle?"

Molly glanced around. "Who's Elle?"

"Rebel," Brynn answered because Matilda was too busy trying to glare holes into Molly's head, Rebel and Harley were talking amongst themselves, and Ava and Wynona were exchanging disbelieving looks.

"But I thought her name was Rebel."

"It's Wynona's nickname for Rebel," Brynn said with the patience of a saint.

"Noooo," Molly disagreed. "Her nickname is Reb. That makes sense. Her name doesn't even start with an 'E', so where does Elle come from?"

Brynn pursed her lips. "It's because of the el at the end of her name."

Confusion wrinkled Molly's pretty face. "Shouldn't her nickname be Bel then?"

"Oh my god," Rebel groaned, then shook her head. "You're fucking with us. Right, Molly? You must be playing a wild joke, pretending you're dumber than a fucking amoeba."

"Actually Amoebas—" Molly started.

"Nope," Harley said. "We're not doing this. I want to win the game."

"We can't win if we're a person short of being even with them," Molly protested. "Or is that the rules of the game? Or are we making our own rules? I've played beach volleyball before. And one-on-one. Ohhhh, isn't beach volleyball in the Winter Olympics?"

Harley squinted at Molly. "It *is* an Olympic sport, but part of the Summer games."

"Are you sure?"

"Positive, Molly," Harley responded. "So listen up. Okay?"

Molly clapped her hands. "Harls is talking," she announced, "and wants us to listen." She smiled at Harley. "My voice carries a greater distance than yours."

Not really, because CJ heard Harley and the other girls just fine whenever they spoke. But no fucking way would he say that, so Molly could hit him with a ridiculous fact that lived only in her pretty head.

"I don't need anyone else to listen to me but you," Harley snapped. "Volleyball is usually played with six players per team, although you can have nine on the roster. We all wanted to play, and the guys refused to break rank and come to our side. We've played like this before, and we've beaten them before. But I need you to focus."

"Everyone wants to play on the side of their privates?"

Mattie yawned. "If you mean pussies against dicks, then, yep. You're right."

"Really, Mattie?" Harley said in exasperation, then pointed to Wynona who was staring wide-eyed at their red-headed cousin.

Poor kid. The heathens on her team would scar her for life.

"I have the remedy," Molly piped in. She ran to the net, scooted under it and positioned herself between Grant and CJ.

"What the fuck are you doing?" Rebel asked, appalled.

"Breaking rank," Molly said happily. "It shows I'm a progressive, twenty-first century woman."

"We'll lose if you're over there," Wynona said with a frown.

At Harley's relieved grin, CJ hid his own. For a second, he'd been annoyed Molly deserted the girls, but fuck it. Harley liked it this way, so he did, too.

Harley ran backwards to her spot. "We got this," she said, picking up the ball from where Molly dropped it.

"Still think her tits are great now, Ryan?" Mark JB asked.

Molly glanced over her shoulder. "What's your name? And who's tits are you talking about?"

"S'up." Mark JB smiled and nodded. "Mark JB, and we're talking about yours."

Molly turned to Ryan. "You think my tits are great?"

"When they're bouncing," he said nonchalantly.

"Forget him, baby," Mark JB called. "Your tits are great all the time to me."

"Dude, you're so fucking lame," Ryder taunted, committing fully to being an annoying little motherfucker.

"Don't be jealous of my game," Mark JB responded, unfazed.

"Game?" Lou snorted. "Only in your tiny little brain. Leave the woman alone, bruh, and retain your dignity."

"The last time you saw a pussy you were being born, Mark JB," Ryder called.

CJ glared at his brother before the little fuckhead gave up their secrets about their porn stash. Dad wouldn't care. *Mom* would.

"Yo, fuckhead," Rebel called to her sibling in blondness, "the last time you saw a twat was a few centuries ago in your former life, so shut the fuck up."

"Nuh-uh!" Ryder yelled, the sunlight glinting off his golden hair. Haloed in the brightness, he looked angelic. "I came out Momma's! Me and CJ both—"

That was too fucking far!

CJ stomped to the wretched little asshole and cuffed the side of his head as Ransom cried, "Momma doesn't have a pussy!"

"Hit me again, fuckhead!" Ryder cried as CJ returned to his position. "I dare you."

Before CJ responded, Molly raised her hand.

"Yes?" Grant said, not bothering to control his laughter.

"I have a question," Molly said.

"We live in a democracy," Rory said carefully. "You don't need permission to speak."

Molly shook her head. "We live in a Republic." She placed her left hand over her chest. "*I pledge allegiance to the flag and to the United States of America and to the republic for which it stands, one nation under God, indivisible, with liberty and justice for all.* See? *Republic.* It doesn't mention a democracy."

"But Molly—"

"Forget it, Rory," Mattie advised, her look wishing imminent death on Molly. "Ask your fucking question so we can restart the game."

"CJ?" Molly called.

"Yo?"

"If Rebel didn't come out of a pussy, is she a test tube baby?"

"*Die!*" Rebel snarled, while the other boys laughed like fucking raving lunatics and the girls stood stupefied.

"There's a website to calculate the date of your death," Molly sniffed. "My date is February 32, 2199."

CJ's raggedy brothers collapsed on the ground and kicked their legs to coincide with their wild laughter.

Ryan's yelp abruptly halted the humor. "You fucking hit me with that ball, you little cunt," he snarled, snatching the ball from the ground and lobbing it at Rebel.

She jumped away, not giving CJ time to stomp Ryan for disrespecting her. She ducked under the net, dodging the punch that asshole threw at her to deliver one of her own to his jaw and knocking him on his ass.

"*Whore!*" Ryan started.

Rebel dove, landing on top of their cousin and biting his chin while digging her nails into his jaw. "I'll show you a fucking whore, bitch."

It was happening so fucking fast, CJ barely registered his little sister pummeling Ryan so badly, he needed rescuing from her. With Grant's help, CJ dragged her away but not before she got in a last kick.

"Let go of me!" She jerked free.

CJ wrapped his arms around her and saved Ryan's life as Grant helped the beaten motherfucker to his feet.

"Ryan, I swear if you ever fucking touch me again, I'll kill you," Rebel said, trembling in fury.

"C'mon, Reb," CJ muttered, hugging her tight just because he loved her, her heart pounding as much as his. He grabbed her elbow to bring her home, not realizing Harley and Mattie were there until they surrounded Rebel and embraced her.

"What about my birthday?" Ryan said around a cough, staggering to his feet.

"You're the jackass who fucked with my sister." Ryder folded his arms. "Fuck your birthday."

CJ *almost* pitied Ryan, but the hurt flashed across his features too fast, replaced by anger. He glared at CJ.

"I *know* you don't want some of me," CJ warned.

"No!" Rebel growled to Harley and Mattie. "I want to play the fucking game."

Ryan blinked, shock entering his battered face.

"You'd prefer to give fuckhead a good birthday than face Diesel?" Mattie spat. "Be a coward and a dumb bitch. See if I fucking care."

Rebel started for Mattie but Harley jumped between them and shoved his sister away.

"*Enough*," Harley ordered. "This isn't a boxing match. You want to play the game, Rebel? If you don't take your position, I'm going home." She turned to Matilda and pointed to the spot she'd been in. "Get over there. You didn't have to broadcast our private conversation. That's pretty low."

"I really hate you right now, Harley," Rebel said, stomping to her spot.

"You don't, so whatever," Harley responded, fisting her hands on her hips and glowering at Mattie until she too took her place.

Walking to Harley, CJ hugged her and kissed her cheek. "How about me and you leave these bozos so we can play Mario Kart?"

"After we beat your team," she said, backing out of his embrace and pointing to his place.

Brynn and Ava left the sidelines where they'd been talking and returned to their spots with Wynona following.

"Winnie, don't tell on us," Rory said.

Her little face, sharing a strong resemblance to Aunt Ophelia, was ashen. Normally, she stayed with the younger kids at the insistence of her parents. Today, she'd begged to participate in the game, and they'd allowed her to do so.

She craned her neck to look at Rebel, her idol. She'd even gotten the drop on Rebel's outfits for the day. At the moment, she wore a smaller version of Rebel's jean shorts and tank top. When he'd been at Uncle Val's earlier, he'd overheard Aunt Zoann laughing at how

Aunt Ophelia revealed Winnie's plans to wear the same denim skirt set as Rebel at the barbeque later today.

"Ro's right, Winnie," Rebel said now. "We might hate each other and regularly try to beat each other to death, but we keep it amongst us."

Winnie glanced at Rebel's bloody knuckles, then at Ryan's split lip, bruised face, and swollen eye.

"It's okay, Wynona," Ava reassured her. "None of us will let you get in trouble."

Brynn walked behind Wynona and squeezed her small shoulders. "Don't stress. Your cousins are never dull."

"You're my cousin, too, Brynn, so aren't they *your* cousins?"

"Nope, Winnie," CJ answered. "Brynn's mom and your dad are brother and sister so you two are cousins. Neither Aunt Georgie or Uncle Cash are related to any of us."

Winnie considered the words. "But aren't they your aunt and Uncle?" she asked after a moment.

Giggling, Brynn folded her arms and looked at CJ to continue.

"Go ahead, bro," Ransom taunted. "Make that shit make sense."

"Fuck off, big head," CJ ordered.

"I can explain," Molly offered.

"No the fuck you can't," Mattie inserted. "CJ tell her."

He nodded. "Aunt Ophelia, Aunt Zoann and my dad are sisters and brother. Since your mom, Ryan and Devon's mom, and my dad are related, we're cousins too."

"Oh," Winnie said after a moment.

"Don't forget Uncle Johnnie and Uncle Christopher are—"

"She's confused enough, Ryan!" Harley said.

"They're what?" Winnie asked.

"Cousins," Rebel said quickly. "They're cousins."

"Exactly," Brynn agreed. "We're all a big family, related by blood and, uh—"

"Love and friendship," Harley supplied.

"Yes!" Brynn smiled at Winnie. Poor kid was staring in wide-eyed confusion. "Our cousins are a happy bunch."

"Tell her the truth, Brynn. They're heathens," Grant said. "Far beneath your beauty and dignity."

Brynn swept her wealth of black hair into a topknot. "You're so full of shit, Harrington. You're as much of a heathen as them. As I am."

"Why don't we talk later and compare our heathen notes?" he suggested.

"Wee-woo, wee-woo," Ransom wailed. "That's the sound of the police coming for your old ass for chatting up Brynn, Grant."

Grant flipped Ryder off. "More time for note comparison from jail," he said, winking at Brynn. She giggled.

Mark JB shook his head. "You say my game is lame, Ryder."

Molly cleared her throat.

CJ lost track of her during the brawl, but she appeared unscathed.

"You have a really strange name, Mark JB. Are you related to the people who make JB Scotch? My dad loves that stuff. Wait 'til I tell him I met one of the founders. Would you autograph a bottle?"

Mark JB scratched the side of his head, while the other boys shifted. Harley glowered and CJ shrugged.

"I don't know nothing about JB," Mark JB admitted. "I'm not related to them. My dad's name is Mark, and I'm a junior. My name is Marcus Banks, Jr."

"Yeah, but if we called him Mark BJ, then—" Rory started.

Molly giggled. "Do you know 'bj' stands for blowjob?"

"What's a blowjob?" Wynona asked.

"Nothing," Rebel said quickly as Matilda blurted, "a dick suck."

"Oh." Wynona looked at Matilda. "What's a dick suck?"

"Well, we all saw that question coming," Rebel complained with sarcasm.

"Speak for yourself, Reb Elle," Molly told her, folding her arms and glaring at Rebel. "I didn't see it coming."

"Shocking," Mattie said with an eyeroll.

"Let me explain something to you, Molly," Rebel told her in a shittier mood than when she'd first arrived. "I can speak for you or whoever the fuck I want to. It's my mouth. If you don't like it, fine. I respect that. But what you're not doing is giving me your fucking looks. I'll pluck your fucking eyes out."

"Yanking her tongue out would be better," Matilda said, studying her nails.

"Can we play the game, please?" Lou called. "Molly's a nice chick. You girls got to ease up on her."

"That reminds me," Molly said before anyone commented. "Mark JB, you said a double negative. Remember? When you said, I don't know nothing...?" Her voice trailed off. She pointed to Lou. "And you didn't intro yourself so I can't thank you properly for defending me, so I'll just say much obliged."

"That's Lou," Harley said. "He's one of my little brothers."

The aggravation on Harley's face tickled CJ, and he laughed, capturing her attention. The moment their gazes met, he winked at her. Her answering smile removed the annoyance from her face and eased the crease in her brow.

"Mark JB's dad and our dad are brothers," Harley explained. "Ryan and Devon—" She pointed in Devon's direction where he stood somewhere behind CJ— "are brothers. Ransom and Ryder—" Again, she pointed at each boy— "are CJ's and Rebel's brothers." She pointed to Rory. "That's Rory, Mattie's older brother. Grant is Lolly's stepson." She nodded in Grant's direction. "And, finally, last but not least is Ava's brother, MC or Cameron Baptiste, Jr., or Mini-Cam—MC. They're the relatives amongst us."

"Who?" Molly asked.

"You don't really want to play volleyball, do you?" Harley said, instead of explaining how everyone was related for a second time.

"Of course, I do! Why would you say I don't?"

"Maybe, because you keep opening your fucking mouth and asking questions that we can talk about at the party," Rebel yelled.

"Isn't this the party?"

"Have we sung happy birthday to Ryan yet?" Matilda said. "We're in the middle of a clearing, playing volleyball. Does this look like a party to you?"

"You know—"

"Wait, Molly!" Ava held up her hand. "Don't answer that. We can have a lot to talk about at the actual party."

Wynona bounced from foot to foot. "Elle, I have to pee, and I'm bored. Can I go home?"

"Sure," Rebel said with a smile and tipped her head back after the little girl ran in the direction of the family homes. "We can't play. We're five short."

Harley threw the ball in the air and caught it again. "Let's see what we can do."

"You're going down, Banks," Rory called in good-natured fun.

"In your dreams, Donovan," Harley returned and poked her tongue out at him. She nodded to Rebel. "Do the countdown."

A short serve gave CJ's side possession of the ball.

Harley and the other girls were athletic and competitive. The guys did their best to keep the ball from Molly, and the girls did their best to get it to her. She managed one or two decent hits, but CJ and the other dudes still worried she'd fault them.

"Fuck, man," Rory grumbled, "these girls are beasts."

Beasts who wanted to run them to the ground and exert their dominance. Finally, the score tied at fourteen, with one rally remaining. Ryan positioned himself to serve.

"Hit that motherfucker to CJ's house," Grant said, grinning.

Laughing, Rebel flipped him off.

Ryan threw the ball up, then volleyed it with all his might when it came within reach. It tracked in Harley's direction, but it was high. Undeterred, she ran forward to give herself the momentum she needed to lift herself off her feet and return the ball to CJ's side with a powerful swing. Grant and Rory both dived for it, making contact with the ball at the same time. Even if the ball hadn't escaped the two of them and hit the ground, the fault caused by the double assist would've given Harley and her team the winning point.

"The motherfucker is duly hit, Grant," Harley said with a smirk, joining her teammates in laughter.

Once the girls accepted their congratulations with common ungraciousness, they talked and laughed amongst themselves. Rebel and Ryan's fight was just a blip in their day, like all their disagreements. The game worked off the last of their hostility and now everything was back to normal. Ryan kept his arm around Molly's neck, whispering to her while she blushed and giggled. Grant stayed close to Brynn, chatting her up and CJ hovered next to Harley.

"What did you do, dude?" Grant asked suddenly, poking CJ and nodding toward trees where the trail to the houses began.

'Law was storming in their direction, Diesel, Uncle Mort, Uncle Johnnie, and Uncle Val trailing behind.

Rebel's demeanor darkened again. Based on Mattie's words, CJ suspected Diesel's presence set her off, but before CJ could question her, his father demanded, "Which lil' fuckhead let Wynona walk the fuck through the forest by herfuckinself?"

"She had to pee." Rebel spared Dad a glare, then turned her head. "We were playing the game, so I told her to go to her house."

"Reb, Cash having a shit fit," Uncle Val said in annoyance. "I told the motherfucker to shut the fuck up. Don't let his bullshit ruin my boy day."

"Yeah, motherfucker acting like Winnie walked ten fucking miles," Uncle Mort put in. "She went to Johnnie. His house the closest to the clearing, so she walked on her own at most three fucking minutes."

"He interrupted our pool game," Uncle Johnnie grumbled, "coming to Christopher's after Kendall brought Wynona to him."

"Thank god, Uncle Johnnie," Diesel added. "I've lost enough to you today."

Rebel eyed Dad. "Why are you so angry?"

He studied her for a moment, glanced at Ryan, then continued with the conversation. "Cuz you the lil' motherfucker charged with babysittin' her."

Fuck, whatever happened, Rebel had really pissed off 'Law. He wasn't demanding answers. True, the kids were expected to settle their own shit, but when there was evidence of physical fighting there were at least questions.

"I ain't blamin' Cash for worryin' about his girl on her own," Dad went on, "but the motherfucker over the fuckin' top with that bullshit. I ain't in the fuckin' mood for him bein' so fuckin' overprotective when we on club fuckin' grounds."

Uncle Val grinned. "This not Psycho Stalker Wildman talking?"

"Uh, Prez, you do remember Meggie girl, right?" Uncle Mort questioned.

"Wynona is a child, Christopher," Uncle Johnnie said. "Megan's a grown woman and you're ten times worse."

"But he said she was a girl," Molly said before his father answered, pointing at Uncle Mort. She giggled. "You can't be a girl and a woman." Her eyes widened. "Oh, wait! You're talking about two different people? A girl named Meggie and a woman named Megan."

"Who—?" Dad started.

"No, shit-for-brains, we're talking about the same person," Rebel interrupted on a growl. "My mother. There's no way you're that much of a dumb bitch. *None.* I refuse to believe it."

Molly poked her lip out. "Reb Elle, you are so, so mean. Why do you stay so angry all the time? You have two emotions with me. Angry and angrier. That hurts my feelings." Before Rebel responded, Molly focused on Outlaw. "Are you related to CJ? You look just like him."

CJ stifled laughter at his father's shock. "That's my dad."

"No," Molly protested. "He can't be your dad if Rebel is your sister. If you look so much like him, she would, too."

"Ryder is my brother, and he's blond like Reb," CJ told her. "Rule is Rebel's twin, and he has black hair."

Molly studied each of his siblings before staring between CJ, Rebel, and Dad.

"I'm very good in science," Molly started with a sniff. "I think your mom needs to have a DNA test to make sure all of you are hers. Your dad might've brought somebody else's DNA home and gave it to her. All the kids might not be hers."

"And you wonder why I want to kill you." Rebel glowered at Ryan. "You're the asshole who invited her. Shut her up before I rip your tongue out so you never do something so stupid again."

"Reb Elle, you really need anger management..." Molly started, her voice trailing off and her eyes widening as she looked past Dad and the other men. "Oh my god! Oh my god! Oh my god! That's Sloane Mason! Sloane Mason." She drew in small, short pants, then began fanning herself. "I'm going to faint. Sloane freaking Mason!" she squealed just as the man reached them.

Molly barreled to Sloane, throwing her arms around him, and bursting into tears. "I love you!"

Grimacing and glaring at the snickers from the other men, Sloane removed Molly's arms from around his neck.

"Brynn—"

"I'm Molly," Molly said, grabbing Sloane's wrist. "She's Brynn." She pointed to Ava. "Our names sound nothing alike so I don't know how you got them confused."

"Wynona didn't need to pee," Matilda said. "She needed to escape before you brought her brain back to the preschool level you exist on."

"That isn't nice, Matilda," Uncle Johnnie chided. "Ladies don't harangue others."

"Harangue?" Dad, Uncle Mort and Uncle Val chorused as Mattie's face fell.

"Yeah, harangue isn't the right word, sir," Molly said gravely. "That goes on a lemon pie."

"I think that's meringue," Harley told her.

CJ admired Harley's patience. Molly was a fucking know-it-all who didn't know shit, didn't listen to what other people said, or just didn't care. He wasn't sure if Molly was truly ignorant, plain dumb, or the best comedian in town. Whatever it was, Harley rarely lost patience with her.

"Meringue is a dance, Harley," Molly said in exasperation.

"Merengue is a dance," Lou corrected, always ready to jump to the defense of his sister. "Harangue means a scolding. Meringue is a kind of icing."

"I'm pretty sure you don't know what you're talking about," Molly insisted. "I am very articulate with big words and there's no such word as merengue."

"Uncle Mort's a music major, Molly," Rebel said. "Of course, Lou, as his son, would know the meaning of merengue."

"Oh my god, you people are so stupid," Molly hissed. "First, music has nothing to do with dancing. Second, if Lou is related to Uncle Mort, then he can't be your uncle."

Mattie gritted her teeth, huffed out a breath, then folded her arms. "Why not?"

"Lou is Black and Reb Elle is White. They can't be related...ohhhhh! Of course, they can be. Southern ancestors."

"What...?" Uncle Mort started.

"Don't ask, Daddy," Harley said.

"My ass got a question," Outlaw said.

Ryder rested his elbow on Ransom's shoulder and grinned. "We want to hear it, Dad."

"I'm pretty sure your brain has a question, not your ass, sir," Molly said as if she spoke to a simpleton.

Dad snapped his brows together, as Ryder and Ransom burst into wild laughter.

"I'll try to answer," Molly continued, "but I really would like to get back to telling Sloane my real name.

For some reason, I'm always interrupted from my original topic and end up way off track."

Dad's growl made Molly jump.

"Okay, so, maybe, your wife doesn't need a DNA test to see if Reb Elle is really hers. Reb Elle growls just like you."

"Why you call my girl Reb Elle?" Dad asked, ignoring the dumber shit for *dumb shit*.

"Wynona calls her Elle, as a nickname, but her real nickname is Reb, so her name has to be Reb Elle, not Rebel like I thought."

Dad folded his arms. "By any fuckin' chance, you eighteen?"

"I'm sixteen," she said with an indignant gasp. "Oh my God! I have wrinkles and my age is showing?"

"Too soon, Outlaw," Uncle Val sniggered. "She a child, so no insults."

"Whisper what you want to say, Daddy," Rebel said with a semblance of real glee, "and I'll be happy to tell it to her in my own words."

Diesel and Uncle Mort snickered.

"CJ?"

"Yes, 'Law?"

"You invited her here?"

Indignation at his father's low opinion roared through CJ. "Ryan invited her. I didn't know she'd be here." If he had, he would've skipped the volleyball game.

"Molly's really pretty, Uncle Chris," Grant said. "I can't blame Ryan for inviting her. I would've if I was in his place."

"Your old man would bar you from club property if he heard that," Uncle Val said.

Molly stared at Sloane as he wrapped an arm around Brynn's neck and kissed her cheek. "Get away from him,

Ava! I saw him first. I need a marker so he can autograph my tits."

"Fuck, that must bring back nightmares for you, Sloane," Uncle Val said around laughter.

Sloane scowled and Dad frowned. Uncle Val held up his hands.

"What happened to you, Reb?" Diesel asked, taking in the cuts and bruises on her face, hands, and legs.

She gave him a nasty look. "None of your fucking business, fuckhead. Don't ever talk to me again."

Diesel stiffened.

"Rebel—" Dad growled.

"You're a disgrace when you should be an example, Rebel," Uncle Johnnie huffed. "You're offending your cousin's tender ears and embarrassing yourself. If you say another foul word, young lady, I'll spank you."

"If you fuckin' touch my fuckin' girl, motherfucker, I'll pound *you*," Dad snapped.

"We don't use such language in Matilda's presence, Christopher," Uncle Johnnie said stiffly. "If you can't control your little girl and *my* daughter wants to be in her company, then it's up to me to step in. If she doesn't want to take a cue from Matilda, maybe she needs to follow Harley's example."

Uncle Mort tossed the cigarette he'd been enjoying. "Son, I know you not bringing my daughter into your bullshit."

CJ watched all three girls. Harley's horror at being weaponized to make a point, Mattie's dejection, and Rebel's crestfallen shame.

Dad guided Rebel to the side and started a low conversation with her. CJ wanted to go to her, but he refused to leave Harley.

"I-I'm not perfect, Uncle Johnnie," she blurted into the tense silence. "I-I...today...I-I said motherfucker."

Uncle Mort raised his brows. "You did?"

"Yeah, Daddy," she said with hesitation. "S-so, um, Rebel isn't the only girl who curses."

"Harley," Uncle Mort said, shaking his head in disappointment. "You not saying motherfucker right, baby."

"Are you fucking kidding me?" Uncle Johnnie snarled.

"Do you see me laughing, motherfucker?" Uncle Mort returned. "Only reason Prez not leaving pieces of your bitch ass around this motherfucker is 'cause of Ryan's birthday. What the fuck is wrong with you, Johnnie? I curse. Bailey curse. Roxanne curse. You think I'm looking down on my daughter for doing it too? Further, Reb not my kid and I feel like beating your ass the way you shamed her."

"You and Kendall use bad language," Uncle Val said, "yet you want Mattie to act like a nun. So what if she says *motherfucker*?"

Uncle Johnnie glared at Mattie. "Do you say such awful language?"

"No, Daddy," she mumbled, staring at her feet.

Rory stepped next to his sister, who stood a head taller than him. "Dad, I say motherfucker, fuck, cock, pussy, and a bunch of other shit. You and Mom don't get mad at me."

"You're a man," Uncle Johnnie said.

"And you fucking clueless," Uncle Mort responded as 'Law and Rebel rejoined their group.

Dad looked at her with expectation, but she clenched her jaw and folded her arms. "I swear to fuck, Ellie, if you ain't greetin' your brother like you got fuckin' sense, I'm chainin' that fuckin' garage for the rest of the fuckin' summer."

She lifted her chin, glanced between Dad and Diesel, then smirked at CJ. "Hello, brother," she cooed. "There, Daddy," she said crisply. "I greeted my brother."

Anger percolated from their father, then he smiled. "Okay, baby, you win," he conceded and walked to Molly. "You a fuckin' kid. Sloane a grown ass motherfucker. Even if he ain't, have some fuckin' respect for yourself and don't fuckin' invite no grown motherfuckers to put their hands on your fuckin' tits."

"They're just tits," she countered, hands on hips. "Duh! You're an old dude, but you should stop being so uptight."

The five men looked at her, then at each other, and guffawed with laughter.

Brynn tried to insert herself between Molly and Sloane.

"He's mine." Molly looped her arm through Sloane's and yanked him back. "I warned you, Ava. You can't have him."

"And neither can you," Sloane snapped, pulling away from her and returning to Brynn's side.

"No—"

"Yeah..." Brynn said, placing her body in front of her father's. "I'm Brynn, Molly, not Ava. And he—" She directed her thumb over her shoulder, in Sloane's direction— "is my father."

Molly's eyes widened and she gasped.

"Reb, since you didn't answer Diesel, would you tell me why Ryan all beat up and you a little bruised and battered?" Uncle Val ventured.

"Ryan's the stupid fuckhead who invited Molly, Uncle Val," Rebel answered sullenly. "I plead temporary insanity at hearing her date of death is estimated to be February 32, 2199."

"We understand, baby," Uncle Mort said. "You don't have to say no more. Your uncle Mort would beat a motherfucker too after hearing that shit."

"I'm just going by what the computer said," Molly said indignantly.

"Yeah, well, stomp that motherfucker cuz it ain't got no fuckin' reason to exist." Not waiting for Molly's reply, Dad looked at CJ. "Diesel stayin' at the house with you when the rest of us go on vacation."

"Wait, what?" Rory piped in. "CJ gets to stay home?"

"No way!" Ryan protested.

Harley frowned. "You aren't coming?"

"Thanks, Christopher," Uncle Johnnie bit out. "We have a mutiny on our hands because of your blithe announcement. CJ should be required to go on our yearly vacation like the rest of the kids."

Dad stiffened. "When I fuckin' ask your motherfuckin' ass to fuckin' think about what the fuck my kid doin', I'll let you fuckin' know. 'Til then, shut the fuck up, cuz it ain'tcha fuckin' business."

"I want to stay with CJ, Dad," Rory said, a plea in his voice.

"We'll discuss it later, Rory," Uncle Johnnie said with annoyance.

"Aww, Dad," Rory went on. "Those vacations suck. They're for the small kids. I'm a young man. I should be able to stay, too."

"If Diesel don't mind, you can stay behind," Uncle Val said to Ryan. "But if you're too old to go, then so's Devon."

"That's not fair!" Ryan cried. "I knew you were handing me bullshit, old man." Not waiting for a response, he stormed away.

Stuffing his hands in his pockets, Uncle Val sighed, but he looked so sad. "I need to finish setting up for the barbeque," he said and started off.

"Wait, Ryan's Mr. Dad," Molly called. "He invited me and now he's gone. Do I have to leave? Is the party canceled?"

"Come on, Molly," Harley volunteered, "you can come with me and Ava to my house. We can shower and change for the barbeque."

"Thanks, Harls, you're so sweet, even if I think of a loud motorcycle every time I hear your name. I would love to drive one."

"Get her the fuck away from my fuckin' ass," Dad snarled. "Ain't givin' a fuck how fuckin' old a motherfucker is. Sayin' you drive a fuckin' bike, cross the fuckin' line."

Harley grabbed Molly's hand. "Come on, Molly. You ride a motorcycle," she explained.

"No, a motorcycle uses a liquid to make it run and it has a motor. You know? Motorcycle? That means you drive it. You can ride a bicycle or a horse or...or a greyhound—"

"Um, yeah, okay," Harley said, yanking her away, with Ava hot on their heels.

"Wait—" Rebel began, starting off behind them.

"Your lil' ass comin' with me, Ellie," Dad interrupted, his voice bringing her to an abrupt halt. "You comin' to fuckin' apologize to Cash for not lookin' after Wynona."

Instead of answering, she glared at him. Dad stared at her until she flushed and looked away.

"My ass almost forgot, Ellie," Dad said, "your ma want you to meet Tabitha. Diesel girlfriend," he added. He smiled, not fazed by the devastation clouding her face.

CJ understood 'Law's tactics. Rebel had disobeyed Dad *and* tried to play him. Still, his little sister's comeuppance was painful to watch.

"They moved in together over the weekend," Dad added.

Even Diesel winced.

"Reb'll get to be in her first wedding when you and Tabitha marry."

"Goddamn," CJ mumbled.

"I fucking hate you, Daddy," Rebel said on a broken sob.

"Ain't givin' a good fuck, Rebel," Dad said. "Cuz whatcha ain't doin' is thinkin' you bitchin' me out. My ass on your side. Every fuckin' day. All fuckin' day, but if you playin' me like my ass the fuckin' enemy, then that's the fuckin' way Ima treat you, baby."

"I'm telling Momma you lied on her."

"Ain't lyin' on Megan. She wantcha to meet Tabitha. And even if she *ain't* sayin' that shit, what the fuck you think *you* doin' tellin' her what I said? Not a motherfuckin' thing. You ain't dividin' me and your ma to conquer us."

"Those are your stupid rules," she spat.

"Nope. They your ma's rules."

"Then not only is she a fucking liar but she's stupid too," Rebel snarled, forgetting the cardinal rule.

Until then, Dad's annoyance showed vestiges of anger here and there. His growl snapped Rebel to her senses and she stumbled behind CJ a moment before Dad tried to snatch her.

"Dad!" CJ said, the buffer between them, though the black fury on his father's face frightened him. "She's upset. She doesn't mean it. Reb loves Mom."

"I'm sorry, Daddy. I didn't mean what I said about her."

"Rebel," Dad said, his voice culled from the depths of hell, "you grounded. I wantcha fuckin' cell phone, your laptop, your tablet, and your keys to the garage. Ima tell your ma no more fuckin' allowance. On second fuckin' thought, gimme your fuckin' debit card too."

"You're ruining my life!" she wailed. "I can't even shop?"

"Your ma too stupid to fuckin' count her money to deposit in your account and too much of a fuckin' liar to keep doing the shit she been doin' since you was ten."

She gave up her spot behind CJ and stepped in front of him. "I'm sorry, Daddy! Please. I can't survive without shopping."

"Oh fucking well. Call my ass a motherfucker, assfuck, fuckhead, what the fuck ever 'til you blue in the fuckin' face. Whatcha ain't doin' is disparagin' your ma when she ain't even here to defend herself. Your problem with me, not her."

"Rebel," Diesel started.

She stiffened. "Fuck off," she ordered, on the verge of hysterics. "You're not my brother. You'll never be my brother and I'm glad because I fucking hate you. You moved out and forgot I existed. You're a stupid motherfucker and—"

"Rebel, baby, come with me," Uncle Mort said, putting an arm around her shoulder.

"No, Uncle Mort. Molly's there and—"

"Go with Uncle Mort. You look like a beet with blonde hair, Rebel," Ryder observed.

"Shut up, stupid," Ransom said. "She looks like a tomato but you don't tell that to a girl."

"Let's go to Roxanne," Uncle Mort said. "Prez can calm down. You can clean up and we can all regroup for the pool party."

She sobbed against Uncle Mort. "I don't want to go to the party."

"I'll send Tabitha home before you arrive, Rebel," Diesel told her, pity in his eyes. "But I'll be there. I haven't spent time with Uncle Chris in weeks."

"I haven't seen Lolly in months," Brynn said. "I'm walking with Grant over there. We can go together. He's telling me about Boston," she explained when Sloane lifted a brow in question.

"Come on, Reb," Uncle Mort said and nodded to Grant and Brynn

“She needs to clean up her mouth, Christopher,” Uncle Johnnie complained again once Sloane walked away with the other four. “She’s a bad influence on my daughter.”

“My ass would be fuckin’ insulted if I ain’t know for a fuckin’ fact, I’m lookin’ at the motherfucker that’s the fuckin’ bad influence on his girl,” Dad said flatly, glanced at Uncle Johnnie from head to heel and sauntered away.

Birth

Patricia

Staring at her tiny son, Patricia Donovan smiled tenderly. At just a day old, the boy was smaller than she'd imagined him because her belly had been huge. Thankfully, her labor went easy and quickly. Barely six hours. Her boy had been anxious to come into the world.

Now, he slept in her arms, his little mouth moving as if he dreamed of nursing. Overwhelmed by a new type of love, Pattie's heart melted. The battle to keep her son had been worth every harsh word and painful lick Daddy gave.

Living at his whims concerned her, but her father meant well. He wanted the best for his children. However, his behavior had been so erratic the past few weeks that she couldn't trust his temper. Everyone tried to placate him, but when life frustrated Daddy he took it out on those he loved most.

Pattie didn't know much about babies. When she was a mom for a week in her Home Ec class, Daddy was horrified and refused to allow Pattie's participation. This year, the teacher didn't bother offering the assignment to Tess. Mrs. Pettigrew was probably still smarting from the hell Daddy brought on her for Pattie's time in her class. *However*, even without the stupid assignment, Pattie knew babies cried a lot.

Daddy's reaction to the noise worried her. He liked peace and quiet most of the time. Besides, out of sight, out of mind. Any sound from her son would remind her father of the boy's presence.

The baby wiggled in her arms. Humming a tune from her own childhood, she reveled in the mid-morning solitude, though her private room at Hortensia General needed a remodel. The peeling paint and dingy window should've depressed her. Instead, she enjoyed the seclusion, not even missing her TV. The one in her hospital room didn't work.

It didn't matter. She had her son. And she intended to *keep* her son. With her. Alive. As much out of harm's way as possible. To achieve her goal, she'd done what she had to.

"Baby boy," she whispered, kissing his little nose.

The opening door interrupted her peace and she lifted her head. Light from the hallway glared into the room.

"Pattie," Tess greeted as she walked in and closed the door, throwing their surroundings into shadow.

Pattie refocused on her son. Tess reached her side and the weight of her stare burned; Pattie didn't look up.

"I came to see my nephew," Tess announced timidly.

Pattie ignored her. Acknowledging Tess would bring her face-to-face with her sister's small baby bump.

Tess sniffled. "Forgive me," she whispered. "Pl-please, Pattie. I-I fought. I-I resisted. I didn't want to," she finished miserably. "I didn't know..."

Pattie snapped her head up and glared at her little sister, younger by eleven months. "What didn't you know, Tess?" she hissed, tightening her hold on her son.

Tess traipsed to the light switch and flipped it up. The brightness hurt Pattie's eyes. Even her boy screwed up his little face. Absently, she wondered if he would be a light sleeper like she and Mama.

"I didn't have a choice," Tess said into the silence, back at Pattie's bedside. Gray eyes beseeched her. "I-I didn't mean for it to happen." She placed a hand on her belly. "But I want this baby like you wanted yours."

Pattie's stomach turned in revulsion and anger. "I don't care what you want, Tess. I had to fight to keep Sebastian's son and Daddy is just turning a blind eye to *your* pregnancy. I don't think so. Abort your baby or don't talk to me again."

When Pattie confessed her condition to Daddy, she'd had to do it on her own.

Tess had had backup from their mother.

Tears slid down Tess's milk white cheeks. Whereas Pattie had dark brown hair like Mama, Tess's was pale yellow and fine as cornsilk. Her bow-shaped lips and fine skin grossly contrasted Pattie's wide mouth and susceptibility to acne. Tess was just as she seemed—delicate and sweet. *Meek.*

At one time, her sister's distress would've moved Pattie. Not now. The last two weeks of her pregnancy had been hell. Daddy had been particularly mean. Mama stayed in tears. And she'd discovered Tess was also expecting.

Her sniffles awakened Pattie's newborn and he whined, squirming in her arms. Unsure how to hold his head, she was afraid to lift him to her shoulder as she'd seen the nurse do earlier. His face reddened and he released a wail.

"Get out. You woke him up with your stupid crying." Pattie wanted to weep along with him at the enormity of her responsibility. Fingers shaking, she fumbled with the opening of her hospital gown. She'd had to put it on backwards for her son to have easy access to her breasts. When she guided her nipple to his mouth, he screamed louder. "Momma's here," she murmured, kissing the top of his head and rocking him in agitation.

Tess took him into her arms. She smiled tenderly, then lifted him onto her shoulder and cradled the back of his head, swaying from side-to-side in a gentle rhythm.

"Mrs. Millstone taught me how to soothe an infant."

Since the age of thirteen, Tess babysat the Millstone children. Pattie had wanted that job, but Daddy refused, then allowed Tess to accept the position.

"Sweet boy," Tess crooned.

Pattie sidled a glance at her sister, shocked at the ease Tess calmed the baby. Falling into a fussy sleep, he rested his little head on her shoulder.

Some of Pattie's anger and despair slipped away. She took her son back into her arms and gave her sister a small smile.

"I'm not getting rid of my baby," Tess said quietly. "Even for you to keep loving me."

Grinding her teeth together, Pattie didn't know what to say. Sebastian Caldwell had been her ticket away from Daddy. She didn't like the biker and he'd used and abused her when he'd first took her, but *he* was the lesser of two evils.

The door opened again. Alarm raced through Pattie as Mama and Daddy walked in. Hating the sight of her mother's black eyes and swollen jaw, she lowered her lashes. Mama paused next to Tess, while Daddy ambled to the other side. Tension tautened her muscles, yet she remained still. Moving might upset the balance and set Daddy's temper loose.

Her little baby whined. The sound hurt her head and sent nausea through her. She feared Daddy snatching her boy away as he had her kitten. She'd loved that little orange ball of fur. Once too many times, Sherbet had meowed in her tiny cat's melody. Daddy threw her in a garbage can and covered it. When Pattie snuck outside hours later, it was too late. Her kitten smothered.

Somehow, she managed not to cry at the memory or shiver in fear.

"What's his name?"

"I'm not sure, Daddy," she said as calmly as possible. She had an idea of what she wanted to call her son, but she was waiting for his father to arrive.

"Give him to me."

She cleared her throat. "He's agitated from all the excitement. I'm trying to settle him and handing him to you will only rouse him further."

It took a lot for her to contradict her father. From an early age she'd been taught that he always knew best. Mama preached what love meant. Forgiving the unforgiveable was a Donovan doctrine. It had taken her months to forgive Daddy Sherbet's death. If he harmed her baby, she didn't know if she ever *could* forgive him.

Mama forgave him over and over. Somehow, she exonerated him of the burns and beatings and belittling.

Daddy leaned closer, brought his hand to the back of her boy's head. He was a tall man with big hands. They could easily crush the fragile skull. The thought exacerbated Pattie's headache and nausea. For the first time since her visitors arrived, her stomach was starting to hurt and the episiotomy stitches burned.

The door to her room opened yet again. Daddy's hand fell away and he stepped back.

"Cee Cee's right behind me, Logan," Sharper Banks said around a cough.

Relief flooded Pattie and she buried her nose against her son's belly to hide her smile. She ignored her mother's sharp intake of breath and Tess's cry of dismay. It wasn't about them or herself any longer. She had to protect her son.

"Why is he here?" Mama's shrill voice cut into the silence.

"Pattie just gave birth to his son," Sharper responded, oversimplifying matters and stating the obvious as usual. He remained just inside the room, holding the door open.

"I don't want him here when I give birth," Tess cried.

For the first time in two weeks, Pattie felt a frisson of sympathy for her sister. Her earlier gentleness with the baby started Pattie's thaw. Hearing her distress completed it.

Even though he entered with the same stealth he had the first night he crept to her bedroom, Pattie knew the exact moment Cee Cee entered her hospital room. She smelled the smoke and leather. She felt his presence. The hot excitement that dipped to cold fear and spiked to anticipation. The spurs on his motorcycle boots jingled as his footfalls clipped toward her.

As he halted at the foot of her hospital bed, she raised her head and met his green gaze. Windswept ebony hair framed his sun-browned skin. His denim vest...no, *cut*...still proclaimed him 'President', while leather chaps covered his jeans.

"Hey, girl."

"Hey."

He removed his black riding gauntlets and threw them on her bed. "I had a boy. Yesterday," she added for good measure.

Cee Cee grinned at her. His eyes remained empty. "Let me see him."

As he approached the bed, he gave Daddy a look and he stepped back without comment. Huffing, he sat in the chair near to where he stood. Pattie's eyes widened. She'd never seen Daddy give way to anyone, especially another man.

She was so confused, she almost missed Cee Cee lifting her baby out of her arms. She settled against the pillows, wishing for pain meds. Now that pain had set in, she was really feeling it. She closed her eyes.

"What's his name?"

Cee Cee repeating Daddy's earlier question made Pattie open her eyes again. "I was thinking about Christopher," she murmured.

"My name's Sebastian."

"I don't like that name," she retorted.

Snickering, he glanced at the baby again. "I approve," he announced. "Good work. Want to see my boy, Sharper?"

He walked over and took her son into his arms. Unlike Cee Cee, Sharper wasn't good at holding a baby.

"You drop my kid, I'm tossing you from the roof, motherfucker."

"You'd have to get me up there, asshole," Sharper responded, bringing the baby to Mama.

"Give him to Tess," Pattie said, shooting to a sitting position. She didn't trust Mama not to hand the baby over to Daddy.

Surprisingly, Sharper followed her directive.

"Bring him to one of the cunts outside so they can take him to the nursery," Cee Cee instructed.

Mama glared at Cee Cee. "Come, we'll go together, Tess."

Suspicion welled in Pattie and she shoved the covers aside. "No. Give him to me and I'll ring the buzzer."

"He'll be fine, Pattie," Cee Cee said with certainty.

Unease slid into her. Cee Cee sounded cold and calm, just as he had when he'd forced himself on her the first time. She'd been hysterical. He'd been unmoved.

The moment Mama and Tess left the room, Cee Cee pulled a big gun from his waistband. It looked like the same one he'd threatened her with. One moment his hands had been free and the next he'd reached behind himself, grabbed the weapon, and shoved it into her mouth.

Exactly what he did Daddy now and dragged him to his feet by his collar.

"Warnings don't work with you, Donovan," Cee Cee growled.

"Cee Cee—" Sharper began.

"Shut the fuck up, dickhead. I don't have the goddamn patience to revisit shit."

"What the fuck are you doing here anyway? Who the fuck told you Pattie had gone into labor?"

At Sharper's question, she tensed, waiting for Cee Cee to expose her. As much as she feared her father and worried about her son's safety at his hands, she loved him and didn't wish to alienate him more than her pregnancy had.

"Does it matter who told me?" Cee Cee asked in that nonchalant way he had.

Yes, if it got her father killed. She wanted safety, not death.

Cee Cee shoved Daddy back into the chair as if he didn't know if he wanted him on his feet or not. The gun no longer rested in Daddy's mouth. It was aimed between his eyes.

"I told you to leave my fucking kid alone, Logan."

"Tess has your spawn in her belly," Daddy spat, unaffected by the imminent danger. "It's yours to do as you see fit."

"Keep it and her," Cee Cee said with disgust. "As long as you don't hurt the kid."

"She isn't Pattie," Daddy said tiredly. "I don't care if Tess keeps the baby. I want better for Pattie."

"I don't give a fuck what *you* want, Donovan. *I'm* not Sharper."

Confusion hit Pattie. In the next instance, she completely forgot the comment. Sharper was escorting Daddy out of the room and she was alone with Cee Cee.

He lit a cigarette and stared at her, blowing smoke out of his mouth and allowing it to pour out of his nostrils. "I want the kid's name to be Sebastian."

His treatment of Daddy peeved her. "I don't remember asking you what you wanted," she retorted.

"It'll remind Logan he's my kid. It'll protect him, Patricia."

"Having your last name will do the same thing."

"You're an annoying little cunt."

"And you're an ass."

His green eyes narrowed. "I don't like annoyances. I get rid of them so be careful."

She threw him a sullen look.

"*You* called *me*."

"I didn't trust Daddy."

Hooting with laughter, Cee Cee squeezed the cigarette out between his thumb and forefinger, then shoved it in his pocket. "If I'm the lesser of two evils, then Donovan is more of a motherfucker than I thought."

"He sold me to you. That says it all."

"You wanted cock from me."

"You brutalized me for three days. I didn't want that."

"I was angry with your old man," he said with a shrug. Unapologetic as ever. But that was Cee Cee.

"He still sold me!"

"Your cunt is as expendable as your mother's and your sister's."

She blinked at his outrageous statement. “My mother? Wh-what are you talking about? What do you mean my mother?”

“Exactly what I said. I don’t like dry pussy, so I’ll punch Donovan if he sends Elmira to me again. And I can’t tolerate a sniveling cunt like Tess. He gave me Elmira to get you back and he sold Tess to me to save his fucking life.”

Tears rushed to Pattie’s eyes. “You’re cruel and vile.”

“I’m crushed.”

Annoyed at the tears sliding down her cheeks, she swiped at them with impatience. “Take Christopher with you. Daddy hates him.”

Swift anger replaced Cee Cee’s shock and Pattie hastened to correct her mistake.

“Daddy wasn’t harming the baby before you arrived,” she added quickly.

“*Yet.*”

She flinched at the growl.

“Did I say that?”

“You didn’t have to.”

“Cee Cee, please! You’ve somehow misread my father. He’s a hard man but he means well.”

“For himself, Patricia. He doesn’t give a fuck about anyone else. Logan is—”

“You’re my son’s only chance,” Pattie interrupted, afraid she’d let slip how much she feared for her son’s life. She’d only just met her boy yesterday, but she’d protected him in her belly for months. Many days, she felt he was her only friend. But to continue safeguarding him, she had to let him go.

Cee Cee tipped her chin up and studied her. He cocked his head to the side. “You’re serious.”

It wasn’t a question. Determination to protect her child steeled her backbone and oozed from her.

"I love him," she whispered. "I don't know how else to protect him."

"By killing Logan."

"You can't kill Daddy."

He snatched his hand away. "Why is everybody always protecting that motherfucker? Well, I understand Sharper's motives."

"And they are?" she demanded, surprised she picked up on his insinuation. But she was no longer the same sheltered girl Daddy had sold. "My father likes women. And he doesn't like anybody who isn't white."

"Does Sharper look white to you?"

Laughter bubbled up and she rolled her eyes. "Not him, dummy. He's Daddy's best friend. He doesn't count."

The amusement curving his mouth fascinated her. Cee Cee was a hard man. She couldn't remember him ever laughing out of joy. He knuckled her cheek, then brushed his lips against hers. "Come with us."

At his husky invitation, hope curled inside Pattie. He was kinder than he pretended. Although she'd decline the offer, hearing it made her believe she'd been right to call him. "I can't."

Amazement widened his eyes. "Why not?" he demanded, hostility seeping into his tone.

"You impregnated my sister." And apparently had sex with Mama. And almost killed Daddy.

"If it makes you feel better, I knocked up two other bitches besides Tess."

Stiffening, Pattie clamped her lips together.

"Careful," he cautioned in the tone warning of impending violence. "You're digging a fucking hole for yourself that I'll be happy to bury you in along with pieces of Logan before covering you both with a ton of wet mud."

“That’s not how you convince a girl to runaway with you.”

“I’m not trying to convince you of a fucking thing, Pattie. I asked you to come with me and my son.”

“He’s mine, too.”

“You pushed him out of your pussy, so that’s obvious.”

She hated his crudity. For all Daddy’s faults, he rarely used bad language.

“I might’ve been wrong about you being a good girl,” Cee Cee said darkly. “Are you like every other twat alive? A scheming, jealous slut?”

“How can I be a slut if I haven’t made love to anyone but you?”

His amusement returned, his mercurial mood as frustrating and frightening as it had been when he’d kept her for three days. “Made love?”

“Didn’t we?” she squeaked. “I-I mean after the first day when you hurt me so badly.”

For long moments, he remained silent, his green gaze touching on her lips, her nose, her eyes, and her hair barely secured in a messy topknot. “We did, babe. You never came when we fucked. That makes you sweet and innocent. *Good.* Not like my mother. No matter what she promised me or what my old man did to her, she forgot it all to get her pussy off.” His hands balled into fists.

Afraid, Pattie shrank back. “Don’t beat me,” she whispered. “I’m still healing from the baby.”

Anger burned in him, steamed from his pores, and reddened his face. “Come with me and my boy,” he snarled.

“I can’t,” she said, trembling. To save her baby, she’d pushed away memories of Cee Cee’s abuse. “I want loyalty and you won’t give me that.” It wasn’t a lie.

“You want away from Logan,” he spat.

"I want Christopher away from Logan."

"So you're throwing *Sebastian* away, instead of being a mother and coming with us."

"I am not throwing him away—"

"Shut up before I fucking strangle you. And this time I won't stop until you're a dead fucking cunt."

He stared at her, then turned on his heel and stalked toward the door, the spurs jingling each step away from her.

"Wait, please!" Pattie cried, desperate. He halted. "Please, Cee...Sebastian. I just want him safe. If I had money, I'd move to my own place to get him away from Daddy. And...and I...his name is Christopher. St. Christopher was fearsome and fearless. Strong and courageous. In Greek, it is *Christophoros*, and it means 'Christ bearer'. Daddy makes us listen to Sharper read and discuss the bible two or three times a month. Sometimes, it is my only comfort. I can't explain what it is doing to me to give up my son. I think he's my only friend. He isn't, though. He's my baby. I'm his mother. I can't be selfish. There's so many reasons I can't come with you. I've been so angry with Tess. She needs me, though."

He returned to her side. "I'm not taking Christopher," he told her, his way of accepting the name she wanted. "I've been hanging close by until you pushed him out. I expected Donovan to not test my goodwill. He's a stupid motherfucker, so I should've known better. Last I heard, the baby was due in ten days. If you hadn't called me yesterday, I wouldn't have known you were in labor. A clear violation of my instructions to Logan."

His disgust alarmed her. She didn't want Daddy killed. However, Cee Cee announcing he wasn't taking Christopher superseded fear for her father. "You have to take him—"

"I'm leaving, Pattie," he said gruffly. "Heading East."

"But your club is in Portland."

He shrugged. "I've made a deal with Sharper. I'm relocating the Scorpions so the Dwellers can get a foothold."

"I overheard Daddy and Sharper talking about the Dwellers soon having support on the Atlantic Coast for cross-country transactions. They must've been talking about you. I..." Her brows snapped together. "Why would you make a deal with Sharper if the Death Dweller MC belongs to Daddy?"

"It's Club business," Cee Cee said sharply. "Nothing you should know about. Opening your fucking trap can get you fucking killed."

"I would never betray Daddy, Sharper, or you. They don't know I overheard."

Cee Cee grunted.

"You can't go if you're not taking Christopher. You'll be on the other side of the country if I need your help. With you so far away, who knows what Daddy might do? You asked me to leave with you and Christopher without mentioning your intentions. If you leave, I'll hate you."

"It's not like I give a fuck, cunt."

"One minute you're gentle and the next you're vile."

"I hate bitches. They're scheming cunts. Only worth fucking and popping out kids. If I didn't have to empty my balls and leave a legacy when I bite it, I'd make it my mission to kill all of you." Blood lust fired his eyes. "You're disappointing me as well. I'm furious that I've misjudged you. You don't give a fuck about me or my kid."

Bewilderment hit Pattie. One minute, he understood her and believed her. In the next, he accused her of lying. She barely kept up with his flip-flopping and didn't know how to respond.

"Killing Donovan would solve so many fucking problems," Cee Cee grumbled, scrubbing a hand over his face. "When I instruct motherfuckers to do shit, they know better than to defy me. I never allow disrespect. If I ask to be informed when a bitch has my kid, my orders are followed. But your old man plays fucking games."

"I called you to protect my son, not to kill my father," she said, a bout of insanity turning her moods as capricious as his. "And how many children do you have?"

"Killing that motherfucker would protect the kid," Cee Cee spat, ignoring her question. "Killing Donovan would protect Sharper, Wally, Kaleb Paul and Joe."

"The mechanics?" She'd never met Joe and Kaleb Paul, but she'd heard about them. "And Wally is called Rack now."

"He's a stupid motherfucker, too," Cee Cee scoffed. "I can't fucking believe the position..." He growled like an angry dog. "Why the fuck do you protect Logan?"

"Because he loves me. All of us." She paused and frowned, thinking of her brother. Maybe, Daddy didn't love Simon. "He's my father. I owe him my allegiance."

"You're a fucking stupid bitch. I don't hide my evil, Patricia. Your *daddy* does, and that's the worse snake in the grass in the fucking world."

"Daddy isn't evil. He's stern. We'd all be lost without—"

"Shut your fucking trap. Logan stays alive because of Sharper. Not you or Joe." Another growl. He began pacing. "I curse the fucking day Donovan ever came to my fucking club." Gripping the bed railing, he glared at her. "I have nine kids besides Christopher and the pup Tess is carrying. Sebastian is my oldest. He lives with me. Bashful little asshole. Afraid of his own fucking shadow. That's why he's called Bash."

"You have a son named Sebastian already?"

"I have two sons named Sebastian. One named Charles. Mikey. Billy. Only daughter I claim is Celia. My little sister, Kimber, took a shine to her. Otherwise, I have no use for girls. I paid off the four other cunts who dropped daughters and sent them on their way."

"If Tess has a girl, you can't send her away!" Pattie cried.

Cee Cee gave her a putrid look. "I can do any fucking thing I wish."

"But—"

"Shut the fuck up. Your entire fucking family is a thorn in my fucking side. If I wasn't riding out, I'd take my kid and bury you, Logan, Elmira, and Tess after she pushes her brat out."

"You're a madman. This is a hospital. If someone overhears you and anything happens—"

"This shitty hospital would've closed years ago without my money. If I say jump, they ask how high."

"This is Hortensia. Your club's in Portland."

"Don't make a fucking difference. *This* is where my money worked best to my benefit."

Small town, less law enforcement and red tape, Pattie guessed.

Stomping to the door, Cee Cee opened it and yelled, "Sharper, bring that motherfucker to me."

He returned to the chair he'd yanked Daddy from and sat in brooding silence until the door opened and Daddy and Sharper walked in.

"Patricia and I are getting married."

Ignoring Pattie's gasp at his casual announcement, Cee Cee stared at Daddy with a look of distaste. Blood drained from her father's face.

"I'm signing the documents to give Christopher my name. Our wedding will take place in a week."

"No!" Daddy managed, on the verge of fainting.

"She's already agreed, fuckhead," Cee Cee said coldly. "You sold her pussy to me. It's mine to do as I see fit. I'm marrying her. She'll be my wife. Christopher will be my legitimate kid. He's untouchable by you or any other motherfucker who values living."

"What about the East Coast?" Sharper asked.

"I'm still going," Cee Cee gritted, getting to his feet, stalking to Daddy, and grabbing his collar. He yanked him closer. "Listen well, Donovan. I want to bury you so fucking bad I can almost taste your blood. But Sharper made that cunt he's marrying cough up money and paid for your fucking life. I'm taking his cue. Extra insurance for my fucking kid. I'm giving you money to keep him alive. Because I don't fucking trust you, I'll buy Joe and Kaleb's lives too. If you take my money and fuck me over, I'll feed you your fucking eyeballs and pull your fucking tongue through the sockets."

He shoved Daddy so hard, he crashed into Sharper, who quickly steadied Daddy, the action oddly tender.

Daddy swept Sharper with a cold glance, brushed off his sleeves, and looked at her, missing Sharper's death glare. "You've agreed to marry him, Pattie?"

At first, she didn't know how to answer. *Yes* would protect her son but make Daddy her enemy. *No* left Christopher vulnerable but her in her daddy's good graces.

"Well, Patricia?"

"Yes," she said softly at Daddy's sharp voice. "I'm marrying Cee Cee."

INTERLUDE

The Good Son

Simon

Agreeing to be a son's father shouldn't have been taken as lightly as Simon Donovan had when his daddy ordered him to do so. He didn't understand why the kid couldn't know the identity of his real parents. But Daddy had a reason for everything, so Simon was a good son, and followed along.

His heart banging in an uncomfortable rhythm, he swallowed and glanced at the casket containing his little sister's body. Even in death, her skin kept that godawful pinkish hue. She resembled a badly painted mannequin, instead of a girl, frozen in death, three months after her sixteenth birthday.

In his arms, Tess's week-old son, John, squirmed. Pattie sat next to Mama on the sofa, holding her six-month old baby, tears sliding down her cheeks.

"Why'd Daddy insist on having a home funeral?" Simon whined, agitated.

He didn't know how he'd ever sleep in the house again. Mortuaries were spooky because of all the dead bodies. And he'd heard murder victims haunted their killers unto eternity. But Tess had been good. She wouldn't want him frightened. Knowing her, she'd understand he'd injected her to hasten her death. She'd been so frail from her days of starvation. The long labor and massive blood loss weakened her to the point of no return.

Christopher made a noise, drawing Simon's attention. Smiling tenderly, Pattie lifted her dark-haired son and situated him on her shoulder. He was a puny thing, unlike John, only days old, but strong and strapping, and showing no signs of the hell Daddy put Tess through.

John whined. Huffing, Simon stood and stared at the boy, swaddled in a thick blanket. His eyes were blue, the same color Christopher's had been, though his were changing.

"Where's your daddy?" Mama asked tearfully, rising to her feet and ambling toward the white coffin to stare at the corpse.

She wore the same styled black dress as Tess in a macabre tribute. Mama had wanted Pattie to follow suit, but she'd refused. She'd changed since moving to her own place after Christopher's birth.

Yards of black bunting decorated the house. Incense covered the scent of death.

Once again, Simon's heartbeat took an erratic rhythm. He wondered if Tess's ghost sought revenge by ruining the mechanics of his heart. Death frightened him, especially now. He wasn't sure if his wish to please Daddy would absolve him of murder. Maybe, his good intentions canceled out a broken commandment. When he got the chance, he'd ask Sharper.

Several sets of footsteps created an uneven pounding across the wood floor.

Mama bent and sobbed against Tess's still form. Wondering if she'd smell almonds, Simon almost dropped John, when he wiped the sweat suddenly beading his brow.

The baby released a furious wail, the sound rising above Mama's weeping. Pattie stood, nervously bouncing Christopher on her shoulder. Though she'd turn seventeen in a few months, she seemed to have aged well beyond her years. If her life didn't change, her beauty would fade quicker than Mama's.

If not for photographs, Simon wouldn't have believed Mama had ever been as beautiful as Pattie.

Daddy walked to Mama and pulled her into his arms.

Guilt pressed into Simon at the display, since he couldn't ever remember such tenderness from his father.

"Come, Elmira," Sharper said kindly, taking her elbow and guiding her back to the sofa.

Cee Cee Caldwell walked to the casket, swept Tess with an impassive look, and turned away. Not once glancing at his screaming newborn or Simon, he went to Pattie and took Christopher into his arms.

"Hi Simon."

He lifted his head at his girlfriend's greeting, frustrated by his crying nephew...*son*. "Hi Mari," he mumbled.

Marissa's thick, dark brows drew together. "He's really loud, isn't he?"

Daddy plucked the baby out of Simon's arms and cradled him with an affection he'd never shown anyone else. "He looks like me," he said gruffly.

"He's a fucking newborn, asshole," Cee Cee said dryly. "He doesn't look like anyone."

"Why are you here?" Daddy demanded, his body stiffening in anger.

"I'm here because I wish to be," Cee Cee responded, without a shred of warmth. "I'm here to see my son." He smirked at Simon. "And to meet his cousin. Or should I say brother?"

"Cee Cee," Sharper chastised.

Keeping Christopher in place with one hand, Cee Cee started off, throwing over his shoulder, "Pattie, Simon, come with me. I need to talk to you." He disappeared, certain they'd follow.

Of course they would. It was Cee Cee. They had little choice but to obey.

Outside, Simon found the cloudy day cool and depressing. Cee Cee had sat Christopher on his bike, holding him tightly. A child, about eight or nine, with black hair and green eyes, smiled between Cee Cee and Christopher.

"Don't let your brother fall, Bash," Cee Cee directed. "I'll beat your ass if you do."

Bash grinned. "Yes, sir."

Pattie leaned against the porch railing, silent. Simon shoved his hands in his pockets. He wanted to go back inside. Surely, Sharper had begun the services.

Grabbing a cigarette from behind his ear, Cee Cee lit it, then shoved the lighter back into his pocket and walked up two steps, not clearing the third to reach the porch.

"I'm sending a motherfucker to you, Pattie."

"I beg your pardon?"

He drew on his cigarette, then released the smoke, his mouth curving into a half-smile. He was deceptively laid-back. If one didn't look closely at Cee Cee and allowed his good looks to blind you, one missed the cruelty hardening his face and the coldness deadening his gaze.

"Fred Sterling," he announced. "Sharper has been accepted into the Masters of Divinity program, so he's leaving too. Wally's a fucking brick head. I'm not entrusting my boy's well-being to him."

"Pa look!" Bash called, roaring with laughter. He'd removed Christopher from the bike, stretched his little arms to hold his hands, and was now helping him to walk. The baby was grinning, encouraged by his brother's giggles. "I got Christopher to walk."

Cee Cee nodded. "You're a good brother. Me and you will have extra bourbon tonight."

"Can Christopher come with us and have some?" Bash asked, his look as hopeful as his tone.

"Absolutely not!" Pattie said. "He's too young." Her glare at Cee Cee showed she felt the same about Bash but was wise enough to withhold her opinion. "How can you send someone to me when *I'm* your wife?"

"Wife?" Cee Cee scoffed. "Five months ago, you declined that position. You're my fucking bitch in name only, cunt."

High color flushed her cheeks, and she sidled a glance at Simon. Christopher squealed happily, accompanied by more laughter from Bash. To be so young and innocent. Carefree.

"I swear if you do this, I'll tell our son I conceived him through rape."

"To hear *you* tell it, you did," Cee Cee replied with a shrug.

"The first day and a half with you was awful," Pattie cried. "It *was* rape."

"Tell the kid whatever the fuck you please, Patricia. I don't give a fuck. I've already forgotten how your pussy feels. What I *do* give a fuck about is making sure Donovan doesn't harm my kid."

"It isn't because you love him," she charged. "It's to best Daddy."

"He's a small kid," Cee Cee said flatly. "If the motherfucker lives to eleven or twelve, and Logan fucks him up, that'll be on him."

Pattie gasped. "He'll still be a child."

"Will he?" Cee Cee fired back. "Either he'll be a fucking sniveling pussy like Simon or he'll be a fucking fighter, but he *won't* be a child if he has to grow up around motherfucking Donovan."

"Hey, you can't talk about my daddy like that," Simon fumed.

Cee Cee glanced over his shoulder and narrowed his eyes. "What the fuck are you doing about it?"

"Simon, shut up," Pattie ordered. "Daddy has just forgiven me, Cee Cee. If he thinks I'm breaking my vows to you, he'll see me as nothing but a whore."

"Here, Pa," Bash interrupted, unperturbed by the arguing. He'd walked Christopher to Cee Cee, who didn't hesitate to lift the baby into his arms. "Can I have a cigarette?"

"Only half," Cee Cee responded. "Look in the saddlebag."

Drawing herself up, Pattie grabbed Christopher from Cee Cee. "You're a fucking madman," she charged. "Bash is a child—"

A slap across her cheek interrupted her. Flicking his cigarette away, Cee Cee hit her again, splitting her lip. Christopher began whining. When Cee Cee raised his fist, Pattie shielded the baby, leaving herself exposed.

"Every time I'm ready to bury you, cunt, you do something to earn a reprieve." He snatched Christopher into his arms as Pattie dropped to her knees, fell back on her haunches and sobbed.

"Here."

It took a moment for Simon to realize Cee Cee was holding Christopher out to him. He scrambled to take his nephew into his arms, horrified when Cee Cee took his cock out and forced it into Patricia's mouth.

Holding her head in place, ignoring her tears and blood, her gagging, he rammed his dick in and out. Ecstasy washed over his face and he threw his head back. His swollen prick stretched Pattie's lips, further ripping the split opened by one of his licks. Sliding out of her mouth, he yanked her head back and shot off in her face, then punched her. She toppled to the concrete, sobbing in a heap.

He allowed her tears for as long as it took him to tuck his cock back into his jeans and zip his fly. Then, he bent, grabbed her hair, and yanked her to her feet.

He stared at her, not caring about the damage he'd done to her face, unmoved by her trembling.

"You fucking think I don't know what a vicious cunt you are, Patricia?" Cee Cee snarled. "It seems mighty fucking odd to me that you found out I was coming to sign John's birth certificate and Tess suddenly ended up dead. Oh, that's right. You were the good sister, looking after her because she was sick in her last weeks of her pregnancy. Not because you were fucking starving her. She's not a corpse in that fucking coffin because you convinced dumb ass to inject her with cyanide." He stared at her. "But you've played yourself. That baby is Logan's atonement for selling Tess to me. I'd leave you to his fucking wrath if it wasn't for Christopher."

Cee Cee punched Patricia in the belly, and the sound made Simon flinch. On the ground again, she curled into a ball. Cee Cee spat into her hair.

"What about the baby you lost? Sharper's kid?" he demanded. "But you didn't lose that kid. You got rid of it. You know Logan would've killed you for fucking Sharper. Trying to steal your daddy's boyfriend is low even for a bitch like you."

Simon reeled back, almost dropping Christopher, who had fallen asleep.

"You're taking up with Fred, Patricia," Cee Cee ordered, sparing a brief glare at Simon before looking at her again. "I'm out of patience with your entire fucking family."

Without warning, the door opened, and Sharper walked out. He looked between Cee Cee and Simon before his gaze found Pattie.

"They're waiting for these two, asshole. How the fuck am I supposed to explain why Pattie is so beaten?"

"The same way you'll explain sticking your cock in her."

Simon shrank back, afraid for his life at the violence in Sharper's eyes.

"You told me to keep her safe, Cee Cee."

"Where in those fucking words, did you hear *fuck her*?"

"She offered. I accepted."

Cee Cee glared at him. "I'm sick of all you motherfuckers. Since Donovan walked into our fucking lives, there's been chaos. Bickering like fucking bitches. Petty arguments. When I blaze out this time, I never want to see any of you fuckheads again. In fucking life. Fuck all of you."

"Really, Sebastian? What about Wally? Goddamnit, what about *me*? We're fucking family—"

"Wally's my brother, not you. You're just a second or third cousin. Because why not? Our family tree is as fucked up as everything else."

"My parents took you and Wally in, when Uncle Novis died. You would've gone to the orphanage—"

"Which is where we all fucking ended up at anyway, Sharper," Cee Cee said tiredly.

"My mother and father died."

"Pa, I'm tired," Bash called, waving at Sharper. "Hey, rev."

Smiling, Sharper nodded. "I'll take Pattie and Christopher inside, while you talk to this sniveling coward."

At his approach, Simon swallowed and stepped back.

"Give me the baby," Sharper snapped.

Trembling, Simon carefully took Christopher from his shoulder and handed him to the minister, who then turned and walked to Pattie.

"Up, Patricia. We need to go inside."

Pattie heaved in a breath.

"Now!" he commanded.

Sniffling, Pattie dragged herself up and staggered to her feet. Seeing her battered face, Sharper winced, then nodded to the door. "Go inside and clean yourself up. If Logan asks what happened, tell him you were playing with Bash and fell out of the tree. Do you understand?"

Her swollen face crumpling, she nodded.

"You're a good girl, aren't you?" he crooned. "And good girls keep secrets. Remember?"

"Y-yes."

When he said nothing more, she took Christopher and limped inside, leaving the door ajar. Sharper started behind her.

"Sharper?"

He stopped at Cee Cee's call.

"Keep your cock out of Patricia."

"You almost sound jealous, Cee Cee," Sharper taunted. Sniggering at Cee Cee's flip off, he turned on his heel and followed Pattie's path, closing the door behind him.

"Are we about to hit the road, Pa?" Bash asked.

"Go play a bit, boy," Cee Cee said, fixating his gaze on Simon. "I have some business to tend."

"Okay, Pa." Without a word, Bash scooted away.

"You got a hard cock when Pattie sucked me off?" Cee Cee demanded.

Wary, Simon shook his head. The sight had turned his stomach.

"Ever had pussy?"

The lifting of Cee Cee's brow told Simon he'd best answer with words.

"Daddy said it's a sin to lie with a woman before marriage."

"Is he chopping your fucking cock off if you disobey him?"

"I want to be a good son, Cee Cee, so Daddy can be proud of me."

"*Daddy* will never be proud of you, numb nuts."

Despair rose in Simon. "He said he was. I got Marissa to play along and sign the birth papers for John."

"*Money* got that cunt to play along," Cee Cee scoffed.

"But—"

Cee Cee stepped in front of Simon, so close their noses almost touched. "Will I have to fucking kill you for wasting space as a stupid motherfucker?"

"No," Simon squeaked, his voice cracking like a young boy's instead of a grown twenty-three-year-old.

"Why'd you commit sororicide?"

Simon frowned. "I don't know what that mean."

"Killing your sister, dumb fuck," Cee Cee growled.

"That's not homicide?"

Snarling like an animal, Cee Cee yanked his .44 from behind him and shoved it between Simon's eyes.

"Please!" he cried, tears rushing to his eyes.

Insanity brightened Cee Cee's gaze.

"Daddy! Help!" Simon screamed. "He's going to kill me! I'm a good son! You told me."

Grabbing Simon's throat, Cee Cee cocked the hammer. "Shut the fuck up. I'm finished being nice and I'm sick to fucking death of giving you motherfucking dirty Donovans a fucking pass. Pattie loves you, and I need that bitch half stable to raise my kid. I'm leaving *for good* and erasing you motherfuckers from my memory."

"Okay," Simon sobbed, his need to pee rising. The fear and tension weakened his bladder. Any minute, he expected to piss himself. If Daddy ever found out, he'd never let Simon live the humiliation down.

"Sharper is marrying you and Marissa, as soon as he finishes with your sister's last rites."

Cee Cee's conversational tone was surreal, like he didn't have a gun pressed to Simon's head and the trigger ready to fire.

"When we get back from the cemetery, I'll change and marry her."

"I don't have fucking time to wait until you bury that bitch," Cee Cee told him. "You and Marissa are marrying *before* the hearse comes to take Tess away."

"But—"

"Shut it," Cee Cee warned.

Immediately, Simon snapped his mouth closed. He had so many questions. He'd never dare ask his father for answers to all the revelations he'd heard today.

"Fred'll contact me if anything happens to my kid."

Christopher.

"*You*, pussy face, along with Marissa, will be John's stabilizers. Understand me? You'll never have the balls to stand up to Donovan, but my kid'll have a fighting chance at sanity if he's not completely influenced by Logan. Nod your head if you think you're up to the task."

Not wanting to discover the consequences of not following the orders, Simon obediently nodded.

"Logan, forever the motherfucker, wants his shabby fucking farmhouse rebuilt."

"Daddy insists I live here with John," Simon pushed out.

"The house will be big enough. You'll get money every month."

Simon widened his eyes. "Daddy'll let me?"

Narrowing his eyes, Cee Cee clipped Simon's jaw.

"Ow!" he moaned, grabbing the spot Cee Cee hit and trembling again, unable to push words out of his mouth to beg for his life

A moment before Cee Cee pulled the trigger, his finger moved.

It clicked.

Simon pissed himself, his shaky legs unable to hold his weight. He sank to the concrete, the stream of pee halting but leaving him in a puddle.

Red-hot humiliation rushed through him at Cee Cee's wild laughter.

"You're your daddy's son, after all." With that cryptic statement and still chuckling, he backed away and called for Bash.

PART TWO
TIME
FLIES

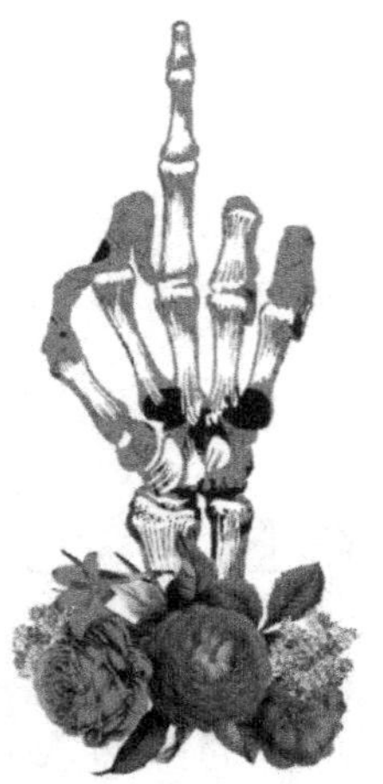

Chapter Twenty

"Come on, Harley." Holding her hand, CJ guided her to the treehouse built for him and his siblings years ago. "I won't let anything happen to you."

Harley feared the dark. Lights along the way helped, but they were still in a forest without enough lamps to remove the scariness. The July night was cool, damp, and foggy. If he wasn't so nervous, he might've played a practical joke or thought of a way to tease her.

With Rebel grounded and Mattie *protected* from devilseeds, Harley had been around him even more. Usually, she was with the girls doing girl stuff and CJ was with the boys doing his things, until a point in the day when they broke off and did best friend stuff. Harley had to either spend hours on her own until CJ was available or run with him and the boys.

She ran with him and the boys. Which made him even more aware she was a girl. On the football field, she had to sit on the sidelines. On the soccer field, she kicked ass. At the mall, they dressed in jeans, motorcycle boots, and T-shirts. She dressed like a little fashionista and smelled of jasmine. At parties, they acted cool. She laughed and danced and socialized. At the pool, they wore swim trunks and sunscreen. Harley wore little bikinis that barely covered her chest and showed too much of her legs.

Weeks ago, fine. One moment she'd been flat-chested and then the next...the next...*Goddamn.*

Even though Ryan was fucking Molly, he noticed Harley more and so did Grant, and CJ didn't like it. She was wary of Ryan, but she entertained Grant. CJ had never been so relieved that Grant would head back to Boston in a couple weeks.

That reminded CJ how time flew by this summer. Only yesterday they'd been in the clearing playing volleyball on Ryan's birthday and the stress of school was just an annoying memory.

Now, the annual family vacation was days away, CJ had two weeks of summer school left, football camp started a week later, and today was *his* big day.

Reaching the treehouse, he released her hand and nodded to the steps, the small lights on each one not denting the darkness. "You go first. I'll be right behind you."

She thumped his shoulder and laughed. "Nice try, but I'm wearing a skirt."

He leered at her. "A very short skirt."

When she bit her lip and glanced at him, he drew in a deep breath and willed his racing heart to slow down. He hoped she liked what he'd done for her.

He took her hand in his again, then led the way up the steps. At the door of the elaborate treehouse, doubt crept into him. If Harley accepted, their relationship would change. She'd go from being his best friend to his girlfriend.

"Everybody will start looking for us," she warned as they stood in front of the door. "We just up and left the party."

"It's *my* birthday," he corrected, not making a move to go in. "The sweet one. I'm allowed to creep away."

She laughed again. Harley was such a happy person. "It can be your sweet sixteen," she conceded, "but I think super would fit you better."

His chest swelled at her words and his nerves calmed. She'd dropped little hints she saw him as more than a best friend for days. Weeks. Months. He'd be a liar if he said the sudden appearance of breasts and curves hadn't also caught his attention.

"How about sexy sixteen?" he murmured.

"That works, too," she agreed with a smile.

He brought her delicate hand to his lips and kissed the back of it, his gaze never leaving her face. Her eyes widened a fraction, but she stayed silent.

"Come on, Harls," he said gruffly. "I made something for you."

"It's your birthday," she whispered. "You're the one who should get the gifts."

Not responding, he opened the door, then stepped aside, allowing her to precede him. The sweet scent of the roses hit his nose and she gave him a curious look.

"Go see," he encouraged.

Nodding, she walked forward to the playroom. He'd thought about decorating the bedroom on the second level but that would've been too blatant.

"Oh my God," she breathed.

He closed the door, then grabbed the remote from the console and pressed play. As *All of Me* by John Legend filtered through the sound system, CJ stuffed his hands in the pockets of his jeans.

Dozens of roses and balloons decorated the room. The lit fireplace replaced the chilly wetness from outside and aided the strings of lights crisscrossing the ceiling. A sign with the words, *I love you, Harley*, hung from the center of the ceiling.

The firelight reflected in her eyes, brightening them to topaz. In preparation for Disney World, she'd gotten box braids. They framed her face, hiding the few pimples dotting her honeyed skin.

Unable to stand still, he drew her into his arms and she smiled, then laid her head against his chest and followed his lead. Mom and Lolly and Aunt Bailey loved to dance. He supposed he'd picked it up from MegAnn, tickled at the times when it was just him, his siblings, and his parents, and she forced Dad to slow dance with her.

As CJ held Harley and felt her body against his, smelled her floral scent, he understood why his father sometimes acted so grouchy after a song ended and Mom turned her attention to him, his sister, and his brothers. He wanted to be alone with his wife.

Harley melted against him, and CJ's erection hurt. Before he led Harley upstairs, he'd text Grant and ask if his cock should be in pain. Normally, he reserved these questions for Dad. However, 'Law would be madder than a motherfucker and Uncle Mort would be gunning for him.

The conversation they'd had in the diner seemed so long ago. Still, the promise he'd made was uppermost in his mind. That night, he'd jerked off, imagining of Symphony's lips around his cock. Coming left him breathless and had his eyes rolling back in his head. The next morning he'd torn up her phone number and hadn't thought of her since.

Because Harley mattered most of all.

Closing his eyes, he kissed her forehead, loving her with everything in him.

"What...How did you do this?" she asked after the song ended.

"Diesel helped me."

"This is so...so..."

"Sexy?" he supplied, sweeping her braids to one side and arranging them over her shoulder.

She nodded, pink undertones staining her honey color.

He pulled out the two rings he'd safeguarded all day. He held them out to her. "Promise rings for you and me. Wear yours and I vow I'll love you the rest of my life. I'll protect you. Cherish you."

She stared into his eyes. "All the things you already do."

"I brought you here to give you my ring and..." His voice trailed off and the first bit of uncertainty hit him.

"And? Tell me. I won't be mad."

"To kiss you," he finished, tired of offering her the ring when she made no move to take it. His hand fell to his side. "I brought you here to kiss you." His face flamed and he dropped his gaze. "I've never kissed a girl before. I've always wanted my first kiss to be with you." His first everything.

She tipped his chin up and they stared at each other. The day she turned eighteen they'd marry. They were meant to be together.

"You've had grown women throwing themselves at you." Harley's sweet, awed voice broke into CJ's thoughts. "Most of the girls on the squad are in love with you. Yet—"

"They don't matter to me, Harley. You do."

Tears rushing to her eyes, she stepped back and looked at her toes. "I-I can't."

He studied her reaction, pondered her refusal. "You're lying."

"I'm not, CJ," she insisted around a sniffle. Still not looking at him.

The high he'd been riding all day teetered, caught between hope and despair.

"Harley—"

"You're my friend," she interrupted, stiffening her spine and finally meeting his gaze. "My best friend. I love you so much. If a relationship between us doesn't work out, we'd ruin our friendship, too."

"No. No, love," he promised, taking her in his arms and hugging her. "We were born to be together. There's nothing that can ever come between us. I love you. I'll never stop loving you."

She melted against him for the briefest of moments, then she stepped out of his arms. Her mouth trembled. At any moment, she'd dissolve into sobs. "I love you," she whispered. "But not the way you want me to. You'll always be my best friend, CJ, and I refuse to allow anything to ruin that."

Clenching his jaw, CJ nodded, obediently leaning down so she could kiss his cheek.

"I want to go back to the party."

Not speaking, he turned on his heel and led the way out, his heart smashed into a million little pieces. His high definitively crashed and burned. He wanted to be alone, but Harley feared the dark, so he couldn't allow her to return to the house on her own.

Walking over one of the brick bridges 'Law had built over the moat surrounding the house, CJ guided Harley to the back door, installed especially to get to the treehouse and play area.

"I'll be in in a second," he managed, when all he wanted to do was...*cry*.

Harley stepped into the coolness of the house, then turned to him. "Please don't hate me."

He pulled his last cigarette from behind his ear, took his lighter out of his pocket, then lit it. "I could never hate you," he told her, blowing a ring of smoke away from her. "You'll always be my number one bro."

His words didn't appease her. She looked devastated.

Without another word, she hurried away. CJ closed the door, then leaned against it, finally giving in to his broken heart.

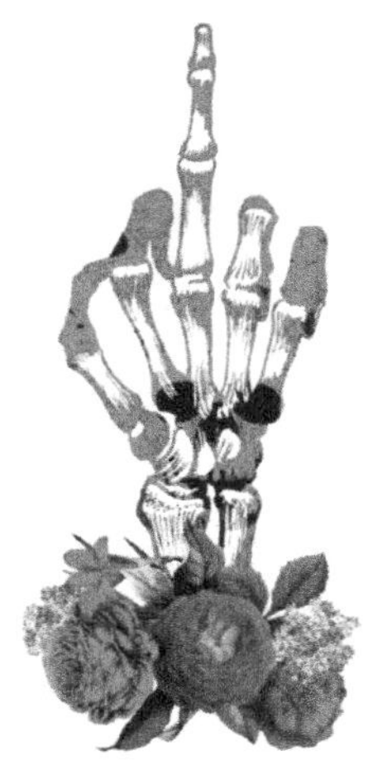

Chapter Twenty One

CHRISTOPHER

"Christopher?"

The sound of his woman's voice traveled to Christopher just as he reached the kitchen after walking through the house to check the door locks.

"Yeah, baby?" he called, waiting for to catch up to him.

CJ's birthday party went well, even if the women had spent most of the evening talking about their fucking Mardi Gras charity ball happening in a few months.

Fuck it and those fucking monkey suits.

"You're in here alone," Megan said as she walked in.

At first, only her mini robe dress and platform heels caught his attention. Her feet in the air while she wore those shoes and he fucked her...

"Christopher, have you seen CJ?"

The concern in her voice registered. Worry creased her brow and brightened her eyes.

He straightened, and his cockstand deflated. "What the fuck wrong?"

"I can't find CJ." She touched her chunky side braid. "He isn't in his room. He didn't even tell Harley goodbye a couple hours ago."

Not finding his boy in his bedroom wasn't a big deal, but not seeing Harley out? That shit was another fucking thing altofuckingether. Christopher hadn't realized she'd left because Mort and Bailey had only headed home ten minutes ago.

As soon as they could, him and his boys had escaped to his mancave to drink and gamble. They'd touched upon a little club business. The Scorched Devils had backed off their bid to be absorbed by the Dwellers. The Noxious Gnomes, with their stupid fucking name, still operated as a non-threat. Rumors of the American Scorpions floated in the air, but no one had found any evidence they were nearby.

Mostly, Christopher and his motherfuckers hid from additional discussions for the Mardi Gras ball and toasting CJ.

"Do you think CJ's at the club?"

"Nope. He here somefuckinwhere, baby," he said, hating to see her distress.

His boy better have a good fucking excuse for upsetting Megan.

"He probably down in the basement." They had every fucking thing imaginable down there to keep their kids entertained.

"He isn't. I went there before I looked for you."

"He here," Christopher stressed.

She rocked on her heels, drawing his attention to her legs. They would feel so fucking good wrapped around his waist. "Aren't you worried?"

Walking around the counter, Christopher drew her into his arms, inhaling her cherry blossom scent. "The lil' motherfucker here. I ain't got no fuckin' alert CJ left the fuckin' premises."

"It's just that today's his birthday."

Christopher glanced at the clock on the wall. "Motherfucker about fuckin' over now. It's 11:30."

"He's been so distracted all day. I thought once everyone left, I'd wish him a proper happy birthday. He's sixteen today, and I wanted to tell him what he means to me. I've been doing it since he turned ten. Sixteen is a special birthday. I definitely wanted to do it today."

"I underfuckinstand, Megan." And he did. CJ was their firstborn. His boy and his wife had almost fucking grown up together.

Her pregnancy with CJ had been the easiest. Her next pregnancy with their second son ended with her almost dying and Patrick not surviving. After Axel's birth, Christopher policed her birth control. One fucking slip-up and she'd ended up filled with Gunner. The lil' motherfucker was three-years-old, and Christopher suspected Megan was getting baby fucking fever again.

Fuck him, they already had eight lil' motherfuckers. True, Diesel was grown, so she couldn't fucking baby his ass. And CJ, her unadmitted favorite, was almost fucking grown. Rebel had lost her fucking mind. Rule wanted to pray and draw. Ryder, Ransom, and Axel, each separated in age by a year were the terrible fucking triplets and Gunner was a terrifying toddler.

Taking her face between his hands, he leaned down and kissed her.

In October, Megan would turn thirty-five. It was a milestone, and he knew he had to do something special for her. Yet, for him, it would be her thirty-sixth birthday that meant even more. They would've been together exactly half her life. They had met the day she turned eighteen, and Christopher's life hadn't been the same since.

Lifting her in his arms, he turned and sat her on the counter, claiming her mouth in another kiss. Tasting her gave Christopher the ultimate high. Her scent, her nearness—*her*—was like the air he needed to breathe.

She remained, now and forevermore, his everything.

"Ima find the lil' motherfucker, baby," he promised after he pulled his lips from hers.

She met his gaze and nodded, believing his words because of her unwavering trust in him. Leaning forward, she pressed her lips against his again and wrapped her arms around his neck.

"I love you," she said.

"I love you, too, baby," he said huskily. "My ass the luckiest motherfucker afuckinlive. My children lucky lil' motherfuckers that you their ma, Megan."

She rested her head against his shoulder. "Maybe, CJ thinks my birthday ritual is boring. He might be hiding."

The lil' motherfucker better not be. "You got every fuckin' right to tell my boy how much he made your life better and cry over his baby fuckin' pictures. CJ come outta *you*. That give you the fuckin' right to tell him how much he mean to you everyfuckinday if you fuckin' wanna. Ima find the lil motherfucker and bring him to you. Just don't take too fuckin' long cuz I ain't fucked you since early this fuckin' mornin'. My cock missin' your pussy."

"You're so bad, Christopher."

"That's why you fuckin' love me."

"Always," she whispered. "By the way, I think I finally found the perfect chandelier for the foyer."

Redecorating the massive motherfucker they lived in fell under the same category as the annual Mardi Gras: minimal interest to keep Megan happy and steer clear of pussy lockouts.

"I gotta find CJ, baby," he said, using a low-motherfucker move to get out of hearing about all the shit she intended to do to the house. She was concerned about their boy. He wasn't. If he really thought CJ had left the premises, *then* he'd worry. But Megan was CJ's ma, so nothing but seeing him would appease her.

Lifting her off the counter, he grinned and stole another kiss from her before setting her on her feet. "Go upstairs, baby," he whispered.

Shifting from foot-to-foot, she rested her hands against her belly.

The action raised his suspicions. Now that he thought about it, his woman had been overly emotional for a few days. And hadn't she fucking thrown up this morning?

"Megan—"

"CJ's had a long day," she said in a distracted tone, dropping her hand to her side. "If he's too tired, just send him to his room."

"CJ sixteen not six," Christopher snapped, wanting to address his worry about a possible pregnancy and annoyed that Megan was so anxious over their boy. He'd slap the piss out of the little motherfucker for concerning her. Meanwhile... "He can keep his motherfuckin' eyes open long efuckinnuff for you."

She sighed. "Okay. I'll make sure the boys are tucked in, then go to Rebel's room and talk to her until you come up."

"What the fuck she doin' that you gotta talk to her?" he asked in suspicion.

His girl had been grounded this entire summer and he might extend it until she turned eighteen. She was barely civil when he saw her, which was rare, since she avoided his fucking ass as much as possible.

"She saw Diesel earlier today when he stopped in to bring CJ his birthday gift. Whatever it was. I didn't see it before they left for a little while."

"Ima make CJ show it to you."

"I tried to talk Diesel into staying for CJ's party, but he said he had business to see to."

"Same fuckin' thing he told me, Megan," Christopher confirmed, leaving it at that.

She wrinkled her nose. "It seems strange that he'd stay for Ryan's party, even if he was with you and the guys, but couldn't do the same for CJ."

Christopher felt the same fucking way. He remained silent, allowing his woman to work shit out in her head.

"What do you think of Tabitha?"

"That she a fuckin' schemin' cunt. Goin' from paralegal at the law firm to movin' in with our kid."

"Kendall said she checked out. Her work history. Her background. Her associate's degree. Everything."

Unfuckinfortunately. "Riley couldn't find nothin'."

"Diesel moved out not long after she started working at the firm. We were weeks away from starting the construction for his house." She sighed. "I was hoping CJ would've turned up by now."

"Go upstairs, baby," he encouraged, annoyance toward CJ *and* Diesel surging.

Christopher didn't have many rules for his children, but as long as they respected their Ma, everyfuckinthing else could be worked the fuck out. It wasn't a rule needing much enforcement, especially from his boys.

They loved her...

Unease slipped into him. CJ wouldn't just disregard Megan's feelings. What the fuck was going on?

Not showing his concern or his annoyance, he escorted her to the central hallway and the main staircase.

She started up, paused to blow him a kiss, then continued on.

Considering all the places CJ might be, Christopher checked his phone, opening the home monitoring app.

There'd been so much activity all day, it would be easier to start searching. Lighting a cigarette, he cut across the central hallway and walked through an archway to a long corridor built in a square grid for easier access to the entire first floor.

It wasn't until he'd made almost a complete circuit, and was passing the den that the sound of glass breaking captured his attention. He grabbed his piece. Rushing forward, he widened the gap in the door and walked into the room, his gun aimed and cocked, ready to fire.

"Don't shoot. It's just me," CJ slurred, shielding his face with his arms. The motherfuckers couldn't stop a fucking bullet. They would get fucked up first.

Scowling, Christopher shoved his .9mm back into his cut.

His boy stood in the center of the room, swaying and staring at a puddle of liquor littered with glass from a broken bottle.

Scrubbing a hand over his face, CJ looked at Christopher. CJ's watery, red-rimmed green eyes hinted at inner turmoil. Christopher scratched his jaw. His boy drinking didn't concern him.

Howfuckingever, his boy drinking to his current state of fuckedupness, where Megan could see him, did.

Christopher went to his son and guided him to the sofa, then cleaned the mess in silence. Once he finished, he grabbed a bottle of rum from the bar, then crooked his finger.

In CJ's room, Christopher closed the door. "Your Ma wanna wish you happy fuckin' birthday, boy." Although Megan wouldn't want to see CJ drunk off his fucking ass. "You hear me, son?"

"Yeah, Dad," CJ mumbled.

Twisting the cap on the bottle of rum, Christopher swigged. He lifted it away from CJ's grasping hands. Already off-balance, CJ pitched forward, bracing himself on his hands at the last moment. At first, he didn't move, and Christopher feared his boy had fucked himself up, then he staggered to his feet and faced Christopher.

"I need another drink."

"No the fuck you don't. As it fuckin' is, you gonna need a new fuckin' head in the mornin', since you gonna wanna blow the motherfucker you got off cuz of that fuckin' hangover."

"I don't care. It doesn't matter. *Nothing* matters. Harley doesn't love me. She turned me down, Dad. I asked her to be my girl and she said no." He hung his head and sniffled. "She doesn't love me."

Fuck him up the fucking ass. Had he ever been so fucking teenagey and emotional? First Rebel with a grown motherfucker who was her fucking brother. Now, CJ and Harley. He *was* shocked Harley turned CJ down, but fuck she was still a little kid.

"Maybe, you shoulda did this shit when she made sixteen."

Tears slid down CJ's cheeks. "I love her."

"How the fuck you know? You ain't ever had no fuckin' pussy. No motherfucker able to say he love a bitch if he don't know how the fuck her pussy feel."

"I was finding out tonight."

Fuck. Him. Fuck, but he needed Aunt Mary to work her magic. What she couldn't handle, Uncle Al would bring up the rear. Suddenly, he wished he could turn back the clock to CJ's sixth birthday. Back then, his attachment to Harley was cute.

Now, it was just fucking concerning. He wasn't talking about a random fucking girl. Fuck no. They were discussing *Harley*.

"Mortician woulda cut your cock the fuck off and I woulda helped him," he growled. "What the fuck is wrong with you? I thought you felt more for Harley than just turning her into some ass."

"Dad!" CJ yelled, his eyes blazing. "I fucking love her!" he slobbered, punching his chest hard enough to knock a fucking hole in it. "I wouldn't have just left her. I want her to be my first! My last! My love! My life! My—"

"Fuck, shut the fuck up!"

CJ tripped to his feet, a surer sign the lil' motherfucker was drunker than a motherfucker. Digging in his pocket, he pulled out two rings and held them out to Christopher.

He snatched the jewelry from his boy. "What the fuck this shit?"

"Rings, 'Law," CJ said with exasperation.

"I know what the fuck in my fuckin' hand, CJ," Christopher snapped. He wasn't a brain-dead assfuck. "This shit ain't lookin' like a I'm-your-motherfucker-you-my-bitch rings."

"A promise ring?"

"What-the-fuck-ever. Hers look like a fuckin' engagement ring."

It was a specially made ring, with gold skulls inlaid with topaz, banded with diamonds and topped with a princess cut diamond. It must've cost a fucking fortune.

What the fuck happened to the days of watching over bikes...taking out the trash...selling blood and kidneys and cum...to make enough money for a movie, a bud, a pint, and some condoms? He had to talk to Megan. No fucking reason his boy could afford a ring like this and still have fucking money. He should've been broke for the next six or twelve months at least. But since the little motherfucker hadn't hit Christopher up for bills, CJ still had money.

"There'll never be another girl for me. I'm joining a monastery like Rule wants to."

"That'll be the fuckin' day your dick fall off and shrivel the fuck up."

CJ sat down again, missing the edge of the bed, and falling flat on his ass. "I notice other girls, but Harley is everything to me." He sniffled again.

Sighing, Christopher set the rings on CJ's bureau and swigged from his bottle again. He wanted to tell his son to stop boo-hooing over a girl, but that would make him a hypocritical motherfucker. Megan had the power to tear him to pieces, too.

Capping the rum and setting it aside, Christopher slid down to the floor, next to CJ.

"Ma'll be so upset if she sees me so fucking fucked up."

"Ain't nothin' but a thing, son. It's okay," Christopher added, his heart hurting for his boy. Megan would be upset, but she'd understand.

"Harley said if we broke up, we'd ruin our friendship."

"She right."

"I wouldn't break up with her. She wouldn't break up with me. I wouldn't let her. We belong together."

What the fuck *that* meant? Christopher was an obsessed assfuck behind Megan. She was his first thought when he woke up and his last one before he fell asleep. Her happiness came before everything, even his own. If, one day, she wanted to walk away and Christopher couldn't change her mind, he'd step aside.

Granted, his behavior *before* he gave up might be a little suspect. He'd take her to one of the club's safehouses and keep her there for a month to plead his case. Then, if she still wanted to leave, he wouldn't stop her.

He'd give Megan *anything*, even a divorce, as long as she was happy.

"I ain't likin' your fuckin' words. If she wanna leave your fuckin' ass, you let her walk the fuck away. Don't ever fuckin' take away her fuckin' free will."

"The tree house was decorated so fucking perfect," CJ said, ignoring Christopher's sharp words. "Diesel really came through for me. It was full of flowers and-and fucking stuff. Harley loves flowers and she likes swings and she likes the wind blowing through her hair and her favorite candy is M&Ms and—"

"CJ, you too fuckin' young to tie yourself to one girl. Women always smarter. Harley probably know what the fuck she talkin' about. You both got your whole fuckin' lives ahead of you."

"For as long as I can remember, Harley has been in my fucking life."

"As your fucking friend."

CJ opened his mouth, then closed it again, his drunk fucking brain drowning coherent thought. Just as fucking well. He was a good kid, but he was fucking stubborn and a fucking teenager. That made the lil' motherfucker a walking recipe to do the opposite of whatever Christopher told him.

The more he said they were too fucking young, the more CJ would insist otherwise. Christopher didn't have the heart to tell his boy that Harley might love him like a brother. He'd monitor the situation, though. See what the fuck Mort had to say about Harley's mood.

"Dad, you of all people should believe in true love. In soulmates."

"Ain't fuckin' started believin' that 'til I met your ma. My ass definitely ain't fuckin' believed in that shit at sixfuckinteen."

"Ma was eighteen-years-old when you met her. She was real young, too."

"My ass just a fuckin' lucky motherfucker. That shit coulda went sideways, CJ. She coulda decided she ain't really fuckin' wanted me."

"Harley turned me down, Dad," CJ mumbled, sinking into a drunken stupor.

Standing, Christopher grabbed his son's arms and dragged him up. He was so fucking happy the bed was right the fuck behind CJ. Keeping him steady, he guided him onto the mattress, then shoved his legs onto the bed and removed CJ's boots, almost identical to his.

After tucking CJ in, Christopher paused for a moment and studied him. Sixteen.

His boy was *sixteen*. Where the fuck had time gone? It seemed like yesterday when he was coaching Megan through labor to bring CJ into the world.

And now?

Time had stolen that baby and grown him into a beautiful boy if he might fucking say so himself. It was kinda fucked-up he'd gotten his first broken heart on his birthday. When all was fucking said and done, true fucking love existed, but it happened in its own sweet time.

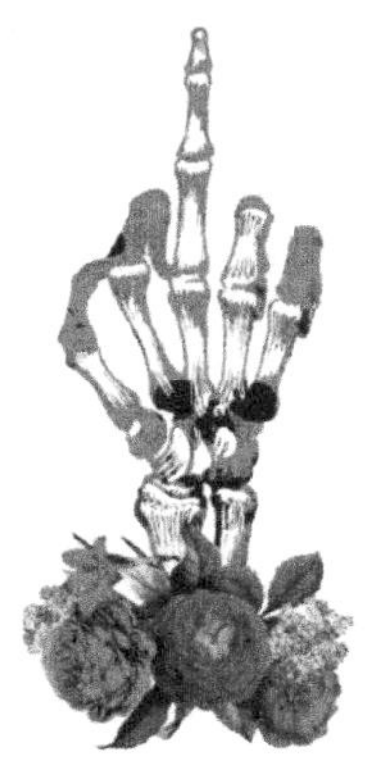

Chapter Twenty Two

HARLEY

"Knock, knock," Mommie said the next morning, opening the door to Harley's bedroom and walking in.

"Hey," Harley mumbled, tired and sad. She hadn't slept a wink all night. She'd never forget the pain in CJ's eyes when she'd turned him down. If only he hadn't asked her last night. *Or* if only her body was normal. Or if only...

There were a lot of *if onlys*. Too many.

Timing shattered her dream of her and CJ marrying. He hated her now. He hadn't even told her 'bye'. Once she'd returned to the house, she left the party within ten minutes. She had no place. Rebel sulked nowadays. Uncle Johnnie barely let Mattie out of his sight. Without CJ, Harley had no place with the boys because of Ryan. Sometimes, it seemed he hated her. Other times, he looked so lost.

CJ was the only one who'd keep him in line.

She sniffled.

Sudden sunlight streamed into her room. Squinting against the glare, Harley lifted her head. Mommie stood in front of the window seat, stylish in stiletto boots, black skinny jeans, a cream-colored sweater, and her cut, with her dark hair in a high ponytail.

She walked to the side of Harley's bed. "What's the matter, my love?"

"Nothing," she lied, unable to keep the tears out of her voice.

The bed dipped as her mom sat on the edge, right next to her. "Did you and CJ argue? I saw him right before we left last night. He was in the den when I went to get mine and your daddy's coats. CJ seemed like his best friend left him."

Weeping, she face-planted on her bed.

If only she'd known the right words to explain the real reason she hadn't accepted his promise ring. She could've at least stayed with him. They were lifelong best friends, so she knew she'd crushed him. Instead, she'd chickened out, unable to stay when her heart was so broken. Not even her fear of the darkness compared to her misery. Her obscure surroundings and cold dampness didn't register as she'd run home.

"Harley?"

She dragged herself to a sitting position. "I still haven't started my period," she said on a sob, the heart of the reason for declining CJ. "All the girls have their periods now. Except me. I'm not normal."

CJ deserved someone who could give him a big family. If she didn't have a period, she'd never have babies.

"You're fourteen-years-old," Mommie soothed in her gentle voice, most of the time having the right words for Harley.

Mommie was the epitome of beauty, while Daddy was the best *girl dad* ever, even though he had two sons. He was wise, smart, funny. Together, they'd given her and her brothers, Lou and Kaleb Paul, a warm, loving home. Her parents adored each other and had the absolute best marriage. Just the kind of relationship she wanted.

Just the kind she'd always dreamed she'd one day have with CJ since, in her mind, they were made for each other.

"He's sixteen, sweet doll. There's not much the two of you could do in terms of a relationship anyway."

She wasn't sure if she wanted to know what her mother meant, so she didn't pursue the conversation. "Molly gives CJ these really annoying stares. She's always licking her lips around him. Sometimes, she gets his attention, too."

"Molly also told me it's a proven fact fifty chickens can kill a lion."

When Harley brought her home after the volleyball game. "All the boys like her." And all the girls—*grown women*—liked CJ. Except he gave Harley all his time and priority.

"Molly's a sweet girl, but I think CJ prefers girls with a little more...ah...more...substance."

"Yes, but did I tell you about Jaleena Davis? Her dad's like this super-smart, super-wealthy, super-handsome tech exec. Jaleena is already talking about joining her dad's company. She has all these ideas. She's the same age as me, and she's thirsty for CJ, Momma. *Thirsty*. How can I compete if I don't ever get a period?"

"You're a late bloomer."

"Like you?"

Mommie pursed her lips. "Well, no."

Harley burst into tears. "You already had your period by fourteen!"

"Yes, sweet girl, but everyone is different." She pulled Harley into her arms and held her until her tears quieted.

"I talked to Aunt Jordan about these emmenagogues I researched and—"

"No, Harley," Mommie said firmly. "You're not taking herbs to try and bring about menstruation. It isn't happening."

"But, Mommie, the emmenagogues are all natural. Parsley, chamomile, rosemary, sage, oregano, and cinnamon."

"There's also pomegranate, celery, papaya, fenugreek, and chicory."

Harley hadn't had any doubt that her mom would know what an emmenagogue was. She was a Doctor of Psychology, and loved not only medical and psychological thrillers, but nonfiction books about physical and emotional health.

"None of those are dangerous," Harley persisted.

"Let nature take its course, sweetheart. Not only have we spoken to Aunt Jordan off the record, we've also spoken to your pediatrician and she said you're perfectly normal. Your breasts are starting to develop and you're getting acne."

"CJ's perfect! He'll think I'm so ugly with my face all spotted."

"*Harley*, baby, stop this," Mommie clucked. "You're overworked for nothing."

"I'm not normal," she insisted.

"You'll be fine. I promise."

Harley broke CJ's heart and she'd never be fine again.

"What about birth control? Can I get on some?"

Mommie blinked, her mouth opening and closing before she licked her lips. She stared at Harley and cleared her throat. "Why?" she asked faintly.

"It regulates your cycle and some types regulate your cycle," Harley mumbled, unable to hold her mother's searching gaze.

"You don't have a cycle yet and not much acne."

Harley wasn't sure what she was saying. She hadn't slept and she did little else but cry. She texted CJ but he hadn't responded, and she'd cried more. If she hadn't awakened her parents and her brothers, she would've gone to the music room and practiced on the drum kit. The couple times she'd calmed herself, she'd arranged entire menus in her head. Cooking soothed her, while preparing food wouldn't have disturbed her parents and brothers because of noise. Except aromas wafted through the vents, so they would've come to investigate and asked why she was preparing a full meal in the middle of the night.

"This is about CJ, I take it."

"It doesn't matter," Harley sniffled. "He hates me."

"I doubt that," she said after a moment. "Get up, sweet girl. Face the day instead of moping in your room. You used that pass at the beginning of the summer."

She hadn't been moping. She'd been healing.

"We'll be late for girls' day out if we don't leave soon."

"Can I skip today?" Harley enjoyed the one day of the month when her grandmother, mother, aunts, and girl cousins all went out. Sometimes, it was to see a play. Other times, it was to shop. And, on other occasions, it was to do volunteer work. "I-I'm not feeling good."

"I'd really like for you to come, but if you need to skip this month, you can."

"Thank you, Mommie."

Leaning over, she kissed Harley's cheek, then stood. "Everything will be fine. Trust me. I love you."

"I love you, too."

Left alone, Harley turned her face into her pillow and dissolved into tears all over again.

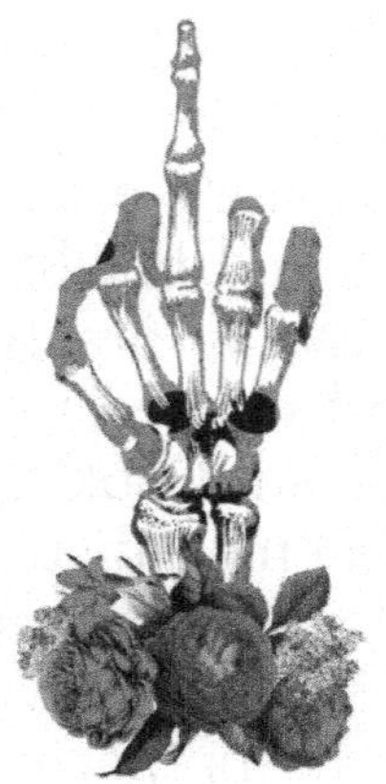

Chapter Twenty Three

REBEL

Cheek-to-cheek with her mother, Rebel offered the camera a wide grin. They changed positions, ending up back-to-back. Pursed lips and fish cheeks were snaps three and four. For the final shot, they put their arms around each other's necks. At the last minute, Momma tickled her, and peals of laughter escaped Rebel.

"That's my absolute favorite shot," Momma said, following Rebel out of the photo booth.

Rebel stood near the photo dispenser, listening to the machine's various sounds. "Our kissy faces are my fave."

"We should give that one to Daddy."

Not responding to the expectation in her mother's tone, Rebel shook her head. "I want that one."

"Aunt Meggie!"

Rebel wrinkled her nose at the sound of unfamiliar high-pitched call. Who was that? Her parents had enough children, without picking up stragglers. Like

Diesel. Luckily, the machine coughed up the photos, allowing her to ignore the newcomer.

Daddy's ringtone pealed in the space. Predictably, Momma turned away.

"Those are cute," the annoying voice rose from right behind Rebel, startling her. "Aunt Meggie looks like your sister, instead of your mom."

Spinning, Rebel shoved the strips of photos into her pocket and glared at the stranger. She was attractive with brownish-blonde hair, dull blue eyes, too much makeup, botoxed lips, and huge tits.

"Yeah, my mom's totally hot." What she wouldn't do to still have her bubble gum. She'd totally pop it in this woman's face. "Now, am I supposed to know you since you obviously know me?"

"Rude much?"

"Give a fuck much?"

"Rebel!" Ava and Mattie's loud chorus rose above the bustle of the mall.

She looked around. "Where's Harley?"

"Aunt Bailey said Harley wasn't feeling good," Mattie explained. "She asked to stay home."

"I'll call her later and check on her," Rebel promised, eyeing Mattie and remembering Daddy still hadn't returned her phone or ungrounded her. Nor had he returned her debit card. If she went home with anything today, she'd have to ask her mother and then she still might not get it. Momma wasn't happy with Rebel's behavior, especially the way she was treating Daddy. Rebel had never been so miserable. She'd sequestered in her room during their weekly get-togethers. Momma, Lolly, and her aunts always tried to coax her downstairs, but Rebel always refused. "What have you and Harley been getting up to lately, Mattie?"

Her cousin shrugged and forced a smile. "Daddy hasn't allowed me around Harley too much."

"That sucks, dude."

"Yeah, Reb. When he found out you were allowed to come, he wanted me to stay home, but Maman had a closed-door discussion with him, then we left."

As angry as Rebel was with her father and as unfair as she felt he was being, Uncle Johnnie was ten times worse. He was foul, and she was fucking counting the days to her eighteenth birthday to tell him all about himself.

"Hey, girls, what are you two talking about?" the stranger asked.

It was one thing to have to talk to her when no one else was around. But this was too much. "We're talking about nothing that would interest a grown ass woman whom I've never met. You're a fucking stranger and creepy as hell. Get lost before I call for help."

"A stranger? That's Tabitha, bro," Mattie said, rolling her eyes.

Rebel choked. Tabitha. Who'd called Momma *Aunt Meggie*.

Tabitha. Diesel's live-in girlfriend.

"I see you recognize my name." Tabitha's smile was hard and cold. "I might be able to offer a few makeup tips if you tell me what you were discussing."

"Maman won't allow me to wear makeup until I'm thirteen."

"Part of the fun of growing up is rebelling against the parents," Tabitha cooed.

"Why would we do that?" Ava asked.

"You're not an adolescent unless you give your parents trouble," Tabitha responded with a condescending cackle.

The woman thought they were idiots.

"So give me the deets," she pressed.

"If I liked you, I'd consider it," Mattie said sharply. "But since I hate your guts, not only won't I give you the details, I'm not fucking talking to you."

Tabitha looked like a fucking cat on the hunt. "I'll give you the tips, Rebel. You can pass them on to Matilda when the time is right."

"You're Diesel's girlfriend," Rebel pushed out. "And Diesel's one of the club's lawyers that works with Aunt Kendall and Brooks, so when my cousin turns thirteen next year, you'll still be around to give tips."

Unfortunately.

"Silly me," Tabitha said with a stupid laugh that grated on Rebel. "Well, I have another idea."

"Well, so do I," Mattie mocked. "Bye."

"I beg your pardon. What does that mean?"

"Leave," Rebel answered. "That's what that means."

A burst of laughter from the crowd of women not far away broke into their little standoff. Still on her phone, Momma waved her hand furiously as Lolly called, "Diesel, boy, what are you doing here?"

"I have business, Lolly," Diesel called, walking into view. He wore jeans and his Dweller cut.

Rebel hated him a little more for being so magnificent and bad ass."

"Hey, Monkey Butt," he greeted Rebel and kissed Tabi Cat's mouth.

Rebel glared at Diesel. "I told you to stop calling me that, you big asshole."

"Ready, Tab?" he asked, ignoring Rebel.

"Yes, my love," she said, leaning in to kiss him.

"Let me say hi to Kendall and Aunt, er, *Meggie*," Tabi Cat told him.

Diesel lifted his brows, seeming less than pleased. "You haven't spoken to them?"

"I haven't been here long. I found her and Rebel already here."

"Yeah, they like to take pictures in those booths," Diesel said. "They usually get here ahead of everyone."

"I didn't think you remembered that," Rebel sniped, on the verge of sobbing and hating Diesel almost as much as she despised Tabitha. Something about her made Rebel uneasy. She glared at Diesel. "You were in such a hurry to move."

"Are you ever forgiving me, Reb?"

Maybe, if he hadn't forgotten she existed and crushed her heart.

Still, she wished she was grown. She'd run stupid, mean-eyed Tabi Cat away and make Diesel love her.

Her phone beeped and she read her brother's message.

Is Harley there?

No.

By the time Rebel typed two letters, Diesel and Tabitha had walked away.

"I want a ciggy," Mattie said. "Cover for me while I go to the bathroom."

Realizing CJ wouldn't text her again and wondering what was up with him and Harley, Rebel sighed. "Go. I won't tell."

"Girls!" Aunt Kendall called. "Come and welcome your new cousin. Diesel and Tabatha married three days ago at the courthouse."

Rebel's world crashed and her stomach turned. She staggered, tears rushing to her eyes. She couldn't believe Diesel would do such a thing. He hadn't even had the decency to tell her himself.

Unable to bear it, she ran. They spent a lot of time at the mall. She knew the quiet spots and the busy ones. Sobbing, she somehow reached the third level, heading to a section with not much foot traffic, near an emergency exit stairwell.

She tripped to an empty bench and swiped at her wet cheeks.

A Kleenex tickled her nose.

"I got more if you need them." Orange, one of Slipper's sons, served as a bodyguard for the monthly outings. He was as soap-shy and greasy as his daddy and just as kind.

"She's there, Meggie." Fuse's voice traveled to Rebel. He was one of the younger brothers who Potter vouched for.

A moment later, Momma sat next to Rebel and put an arm around her. She leaned against her mother's shoulder and sobbed. Her tears came in an endless stream, until her head and throat hurt and her eyes ached. The entire time, Momma whispered soft, comforting words to her.

When Momma placed a wet cloth against Rebel's head, the scent of sweat and motor oil hit her nose.

"I got a handkerchief, too, Meggie."

"Thanks, Orange, but Fuse's is enough."

"You want a swig of something, Rebbie?"

"She isn't old enough to drink, Orange."

"You sure, Meggie?" Orange asked. "She's not fifteen or sixteen yet?"

"Nope."

"Meggie, I don't know about that," Orange protested. "I'm sure she at least sixteen."

"I'm sorry to disappoint you, but she's younger. I was there when she was born."

"Oh, yeah. That's right." He fell silent and then, "Even though she's not fifteen or sixteen, she can't have a little nip?"

Rebel sat up, frowning at the green tint to her mother's skin.

"You do know that's not legal drinking age?"

Orange scratched his greasy scalp. "No?"

"Meggie's right," Fuse said, shaking his head. "You got to be twenty-one to drink in public, dumb fuck."

Orange's eyes widened. "Fuck! Where've I been? How long that law been in place?"

Fuse clapped Orange's shoulders. "Years, motherfucker. Years."

"Can I talk to Rebel alone?"

"We can't leave you by yourself, Meggie," Orange protested. "I'm the lead today and I'm not failing Prez."

"You don't have to leave us *alone*-alone. Just walk a few feet away so my daughter and I can have girl talk."

"Oh." Orange didn't move. "How can you have girl talk when you're not one?"

"She got a pussy, Orange," Fuse snapped. "What the fuck that make her?"

"She not a girl, Fuse. She Prez old lady."

They sounded as stupid as Ryder had at Ryan's birthday. Were all guys this fucking stupid when they didn't know how to classify a woman?

"She can't be an old lady if she don't have a twat!"

Oh, for God's sake.

"She have all them babies, so she *must* got a pussy."

"Orange!" Momma screeched. "Fuse! Enough!"

"Fuck off, Fuse. If Prez hear you say something about what's between Meggie's legs, he burying you."

Rebel didn't have the patience for another moment of their nonsense. "Dickheads!" she yelled, wanting to talk to her mom. Fuse and Orange would never leave unless she adapted her daddy's style. "I'm hungry. Leave me alone with my mom and find something for us to eat."

"I don't like you calling me a dickhead, Rebel," Orange objected.

"It's either me or Daddy," Rebel said.

"*You* is fine." Fuse yanked Orange by the arm and dragged him away.

Momma tucked some of Rebel's hair behind her ear. "When you grow up, a man who worships you and whom you adore will come along."

"I love Diesel."

"Sometimes, we don't get to be with the people we love first. We wish them every happiness and move on with our lives."

Tears slid down Rebel's cheeks again. "D-daddy was your first love."

"I was lucky, blessed, and fortunate. What your daddy and me have is a gift and can't be taken lightly. You *will* find the man for you just as Diesel has found the woman for him."

"Suppose they're divorced by the time I grow up?"

"Then you'll get to see if you and Diesel were meant to be together. If it's before or after your daddy kills him depends on how soon you let him know."

"Momma!" Rebel said, appalled. "You couldn't allow Daddy to kill Diesel when we get together."

"I want you happy, my love, but Diesel is your brother—"

"I have enough of those. I don't need a stray."

"That's enough, Rebel," Momma warned in a steely voice. "You might not agree with our choices, but you will respect them. Your daddy and I adopted Diesel. He's a Caldwell. My son. Your brother. You *must* accept that because you have no choice. It won't change. Diesel also married Tabitha. Don't wait for them to break up or scheme to come between them when you're older."

Not answering, Rebel faced the empty cavern of the area they sat in and glowered.

"Whatever is meant to be will be. Enjoy today and worry about the future tomorrow."

Staring into her mother's blue eyes, looking at the kindness on her face, Rebel would concede for now.

"Aunt Meggie!" Tabitha called, rushing toward them with Aunt Kendall and Mattie hot on her heels. "How are you feeling?"

When Diesel's wife knelt in front of Momma, Rebel recoiled and jumped to her feet, her anger sweeping in again.

"Get off your fucking knees," Aunt Kendall snapped and glared at the back of Tabitha's head. "I couldn't catch her before she came up, Meggie."

Turning greener by the second, Momma nodded and eyed Tabitha as the girl stood.

Rocking on her heels, she smiled. "I hear congratulations are in order, aunt." She looked at Rebel, her eyes gleaming. "I wonder if the new baby will be a girl."

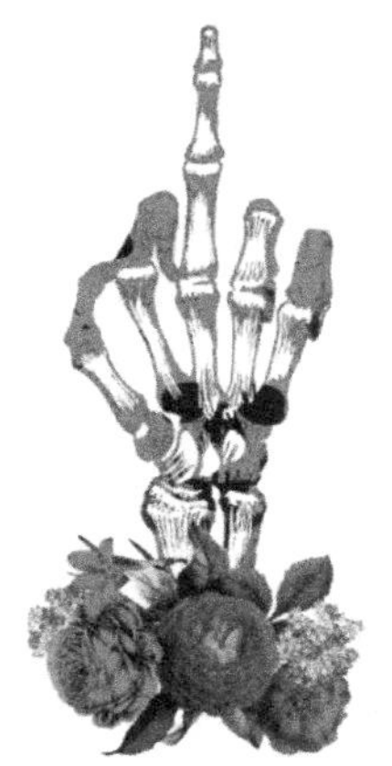

Chapter Twenty Four

CJ

"Knock, knock."

Scowling, CJ tossed aside the book he'd been trying to read as Diesel opened his door and breezed into his bedroom.

"You look like shit."

"Suck it." CJ wouldn't admit how shitty he felt. He'd awakened with a terrible hangover. Every time he sat up the room spun. Somehow, he'd dragged himself into the shower and tried to wake up. It was only after Outlaw gave him a hangover remedy, which in turn made CJ throw up for what felt like hours, did he feel better. At least, physically. Emotionally, his mood was in the pits.

"You need to talk to your sister," Diesel said, cutting into CJ's misery.

"Rebel?"

"Do we have another sister I'm unaware of?"

Pushing his own problems to the side and ignoring Diesel's sarcasm, CJ ran a hand through his hair and sat up. "What's wrong with her?"

"I told her about Tabitha and me."

"What about Tabitha and you?" CJ grumbled. "Having a live-in girlfriend is old news in this house. Rebel's still suffering the consequences of her meltdown. Whatever else Rebel knows is more than what I do."

"We're married."

The startling news yanked away CJ's misery over Harley. "Married? You? To her? Tabitha?"

Diesel had taken him to lunch to introduce them, since she'd already left by the time Ryan's party began. And he hadn't dared invite her to his own birthday party out of respect for Rebel.

"Isn't today Saturday?"

"We were married three days ago."

CJ widened his eyes. "And you didn't mention it to us yesterday?"

Diesel shrugged, unbothered by the secrecy. "We married at the courthouse. Just like Uncle Chris and Aunt Meggie did."

"Which they followed up with a church wedding," CJ reminded him. Later, he'd think about why Diesel didn't want to know the end result of all CJ's hard work in the treehouse since he'd known the plans. "Nevermind. Why do I need to talk to my sister because you're married? It seems like you're the stupid motherfucker that needs talking to."

"Keep your friends close and your enemies closer."

Whatever the fuck that meant. "Nowhere is it written you should marry your enemies. Dad know?"

"Not yet."

Diesel rarely shared the reasons behind his actions. Sometimes, CJ was suspicious of Diesel. Maybe, he wasn't as loyal as he pretended. Then, he'd chalk it up to jealousy, call himself an ass, and his doubts faded.

"About Rebel."

"I'll check on her."

"Yeah, well, Aunt Meggie's expecting and Tabitha let the cat out of the bag by wondering if the new baby would be a girl."

That fucking bitch. He hadn't liked Tabitha when they first met and she was dead to him now. She'd hurt Rebel.

Scowling at Diesel, CJ headed to his little sister's room.

DIESEL

"Go away!" Rebel said around sniffles, picking up a teddy bear and flinging it at Diesel's head.

"Stop that, Reb," CJ ordered, sitting on the bed next to her and hugging her.

Unsure of what to say and how he fit in, Diesel lingered in the doorway. He felt awful for so many different fucking reasons.

First, Rebel. She was developing before his fucking eyes and already gorgeous. But she was a child and he'd never see her differently. Even if she were older and he thought her more than a little sister, he'd never pursue her. Uncle Chris and Aunt Meggie accepted him as a member of their family, gave him a life he'd once only dreamed, and trusted him to live under their roof around their children. Eighteen or eighty, Rebel would always be off-limits to him out of loyalty and respect.

"Diesel?"

At the sound of Tabitha's voice, Diesel backed out of Rebel's doorway, nearly colliding with his new wife.

"How's little Rebel?"

Only Tabitha's round ass drew more attention than her double D tits. He wished she had a better attitude. More than anything, he wished he could trust her. Recently, he'd discovered her very concerning family ties. Over the past few months, he'd run his fucking mouth, believing she was really into him. He needed to know what she'd divulged to protect his family.

Yet, time was running out. Kendall *despised* Tabitha. She'd warned Diesel to keep watch on her because she didn't trust her. She'd also warned Diesel to keep her out of her path. He suspected Aunt Meggie didn't like Tabitha either. She wasn't cutthroat like Kendall, but she had amazing fucking instincts. Whenever Aunt Meggie was in Tabitha's company, she studied her.

Closely.

All it took was Aunt Meggie mentioning to Uncle Chris that she wasn't comfortable with Tabitha. After Tabitha betrayed Diesel's confidence and played on Rebel's fears with a new baby, Uncle Chris might hold him responsible.

Fuck.

Rebel's sob reached Diesel and he scraped his fingers through his hair. "Don't call her little Rebel."

"Why not?" Tabitha glared at him. "She isn't an adult."

"No, but she *is* my sister with little tolerance for patronizing."

"She's a child," Tabitha snapped. "She needs to act like one."

"Look at it from my perspective—"

"There's no reason to," Tabitha interrupted. "This is about me, not you. She's a snotty brat and needs to be put in her place."

Irritation surged into Diesel. "Rebel is a part of my family."

"She shares no blood with you."

Almost Rebel's exact words. "That doesn't matter. She's still my family *and* a child. Step back, take the fucking high road, and leave her alone."

"I love you," she said, tears rushing to her eyes. "I don't want anything to jeopardize our happiness. I'm your wife. My happiness should be the most important thing to you."

"Your happiness depends on your understanding that I expect to be happy too. That's achieved through compromise."

"I don't like that word."

He grinned at her petulant tone.

"Can I talk to Rebel myself?"

"Fuck no. What you did at the mall is inexcusable. I'm telling you this one last time: don't fuck with my family."

Chapter Twenty Five

HARLEY

Sliding off the passenger seat of her father's bike in front of their favorite diner, Harley handed over her helmet and watched as he hung it on one of the handlebars, then copied the action on the other side with his own.

Their yearly trip was behind them, though it hadn't been the same without CJ. Ryan, Devon, and Rory had also stayed behind, but it was CJ's absence that made Harley the most miserable. If only he would answer her calls and texts. But since his party, three weeks ago, she hadn't seen him. One good thing from the trip was Uncle Chris and Rebel mending fences, and Uncle Johnnie easing up on Mattie.

Aunt Meggie was wretchedly ill the whole time and Rebel didn't smile much anymore. Harley understood because she didn't either and neither did Mattie.

Since the Scorched Devils meeting, nothing was the same for any of them. The blow-up at the volleyball match ruined the summer and the scene in the treehouse destroyed her life.

Because of all the costs associated with the changed travel arrangements, Daddy canceled their hotel reservations and stayed at the mansion he shared with Uncle Digger. Winds of past violence floated in the club sometimes and rumor had it the luxurious estate was rebuilt after Daddy and her uncles blew up the original one. From what she understood, it was her granddaddy's house, where Daddy and Uncle Digger grew up.

Whether it was true or not, she didn't know.

Since the place was so big, everyone canceled their hotel reservations and stayed there. She, Mattie, and Rebel each had bedrooms in a massive suite that included private staff. It made her wonder how much money her parents had.

She texted photos to CJ. She sent videos of the little kids' awe at their private audience with Disney characters. From experience, she knew her six-year-old cousin, Link, was at the age when his delight at the privilege of one on ones with Mickey, Minnie, Donald, and the others was fading. But that observation hadn't mattered.

CJ refused to answer her.

This morning, Daddy took her to school to register for her classes. The new school year would start in just under two weeks and everyone was gearing up. She didn't care.

After dismounting, Daddy lit a cigarette. "I can already taste that burger and fries," he said, smoke pouring from his nostrils.

Silent, she nodded. She didn't have much of an appetite. Everything was different and she didn't know how to make it better.

Discarded notes filled her trash bin. Explaining the real reason she'd turned CJ down was just too embarrassing. Each time she came up with the right words, she second guessed herself and changed her mind.

Daddy dragged on his cigarette again. "Do I need to bust a motherfucker head, baby? Why you been moping for weeks?"

"Me and CJ aren't friends anymore," she confessed and burst into tears, barreling into his arms and sobbing against his chest. "I hurt him really bad, Daddy, and he hates me."

Ever patient, her dad hugged her while she cried.

"CJ never hating you," he promised once her tears quieted to sniffles. "He like your company over anybody else."

Swiping her eyes, Harley stepped back. "He asked me to be his girlfriend and I turned him down. I br-br-broke his heart."

Daddy frowned. "You can't be no motherfucker girlfriend until you at least forty, Harley. You got over two decades left before you can even think that way."

"By then, he'll be married to someone else."

He gave her a considering look. "I can't say I'm not happy you turned him down, but why you did it when all you ever want to be is around his little ass."

Harley couldn't reveal the truth. "I'm not right for him."

As Daddy contemplated her words, he dragged on his cigarette. His dreads were queued today, revealing the skull-shaped diamond studs. It reminded her of the ring CJ had offered her.

Harley sniffled.

"Explain what you mean by not right and why you think that? Did he say that to you?"

"Of course not, Daddy!" Harley cried in frustration. "He would never. He's perfect. Kind. Protective. Funny. That's why I love him. I want to spend the rest of my life with him and give him a lot of children."

Blowing more smoke, Daddy glared at her. "You can always join a convent."

"I might have to," Harley said glumly. "Not only won't CJ want me, but no other boy either."

Finished with his cigarette, Daddy placed an arm around her shoulders and guided her into the diner. Harley welcomed the inside warmth and waved at the people who greeted her or waited patiently while Daddy spoke to an acquaintance. It didn't matter if he stopped in often or stayed away for weeks, someone always wanted his attention.

"Hit me up on my cell," he told a man with a long gray beard and a leather jacket. "We'll talk about it later. I'm here to spend time with my daughter, not conduct business."

The older biker nodded, gave her a quick glance, then turned on his heel and walked away.

As soon as they sat, Symphony rushed to the table. She was tall and pretty with dark skin and long braids. Ever since she started at the diner, her parents requested Symphony whenever they brought Harley and her brothers. Mommie always asked about her well-being and made a point to leave huge tips.

Enormous.

Even Lolly liked her and told Symphony to put her on speed dial for anything she might need.

Mommie and Lolly marshalled Harley's aunts to give Symphony a sick present for her twentieth birthday. Harley couldn't wait for that day. She only wished CJ would be around to share her anticipation.

"Hey Mort." Symphony nodded at Harley, then swept her dad with a look, leaning so close her abundant cleavage almost touched him. She met his gaze and smirked. "How's it hanging?"

Everyone knew how happily married her parents were, especially Symphony, who bombarded Mommie with questions about everything, even what it was like being an old lady.

Being so emotional the past few weeks messed up Harley's perception. Therefore, Symphony *wasn't* flirting with Daddy.

Oh, but she was. Harley had grown up around the biker girls. Even if she hadn't, Symphony blatantly brushed her breasts against Daddy's arm before she stepped back.

"Can I get your usual, Mort?"

"Give us a few minutes."

Daddy sounded annoyed.

"But my shift's almost over," Symphony pouted. "I want to be the one to serve you."

Harley folded her arms.

"You leave such a big tip."

"That's so gross. That's my dad. And my *mom* leaves your raggedy tips," Harley snapped. "Not Daddy."

He threw Harley an amused grin.

She sniffed. "Bye, Symphony."

"Next time, Mort."

"I don't think so," Harley inserted. "Next time, I'll make sure my mother is here."

Symphony stomped away without responding to Harley.

"If your momma was here we wouldn't have a father-daughter outing," he pointed out.

"Mommie has been so nice to Symphony and she acts like she doesn't care. She's throwing herself at you right in front of me."

"No woman ever coming between me and your momma, baby doll. And there's a lot of Symphonys in the world. I didn't expect it from her 'cause you right. She biting the fucking hand that's looking out for her."

"Tell her to stop. No, tell all those women who don't respect your marriage to stop." Harley couldn't remember a day when Daddy hadn't proudly worn his wedding band.

"I don't have time to waste my breath on bitches who won't listen anyway 'cause they think they bad enough to make me break my vows. I'm so used to it, it barely registers, so pull in your mini-claws."

"It registered this time. I heard it in your voice."

"You right, baby doll. It did." He rubbed the back of his neck. "It's good to see your fire returning. You been moping for days."

Harley nodded. "Yeah."

"Let's forget CJ for a moment."

"I can never do that, Daddy."

"Okay, let's put the little motherfucker to the side for a moment, so you can explain why you think no man will ever want you?"

Harley searched for the right words, her misery battering her.

Daddy reached across the table and grabbed her hand.

"Harley, baby, I'm your old man. There's nothing you can't tell me."

"I have Amenorrhea," she mumbled. She'd looked up her symptoms and discovered the term.

"Ameno*WHAT*? How bad is it? Aww, baby, no wonder you so sad. Bailey must be too broken up to tell me." Releasing her hand, he slid out of the booth and came over to her side, dropping next to her and grabbing her in a big bear hug. "If CJ the best friend you think he is, and I know him to be, it won't matter."

Concern for her dad worrying needlessly stole her embarrassment. “That means I don’t have a period,” she blurted.

He froze, then abruptly stood and returned to the opposite side of the booth. He scratched his jaw. Stretched a leg.

Despite the awkwardness, Harley forged on. “Momma said it’ll come, but if I don’t get it, I can’t marry CJ because I can never have children.”

“Your momma right, Harley. You go to all your checkups and your doctor would’ve said if something was wrong. Maybe, this a good thing. You and CJ are always up under each other. You live in your own little world. This’ll give you both a chance to grow up and meet other people.”

“But we wanted to be each other’s firsts!”

If she’d announced she’d just robbed a bank, she doubted her dad would’ve looked as horrified.

“I need a fucking blunt,” he managed. “You can’t be nobody’s first until you married, and you can’t date until you marry...”

Harley scowled.

“You used to laugh at that joke.”

“It used to be funny, Daddy.”

“Tell me this, baby. You all upset cuz you don’t have...you know, uh, *that*. Why that shit important? You and CJ friends. Not to mention you just a little girl. You shouldn’t worry about grown people business for another fifteen, twenty years, when you a adult. You CJ girl friend. You a girl *and* you his friend. I won’t mind chaperoning the two of you to the petting zoo, the Children’s Museum, or the library. Ice cream.”

Harley gauged her dad’s expression, searching for signs he was joking about little-kid outtings, and finding zero. “We’re not chaperoned now, Daddy. He comes to my room. I go to his—”

"No, baby," he said, shaking his head in denial. "That shit stopping, and I'm talking to your momma later tonight about buying a new wardrobe for you." He pointed to her shirt. "That shit not working. I can see your neck." He peeped around the table. "You got boots on, so your ankles covered."

"Really, Daddy? This isn't the late 19th century or early 20th century. I'm a 21st century woman."

"No!" he barked, slamming his hand on the table and drawing a couple of stares. "Goddamn it, Harley. You not a fucking woman. You a child. A little girl. My little girl. My first born. You not ready to grow up."

"In three and a half years, I'll be an adult."

"The fuck you will," he snapped. "Adult a relative fucking term. Eighteen barely legal."

"Aunt Meggie met Uncle Chris when she was eighteen and she had CJ a couple of months before her nineteenth birthday."

"They a special case," he responded, waving away her answer. "You can't go by them."

"You and Mommie—"

"No," he interrupted. "Don't go by me and your momma. Your momma was twenty-one when we met. Then, after your grandpa was killed..." His voice trailed off. "Fuck," he mumbled, and heaved in a breath. "I'm being a hypocritical motherfucker, baby, and I don't give a fuck. Stay away from dudes. Dudes are motherfuckers. Dudes just want pussy," he said flatly. "Then, they skip out. Boys...boys dirty. Filthy. Nasty. I know cuz I got a dick so that make me a boy, too. I was a dirty, filthy, nasty motherfucker that just wanted pussy. You don't want to have no shit like that in your life. Never. Ever."

"Do you want me to become a nun?"

"You willing?"

"I'd be cloistered away, and you'd see me very rarely. I would miss you, Mommie, and my brothers too much.

Besides, I don't want to become a nun. I want to marry CJ. And he isn't dirty, filthy, or nasty. He's perfect. He's beautiful." The memory of the scene in the treehouse sent tears rushing to her eyes again. "He wanted us to be each other's first kiss," she said around sniffles. "If you were CJ and your best friend told you she didn't want to go steady with you, would you ever give her another chance?"

"Harley—"

"Daddy, please. Tell me what to do. He won't even text me back. In my entire life, this is the longest I've ever gone without some form of contact with him."

Daddy returned to her side, placed an arm around her and pulled her close. "You my pride, Harley. I want...fuck, this not about me, huh, baby? If I was CJ, my ego would be hurt and I'd feel my best friend betrayed me. I would feel stupid for misjudging her feelings."

"But—" she started around a hysterical sob.

"No, Harley. No buts. That's on the real."

"I've lost my best friend!"

Frowning, he swiped at her tears with his thumbs. His eyes seemed suspiciously moist, but Harley viewed him through her own tears.

"I'll make sure he contact you before your bedtime tonight."

Harley grabbed her father's shoulders. "No, you can't. Uncle Chris...you can't say or do anything to CJ, no matter what he does to me. Uncle Chris would...would..." Sadness and regret bubbled in her. "Don't confront CJ, Daddy."

"'Cause of Outlaw?"

She nodded. "He might...he might..."

"Kill me," he finished. "But you mine. My first born. My only daughter. My baby girl. If I got to die cuz CJ fucked over you and I break the little motherfucker in two, then so be it. I love that boy like we true blood. When it comes to you, all that shit goes out the window, Harley, and if Outlaw got to kill me over it, then I go out defending you."

That didn't make her feel much better. She didn't want anyone to die. "He's a virgin, like me. He doesn't have experience and would never try to seduce me."

"Why the fuck your mind stuck on sex?" he growled. "I wasn't talking about dick experience, Harley." By the sound of his voice, he was more than a little exasperated with her. "CJ shoot. He ride. He smoke. He drink. He well-traveled. And Outlaw his old man. CJ his mini-me. That shit alone say a lot."

"Has he ever killed?"

The question startled her dad and his eyes widened. "No." He sidled a glance at her. "Would that make a difference if he had?"

Discomfort squeezed her stomach. She wasn't sure how she should answer that. She'd spent the majority of her life in a motorcycle club, with the Bobs, club girls, and the bikers. She knew...*stuff*.

She met his gaze. "It doesn't make a difference to Mommie and Aunt Meggie. Or none of my other aunts."

He contemplated her for a moment, then nodded. "You not them. You you. One lesson I hope I taught you good is always staying true to yourself. No other motherfucker got to live your life. If they got a issue with what the fuck you do, they don't have a fucking thing to say. My father loved to quote the bible and claim sinners go straight to hell. How the fuck he knew? And he wouldn't go to hell for another motherfucker sins. He was too fucking busy making sure he got there 'cause of his own damn evilness. You not your momma. You not your grandma. Don't gauge what the fuck you accept 'cause of how the fuck other people react."

"Okay. And no. It wouldn't make a difference to me, if CJ had killed someone."

Bowing her head, she put her elbows on the table, just then realizing they hadn't yet ordered food, and no one else had approached the table after Symphony.

Tears slid down Harley's cheeks.

"Aww, baby girl." Daddy hugged her close. "Cry if you got to, Harley, but don't worry. Things always fall into place."

"Okay," she sobbed.

"You trust me, right?"

She nodded. "Yes."

"Then trust me now. This shit'll blow over and you and CJ will be hanging out again."

"It doesn't matter if you're setting new rules in place. We like to play games in each other's rooms."

"Play those motherfuckers in the open."

"It's just a bedroom, Daddy," she said, still heartsore.

"To you."

"If you're talking about making love, we can do that anywhere."

His brown skin turned gray and he responded much the same as her mother when Harley had brought up birth control.

"Make love?" he finally got out. "You don't know nothing about making love. That's reserved for motherfuckers you fall in love with when you fifty. That's the earliest you can marry."

"I'll be old," she protested.

"I'm almost fifty, you little ageist. I'm not old," he grouched. "You ready to order?" he asked a minute later.

"I'm not real hungry."

"This your favorite burger place."

She shrugged.

"I'm torn between sticking a turkey baster filled with bleach in my ear, to erase the memory of this entire conversation, or hiding you away in a closet and never letting you out—"

"Until I'm fifty," she reminded him.

"Sixty at the earliest." He pinched the bridge of his nose. "The other part of me want to...fuck, Harley. I want to tell you, you my daughter, and a Banks don't give up. CJ adore you 'cause you just full of life and fire. But, lately, you been brooding. Don't face obstacles like this, baby. Fall back and reassess the situation. Figure out a new tactical maneuver. Stand up to CJ, like usual. He being a fuckhead to you, and that shit not right. You hurt him, so apologize. You don't owe him a motherfucking explanation for why you told him no. Just don't...don't...just...fuck! Just stop being so sad."

"I will, Daddy," she swore. "For you. It makes you sad when I cry."

"It depends on what you crying about. And, no, I don't like to see you cry, but I'm your old man. My shoulder's always here for you to lean on or sob on. No explanation ever needed."

"Okay," she said, feeling a little better. A rumble stirred in her stomach. When she got home, she'd go talk to CJ. Daddy was right! She was a Banks. Her father's daughter. She straightened her shoulders. "I am hungry."

He smiled at her.

"CJ can't deny you anything, especially face-to-face. Go knock sense into the stubborn little motherfucker."

"I will."

"That's my girl. But you doing it in the open. You not going near his bedroom ever again and he not coming near yours."

"We both like being there, to share secrets and talk about things at school. CJ won't agree to us not spending time amongst everyone, all the time."

"I don't give a fuck what *he* want. *You* my daughter, so *you* follow my rules."

She'd never had a problem listening to her parents. Of course, there'd never been a conflict. Her parents always trusted CJ and Harley.

However, she faced a dilemma. If CJ saw things differently, she might not follow her daddy's rules.

Chapter Twenty Six

CJ

Baseball cap backwards on his head and hands shoved in his pockets, CJ walked through the opened gate to the custom-made swings, monkey bars, slides, and tunnels. Nowadays, he only ever visited with Harley. Otherwise, the playground equipment installed when he was little wasn't his thing. He preferred the treehouse or his father's mancave.

The creaky swing chains quieted as Harley planted her feet on the ground to stop. "You came."

The words were meant as a statement, yet he heard the question in her tone.

"You invited me," he replied, speaking to her for the first time in almost a month. He'd been angry, hurt, humiliated, and unappreciative at how far off he'd been about Harley feelings.

The next day, bullshit piled on top of bullshit at the discovery of his mother's pregnancy and Diesel's marriage. Both events wrecked his little sister and the revelation Mom was expecting a girl worsened Rebel's anguish.

She intended to throw hands on sight of the new baby. CJ wished Mom hadn't paid for the blood test for the early discovery. She was in her twelfth week and he would've welcomed the peace if she'd waited another month.

He'd endured every single incident without Harley and he'd been as miserable as Reb, but he'd swallowed his pain and managed not to respond to Harley's texts or answer her phone calls. Somehow, he'd avoided her at the clubhouse and at the weekly family dinners. He'd told himself the change in their relationship was for the best. He'd tried to bond with Ryan over alcohol, cigarettes, and porn and encouraged Dev and Ro to do the same. But some shit never changed. Ryan was still a dickhole and as big of an asshole to Devon and Rory as ever.

To disregard his misery, CJ convinced himself he'd ignore Harley for the rest of their lives. Until she'd asked him to meet her at the swings.

Like the rest of her texts, he hadn't answered her, not intending to come. But, fuck his life, he hadn't been able to stay away. One moment, he felt justified acting like a dick, and the next he felt...*like a dick* for ghosting her.

She was still the prettiest girl he'd ever seen. Her braids were gone. Her long, dark hair was parted in the middle and straightened from the flatiron, accentuating her heart-shaped face and delicate pink lips. Her honey-colored skin had a peachy undertone that made her skin glow, while her eyes reminded him of topaz. Brilliant and bright and beautiful. Like her.

She paired tall equestrian boots with a fitted turtleneck sweater, leather mini skirt, and opaque tights.

He scowled and glanced around, as if his thoughts hung like a banner in the sky. But who gave a good fuck if he could identify opaque tights?

Harley stared at him, gazing at him through her lashes, silently asking for his attention.

“What do you want?” The words were sharp.

“To talk to you,” she responded in a tone CJ couldn’t read. “This is hard, so please sit next to me.”

“On that swing?”

Harley nodded.

“Absolutely not. I’m not six.” Neither was she! Since his birthday party, her tits had grown even rounder.

She moved the swing again, slow enough to skim her heels over the ground. Bowing her head, she stared at her feet. “I-I...” she started, heaved in a breath, and tried again. “There’s things...I mean I’m not.” Another inhale and a glance at him. “I’m not. Other girls have theirs. But I don’t...Mine...It doesn’t.” She met his gaze. “Anyway...yeah...that’s the reason. I-I think you need it for you know. And, you know, children. And, well, you know—”

“Actually, I don’t know,” CJ interrupted. “I can’t make heads or tails of what you’re saying.”

“Because I don’t know how to say it, CJ!” She jumped off the swing and walked to him. “This is really, really hard for me. And embarrassing.”

CJ lifted his cap and ran his fingers through his hair, then settled the cap back on his head bill-forward. “What the fuck, Harls? We’ve talked about everything.”

“Not exactly everything,” she mumbled.

“There’s nothing so bad that you can’t tell me. We’re best friends.”

“Are we?”

He didn’t answer because he didn’t know how to. *Were they*? Calling her his best friend was like breathing. It just happened. But best friends understood each other and didn't take feelings for granted.

Betrayal rose in his gut again and he glared at her.

Tears rushed to her eyes and he thought she might cry, then she blinked and shifted her weight. "I miss you so much. I can't take that you're mad at me or that I hurt you. I'm so sorry that I did. Don't hate me."

"This is so fucking annoying, Harley. You're trying to tell me something and I can't figure out what that is." CJ pulled her into a hug, then kissed the top of her head, instead of on the cheek, like normal. "I can't ever hate you, even though you fucked up my ego pretty bad." Something only she—and his father—had the power to do. "But I'll live. I'm sorry for acting like a fucking jerk."

She wrapped her arms around him, and CJ smiled into her hair, pressing closer to her. Immediately, desire pummeled him, and his body reacted.

Awkwardly, they stepped away from each other. The red tinge in her face made him sigh.

"I'm sorry, Harley."

"Don't apologize. It's...you can't control that stuff."

Despite her words, she was embarrassed. Shocking, when the club had the Bobs and was *the club*. Sex was part of their everyday lives. So...

"Harley!" CJ grabbed her hands and held them, drawing her closer. He pressed his forehead to hers. "Harley, listen to me. I just want to say you're my girlfriend. That doesn't mean I expect you to have sex with me right now."

"But you want to kiss me."

He wanted to do more than that...nope. *Nope*. Scratch that thought right the hell out of his head. He nodded. "Yeah."

She pursed her mouth. CJ would jerk off all night to the memory of her pretty lips, made for him to worship.

"Really kiss me," she clarified, like he was stupid.

"Uh huh," he confirmed, staring at her mouth.

"We're so good as best friends. I don't want to mess that up."

He took in every inch of her face and combed his fingers through her hair. "I'm being unfair, putting all this pressure on you. You will always be my best friend, Harley. Nothing in the world will ever change that."

Instead of the relief he expected, sadness marred her face. When she didn't respond, he smiled at her, then tugged her forward.

"Come on. Let's swing a little while."

"I can swing higher than you!"

The familiarity of her boast felt good. He smirked. His legs were longer than hers and she wore a short little skirt. "We'll see about that."

They kicked off at the same time, though he didn't put the full weight of his body into maneuvering the swing until she had a good momentum going. Just as he'd suspected, she didn't exert herself and go full force; she must've remembered her short skirt, when he couldn't forget it.

Her hair fluttered about her when she swung forward and whooshed away during her backward motions.

"I'm swinging higher than you," she crowed.

Yes, she was.

CJ stopped swinging, got to his feet and then climbed onto the seat. When he was a kid, he loved to swing while standing. Now, he was far too tall.

Harley jumped mid-swing, landing on her feet like a little cat. She stood on the seat and set it in motion.

"How many hours did we spend perfecting this?"

"Too many to count," he said, walking behind her, far enough where she wouldn't hit him, but still so close he smelled the sweetness of her body spray.

"Are you going to push me?"

He wanted to. Then, things might feel completely normal again. However, no matter how he tried, he noticed things about her that never registered before. The swing of her hips were she walked; the softness of her voice when she talked.

"Can we just talk?"

She jumped off the swing and came to him. They stared at each other for a moment before she looked away and shifted her weight.

"I want to kiss you too, CJ," she blurted. Resuming their earlier conversation would make things even more awkward.

"Then what—"

"I can't be your girlfriend," she said in frustration.

He scowled at her. "Listen up, Harley. I don't know what I've done to you that has you so adamant—"

"Nothing, CJ. You're beautiful and perfect and I can't imagine my life without you. This has nothing to do with you."

The incredulity at her lame-ass line must've shown on his face because she flushed. Anger suffused him, and he glowered at her.

Her chest heaved, rising and falling in agitation. She stepped closer, met and held his gaze, unintimidated by his look.

"You could've said anything except the 'it's not you, it's me' line, Harley," he snarled, bitter. "Fuck, you could've said I'm fucking hideous and it would've hit better than that tired excuse."

"You know me. If it was about you, I would tell you."

He stepped back, scrubbed a hand down his jaw, and sighed, regretting his temper. He came to mend their fences, not tear them down any further. "You said you wanted to talk to me when you invited me here. I have to go in a minute, so let's discuss whatever."

Turning away, she went to one of the tunnels and reached inside, pulling out her cellphone, before returning to him. She opened her browser and typed in a word. The fall of her hair blocked him from reading exactly what she searched for.

"I have Amenorrhea," she said softly, holding her phone out to him. "Once you read about it, you'll understand why I can't be your girlfriend."

Snapping his brows together, CJ grabbed the device from her, telling himself not to panic until he followed her instructions and read what the fuck kind of disease she had. It took a moment for Harley's exact issue to register in his worried brain.

"Oh," he said, handing the phone back to her. "Uhhh..."

This was Harley. Hadn't he just told her they discussed everything? The two of them discussing girl and guy stuff was one thing. This right here, though? This was a female issue on another fucking level.

"What does you getting your...er...that...um...have to do with being my girlfriend?"

"I'm not normal. And you deserve someone who is."

"If you're not normal, then exactly what the fuck do you consider abnormal, Harls?"

She chewed on her lower lip and bowed her head.

"Awww, Harley." CJ drew her into his arms and hugged her. "You're not abnormal. You're just a late bloomer. Your tits are popping out, so everything else will fall into place."

Her arms tightened around his waist and she groaned. "Oh my god, you've noticed they've grown?"

"Fuck, yeah! I have eyes in my fucking head."

Still holding onto him, she leaned back and gave him a disapproving look.

He grinned at her. "Would you prefer if I didn't notice?"

She lowered her long lashes. They were thick and enticing. "Yes," she said finally, then met his gaze and shook her head. "No," she amended. "I'm so confused, CJ. I wish we could go back."

His heart sank and his gut tightened. "To before my birthday?"

"No, of course not. To...to...to weeks ago. When you were still just my friend and I didn't yet notice how tall you've gotten or, um, or all your muscles."

He pondered her confession, fascinated at how red she was turning. His disappointment and pain disintegrated, and peace settled into him. Harley was his. She always had been and always would be. Perhaps, her body's physiology needed to catch up. If it took the next twenty years to happen, he'd wait.

She stood on her tiptoes, and he leaned down, allowing her to brush her lips over his.

Immediately, his heart began pounding. She kissed him again and stared into his eyes.

As CJ took in Harley's lovely face, he wanted another kiss from her. The touch of her mouth against his set his blood to boiling.

Taking her face between his hands, he took over. Pressed a little deeper. Yet, this new side of Harley was slightly more delicate, like a little flower on the verge of blooming. This Harley wasn't his bro. She was the girl he wanted.

He slid the pads of his thumbs over her cheekbones, before tipping her chin up. "Open your mouth, Harley," he murmured.

Without hesitation, she did as he asked, not protesting when he covered her mouth with his and tentatively pushed his tongue into her warm recesses. Her taste exploded in his brain, and he grunted, reminding himself to take things slowly. If he slobbered on her, he would die of mortification.

She pulled back. "Stop thinking so much," she told him. "I don't know what I'm doing either."

He nodded. This time when he kissed her, their tongues met, the tips touching. He focused on her, on the one tiny noise she made. On how sweet and minty she tasted, blocking out the closeness of their bodies and how much more he wanted from her.

The kiss went on so long, he felt completely drugged by the time they broke apart. Not ready to let her go, he explored the contours of her face, and allowed her to do the same to his, melting at her touch. His body felt weightless, his head light and giddy. Everything about Harley was suddenly new. She was his little angel, just dropped into his life from heaven, and he was the luckiest guy on earth.

He bent and kissed her again. "Harley," he whispered.

"CJ," she said, leaning her head against his chest. "I want to be your girlfriend so much. I just—"

"You're not ready."

Her eyes watered and she sniffled. "No."

He closed his eyes, unable to bear her tears. It was the one thing he hated most in the world. "Shhhh," he soothed. "When you're ready, I'll be here," he promised. "I'm not going anywhere."

"I've been so sad and angry," she muttered.

"Me, too," he admitted.

She tugged out of his embrace. "Is it bad that I want us to kiss again?"

"I want to kiss you for the rest of my life. I don't think we should risk it, though." She'd shared very personal things with him, so he wouldn't hide from her. "The more we steal kisses, the more we risk doing other things, love. And, if you aren't ready to be my girlfriend, you're not ready for us to be lovers."

She pursed her mouth. "Maybe, on my sixteenth birthday, things will be different, and we can—"

"Stop!" he ordered, his cock hardening. "Let's just take it a step at a time."

"Okay," she agreed, then swallowed. "CJ, if you meet another girl, don't let me stand in your way of finding happiness."

"Harley—"

"No," she interrupted. "We're meant to be together, so no matter what we face, we will eventually find our way to each other."

He didn't know what to say. Her words triggered a deep sense of loss within him. Somehow, he knew ill winds were blowing in to sweep her out of his life forever.

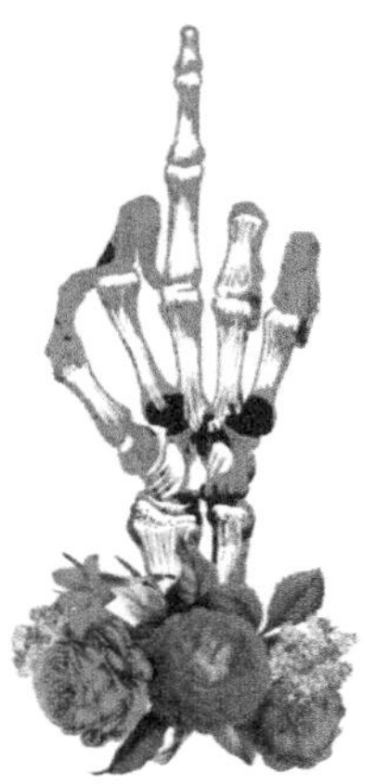

Chapter Twenty Seven

"Mr. Caldwell and Miss Harris will be partners for the year," Mr. Billson, the chemistry teacher, announced. He waited until CJ moved to Molly's lab station before returning to his seating chart.

"Hey, CJ," Molly greeted with a giggle.

"S'up," CJ said lazily, smiling at the pretty girl.

Out of the corner of his eyes, he noticed Ryan craning his neck in their direction. As far as CJ knew, Molly still fucked Ryan on occasion. He didn't intend to compete with his cousin for her attention because he had no interest in her. Still, she *was* fucking cute and like Uncle Mort had told him in the diner, there was no harm in looking.

"I can't believe you're my partner," she gushed, a blush creeping up her neck. "If Mrs. Campo hadn't passed me after my dad visited her last semester, this wouldn't be possible."

Clearing his throat, CJ shifted in his seat. Molly believing platypuses were frogs still alarmed him. Either

Campo was bribed into promoting Molly or the woman was threatened.

"Mr. Byrd move to Miss Davis's station please," Mr. Billson instructed. "Mr. Taylor—"

"I'm not moving nowhere—" Willard interrupted. Over the summer, he'd gone from wild pig to feral hog, growing taller and more muscular. His close-cropped hair widened his square face and narrowed his beady eyes. "Especially next to *her*."

"I'm crushed," Jaleena sniffed, shooting daggers at the dickhead.

"Man-bitch, respect your betters," Willard snarled, "before you're sorry."

CJ snapped his brows together, his hatred for Willard slashing his better judgment. "Fuck off, pig bastard. I have no fucking place in my life for your hogshit."

"Mr. Caldwell?"

Sighing, CJ clenched his jaw at Mr. Billson calling his name. He had enough happening without being on the radar of another teacher. Mom's pregnancy kept her sick a lot, so she usually stayed close to home. Dad was a nervous wreck because of Mom's pregnancy. Rebel had turned into hell child. Harley and CJ's friendship limped along, still not recovered from his miscalculations. For the first time in memory, CJ hadn't seen Harley on their first day back to school nor had they talked or texted. He'd waited as long as possible before leaving this morning. Once he realized she wouldn't contact him and he'd waited too long to contact her, he'd hopped on his bike and headed to school, believing he'd see her at lunch.

It hadn't happened.

Somewhere, during the course of the day, CJ resolved to mind his business if Willard wasn't fucking with him, Harley, Rebel, or Mattie. Yet, the motherfucker couldn't shut the fuck up, which meant neither could CJ.

"*Mr. Caldwell?*"

"Sir?" he said mildly, thinking of football practice in an hour and a half. Unfortunately, the next class, his last of the day, was Language Arts III – Lumbly.

"Let's talk in the hallway." Mr. Billson glared at Willard. "Mr. Byrd, gather your things and report to the principal's office."

"Fuck you—"

Nodding at CJ, Mr. Billson stalked into the hallway.

"Get your shit, CJ," Willard taunted. "Billson will be eating out of my hand just like Lumbly, and you'll fucking suffer, bitch."

"Shut up, stupid," Molly huffed to Willard. "You're so mean. CJ isn't a girl, so he can't be a bitch. He can be the son of a bitch, so ha ha, joke's on you."

"You're insulting my mom, Molly," CJ gritted, holding onto his temper since she tried to defend him. "Don't call her a bitch. *Ever*."

"He's right." Willard made no move to follow the teacher's orders to go to the principal's office. "Your momma isn't a bitch. She's a fucking cunt."

"Motherfuck you, Willard." CJ jumped to his feet and barreled to Willard's station, fist already raised.

Willard stood and swung. CJ ducked and punched the asshole's jaw. Yells and curses flew around him, but he blocked the distraction. 'Law always warned him to never lose sight of an opponent.

"The bell's ringing," Ryan said, physically pulling Willard out of CJ's reach.

"What is...are you fighting, Mr. Caldwell?" Mr. Billson's outrage broke through CJ's anger.

"He punched me for no reason, sir!" Willard whined.

"Bitch, please," Ryan snorted. "You mistook Aunt Meggie for yourself and called her a cunt."

"Shut your fucking mouth, Banks!"

Ryan smirked. "Make me, motherfucker."

"I call Zoann a cunt and you don't hit me."

"She is," Ryan said with a shrug.

CJ stared at his cousin, appalled.

Appalled.

"All those bitches are," Ryan continued.

"Get to your next class, son," Mr. Billson warned before CJ moved on Ryan. The sympathy in his dark eyes shocked CJ, so used to Lumbly blaming him for everything. A teacher seeing his point-of-view was a novel experience. "Keep your cool, Mr. Caldwell," he warned under his breath. "Let administration handle this."

That wouldn't happen without his parents.

Dejected, CJ gathered his two pencils and his phone, and walked into the hallway. It was only the first day of school, so his chemistry and math textbooks hadn't been assigned yet. For his other classes, he'd opted for digital textbooks. It just made life easier.

"CJ!"

Molly and Jaleena called his name at the same time. He slowed his stride but didn't halt, not wanting to be late to Lumbly's class. Washington Hall was crowded with students crisscrossing the hallway, some heading toward the steps and others, like CJ, outside.

"Thanks for confronting that dickhead," Jaleena said when she fell into step on his right side. She was tall and pretty with smooth chocolate skin, dark brown eyes, and a nearly bald hairstyle. He was familiar with her because she was a member of the cheer team. Sadness replaced her normal chill. "He's so awful. I hope you don't get in trouble. If you need me to talk on your behalf, I will."

On his left side, Molly looped her arm through his. "We're in Lumbly's class together, babe," she announced before CJ responded to Jaleena.

"I have Lumbly, too," Jaleena said, sidling closer to him and grabbing his hand.

"Ladies, I know I'm irresistible, but I can't walk right with both of you hanging on me. If I fall, then you two are fucked up too."

Molly giggled and held him tighter; Jaleena released him as they stepped outside and the cool September afternoon greeted them. It was a three-minute walk between the science and language buildings. The steady flow of students slowed the pace, especially with Molly refusing to let him go.

"The campus has a baker's dozen of halls," she said as they approached the main entrance of Franklin Hall. "Plus the athletic center. So thirteen buildings."

"It's fourteen," Jaleena said. "A baker's dozen is thirteen."

"Nooo," Molly said, wrapping CJ's arm around her shoulders.

He tried to move away but she tightened her grip.

"A dozen is twelve."

CJ could shove her the fuck off him; his father wouldn't be pleased. Hurting girls was a big no-no.

"It's called a baker's dozen because they use a lot of eggs."

"What do eggs have—"

"Don't worry about it, bae," CJ interrupted Jaleena, pulling away from Molly to hold open the door for the two girls. He winked at Jaleena as she slipped past him and gave a slight shake of his head. "Jaleena's right, Molly," he said, once he stepped into the building. "A baker's dozen is thirteen. Bakers in the Middle Ages didn't want to come up short and get their asses beat since bread prices were so strictly regulated."

"That is so dumb," Molly complained. "You're discussing the Middle Ages as if they're the past when we're living in them now. Otherwise, this would be the End Ages, and I'm not ready for the sun to burn us to bits and pieces."

"We're in the Modern Era, Molly," Jaleena said. "What—"

"You're right!" CJ blurted, pausing outside Lumbly's class and drawing in a deep breath. Skipping appealed to his common sense.

"Do you intend to step into my classroom, Mr. Caldwell, or should I write you up? We can set the precedent early."

Between Willard and Lumbly, he wouldn't be able to take it. School was a battlefield nowadays, no longer a place for learning.

"You got this," Jaleena whispered as Molly said, "Come on, CJ. He'll write you up. He suspended me last year when I told him I was ten minutes late because I kept losing my place after I counted the one trillionth step between the parking lot and his class."

"And I'll suspend you again unless you tell me how many steps are in a mile, Miss Harris."

Buying time so Molly could come up with a number, CJ guided the two girls in. Somehow, Ryan and Willard were already seated next to one another.

"Mr. Lumbly," Molly said on a sniffle. "Please, don't suspend me. My momma will whip me, and my daddy won't give me any food."

"Too bad for you. Give me the number now or be prepared to get beaten and starved."

"Molly, your parents can be charged with twenty-one hundred twelve different types of child abuse," CJ said, hoping she picked up on the answer.

"They can't!" she wailed. "My daddy's a sheriff's deputy and—"

"Shut your fucking mouth, cunt," Willard blared, because he had a limited fucking vocabulary and a limited vocal range. Roar and trumpet.

"Take your seats," Lumbly ordered, glaring at Molly.

Concerned for her, CJ took Molly's hand and escorted her to a seat close to his, nodding to some of his friends whom he hadn't seen since his birthday party.

Lumbly's classroom was smaller this year, its length cut in half by a divider with a door at the far end. Like the entry, the partition door was slightly open. The low hum of voices filtered through, but nothing too disruptive.

"Settle down, ladies and gentlemen," Lumbly called, still afflicted with his sucked-lemon face and sphincter-lip pucker. He walked to his desk and opened a drawer, then set a magician's cap with *dunce* sewn down the front and back. The neon yellow word stood out against the stark black material.

Vague memories of Pete Hart's abuse and humiliation invaded CJ. 'Law had been called to school and rescued CJ, allowing him to stay home an extra year. Now, the only way he'd escape Lumbly was by dropping out of school. Even telling Uncle Mort wasn't an option. He'd get 'Law involved and, in turn, add stress to Mom.

Lumbly leaned against the desk and folded his arms. "Mr. Caldwell, please go to the chalkboard."

Clearing his throat, CJ got to his feet and called himself fifty thousand stupid motherfuckers. He should've told 'Law months ago about the teacher's behavior. If he had, Lumbly would already be taken care of.

"This semester, we will read *The Crucible*. Today..."

Commotion just beyond the classroom drowned out Lumbly's voice. Stiffening, he glanced toward the hallway; however, the almost-closed door blocked whatever was going on.

"Mr. Caldwell," he began the moment silence fell, "I will say a word and you write it on the chalkboard, along with a short definition. If you get *one* wrong, you will wear the cap for the duration of the class."

"Caldwell, don't need no dunce cap," Willard said around a yawn, his swollen jaw and black eye not severe enough to shut him the fuck up. "We just look at him and know he's a dunce."

Ryan and Willard were the only two dickheads laughing.

"You've sharpened your wit, Mr. Byrd," Lumbly congratulated, then turned to CJ. "Amelliorate."

Either Lumby was a dumb fuckhead or he was mispronouncing the word on purpose. To be safe, CJ spelled the word as the teacher said it and added the correct version without the extra 'l', then wrote a simplified definition.

"Quail."

CJ debated a moment, then wrote his answers.

"Effervescent." He allowed CJ thirty seconds. "Giblet."

Chalk against the board, CJ rolled the word over in his head. "Are the words only from *The Crucible*, Mr. Lumbly?"

"Where else would they come from, Mr. Caldwell?" the teacher retorted.

CJ wrote the word given, the definition, and the word Lumbly *should've* said. Three years ago, Harley roped him into a summer theater workshop, focused on Arthur Miller's play, so CJ knew the terminology. He wished he had a fucking *gibbet* to display Lumbly's beaten and broken body.

"Gull."

The little motherfucker chose words with modern usage completely different from the play's seventeenth century setting.

CJ scribbled the word and the two meanings.

"Congratulations, Mr. Caldwell, you're the year's first dunce."

CJ froze, his pulse thrumming through his body and competing with his rising humiliation. “You’ve only given me five of the ten words.”

“None of your answers are correct, so five are enough. Not the spelling or the definitions.”

They were and CJ knew it, but he had no recourse. Stiffening his spine, he turned and snatched the hat from the desk before shoving it on his head and folding his arms. He wasn’t sure if he wanted to cry—which he’d *never* do in front of anyone, but Lumbly, Willard, and Ryan especially—or kill.

The door to the divider opened and Mattie scooted in just as Jaleena got to her feet.

“All of CJ’s answers are correct, Mr. Lumbly,” she said on a swallow.

“Shut it, Miss Davis, or you’re next,” Lumbly growled, not looking at Jaleena for glaring at Mattie.

A little tremble passed through Jaleena. “But, sir, it isn’t fair—”

“Sit your fucking ass down, man-bitch,” Willard said.

“Get out of my class, Miss Donovan,” Lumbly ordered, not flinching at Byrd’s insult.

“I can’t do that, Mr. Lumbly. Please just listen a minute because I’m coming in peace.”

“I don’t have to listen to you or your threats. I’ve been promoted to Dean of Upper School Language Arts, so I must have done something right. Get out of my classroom.”

“But Daddy and Maman are—”

“Shut your mouth!” Lumbly cut in. “I don’t care what they are since they *aren’t* here. I’m counting to three. If you aren’t gone, I’m suspending you.”

Mattie smirked and stepped aside.

Instead of Uncle Johnnie and Aunt Kendall, the opening door brought in Rebel and CJ’s biggest nightmare. *Harley.* Her beautiful eyes widened at seeing the dunce cap on his head and her mouth fell open.

"CJ?" Rory asked in confusion, appearing next to Harley.

Mark JB walked in, his eyes bugging in shock. "Bruh, why you got that dunce cap on? Shouldn't that be on Ryan and Willard's jacked-up head?"

"Watch your fucking mouth, boy," Willard sneered.

"Bitch, I will paint these walls with your blood," Mark JB growled. "I hunt pigs like you for fun."

"This is out of hand!" Lumbly shouted. "I'm calling security to remove you hooligans." He turned to CJ. "You should be ashamed of yourself. Wherever you are, chaos follows, Mr. Caldwell. You're a waste of space with no good reason to have been born."

The classroom door pushed open and Uncle Mort sauntered in, cigarette hanging from the corner of his mouth. He smoked in silence, not speaking, staring Lumbly into submission. At any moment, CJ expected the motherfucker to grow a fucking tail just to tuck it between his grubby little legs. Finishing the cigarette, Uncle Mort threw it on the floor and crushed it underneath his boot, then cleared his throat.

Uncle Digger, Uncle Val, and Uncle Johnnie walked in.

Still, no one spoke. CJ hadn't gotten permission to remove the fucking hat so he left it on his head like a fucking moronic dumb ass. He wasn't sure what everyone was waiting for.

Then, he heard spurs jingling and the pounding of bootfalls. He'd know his father's footsteps anywhere. They were one of the last sounds he heard almost every evening when 'Law came to wish him *goodnight*. Most of the time, he didn't wear spurs. Only when he was in full leathers or on a special date with Mom or going on or returning from a run.

Outlaw paused in the doorway, swept his gaze over the classroom, touched on Lumbly before focusing on CJ. Like Harley, 'Law's eyes widened. Unlike hers, they iced and narrowed.

"Mr. Caldwell, I can explain," Lumbly began.

"Come on, bruh." Uncle Digger walked to Lumbly, yanked him to the desk, and shoved him onto his seat, then took up guard next to the trembling man.

"Daddy, CJ gave all the right answers." Harley pointed to the board. "Jaleena stood up for CJ, but Mr. Lumbly threatened her too. He didn't even allow CJ the full ten words. He only gave him five. He mispronounced the first one and the fourth one was entirely wrong. Giblet instead of gibbet. Then, he gave him quail and gull, to confuse him since they are both birds as well as words from the play."

"Shut the fuck up, Harley," Willard said, "you weren't even in this class."

"You, fuckface, are stupid," Rebel said in the same hell-child tone she'd used for weeks. "One, you're eighteen and a junior in high school. That says everything, doesn't it, dumb bitch? Two, do you want Uncle Val to replay the recordings? Ryan might know technical shit, but he learned it from his father." She smiled, not nice. "Oops, should I have let it out you're an adult?"

"I am, too," Molly called. "Will I be arrested for being a junior?"

"It's okay, Molly. You won't be eighteen for a bit," Harley reminded her, rushing to her side. "You're fine."

"Th-then wh-why are tears in Willard's eyes?"

"He's eighteen," Harley explained. "You're not."

Dad walked to CJ and removed the cap, then placed his hands on his shoulders. "Why you not telling me about fuckhead?"

"If I came to you for everything, you'll never respect me, Dad," CJ said, shame raging in him at wearing the cap in front of Harley and his father.

"This not *everyfuckingthing*. This a fuckin' adult bullying a kid, *my* boy. You come to me immediately for bullshit like this, son. Ain't lookin' at you no different. Hear me?"

CJ nodded. Dad lit two cigarettes and handed one to him, then signaled Uncle Digger to step aside. The uncles and Rory closed in, forming a semi-circle around the desk, while the others engaged Lumbly's students in conversation. Harley, Rebel, Mattie, Rory, and Mark JB distracted attention away from the front of the classroom.

Dad snatched Lumbly to his feet, then dragged on his cigarette and blew the smoke in the teacher's face. "You like your fuckin' guts in you or you prefer seein' them motherfuckers next to you on a fuckin' table?"

Rory's eyes lit up, but Uncle Johnnie gave him a look and Ro's expression closed.

"I do believe you're threatening me, Mr. Caldwell."

"Ain't threatenin' you, motherfucker. I'm vowin' you fuck with my boy afuckingain and I'm fuckin' killin' you more painfully than I did your fuckin' cousin."

CJ started and Lumbly paled.

"You wanna visit all *Dr.* Hart graves?" Dad asked casually.

"I do," Rory piped in.

"Hush, son!" Uncle Johnnie ordered.

"I'm having you arrested for intimidation, Mr. Caldwell," Mr. Lumbly said in triumph. "This is a public institution with governing laws. You cannot threaten me and get away with it."

"Wrong, motherfucker," Uncle Mortician said. "This a private institution that we keep running. We make the laws here."

"I don't care!" Lumbly snapped back. "I have a contract and I'll sue for breach. Imagine what a court case will do? Discovery will expose your dirty secrets."

"Jake, there isn't a need to bring this to court," Uncle Johnnie soothed. "We're all about peace nowadays." He smiled at Dad. "Especially with all the difficulties of Megan's latest pregnancy."

"Then tell them to backoff, John," *Jake* ordered.

"Ain't fuckin' backin' off cuz you fuckin' with my boy," Dad snapped, shooting daggers at Uncle Johnnie, promising painful revenge. "CJ switchin' to another fuckin' class if you locked in a fuckin' contract."

Harley squeezed next to CJ. "Willard is getting out-of-hand."

"If he wouldn't have backup from dumbass, he'd shut the fuck up," Rebel scoffed, popping bubble gum into her mouth as she scooted next to Uncle Mort.

"Ryan?" Uncle Val asked on a sigh.

Rebel nodded.

"I have an idea," Mattie said, taking Uncle Val's spot as he headed to his fucked-up son. "Maman and Daddy went through a lot of trouble settling the contracts and salaries. Mr. Lumbly teaches the accelerated classes, so why don't we attend this class at the same time as CJ? We could rearrange our schedules."

"Who are you thinking, princess?" Uncle Johnnie asked. "You're smart enough to keep pace in Language Art III, but we don't want to put anyone on the spot."

Rebel made a face at Uncle Johnnie.

"Matilda?"

"Uh, Daddy, well, I-I was thinking me, Rory, Harley, Rebel, Devon, Lou, and Mark JB."

Uncle Johnnie patted Mattie's shoulder and smiled indulgently. "Lou and Mark Jr. are too young."

"I'm the same age as they are," she whispered, bowing her head. "And we call him Mark JB." She offered a timid smile. "It's snarky and fun."

"It's ridiculous," Uncle Johnnie announced, ruffling her hair. "You're special, princess. It's kind of you to include them, just as a lady should be."

"Yeah, if she was a lady, Uncle Johnnie," Rebel snapped. "Just like I told Dumb Ass, he wasn't an adult and should've told Dad about Lumbly, I'm telling *you* your daughter's a child and all the pressure you're putting on her is stupid, unfair, and not a good look for you. Treat her like she's human. Treat Mark JB and Lou like they're our family, instead of sounding like fucking dickhead Willard."

"Efuckinuff, Rebel," Dad barked. "Johnnie grown. A fuckhead yeah, but a grown fuckhead and you ain't got no fuckin' place talkin' to him like that."

Rebel threw Dad a hateful glare. Undaunted, he narrowed his eyes at her and she flushed, dropping her gaze to the floor.

"Yes, of course, Mrs. Caldwell, right this way."

All movement stopped at the sound of Dr. Marvey's voice as he walked into the classroom and stepped aside to allow Mom to enter. Rebel swept Mom with a look of disgust, anger darkening her face. CJ saw nothing wrong with Mom's fitted mini dress that showed off her baby bump. Paired with hi-top Chucks and thick socks, he thought their mother looked adorable.

"Megan, baby, whatcha doin' here?"

"Hey, you," Mom said to Dad, all smiles as she walked to him turned her face up for a kiss.

"Hey, baby," Dad breathed after kissing her.

"It's my day to pick up the girls," she said, "and I saw your bike."

"We have practice, Mother," Rebel said, barely civil. "I told you I didn't need you. You should've stayed home and nurtured your new princess."

"Rebel, I ain't—"

Mom laid a hand on Dad's arm. "You're still our princess, love," she said softly. "But this isn't the place for such a discussion. Let's talk when we get home. And, remember, practice starts next week. We were going shopping today."

"I don't want to go shopping with you," Rebel said.

"I'd like to go with you, Aunt Meggie," Mattie said quickly, forestalling Dad blasting Rebel to hell.

The fury in his eyes frightened CJ on his little sister's behalf.

"Can I, Daddy?" Mattie persisted.

"If your aunt's feeling up to it," Uncle Johnnie said blandly. "She hasn't been up for much lately."

"Motherfucker—"

"Dr. Marvey!" Mom called, interrupting Dad.

The dean stepped next to Mom and gave her the once over. "Mrs. Caldwell?"

"I received very disturbing text messages from my nephew," she started, setting her purse on Lumbly's desk and pulling out her phone. "Ryan informed me that Jake Lumbly isn't qualified to teach at Ridge Moore. He especially isn't qualified to head the department."

"*What*?" Ryan cried. "I didn't send you anything, Aunt Meggie."

Mattie rocked on her heels and Harley pressed her lips together.

Mom offered an innocent smile. "You did. It's right here on my phone."

Jumping to his feet, Ryan rushed to her. "You're lying!"

"Don't disrespect your aunt, boy!" Uncle Val said, dragging him away before Dad got to the motherfucker.

Ignoring his father, Ryan rifled through his phone, growing more frantic by the second. “No! No! No! That wasn’t me. Dad...Val...I didn’t send these!” Eyes wide, he looked at Mom. “I didn’t send the texts to you, Aunt Meggie.”

“Where’d they come from then, cousin?” Mattie asked. “How else would Aunt Meggie get them?”

Sweat beading his brow, Ryan continued sliding his finger over his phone screen.

Mom cleared her throat. She smiled at CJ. He saw how badly she wanted to take him in her arms and hug him but respected how she thought he wanted to be perceived by his peers.

“I expect Mr. Lumbly’s termination effective immediately,” she said. “I can’t have my children and my nieces and nephews receive an inferior education.”

“You can’t do that!” Uncle Johnnie said. “I worked out the contracts.”

“Yeah, for teachers with an education,” she retorted. “Not vengeful idiots who target my child to get to my husband.”

Dad hadn’t been himself for weeks and it was never more evident as the scene grew increasingly out of hand. Mom’s pregnancy messed with his head, but his glare at Rebel revealed how deeply his sister’s behavior hurt their father. Add Uncle Johnnie’s bullshit in and it surprised CJ his father hadn’t gone mad.

“You don’t have the authority, Megan,” Uncle Johnnie said with finality. “Christopher put me and Kendall in charge of this. Jake stays.”

Mom glanced at Dad and he gave the barest nods.

“Furthermore, if he sues for breach of contract,” Uncle Johnnie continued, “whether he’s right or wrong, *our* secrets will come to light.”

“Ain’t goin’ nofuckinwhere, baby,” Dad soothed, seeing her sudden fear. “Especially not jail.”

She nodded, trusting Dad that he spoke the truth. "Well, I like Mattie's suggestion. I think Teacher's Aides might work too. I happen to be free around this time as is Roxy."

"I'll go with Mattie's suggestion, but you aren't interrupting classes," Uncle Johhnie declared. "Hell no. Fuck no."

"You ain't got that fuckin' right to tell my woman when the fuck she comin' here," Dad said.

"Why? Big Joe's money and all her brilliant investments to make it grow doesn't make her the queen," Uncle Johnnie snapped. "I have a say-so in the hiring and firing. *I* have a contract."

Mom rolled her eyes.

"You got the fuckin' contract, Johnnie," Dad said with a vicious grin. "But *I* got the fuckin' keys. Megan and me bought this motherfucker last Friday."

Chapter Twenty Eight

MATILDA

"Harley's a traitor."

"And you're a fucking idiot," Mattie retorted, *over* Rebel's shenanigans and wishing she hadn't changed her mind about the shopping mall. Mattie and Harley would've fared much better on their own with Aunt Meggie.

Mattie glanced at her new set of nails, pale pink and cut short, just the right length for a 'young lady'. She appreciated her aunt's foresight. Aunt Meggie didn't allow Mattie to dwell on what *could be*. Instead, she'd went into the nail shop, announced she wanted a new look and told the manicurist they all wanted the same style. Of course, Rebel balked and insisted on long, red nails. When Aunt Meggie refused, Mattie realized even she was sick to death of Reb's spoiled assery.

"Go away, Rebel. I don't feel like talking to you."

Rebel sat on the bench next to Mattie. While Aunt Meggie and Harley went into another store, Mattie waited outside. She needed to text her father and beg him for an advance on her allowance. She already owed Aunt Meggie several hundred dollars for an outfit. Mattie needed shoes and a handbag to complete her look as well as the right makeup palette and jewelry. She'd just whipped out her phone when Rebel spotted her from wherever she'd stomped to after leaving the nail shop.

"The minute CJ arrived, Harley abandoned us," Rebel complained, ignoring Mattie.

"Harley didn't abandon us, doofus." Mattie slammed her phone on top of her purse, next to her on the bench. "She and CJ are best friends. They always prefer each other's company over anyone else's. Besides, she's with Aunt Meggie and so is CJ. If anyone's the traitor, it's you."

"Fuck off. My life is ruined and you're chickenshit not to recognize my pain."

"All fucking self-inflicted, so I have zero sympathy for you."

"Self-inflicted? It's Megan Caldwell inflicted. If she'd act like a woman in her thirties, I wouldn't be in this predicament."

The noise in the mall added pressure to Mattie's suddenly pounding head. From the outside looking in, Rebel had a perfect life. Mainly because she could be herself and not worry about her parents' reaction. Even now, when she'd turned into Super Bitch, Aunt Meggie wasn't berating her or making her feel unladylike. She was giving her space while trying to soothe Rebel's fear and jealousy.

If Mattie had acted in such a way, Daddy would've reduced her to tears and Maman would've backed him up.

"She's disgusting. She needs to keep her legs closed or tell Daddy to stay off her."

"Your mom's disgusting?" Mattie asked for clarification. "Because she likes sex?"

"*Eww. Images.*"

"*Eww. Hypocrite.*"

"I don't know why I bother talking to you, Matilda."

"That makes two of us, Rebel. I *told* your ass I didn't want to hear what you had to say."

"You're supposed to be my friend." Some of Rebel's anger dropped from her and her face crumpled. "I'm suffering and you don't care."

Mattie wanted to turn her back on Rebel, but the two of them, along with Harley, were in a very exclusive club as the daughters of bikers belonging to one of the most notorious MCs around.

As the *first* daughter of Outlaw and the *first* granddaughter of Big Joe, Rebel was at the top of the food chain, no matter how many other sisters she had. Aunt Meggie took the brunt of the negativity as Uncle Christopher's wife and Big Joe's girl, leaving Rebel to bask in the glory of her enviable position. If only Rebel focused on the positives of their status.

She couldn't even look at it from the perspective of the only other girl in their family, Wynona. Winnie was too young and her parents kept her much more insulated, probably because of the dynamics of Uncle Stretch, Uncle Cash, and Aunt Ophelia's relationship. Harley, Rebel, and Mattie were the princesses of the club, beloved as the only three girls from the first baby boom that produced fourteen boys and ended ten years ago with the births of Axel, Rebel's brother, Harley's brother, Kaleb, and their cousin, Ephraim. Since then, eight more kids were born, including her little brother, Blade.

Harley, Rebel, and Mattie were the three musketeers, and they had each other's backs. Mattie wrestled her annoyance under control.

"I do care, Reb," she said tiredly. "But you're not being fair to your mom. She's a month away from *thirty-five,* Rebel. She isn't old and she loves Uncle Chris."

"Then she needs to get on birth control, and yes, she *is* old. She's over thirty with a nearly grown son."

"With *a* grown son," Mattie supplied, adding, "Diesel," when Rebel lifted her brows in question.

"Diesel isn't her son! It's physically impossible. Dad's old ass could've fathered him." Rebel shrugged. "Who knows? Maybe, he did, and he's just passing him off as a runaway. That would explain why he's so adamant I do not marry him."

"I need a smoke," Mattie huffed. But she wouldn't have money to buy any marijuana, thanks to her shopping spree and her head was hurting too bad to exchange favors. "Maybe, then, I can find the right words to explain how fucked up you are. Uncle Chris wouldn't lie to Aunt Meggie about Diesel's parentage. And, now, you're going in on your dad because you're angry with your mom."

"I'm not angry with Momma. I love her. I hate that stupid baby. I want it to die."

"You love Gunner."

"Gunner's a boy!"

"Aunt Meggie can't control the sex of her baby."

"She can! She can abort the girls. Or she can freeze her eggs and have them fertilized to make sure they're boys."

Mattie's mouth fell open. Her cousin was delusional! But she knew how soul-crushing name-calling was, so she drew in a deep breath. "Reb, we are the first three girls born amidst a surplus of swinging dicks. Harley was first, then you, then me. That makes us special. And your parents adore you. Aunt Meggie loves hanging out with you. She taught you how to walk in heels, for fuck's sake." What she wouldn't give for that. Maman promised when Mattie turned sixteen, she'd get her a pair of designer pumps. Guilt pressed into her. She loved her mother and she hated moments like these when she wished Maman followed Aunt Meggie's lead.

"Aunt Bailey taught Harley, so Momma didn't do anything special," Rebel grouched. "Just gave me stupid lessons like we were models. In her dreams."

"It wasn't so stupid because Aunt Bailey did the same with Harley. They walked with books on their heads for balance and played music. She said how they danced and pretended they were on a catwalk. Just like Aunt Meggie did with you."

Just as Mattie wanted her mother to do with her.

Harley and CJ walked out of the store, all hugged up. Seeing the two of them together called attention to CJ's height. Over the summer, he grew three inches. The past months changed Harley too. She now reached his shoulder and had curves and acne.

"I'll bet they're fucking," Rebel whispered. "Just look at them. She's no longer Saint Harley."

Rebel's speculation worsened Mattie's mood. She'd done a fair amount of virgin-shaming and bullying to Harley.

"Aren't you?" Mattie retorted.

"Not yet," Rebel said darkly. "But I'm curious. How can I not be, living with two nymphomaniac parents? Besides, Diesel will be my first."

"Diesel's married and your brother, weirdo."

"Men cheat all the time, and he isn't my brother."

"He sees you as his sister and I'm not even commenting on how disrespectful you are to his vows. He can't be your first if he isn't willing. Since he's not, you need to forget your obsession."

"I want Diesel and I intend to have him. I'm seducing him. On my eighteenth birthday, I'll find a way to get in bed with him. Even if I have to pretend I'm someone else. No one can tell me what to do."

"You're right but someone *can* say what the hell they want to do, dumb bitch. And Diesel doesn't want you. You can't trample over his rights to have your stupid way. What is wrong with you?"

"I hate Mom's baby and I hate Tabitha."

"I hope I never hate anyone if it eats *me* alive, instead of the motherfuckers I'm hating."

"We're starving," Aunt Meggie announced, startling Mattie.

She'd been so focused on her stupid cousin, she hadn't seen Aunt Meggie, Harley, and CJ approach.

"I'm not, MegAnn," he said with a shit-eating grin, "so by 'we' you mean you and Squiggles?"

Aunt Meggie laughed. "You're calling your little sister *Squiggles*?"

He nodded and pulled Harley closer to him. "Harley thinks it's adorable. Don't you?"

"Yep," Harley said with a grin. "We came up with it together."

"Meggie, you about ready to head home?" Slipper asked, walking up to their little group from somewhere. "Prez wondering how much longer you going to be?"

Mattie hadn't realized Aunt Meggie had a detail with her, since she hadn't seen them.

"Squiggles and me are hungry," Aunt Meggie said happily. "If you, Orange, and Fuse could find seats for all eight of us in the food court, I'd really appreciate it."

"Who's Squiggles?" Slipper asked, scratching his long, scraggly beard.

Aunt Meggie placed a hand on her baby bump. "The baby."

"Squiggles Caldwell is a lovely name, Meggie."

"It's CJ's nickname, Slipper. We haven't come up with a name yet."

"Thank fuck. That's the worst fucking name I ever heard if you stuck with it for life."

"Dude," CJ said, laughing like a lunatic, "find the fucking seats and stop being a lying asshole."

Slipper grinned. "Fuck off, boy. I can be a lying asshole if it keep Meggie happy."

"And you alive," Rebel inserted, ruining the fun. "Daddy would kill you."

Bowing his head, Slipper shifted.

"Ignore my sister," CJ said, glowering at Rebel, "she's mental. Dad trusts you with Mom, so you have nothing to fear."

"Thanks, CJ." Slipper ambled off. "Come on, Orange! Fuse!"

"Mattie—"

"Why were you in that stupid store so long if you didn't buy anything, Momma?" Rebel demanded, getting to her feet, already several inches taller than Aunt Meggie.

CJ abandoned Harley and inserted himself between his mom and his sister. "Back the fuck up, Reb. Mom doesn't have to answer to you."

"What will you do, dickhead? You can't hit me."

"Of course, he can't," Mattie said with sarcasm, standing and realizing even she was taller than her aunt. "He dropped me, but he can't hit you."

"You dropped your cousin?" Aunt Meggie asked.

"Fuck you, whiny bitch," Rebel said, ignoring her mother and not giving CJ a chance to explain. "He bent down before he let you go *after* you told him to and called him an asshole."

Aunt Meggie's whistle got their attention. "Enough!" she ordered. "Rebel, we're having a long talk this evening. You're upset about the baby—"

"It's *you*. You're gross."

"Shut up, Rebel," CJ ordered, though he stood next to his mom and didn't see how his sister's words crushed Aunt Meggie because he didn't turn to her.

"Rebel, you're out of line," Harley said, hugging Aunt Meggie.

"You aren't gross at all," Mattie added, wanting to cry at how unfair life was. She told herself if Aunt Meggie was *her* mom she'd never be so disrespectful, but was that a fair speculation? Maybe, she would've felt as threatened as Rebel did at the prospect of another girl instead of wishing Maman *did* have another baby and it *was* a girl to take away some of Matilda's scrutiny by her parents.

Life would be a comedy if it wasn't so tragic.

Aunt Meggie drew Mattie into her arms and hugged her tightly.

"I love you, Aunt Meggie."

"I love you too, Mattie," she said kindly, pulling away and taking Mattie's face between her hands. "I was in the store buying accessories for your and Harley's outfits as payment for your help with Ryan."

"Mattie knows that stuff," Rebel inserted. "Harley doesn't. You didn't need to buy her anything."

"That's the same thing I said to your mom," Harley said flatly as Aunt Meggie stepped away and rested a hand on her belly.

Rebel's hateful glare at Aunt Meggie's baby bump saddened Mattie. "Stop being a drama queen and calling attention to that stupid baby. If you want to do anything, tell Daddy to stay off you. Having all those children doesn't keep his interest. You're baby trapping him. But the joke's on you, Mom. He's old, so he'll die soon and leave you all alone."

Sometimes, Mattie watched Aunt Meggie and wondered where she got the wherewithal to ignore so much verbal abuse. Usually from Daddy, but Mattie didn't understand why that was, so she wouldn't speculate. He was the only one brave enough to risk Uncle Christopher's wrath. Here and there, she side-eyed her aunt. Mostly, she admired Aunt Meggie's ability to overlook dumb shit and move on. Uncle Chris was the disciplinarian and Aunt Meggie was the coddler.

But everyone had a breaking point.

Aunt Meggie stepped in front of Rebel, on the verge of bursting into tears. Then, she drew herself up and slapped the side of Rebel's face before stumbling to the bench.

Rebel grabbed her cheek. "I hate you!" she screamed and ran off.

"Stay there, Mom. I'll get her," CJ said darkly. Not waiting for a reply, he stalked after his sister.

"I'll tell Slipper that we need to-go order," Harley said, and left too.

Mattie sat next to her aunt and put an arm around her shoulder. "Aunt Meggie, I must teach you how to hit. That bitch should've been knocked the fuck out."

Chapter Twenty Nine

REBEL

Hating her whole family, Rebel glared out the window the entire ride home. She drowned out the concern Momma mightn't be able to drive home. She despised CJ for catching up to her and yanking her by the collar, then dragging her to the SUV, unconcerned by the names she screamed at him. She loathed Diesel and *everyone* who insisted they were related.

And she abhorred her unborn little sister. Each mile closer to home, Rebel prayed for Divine Intervention on her behalf. She wanted the clock turned back to before Momma's pregnancy. Maybe, she could've insisted Momma and her have a girls' night in Rebel's room, where they laughed and talked and danced, and spent the night gossiping.

It would've kept Daddy from Momma.

At the turn onto the dead-end street that led to the club entrance, Slipper gunned ahead and CJ took the lead on his moped with Orange and Fuse on each side of the SUV. Momma barreled through the already-opened gates, speeding behind CJ toward the private access road.

Of course, Daddy was waiting when she swerved to a stop in front of their house. Rebel intended to sit until everyone else went inside. Instead, the back passenger door swung open and Daddy snatched her out and carried her like a ragdoll all the way to the house.

"I'm sorry! I'm sorry!" Rebel chanted, though he ignored her.

Inside the foyer, he released her, not caring that she fell on her ass.

"Mom, do you need anything?" CJ asked, guiding Momma to one of the benches.

"Aunt Meggie, Maman is bringing dinner."

"Slipper didn't know what to order for everyone," Harley said, "so I told him to only order for him, Orange, and Fuse."

"Tabitha, can walk to Aunt Kendall's," Diesel said.

Knowing he was present infuriated Rebel again and made her forget fear of her father's wrath. "No one asked for her help," she snarled, scrambling to her feet.

"Shut the fuck up, Rebel," Daddy warned, in a tone he never used with her, as her pack of brothers descended on the hallway. He looked at CJ. "Next time, boy, beat her fuckin' ass. Appreciate your lil' ass callin' me and askin' permission, but when she actin' spoil and disrespectin' your Ma, fuck her up."

"You're nothing but a bitch, CJ," Rebel yelled, swiping angrily at her tears. "Lumbly's right. You're just a waste of space. *Die!*"

The hurt on CJ's face vindicated her as much as the silence because her words left everyone speechless.

"Rebel, shut up," Momma ordered. "You're embarrassing no one but yourself."

Rule set Gunner on his feet and he ran to Momma, climbing next to her then crawling onto her lap.

"Apologize to CJ," she continued. "You were out of control, and I certainly couldn't handle you." She kissed the top of Gunner's head. Unlike earlier, when she'd been so lively and gorgeous, she was frighteningly pale. "Diesel, find a way to vacate Lumbly's contract. Buy him out. I don't care."

"Mom, don't worry about that now," CJ said, scooping Gunner into his arms.

"Are you hungry?" Diesel persisted. "Tabitha's at the club, waiting for my text."

Mattie shook her head and glanced at Rebel. "Maman's on the way, D. Tell, uh, let Tabitha chill at the club."

Momma got to her feet. "I'm going upstairs. I'm not too hungry right now.

Daddy started toward Momma. "Rebel, stay your fuckin' ass here."

"No, Christopher, deal with her." Momma nodded to Rebel, not looking at her. "I'll be waiting for you upstairs," she said, leaning into Harley as they started toward the staircase.

In silence and carrying Gunner, CJ followed Momma and Harley. They'd just disappeared up the stairs when Uncle Johnnie, Aunt Kendall, and Rory arrived.

"Here, son." Aunt Kendall handed Rory a covered dish. "Bring it to the kitchen. Mattie, set the table for your aunt, uncle, and cousins."

"Okay, Mom." Rory headed right, toward the hallway that led to the kitchen, dish in hand.

"Aunt Meggie is upstairs, Maman," Mattie said timidly because she was a stupid, fake bitch. "I don't think she'll be able to eat at the table tonight."

"Fix her a tray, darling," Aunt Kendall responded. "Me, you and, Rebel will set up a buffet for your Uncle Christopher and your cousins."

"*Not,*" Rebel said. "I'm not a fucking maid, Aunt Kendall."

Daddy released smoke from his cigarette. "You *is* a fuckin' child and if you ain't wantin' another ass whippin' *tofuckinmorrow* night, you apologizin' to Kendall and treatin' her with respect."

"You can't spank me! I'm a girl."

"Can I beat Rebel's ass, Dad?" Ryder asked. Even though he had blond hair like her and Momma, his expressions and mannerisms were all their father.

"Apologize to Kendall *now*," Daddy ordered, barely recognizable in his anger.

Even at Ryan's birthday party, when he'd taken all her privileges, he had an air of parental exasperation. Now, disgust and fury percolated in his eyes. He'd forgotten how he spoiled her for her entire life. Given her whatever she wanted. Sometimes, without Rebel asking. Suddenly, her anger toward Diesel and her parents made *her* the bad guy. Well, she wasn't.

After discarding his cigarette in the standing ashtray, he unbuckled his belt. Pulling the leather through the loops took forever. Catching both ends and halving it didn't minimize its length.

He stepped toward her, the belt raised. Regret softened his anger. "Apologize, Rebel," he said, gentler, almost a plea.

"Will you still beat me?"

"For the way you disrespected your ma, fuck yeah," he answered without hesitation.

Of course, he would! "You're such a fucking simp," she snarled.

"I ain't givin' a good fuck if you think my ass a simpleton, Rebel," Daddy snapped, ignoring the laughter of his sons and Diesel.

Mattie bit her lip to stifle her amusement. Stupid bitch. Uncle Johnnie and Aunt Kendall stared as stupidly as Daddy.

"Dad isn't a simp, Reb," Ransom said with disapproval.

"At least one of you lil' motherfuckers think my ass got fuckin' sense," Daddy grumbled, setting off Diesel and her brothers' guffaws again.

"Dad, stop being old!" Axel ordered. "Simp don't mean simpleton, man."

"Dad's old, dummy," Ransom responded, shaking his head.

"Draw Dad some word art with current slang and the meanings, Rule," Ryder suggested, nodding to Rule.

"Dad doesn't need a dictionary," Rebel chirped, her panic settling. Her father didn't intend to spank her. He wouldn't have allowed this stupid conversation to continue. Whenever he punished her brothers, *nothing* deterred him. Along with everything else, he was full of fucking hot air. "He *is* a simp behind his wife."

Dad snapped his brows together and all the humor died.

Condemnation slipped into Rule's green eyes. "Reb that's so unworthy of you. What Dad shares with Mom is a blessing."

Rebel narrowed her eyes at her twin. "Shut the hell up. You've been ignoring me for months, fuckhead. Keep the tradition going."

"I love you, Reb," Rule said quietly. "I'm going to say an extra prayer for you."

Axel frowned. Until Gunner, he'd been the baby of the family, but took the new baby in stride. Being seven with their little brother was born might've helped. Or, maybe, because there were so many boys in the house, another one hadn't mattered. Being the only other girl aside from her mother set Rebel apart. Now, with a little sister on the way, she'd become Momma's afterthought, too. "In between your chants and devotions, do what Ryder suggested, Rule."

"This gettin' the fuck outta hand. What the fuck a simp?"

"In *simple* terms," Axel started with a grin, "simp's an acronym meaning sucker idolizing mediocre pussy."

"*What*?" And then: "Boy, you fuckin' *ten*. How your lil' ass know what and my ass don't?"

"'Cause you're old, Dad," Axel said. "And we can't give away all our state secrets. Before we know it, parents will be invading our territory, trying to be cool."

"Sucker idolizin' mediocre pussy," Dad repeated, the meaning finally dawning on him. He glowered at Rebel. "You callin' your Ma pussy ordinary?"

"Is that what you got from the definition?" Rebel yelled in disgust. "I wasn't referring to Momma at all, Daddy. I was talking about *you*. A simp also means a man who is stupidly obsessed with a woman. In your case, Momma."

"If you meanin' that to insult my ass, you ain't. I *am* stupidly obsessed with your Ma."

Diesel folded his arms. "It refers to men with—"

"Not only men, Dee," Axel said. "It's gender neutral."

"Yeah, weirdo fits the bill more than Dad," Ransom piped up, thrusting his chin toward Rebel so everyone knew the 'weirdo's' identity."

"Fuck you, crybag motherfucker," Rebel managed, livid. They didn't mind labeling *her*, instead of their stupid, baby machine mother. "I'm not a fucking simp."

"Simps, no matter the gender, are generally ignored or unwanted by the object of their desire," Diesel said through tight lips. "They have an unsuccessful expectation of earning sex and attention."

"*Entitled* sex and attention," Ryder said.

"Shut up, stupid," Ransom commanded. "Before you spill the beans about Simp Nation, the best porn movie I've ever seen!"

Uncle Johnnie clapped his hands over Mattie's ears.

"You watch porn?" Aunt Kendall gasped.

"Dickhead!" Axel hollered. "CJ said don't tell nobody Diesel burns pornos for us!"

"You little motormouth assfuck," Ryder bit out, stalking toward Axel.

He ran behind Dad and wrapped his skinny arms around Dad's waist. "If you hit me, fuckbag, I'll dig up ten tons of earthworms and unleash them while you're asleep."

"*Efuckinuff!"* Dad roared.

"Uncle Chris," Diesel started.

"Shut the fuck up, boy."

"Don't kill Diesel, Dad," Axel begged. "If it wasn't for all those stupid firewalls, big bro wouldn't have been involved."

"We even asked Mat..."

Ryder shoved Ransom and shut him up before he revealed some of perfect little Matilda's secrets.

Ouch!" Ransom cried, starting for Ransom.

Dad snatched Ransom by the collar and dropped him next to Axel. "Shut the fuck up. This fuckin' chaos workin' my last fuckin' nerve. Ima deal with all you lil' motherfuckers later. Right now, I need to check on Megan. All this fuckin' bullshit gotta be disturbin' her."

"Can I explain, Uncle Chris?"

"Ain't interested in hearing right now, Diesel, so—"

"You should be!" Aunt Kendall inserted. "Your children are watching porn supplied by their *adult* brother."

“No one asked for your opinion, Aunt Kendall,” Rebel said, bringing the situation full circle. Her words brought the original bullshit back front and center.

“You ain’t knowin’ when to shut the fuck up, Rebel,” Daddy said coldly.

“*You* threw the gauntlet, Father,” she responded. “I’m merely picking it up. If we’re keeping score, I’d say it’s your move. By the way, unless you change your mind about punishing me for dissing your wife, I’m *still* not apologizing to Aunt Kendall.”

Her brothers had gotten spankings and all Daddy did was hit them on their ass and legs three or four times. She could handle that. She lifted her chin.

His face hardened again. “Fine, Rebel.”

Axel slid in front of their father and wagged a finger at her. “You’re stupid. Dad’s so old, he’d forgotten he was beating your ass.”

“Until you opened your big mouth again,” Ransom added with disgust.

“Learn the art of subterfuge, sister,” Ryder said sternly.

Daddy glared at the three little idiots and started toward Rebel.

“Wait!” Mattie cried, rushing to Daddy and grabbing his wrist. “Reb’s been horrible today, Uncle Chris, but she’s hurt and confused. She doesn’t mean it. She loves Aunt Meggie and appreciates everything. Give her tonight. To think about her actions. Please? For me.”

Daddy placed a hand on Mattie’s shoulder. “Baby, listen up, I ain’t even able to exfuckinplain how much it’s tearin’ my ass the fuck up, knowing I gotta spank Rebel. But she did the fuckin’ crime, so she gotta do the fuckin’ time. And if the shit Rebel doin’ ain’t bad, her ma wouldna left her lil fuckin’ ass to me. That your Aunt Meggie turnin’ her fuckin’ back on her princess tellin’ me everyfuckinthing I need to know.”

"But—"

"Shut up, Matilda! Just shut up," Rebel cried, hurt and angry and tearful. "You're just a fucking pathetic fake loser! Trying to get in my mother's good graces by tapping Ryan's fucking phone and mincing around Uncle Johnnie and Aunt Kendall because you're too chickenshit to be real. And, now, you're trying to steal *my* father." Not thinking, she charged into Mattie. On the floor, she rose up, ignoring the screams and curses. "I hate you. They're *my* parents. Tabitha stole Diesel from me and that stupid fucking baby stole Momma. I hate all of you. I hope they both die." She didn't know the 'both' she referred to and didn't get a chance to ponder it.

Somehow, Mattie got the upper hand and punched Rebel so hard, stars twirled in front of her. Dad plucked Rebel from the melee and the first blow of his belt landed on her ass, the second on her legs. Even though he alternated, she lost count of the number of strikes he gave her. At least twelve! The fucking gall. Then, he let her fall onto the floor to scream and cry in anger, pain, and humiliation.

"Get up," Aunt Kendall ordered later.

Rebel couldn't be sure the amount of time that passed, but her head was pounding from all the crying she'd done and her ass and legs were burning from her spanking.

Shuddering, Rebel turned her head to the floor and cried again. Aunt Kendall's heels clipped to her. A moment later, her aunt drew her into her arms and hugged her.

"You're sitting on the floor, Aunt Kendall," Rebel realized after a few minutes.

"You're on the floor, darling," she whispered, stroking Rebel's hair.

"I hate my parents!"

"You have extraordinary parents, Rebel. Meggie dotes on you and your father adores you. Stop acting so spoiled and ungrateful and cherish their love and support."

Rebel pulled away from Kendall. "*Support*? Daddy said I can't be with Diesel and I'll bet my life Momma's abiding *his* decision."

"That's her husband."

"I'm her daughter."

"She's not here to uphold wrong choices, Rebel. Nor can you love her only when she agrees with you."

"If she loved me, she'd welcome my choices nor would she bring another daughter into this house."

Lifting a brow, Aunt Kendall got to her feet and dusted off her backside, elegant in gray, wide-legged pants and a black silk blouse. She leaned against the console and folded her arms. "I didn't know Meggie had the power to decide her baby's sex."

Rebel hopped to her feet. "She's gross. If she kept her legs closed, this wouldn't be a problem."

"You have all the answers, don't you, honey?"

"At least someone does, Aunt Kendall."

"I thought I did at one time, Rebel," she said after a moment. "I almost destroyed my life, my marriage, and the friendship I had with your mother. Take someone's advice—"

"No, never. I'm not stupid. I know what's right for me."

"You're in an enviable position, Rebel," Aunt Kendall said, changing tactics. "Not only are both your parents alive, they love you. My father was killed when I was very young. When he died, I lost the only support system I knew, and I was angry at the world. I blamed Meggie for shit that happened when she was *three* and didn't know I existed. I blamed her for Johnnie's behavior. For your daddy's behavior. No, she was my main target, but everyone was within my site. If they came into my scope, I took aim. I was hurting and in so much pain. If I would've had what you've had your entire life, *I* would've been different. Rebel darling, it sounds like excuses. I wish I could change things, but I can't. I can only tell you—"

"Stop telling me and focus on your own fucking daughter. You're not a good mother or a good aunt or a good nothing because she's fucked up. I have parents. I don't need you."

High color swept into Aunt Kendall's face, and she straightened, stepping toward Rebel.

"Are you ready to go, gorgeous?" Uncle Johnnie asked, walking into the foyer carrying an empty dish.

Pasting a smile on her face, she nodded, fake.

Telle mère telle fille.

Stupid Mattie. Rebel knew French too. She didn't even care where Matilda or Rory were.

After her aunt and uncle left, Rebel locked the door, then leaned against it and sobbed.

"Reb?"

"Go away, CJ," she sniffled, hoarse.

"I don't ever remember seeing Mom and Dad so angry with you," he said, standing in the opening between the foyer and the central hallway. As if he feared her. "I've never been so furious with you either."

As the words sank in, she spun and narrowed her eyes.

"Shut the fuck up," he told her before she spoke. "I feel like putting you over my fucking knee myself. You're a fucking brat and if any of us shoveled the shit you did, we'd be picking up our fucking teeth off the floor."

"That's child abuse."

"You abused Mom. Abuse for abuse," he said viciously. "And what you said about Dad, being old and dying soon? Get over your fucking self. You're on Mom's ass for having another baby because she loves her husband when you, fucking weirdo, want to fuck our brother."

"Shut up before I punch you."

"I wouldn't. We'd fight in this motherfucker, Rebel. You have a hot ass, so you're turning into a super bitch. If that's your problem, find a motherfucker to fuck."

"You're a disgusting pig."

"Am I?" he retorted. "So, what does that make you? A callous cunt? An ungrateful leech? You want Mom and our baby sister to *die*, Rebel. Wrap that around your miserable fucking head."

"I love Momma!"

"You're a liar. You fear Dad. You don't love Mom. Anyone who loves someone wouldn't break their hearts the way you did. If she was a bad mom, I'd understand. But look around you. *Look*!" he ordered when she didn't follow his instructions.

Rebel glanced around the elegant foyer with the high ceiling, marble floor, and three entryways leading to various sections of the house.

"Mom made this house into a home. She keeps it running so Dad can do his club stuff. She keeps us entertained and fed and gives us the fucking best."

"Mom only does what Dad allows her. That little show where she was ordering Diesel to fire—"

"Rebel, get your fucking head out your ass. Something's wrong with Dad. Can't you see he's not acting right? He's worried about Mom, but she's stepping up and protecting him so I'm stepping up and protecting her." He started to turn away, then paused. "Dad sent me to see that you got to your room. He's already taken all your electronics. As I was leaving him and Mom in their room, I heard him say he was canceling your debit card and you wouldn't get another one until you opened your own. Have a good night, little sister."

Chapter Thirty

MATILDA

The next morning, Mattie sat in the back of her father's Navigator, between her brothers, Rory and JJ. At two, Blade didn't attend school yet. The headache that began in the mall yesterday and worsened after her fight with Rebel plagued Mattie all night. She wished she could've stayed home, but her parents never allowed sick days. Her face was bruised and swollen and she just felt down.

Even with all Rebel's bitchiness, Mattie couldn't stay and watch Uncle Chris spank her. Seeing his despair, remembering Aunt Meggie's pain, and watching CJ's hurt stung. More for their sakes, then Rebel's. She deserved to be dragged to the roof of the house and thrown the fuck off. Dropped in boiling tar. Stung by ten thousand bees. Tongue stabbed. Gutted. Chopped into—

"I'm talking to you, young lady!"

Daddy's voice blared in the enclosed space and Mattie shrank at her unladylike thoughts. Neither Maman or Daddy had spoken to her once they arrived home last night. At breakfast this morning, Maman announced Daddy would drive them to school.

"I'm sorry, Daddy. I didn't hear you."

JJ patted her knee and Rory took her hand in his and held it, resting their entwined fingers on his thigh.

"You're barred from visiting Rebel ever again and she's no longer welcome in our home. I'm talking to Mortician. If he allows Harley to continue to associate with that little girl, you can't associate with Harley either."

Harley and Rebel were her best friends. No matter how much they fought, they loved each other, and she'd be lost without them.

Tears rushed to Mattie's eyes and her chin trembled.

"Dad, that's harsh," Rory said with disapproval, looking out the window, but still holding Mattie's hand. "Harley's innocent."

"When I want your comment, son, I'll ask for it."

"Dad, I love you and I respect you so much, but either I'm a man or a boy. You call me a man all the time. As one, I'm *telling* you, you aren't being fair to Harley or to Mattie. You're punishing them for Rebel's stupidity."

Fear turned Mattie's muscles rigid. She waited for Daddy to scream at Rory.

"You're right, son," he said instead.

Rory squeezed her hand. "Mattie isn't feeling good. She shouldn't have to sit through the second day of school."

"Yeah, Dad," JJ said, encouraged by Rory's bravery. "You and Mom pay enough to the school. Mattie should be able to stay out for the next month and have her work delivered to her."

"I'm removing you three from Ridge Moore," Daddy announced sharply. "Megan and Christopher are the school's owners. I'm not lining their fucking pockets."

"No, Daddy!" Mattie cried, bolting upright and pushing to the edge of her seat. She leaned forward and touched his shoulder. "Please, don't. Rebel and Harley are my best friends. Please."

"You were fighting and cursing like a common slut, Matilda," Daddy reminded her with so much displeasure in his voice, she slid back and doubled over. "I'm so disappointed in you. Whatever you purchased yesterday, we're returning it after school. You don't deserve a reward."

"I don't have the receipts," she sobbed. "Aunt Meggie bought me my stuff because I—"

"Helped her with Ryan," Daddy snarled. "You should've come straight to me when she made her out-of-pocket request. Who does she think she is, involving you in *her* son's bullshit?"

"She's our aunt, Dad," Rory said flatly. "We're her nephews and niece. Family. If she can't call on us, who can she call on? If you or Mom needed help, Aunt Meggie would send *our* cousins."

"I've had enough of your backtalk, Rory."

Rory snapped his attention to the back of Dad's head and glared. Something about the light in her brother's eyes chilled Mattie. It hit her that he'd grown, too. His shoulders were wider and his legs longer. His voice still wasn't as manly as CJ's, but it wasn't boyish anymore either.

"Dad, again, I love you—"

"Enough with the pandering. If you love and respect me, you'll follow my orders, and you won't preface every infraction with that bullshit."

Releasing Mattie's hand, Rory stiffened. Afraid at the anger brewing in her brother's eyes, she grabbed his hand again.

"Ryan's a fucking asshole, Dad," Rory stated, squeezing her hand and calming a little. "He calls his own mother a cunt. He's aligned with the Byrds and they're worse fucking assholes than he is."

At the thought of Wallace, Mattie shivered. Yesterday, she'd successfully avoided him. If she had to go to school today, maybe she'd be as lucky.

"Then why did Megan have to involve Ryan?"

"Maybe, to make the other boys believe Ryan was helping his family," Maman finally snapped after not speaking since announcing Daddy's plans at home.

"You're talking to me again, Kendall?" Dad barked.

"I can always change my mind," she sneered. "Don't fucking tempt me."

"Just what the fuck are you angry about?"

"Oh, my love, you mean what am I *angriest* about?" she asked with venom. "For starters? You're a fucking asshole. You had the fucking audacity to say the words *if I'd fathered Rebel* and topped it off with *I would've found a way for Megan to stop having babies if I were her husband*. Motherfucker," she spat.

"Are you fucking serious? As her brother-in-law, I was making speculations. Jesus Christ, woman, don't start this bullshit again."

"Then don't fling it, fuckhead. After all these fucking years, after *everything*...fuck you, Johnnie."

"You're concerned with what I said about that little cunt instead of our daughter's behavior?"

Maman sniffled. "Mattie didn't do anything wrong. She helped her aunt and she defended herself. Would you prefer our daughter have gotten beat to a pulp by Rebel? I'm all for Mattie being a lady, but I applaud her defending herself, fuckhead. And Rory's right, jerk. Anything we need from any of the kids, they are there for us, and you're *not* setting our children apart from their cousins."

"Wait a fucking minute!" Daddy pounded the dashboard. "At one time, *you* didn't want our children associated with the club."

"Pull the Navigator over before we crash, John Donovan," Maman said in a steely voice. "Calm the fuck down or I'm getting out of this motherfucker, taking our kids, and walking."

"We're twenty minutes away from the school, Kendall. I'd like to see you hoof it in heels."

"I can take those motherfuckers off," Maman snarled.

"Kendall…*fuck*!" Daddy followed Maman's orders the first chance he got, pulling into the parking lot of the local bank. "Now, what?" he asked after long moments of silence.

Maman opened her window and brisk morning air swept in, lifting her red hair from her shoulders.

"Our children love their school and their cousins. I love my life, Johnnie. I love *you* and our kids. I have a place in the law firm and at the club. Don't bring up dumb shit and fuck everything up. And I'm Rebel's aunt. I wanted to try and get through to her."

"Kendall, I don't want Mattie around—"

"I don't care, Johnnie. You don't want her around Rebel because of *Meggie*. And even if it was because of how she's acting out, how dare you turn your back on her? She needs love and support. Does she need to be disciplined? Yes! Of course! Christopher and Meggie took care of that. I checked on Meggie last night and she told me she slapped Rebel. That's how out of hand our niece is. We all need to rally around until Meggie is better and Outlaw isn't so worried about her. She might not even be well enough to continue helping with Roxy's annual ball. This pregnancy is so hard on Meggie."

"It's her own fucking fault. Since she hasn't gotten herself killed by standing at Christopher's side despite everything, she's killing herself because she won't stop having his fucking babies."

Mattie exchanged looks with her brothers at the bitterness in Daddy's tone, their eyes as wide as hers.

"You talk about keeping the peace all the time," Maman said after a few moments. "Is it really for us or is it for her?"

"I resent that fucking question."

"I don't give a fuck. Answer it!"

"Goddamn you."

"Answer," she gritted.

"Of course, it's for you and the children!"

"And Meggie," Maman insisted.

"Fuck, Kendall. No! If I had my way, I'd run her away. She's been fucking shot, stabbed, kidnapped, and almost killed too fucking many times to count. She *killed* a motherfucker."

"And she doesn't know," Maman snapped.

"Maybe, she needs to. She's the most notorious fucking pacifist around and she shot a man to death—"

"Jesus, Dad, would you stop!" Rory said in exasperation. "We didn't need to know this and if we hadn't heard Mom say Aunt Meggie doesn't know, we might've let something slip."

Like Mattie had. She was only grateful Rebel, Harley, and CJ hadn't repeated her claim to Uncle Chris. Not long after school ended, CJ had texted Mattie and told her Uncle Mort said what she'd overheard wasn't true. Even if CJ and Uncle Mort knew the facts, they were protecting Aunt Meggie.

"Tell Megan!" Daddy said. "She needs to know she killed that motherfucker."

"No!" Maman screamed, shoving the visor down and opening the mirror to meet Rory's gaze. "Your Uncle Christopher will kill you—"

"He wouldn't touch my son—"

"Shut the fuck up, Johnnie," Maman said. "You want to run Meggie off? I'm not even exploring your reasons. Even if I agreed, which I don't, why would you send her away with murder on her conscience?"

"Why would it bother her?" he demanded with jarring sarcasm. "It was to save her beloved Christopher."

"Maybe, if she'd found out when it first happened, it wouldn't have been as bad," Maman said tiredly. "But CJ was seven or eight months old when this happened. So far removed from seeing Traveler pull that gun and she had a split decision to make will affect her differently. Meggie knowing she put that asshole out of his misery serves no purpose, especially while she's pregnant."

"Whatever, Kendall. Now, what?"

"We bring Rory and JJ to school, then take Mattie home so I can see to her bruises."

"I see. So, we're rewarding unladylike behavior now?"

"If her behavior was unladylike, the answer would be no. But it wasn't. She was helping her aunt, using her brain, and defending herself. You should applaud her."

Daddy pulled out of the parking lot and back into the road. "You're right, gorgeous."

"I always am," Maman said primly, her window back up and the heat from the vents giving off a welcome warmth.

"Matilda, sweetheart, I apologize for my behavior. That was unworthy of me."

"Apology accepted, Daddy." Mattie moderated her tone and lowered her lashes. "Thank you."

"Boys, do you want to take off with your sister?" Daddy asked.

"I do!" JJ said. At eleven, he wasn't concerned with much.

"Not me," Rory announced. "Today's my first day in Lumbly's class with CJ. I changed my schedule online last night."

"Of course, son," Daddy agreed with mild politeness and accelerated the Navigator forward.

Chapter Thirty One

CJ

As soon as CJ dropped off the soup for Mattie, he'd stop at Uncle Mort's to see Harley.

Yesterday, at the mall, they acted normal. Of course, Rebel's bullshit dampened everything, so maybe that's why he hadn't seen Harley at school again today. Or, maybe, it was because he hadn't been able to keep his hands off when he'd found her in the mall. Hanging out with her was an unexpected opportunity and he'd used it to his advantage.

The kiss they'd shared lived in his fucking memory and he wanted another one from her. She wasn't ready, so he'd kept his distance. He didn't want to unfairly influence or somehow pressure her.

At times, he wondered if she regretted their kiss. The thought pained him. But, fuck, he missed her. It cut him so fucking deep that she no longer required seeing him every day.

However, Harley's strange behavior at the end of last school year also haunted him. He was concerned something similar was going on.

Then, there was Molly. Still dumb as a fucking brick, but a little sad and kind of sweet. Though chemistry and language arts were their only two classes together, she'd somehow attached herself to his side between their other classes. At lunch. During study hall. She'd even skipped cheer to hang out at his football practice.

Her behavior further alienated Ryan, while Willard wanted CJ's position as starting quarterback, so his mad cow little brother hit CJ harder than necessary whenever possible.

Coach Yancy was having none of it and suspended Wallace from the team, pending an internal review. Meanwhile, Ryan was a mean fucking kicker. Bro had mad skills, if he wasn't such a hardheaded jackass.

Mom hadn't recovered from Rebel's bitchery, so she hadn't come and sat in Lumbly's class. Mattie and Harley were absent, though Rory, Lou, and Mark JB were now in the class.

As for Rebel, CJ still wanted to shake the fuck out of her. What the fuck was *wrong* with his little sister?

Diesel was their brother. Period. To *him*, it was fucking disgusting Rebel even had a crush on him. But, fuck, could he fucking talk? He and Harley had been joined at the hip for their entire lives. One day, seeing her as his best friend changed to wanting her as *his*.

Yeah, it was different. Diesel was *legally* a Caldwell. By law, he was Rebel's brother. While CJ might have a modicum of understanding, Mom and Dad didn't, sending Rebel into fits.

The spoiled little witch. Her behavior hurt Dad. In his memory, he couldn't recall a time when 'Law spanked Rebel. He hadn't wanted to do so yesterday. And she'd absolutely crushed Mom.

The heifer got her just desserts.

Usually, the walk through the forest calmed CJ, but his thoughts weighed him down. At the edge of the forest sat Uncle Johnnie's house. As CJ crossed the clearing, the sound of the waterfall pounded in the silence.

It was the most idyllic part of their land, complete with a small stream and a cave. Sometimes, he wished his parents had chosen this area. Not only for its beauty, but the privacy, too.

Sighing, he climbed the elegant steps of the Donovan mansion and crossed the wide portico. At the door, he rang the doorbell. A moment later, a buzzing indicated the unlocking of the door.

Upon entering, CJ halted. The operatic notes of Carlo Bergonzi, whom Aunt Kendall described as a great Verdi tenor, drifted over the sound system. The opera halted CJ. He didn't hate it as virulently as his father, but it still hurt his goddamn ears. He could leave the thermos on the console in the foyer and head to Uncle Mort's house.

"We're in the den, honey." Aunt Kendall's voice drifted down the hall. "Come on."

"Run while you can, CJ," Rory called, less than pleased.

CJ laughed, wondering what bullshit had Rory so put out. Curious, CJ strolled down the hallway. Unlike his mom and dad's house, Uncle Johnnie's had a simple layout. The foyer opened to the main hallway with the staircase to the second floor at the midway point. Passing it brought him to the den, the first door on the left.

Before he walked fully into the room, Blade's little naked ass barreled into him. "CJ!"

Stooping down, he shook his head. "Where's your fucking clothes, dude?"

He pointed a chubby finger up. "Stairs," he announced, tugging CJ's hand.

"Where's Mattie?" CJ asked, getting to his feet and allowing his two-year-old cousin to drag him into the room.

He screamed and spun around. "Where's your fucking clothes, Aunt Kendall?"

"This is my fucking house, CJ," Uncle Johnnie said tightly, "and you'll respect your aunt."

The words went over CJ's head. Anger surged into him. "Understood, uncle," he snapped, "but you could've given me the option at the door to come in and see my aunt and cousin without fucking clothes!"

"We're all without clothes, bro," Rory said, both annoyance and mortification vibrating in his words. "It was Mom's idea."

"To show what a whimsical, progressive mother she is," JJ added.

CJ wouldn't be able to look Aunt Kendall or Mattie in the face again without dying of embarrassment. Where the fuck she cooked up this birdbrained idea to show her fun side, he'd never know.

"It's liberating. You should try it, but of course Megan would pitch a hissy fit."

"As well she fucking should, Uncle Johnnie," CJ snarled, madder than a motherfucker. His confusion over Aunt Kendall's reasoning deepened at his uncle mentioning his mother. "There's no way I should see my mother's naked body and my little sister should see my father's swinging cock!"

Mattie sniffled.

"Your language is offensive to my daughter."

Unable to believe his fucking ears, CJ spun around. He sat the thermos on the table so he wouldn't pitch that motherfucker at his uncle. "You're fucking touched, uncle," he stated coldly, removing his T-shirt with jerky movements and stomping to his teary cousin. He held it out to her. "Put it on, Mattie."

"You will *not* disrespect your mother's wishes," Uncle Johnnie stated. "Take your fucking shirt back and get out, CJ."

Sure he was in the Twilight Zone, CJ stared at his uncle.

"Mattie mentioned how Aunt Meggie was teaching Rebel to walk in heels," Rory said carefully, sending his father a putrid stare. "My mom and Dad got into an argument. Another argument, aside from the one that happened this morning."

"Shut your fucking mouth, Rory," Uncle Johnnie ordered. "We don't know everything that goes on inside their house."

"Bite it, Dad," Rory spat. "I've been sitting in this room since I got home from school without fucking clothes on."

"I'm so sorry, Mommie," Mattie said in a small voice.

"You're not two," Uncle Johnnie blared. "She's *Maman* to you, young lady."

"Mom, Dad, *please* let Mattie go to her room," JJ begged. "This is traumatizing her."

"Put on CJ's shirt, Mattie," Rory soothed.

"You're not her fucking father, Rory," Uncle Johnnie said, his eyes wild. Whatever happened unhinged him.

Meanwhile, Aunt Kendall sat on the sofa, her face blank. CJ tried not to look below her neck.

"You're not *a* fucking father, Dad," Rory shot back. "This is bordering fucking child abuse."

Mattie jumped to her feet, still naked. "Stop, please!" she sobbed. "I can't take it."

CJ covered his face, then pulled out his phone. He'd text Uncle Mort first. He was closer than Dad. As he started typing, Uncle Johnnie snatched his phone and pitched it against the wall. It slammed to the ground.

Shocked, CJ stared at his phone, then met Uncle Johnnie's cold gaze.

"I'm not a child to report. You'd do well to remember that, boy."

"If you broke my fucking phone, I won't have to report a motherfucking thing. You'll be fucked up."

Without warning, Uncle Johnnie shoved CJ and sent him sprawling. As he scrambled to his feet, his uncle started toward him. Rory jumped in front of his father, allowing CJ the time to stand.

"All three of you sit down this minute," Aunt Kendall ordered around sniffles.

"Mom, it's okay," Rory said, his voice cracking and his nose reddening.

CJ drew in a deep breath, unsure of what to do to help Rory and Mattie. Aunt Kendall, too. *All* of them. They were all in a dark place. Possibly, in danger. As long as he was under their roof, he wasn't safe either. But he didn't know how to extricate himself from the situation. He certainly didn't know what to do to save the rest of them. He wished he'd been able to send the message before Uncle Johnnie broke the phone.

CJ backed toward the door.

"Don't you fucking move!"

"Uncle Christopher will kill you if you fuck with CJ, Dad."

Uncle Johnnie transferred his wild gaze from CJ to Rory. "First, I'm not a good husband to your mother because, according to her, I would've jumped at Megan's request to walk the fuck around naked with our children but didn't love her enough to even consider her idea. Now, according to you, I'm a fucking weak-ass bitch."

"Nope, but you are a stupid-ass bitch," CJ said, fed the fuck up. This shit was beyond the fucking scope of sense. "I don't know how the fuck my mom led to *this* fucking travesty, but it's all on you. You didn't have to agree to this stupid shit." He backed toward the door. For now, he'd leave his phone. While Rory blocked his dad, CJ would make his escape.

"You're fucking crying *now*, Kendall?"

Uncle Johnnie's bitter words froze CJ.

"Why?" He kicked the table with the thermos and sent it flying in Mattie's direction, in a blind rage.

Covering her head, Mattie screamed and dove out of the way of the soaring objects.

"I told you I didn't want to do this bullshit. Did you fucking listen?" He yanked Aunt Kendall to her feet and shook her. "Did you?"

Rory and CJ rushed Uncle Johnnie and dragged him away from Aunt Kendall. Blade was screaming. Although JJ was shielding Mattie, tears streaked his face, too.

"Get Blade, Rory," CJ said, wanting to cry as well. He'd never, ever witnessed such a powder keg of wrongness and negativity. "Uncle Johnnie, please, calm the fuck down. Something set off Aunt Kendall. Instead of giving in to her, you should've called Lolly. Tell Mattie she can leave the den. Go and calm down."

"What the motherfuck is goin' on in this motherfucker?"

Dad's outraged question alarmed and relieved CJ.

"Why all you motherfuckers got no fuckin' clothes on? Fuck me! Mattie, go to your fuckin' room and get dressed."

On a sob, Mattie ran out of the room.

"Rory, take Blade and cover his cock. Cover yours, too. JJ, you ain't needin' help. Just go find some fuckin' clothes."

CJ was afraid to release Uncle Johnnie because anger still vibrated from him.

"Boy?"

Clearing his throat, CJ pressed down on his lips before answering. "Yes, 'Law?"

"Why you holdin' back a naked motherfucker in front of his naked bitch?"

"Oh, yeah, that. It's a long story."

"What are you doing here, Christopher?" Uncle Johnnie asked.

"Kendall, go upstairs and get dressed," Dad instructed.

"This is my fucking house."

"Where *my* fuckin' kid at, Johnnie. If his fuckin' phone ain't suddenly stopped workin' *my* fuckin' ass would still be home with Megan. *Get dressed, Kendall*!"

Sniffling, Aunt Kendall stumbled away. CJ drew in a sharp breath and released his uncle.

Dad stepped to them, glaring so long Uncle Johnnie began to turn ten shades of red.

"I swear to you, motherfucker," Dad snarled, low, "if you fuckin' settin' Kendall on her psycho cunt road afuckingain, I'm fuckin' killin' you."

"This is my wife and it's my life."

"Well and fuckin' good, but *my* wife the *only* fuckin' thing that set Kendall off efuckinnuff to orchestrate bullshit like this. I ain't interested in knowin' what the fuck happen. Just nip it in the fuckin' bud befuckinfore it grow outta fuckin' hand." He looked at CJ. "Your phone?"

Uncle Johnnie walked out of Dad's reach. "I threw it against the wall," he announced casually, stooping to pick it up, and holding it out to CJ. "The perils of interference."

Although CJ started forward, Dad pulled him back. Smiling, he sauntered to Uncle Johnnie and snatched the phone. The punch sent Uncle Johnnie flying. He slammed into the wall, then thudded to the floor.

"The perils of assfuckery," Dad said, planted his hand on CJ's shoulder and guided him away, leaving Uncle Johnnie groaning and writhing in pain.

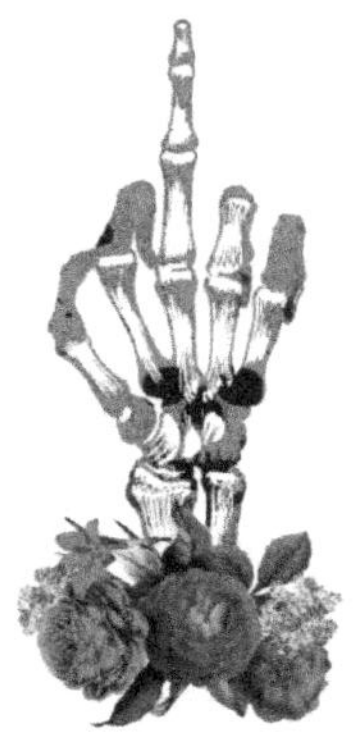

Chapter Thirty Two

HARLEY

Staring at her book but not seeing the words, Harley ignored the commotion swirling up the stairs and invading her bedroom. Uncle Chris, CJ, Lolly and Pop were downstairs. Every now and then, their bursts of laughter echoed in the house.

Any other time, Harley would've been downstairs, commandeering CJ's attention. Now, she never wanted to speak to him again. Tomorrow, she'd take her lunch in the library, just as she had today.

She glared at her phone again, showing a photo of Molly and CJ snuggled together on a bleacher with the message, *at practice with CJ.*

The photo came from *Pillar of Earth.* In other words, Molly. A few days after she accepted the requested, it came to her that Molly said her username was *Pillar of Salt.* To double check she hadn't made an error by approving someone unknown to her, Harley had asked about the day they'd friended each other on their socials. After receiving all the right answers, she'd been satisfied it was Molly and hadn't thought about it again.

At the moment, she was questioning her wisdom. Molly *knew* how much Harley liked CJ. They'd kind of discussed it that day in the locker room when Harley had lost her mind and thought meeting Willard was a good idea.

Neither could she remember ever giving Molly her cell phone number, which very few people had. On the other hand, until today, she'd seen the girl as harmless. A little ditzy but not malicious.

Her lower lip trembled. How wrong she'd been.

"Knock, knock."

Speak of the devil.

CJ pushed her door opened and stepped in. She ignored how broad his shoulders were as well as the amusement in his emerald eyes when he saw the hardening face mask she'd covered her skin with to treat her acne.

"Hey, Harls."

She forced a cursory glance. "Go away."

"Harley, you're not happy about Reb's bullshit," he said, closing the distance between them and sitting on the edge of her window seat. He forced her to scoot closer to the window so he wouldn't touch her. "I missed you at lunch and—"

"Lies!" she hissed, throwing the stupid book aside and huffing. "You were with Molly *all day*. She even came to your football practice. Something you've never allowed me to do."

"I've never stopped you," he snapped. "You're usually at cheer anyway."

"So you admit you were with her?"

"What the fuck are you talking about?" he shouted. "She was there—"

"And you two were cuddled on the bleachers together."

"No—"

Not interested in his lies, she crawled around him, got to her feet, and shoved her phone into his hands.

He knew her passcode, so he unlocked the phone, went through her photos, then looked at her. "If you would've allowed me to finish, I would've told you we weren't cuddled on the fucking bleachers, Harley. We were talking about our chemistry project. She's my partner for the year."

The news wilted her. Molly had the perfect reason to stay in CJ's company. Folding her arms, Harley lifted her chin. "I see."

"Don't you fucking dare. I didn't have a choice. Billson assigned the partners."

"Don't I dare what?" she challenged. "Obviously, there's smoke. Otherwise, you wouldn't try to douse the fire. You would've told me yesterday she was your partner."

"I can't take one more emotional bitch tonight," CJ snarled. "Uncle Johnnie was enough."

His words startled a laugh from her. "What do you mean?"

Groaning, CJ scrubbed hand over his face, then told her what happened an hour ago when he'd brought soup for Mattie since she'd missed school.

"She isn't sick," Harley said. "It was because of the fight she had with Rebel."

"If Mattie is bruised, I didn't pay attention," he confessed. "I was too fucking shocked and outraged Uncle Johnnie and Aunt Kendall saw nothing wrong with being bare-assed naked in front of their children. Blade's a toddler. Fair enough. It won't affect him because there was nothing sexual about what they were doing. They're just fucking weirdos."

Harley frowned. "And they blamed Aunt Meggie for their stupidity?"

"Blows my fucking mind, too. Now, my phone's fucked up because my dumb ass never put the case on it." Sighing, he got to his feet. "Dad wanted to go straight home, but when I realized I couldn't text you, he agreed to stop by. You don't want to be bothered, so I'm heading home."

"Wait!" Harley called just as CJ reached her door and stepped into the hall. She raced to him, though she kept a small distance between them by remaining in her room. "I can't stop thinking about our kiss and then yesterday at the mall, we were best bros again, but it was different." A new awareness that she didn't understand. "When I got home last night, I was so exhausted I went straight to bed after dinner."

The aftermath of Rebel's behavior wore Harley out. She'd told Mommie and Lolly, so they'd check on Aunt Meggie and Uncle Chris, while Harley texted Mattie and Rebel. Mattie had been as heartsore as Harley. Rebel was just vicious.

"Then, during first period, I started getting the messages about you and Molly."

"I don't want her, Harley. I swore I'd wait for you, and I will."

She wanted those words to suffice. Except they didn't. She wanted to kiss CJ again and feel as she had yesterday with him at the mall. Best bros, yes, but something else, too. He was two grades ahead of her, though, and she had responsibilities to her own education. She'd opted for theater as one of her electives. Yesterday, auditions were held for the entire day with hers scheduled during lunch. Early this morning, she was informed she'd been chosen to play *Juliet* for the spring production that would comprise a big part of her grade. Today, during lunch, she'd met with her theater teacher and the guy cast as Romeo. Nardo Grevenberg reminded her of Michael B. Jordan when he first started acting. If she didn't love CJ so much, she'd be totally smitten with Nardo...

Wait! *What* did she say?

Harley drew in a sharp breath. Of course, she loved CJ! But she didn't think she meant the type she'd once had for him.

"Well, uh, I'm heading downstairs," CJ said, awkwardness thick between them. "My dad's probably ready to go home." He leaned down and kissed her cheek. "See you around, Harley."

Harley grabbed CJ's hand. "I've been cast as Juliet," she blurted. "I wanted to surprise you and invite you to rehearsal in a couple weeks."

"For real, bae?" Without waiting for her answer, he swept her into his arms and twirled her around, kissing her cheek again. "I'm so proud of you. You've always loved Shakespeare. You'll kill it."

Giddy from his arms around her, she stumbled when he set her on her feet without warning. He grabbed her shoulders to steady her.

"Yesterday, at lunch, I tried out for the part. Today, I had to meet Romeo."

"So that's where you were."

She nodded.

"CJ!" Uncle Chris called. "We gotta get the fuck."

CJ grinned, then kissed her cheek again. "Congratulations, bae. I've been missing you at lunch but at least I know why you haven't been there." He started to walk away.

"Let's go to the movies," she said quickly. "Just me and you. This weekend."

He stilled. "A date?" he asked after a pause.

"Daddy won't like that, so I-I'll ask Reb...Mattie to cover..."

That wouldn't work either. Uncle Johnnie had already barred Mattie and Harley from spending time together once. If she involved Mattie in her schemes, Uncle Johnnie wouldn't ever let them be close again.

"We can always have a movie night in the basement at my parents' place," CJ suggested.

"It's always a free-for-all, though."

CJ gazed at her mouth and she shifted from foot-to-foot. "What do you want—" He drew in a deep breath. "Why do you want us to be alone so badly?"

Because she wanted to kiss him again and make him forget Molly. He said he'd wait for her, but Molly was fun and comfortable with her body. With sex. Harley was just...just *Harley.* The good girl and the peacemaker.

"Hey, boy," Uncle Chris said, coming into view at the end of the hallway as he topped the staircase. "I been calling you." He nodded to Harley. "You doin' okay?"

"Yeah, Uncle Chris. How are you? How's Aunt Meggie?"

"She fine. My ass straight, too." He looked at CJ. "Let's fuckin' go, son." He turned and started off.

CJ kissed her cheek for a third time and winked at her, then shoved his hands in his pocket and followed Uncle Chris. "Dad, I need to ask Uncle Mort if Harley can come with me and Rory to the mall tomorrow evening. We want to see this new movie, grab a bite, and get Aunt Kendall a birthday gift."

"Johnnie might not let..."

The conversation faded away as they descended the stairs. Smiling, Harley leaned against the doorframe, certain CJ would handle the details.

The next evening, Harley rushed home to jump in the shower.

When Aunt Meggie dropped her and Rebel off at school this morning, she'd passed a note from CJ to Harley, where he'd informed her everything was taken care of and he'd pick her up for seven. After that, her day passed in a blur. She couldn't say what was happening from one minute to the next because she was so focused on her date with CJ.

Now, less than an hour from seeing him, she hurried out of the bathroom with a towel around herself and another one around her hair and went to her closet. She had the entire day to think about her outfit, so she immediately went to the rack with all her new clothes and snatched a denim rope mini skirt with a metallic flower on the back pocket and a black crossover waist crop sweater. She paired her clothes with tall black boots and matching gold chain link earrings, bracelet, and necklace.

After drying her hair and dressing, she stared at herself in the mirror, wishing, for the first time in her life, for the finer texture of her mother's hair. CJ had never commented on Harley's corkscrew curls when she didn't flatiron her hair or have them in box braids, but she was competing against Molly and girls like her. To Harley, her mother's wavy hair was just perfect.

At the sound of the doorbell, Harley squealed, ran to her nightstand and grabbed her pink crossbody bag and hurried out of her room. In the entry hall, she skidded to a halt. CJ was dressed all in black, including the Timberland boots she'd never seen. The silver chain attached to his jeans gleamed against the darkness of his clothes and the scent of leather from his jacket combined with the smoke from his cigarette.

Male voices buzzed in her head, but all she saw was CJ. His fresh hair cut styled into a short messy shag, the color seeming inkier thanks to his dark clothes.

"*Where* the fuck you going dressed in *that*?"

Daddy's blare startled her and she jumped, blurting, "Out with CJ," before she remembered they were supposed to be going with Rory and two or three more people. She wasn't sure how they'd end up alone, but trusted he'd get it done. "We're buying Aunt Kendall a present."

"Not in that," Daddy said, in a tone more unreasonable than he'd ever used.

She glanced down at herself. "What do you mean? Mommie liked the outfit when we bought it at that store."

Daddy scrubbed a hand over his face. "She still at her meeting, so she not seeing you *in* the motherfucker. I am and you not walking out this house dressed like you going on a fucking date." He pointed toward the staircase. "Go and change."

"But Daddy—"

Rory pushed open the door and stuck his head in. Giving her a cursory glance, he nodded then looked at her dad. "Uncle Mort, Harley isn't going on a date. I wanted CJ's opinion on a gift for my mom. We're seeing a movie and getting some burgers and fries. They haven't hung out in a while, so I guess that's why he wants her to tag along."

Her excitement evaporated. Rory made it seem like she'd be a third wheel. Perhaps, CJ and Rory really did have plans already and CJ included her as he always did.

Her shoulders drooped and she opened her mouth to bow out of the evening. Suddenly, CJ was there, taking her hand in his and tugging her toward the door.

"I'll have her back by midnight, Uncle Mort," he promised.

Daddy glared at him.

"What's the hold-up?" Diesel asked with irritation, brushing past them and walking into the house. "Tabitha—"

"Have my daughter home by midnight, Diesel," Daddy growled.

"Sure thing, Uncle Mort. I'm dropping them off. Tabitha just called. She's ovulating so I have to get home and take care of business."

Harley frowned.

"Just another way for girls to manipulate dudes," Rory grumbled.

"Motherfuckers are manipulative, too, Rory," Daddy said with a shake of his head, sounding more like himself. "And, sometimes, when a woman scheme, dudes are the beneficiaries."

"Aunt Meggie flirts with Uncle Christopher and Aunt Bailey with you to have their way. What *they* do is mostly innocent, Uncle Mort. But when Mom gets on her cunning train, all hell breaks loose."

"You think Tabitha is manipulating me because she wants a baby?" Diesel asked, his brow lifted.

"If *you* don't think so, *I* don't have anything to say," Rory retorted. "You haven't been married long, so unless you started trying for a baby before the wedding, there's no fucking reason for her to do all this extra shit. Letting you know she's ovulating is the perfect way to make you drop everything and get you home. Congratulations. You have years of this same behavior to enjoy. I'll be outside."

Before Diesel replied, Rory stomped off.

"Goddamn, their latest bullshit has really affected Ro," CJ said woefully. "We'll call you when we get to the mall, Uncle Mort."

"You better," Uncle Mort said darkly, before Diesel closed the door.

"Behave yourself, little brother," Diesel warned as he stopped in front of the movie theater complex about fifteen minutes from the club. Hortensia was steadily building up, going from a town with a park, a hospital, and the MC as its focal points to shops, business parks, apartments, restaurants, amusements, schools, and a medical center. It was still famous as being the home of the Death Dwellers' mother chapter, but it had so much more to offer nowadays.

CJ got out of the front passenger seat and opened the back door. She'd sat behind him, while Rory was behind Diesel. On the ride over, he didn't have much to say, staring out the window and into the darkness for almost the entire time.

Out of the car, Harley smoothed down her miniskirt, self-conscious under the glare of the bright light from the glass building. As Rory got out, CJ leaned into the Mercedes and talked to Diesel.

"You look so pretty, Harley," Rory said, standing next to her, as they waited for CJ.

"Thank you, Rory," Harley responded, realizing she hadn't paid attention to him other than to acknowledge his presence.

His blond hair was neat and tapered with a hard side part that somehow drew attention to his pimples. Anger and sadness swam in his gray eyes and his mouth was drawn into a tight line.

"I can text you a link to what I use for my acne," she said. "It has helped my skin a lot."

His gaze flew to hers. "Mom said I'll outgrow it."

"She's probably right and—"

"Besides, you barely have pimples compared to me. My sister told me to make a mask of fish eggs, snail mucus, pig manure, toothpaste, and turmeric."

"Oh, my."

CJ slammed the door shut and walked to them. He took Harley's hand in his. "You're so fucking pretty, Harley," he whispered, bring her hand to his mouth and kissing the back of it. "I've been dying to tell you since you rushed into the entrance hall, but Uncle Mort wouldn't have let you leave."

She ran her fingers over his leather jacket. "And you're so handsome, all in black."

At the gleam in his eyes, butterflies swooped in her belly.

"We'll meet you in the food court at 11:00, Ro," CJ said, shocking her. He dug in his pocket and took out some money, handing it to his cousin. "Buy whatever you think your mom will like. Don't be a cheapskate but keep the change."

Rory stuffed the money into his jacket and started off.

"Focus, Rory," CJ said. "We need to know what happens in the fucking movie so we can answer Uncle Mort and my dad's questions."

"Whatever—"

"Rory, I'm counting on you. If you don't want Uncle Mort to kill me, you have to do this shit right."

That dented Rory's simmering emotions and he nodded. "I won't let you down."

"I trust you, Ro. Give Rory your phone, Harley. I'm getting another one tomorrow, so I don't have to worry about tracking tonight."

Without hesitation, Harley complied. Soon, CJ was guiding her away from the movie theater and skirting the mall, heading in the direction of Ridge Moore.

Hortensia's mall in no way compared to any of the shopping centers they enjoyed in Portland, but it held enough shops and restaurants to serve its purpose. The small food court had five places to eat but it would do too.

The night was cold, cloudy, and damp, but CJ kept them moving at a brisk pace. When they left the bright lights of the mall and veered into the forest, he wrapped his arm around her shoulder and drew her close to his side. She shivered at the pitch-black surroundings. The vague outlines of the trees coupled with the sounds of nocturnal activity frightened her.

"I have you, Harley." CJ's confident voice eased her somewhat. "I won't ever let anything happen to you."

She nodded, although she doubted he saw.

The lapping of water reached her ears. Ahead, dim lights offered a glimmer of hope that the darkness would relent. And she was right. Once they cleared the trees, Turn Creek Bridge stood before them. She knew about it from Mattie, though Harley never visited in person.

CJ halted their stride before crossing the bridge's access road that ran parallel to the woods. Instead of stopping when they reached the summit, they continued to the other side. At the bottom, he veered right, unbothered by the thick grass and the returning darkness.

"Where are we going?" she finally asked, wondering if they'd ever stop walking.

"Finally gave in to your curiosity," he teased, the smile in his voice pulling a grin from her. "It isn't much longer."

Another fifty yards through brush and brambles, the silhouette of a structure came into view.

"Fuck, I forgot a flashlight."

"And we don't have our phones," Harley squeaked.

"Even if Uncle Johnnie hadn't broken mine, I would've left it with Rory. I'm pretty sure Dad and Uncle Mort are tracking us to high fucking hell."

They halted in front of the small building.

"It's an old picnic shelter," CJ said, "but the concrete floor is cracked and some of the bricks are missing, so we have to be careful."

"Why are we here?"

"I'm sure there are matches and a candle under the picnic table," CJ said, more to himself than to her. "Wait here."

"Not happening, bud," Harley said. "I can barely see in front of myself. Who knows what lurks around us, waiting to pounce."

He responded by grabbing her hand and tugging her forward. They paused and he settled his hands on her hips. "I'm not leaving you. I'm just crouching to feel under the table. Okay?"

"Fine," she gritted. "Just be quick."

The moment he turned away, Harley shuddered in fear and discomfort. Frigid air swept through the four sides of the shelter and took aim at her and the abundance of skin she left bare. Her mini skirt with the big heart was so cute, but it showed most of her thighs. Her black sweater was long-sleeved, but cropped at the midriff, while her black boots went up to her knees. She had no jacket, gloves, or hat, and—

Dim light flickered as CJ lifted a candle between them.

He grinned. "Hey, beautiful."

"Hey," she said, the butterflies rising again in her stomach.

The candlelight wavered, then extinguished as more wind whirled around them.

"Fuck, I didn't think this through."

“I disagree,” Harley countered, reaching out to touch him but finding him gone. “You planned for everything except the darkness.”

“I couldn’t think of anywhere else for us to go to be alone. Even if we’d gone to the treehouse, I’m sure we would’ve had company.”

He was probably right. Harley drew in a deep breath. “I can’t believe how Daddy shouted at me.”

“If you were my kid, I would’ve too,” CJ admitted as the faint light flared up again. “When I first saw you, my eyes almost popped out of my head.”

Harley snapped her brows together as the flame died again, and CJ growled. “I didn’t think you noticed. You didn’t say anything.”

Two thuds hit her ears.

“The fucking wind keeps fucking up the candlelight. There’s a lean-to about a mile away, but it’s a mean walk and we’ll never get back to the mall in time.”

“It’s also dark,” Harley said as if he didn’t have eyes. Chilled, she wrapped her arms around her waist. “Besides, Rory is all alone and I feel bad for leaving him. He doesn’t seem to be in the best headspace.”

“Fuck, with Aunt Kendall and Uncle Johnnie as my parents, I wouldn’t be in the best goddamn headspace either.”

Harley giggled, then slapped a hand over her mouth. “They aren’t that bad.”

“Yeah, Harley, they are,” CJ said flatly. “Before I walked in on Uncle Johnnie having his dick swinging in front of his children, *Mattie*, I would’ve given him a pass. He hands her such fucking bullshit and he does that because Aunt Kendall wants to prove she’s fun? Fuck him and fuck her. I felt so fucking sorry for Mattie. She was in tears. Rory and JJ were *begging* to let her leave and that motherfucker said no. He was angry with Aunt Kendall, so he made Mattie suffer. That asshole.”

"It was traumatizing for you. I can't imagine h-h-h-ow i-i-t w-w-was for Rory," she said, her teeth chattering.

CJ wrapped her in his embrace, cocooning her with the heat of his body.

She clung to him, breathing in his scent, and smiling. "You're wearing cologne."

"My favorite girl in the entire world wanted to go on a date," he revealed, "so I had to make it worth her while." His fingers tangled in her hair. "Dad and Uncle Mort noticed, too. Although I intended to leave our phones with Rory before, I knew it was even more imperative once my behavior raised their suspicions."

"Do you think Uncle Chris has any other tracking devices on you?"

"I left school early and bought new everything, including a wallet. Since I have favorite shoes and one wallet, that's the only logical places Dad could've fucked with to monitor my whereabouts. Unless he decides on a hypodermic tracker."

Harley tightened her arms around CJ's waist. "You'd know if he implanted something under your skin."

"Unless I was asleep when he jabbed my ass," CJ replied. "However, he's paranoid about Mom's safety, so I think I'm good."

"He loves her a lot and wants her safe, although sometimes it seems over the top."

"I feel that way a lot," CJ said, releasing his hold on her and stepping back. "Then, I have memories of Mom's kidnapping. That was real. Mystic, that motherfucker, took her and left me." He settled his jacket around her shoulders. "Other times, I have memories of my mom falling and full of blood. Or I see her and her neck is bruised with clear impressions of fingers. If I was Dad, I'd be paranoid, too," he said quietly.

CJ never discussed such grim recollections. As far as Harley knew, he had only happy memories and a childhood as idyllic as hers. She stuffed her arms into the sleeves of CJ's jacket. It was ridiculously big for her, but it smelled of him and the giddiness from hours ago returned. She tipped her head up, wishing she could see him.

"What do you—"

His hands cupped her waist and he brushed his lips across hers. "We can talk about this some other time, bae."

Standing on her tiptoes, she nodded, not hesitating to wrap her arms around his neck when he bent his head. His tongue tapped against her mouth and she parted her lips ever so slightly. Closing her eyes, she caressed the fine hairs at the nape of his neck. He tasted minty and—

Without warning, their foreheads got in the way, their teeth gnashed together, and their noses bumped, breaking them apart with a simultaneous, "*Ow*!"

"I'm so sorry!" Harley cried, caressing her forehead before checking the bridge of her nose.

"I am, too. It wasn't your fault, Harley. We just need more practice."

"With each other?"

"No, with fucking Martians. Of course with each other!"

"I was just checking," Harley grouched.

CJ sighed. "Talk to me, Harley. It's like I don't know you anymore. We don't text as often. I rarely see you. Then, suddenly, you want us to go on a date. Is it because Homecoming is coming up and I can't take you to the dance?"

Homecoming? Harley had forgotten about the mid-October celebration. As a cheerleader, she'd participate in the football game, but as a freshman she wouldn't be allowed to attend the dance. It never crossed her mind CJ intended to go.

"You're going without me?" she asked, hurt and outrage blooming in her.

"I'm a football player and a junior. It's a rite of passage. Besides, if I don't go, I can't be crowned Homecoming King."

"No way!" she screeched. "You can't become Homecoming King until I'm eligible to be Homecoming Queen."

"Yeah, way," CJ snapped. "I'll have graduated the year you become eligible."

It would be the same with Prom. And that night was even bigger than Homecoming. Losing one's virginity was as much a tradition as the dance itself.

"You can't go to the dance without me," she said, focusing on Homecoming for now. Prom was months away.

"You can't be so selfish and ask me to sit Homecoming night out because you can't go."

The photo of CJ and Molly cuddled on the bleacher rose in Harley's head and panic flared in her. "Please—"

"I'm going, Harley."

She stiffened. "I suppose you're taking Molly."

"Or Jaleena," CJ confirmed.

"*Jaleena*?" Frowning, Harley patted her hair. "Y-you're okay with her close crop?"

"*What*?"

"Her...her...Molly...Aunt Meggie and Rebel...and you're used to that t-texture and—"

"What the fuck is *wrong* with you, Harley? Have you lost your fucking mind? Since when does hair texture matter to me?"

She wanted the ground to open up and swallow her. Confused and humiliated, she turned and stumbled into the darkness, tripping over an unseen obstacle and sprawling to the ground. Crying out, she landed on her hands and knees. A creature ran over her fingers, and she screamed.

CJ swept her into his arms.

"A rat just assaulted me," she cried.

"Or a small snake."

She screamed bloody murder, kicking and flailing so frantically he almost dropped her. His brutal grip brought her back to her senses.

"I want to go home," she said, on the verge of tears. Lately, she'd been so emotional, and she wasn't sure why, but it was taking over her life. "Go to your stupid dance. I don't care."

He started walking with her in his arms. "Good, because I wouldn't give a fuck, since I'm going whether you like it or not."

Sniffling, she clenched her jaw and stiffened her spine. As they walked across the bridge, she gazed at him, surprised to see anger blanketing his face.

"Stop," she ordered. It worried her that if they didn't clear the air between them, their friendship would be forever changed. As it was, it still hadn't recovered from the fiasco of his birthday.

Immediately, he halted.

"Put me down."

He did so without comment.

She sank deeper into his jacket, annoyed the bridge lights threw him into shadow. "My hair started mattering while I was dressing," she confessed. "How can I compete with Molly if I don't have what she has?" Lost, she lowered her gaze. "For the first time ever, I envied Mommie's hair and felt *different*."

When CJ leaned against one of the beams, it allowed her to see his face. His tender look eased her and she relaxed ever so slightly. He lifted her curls and let go, allowing the strands to flutter in the wind.

"Your hair is gorgeous, Harley. Because *you* are. I can't believe I have to say this to you, but I don't see texture or skin color. I like Molly. She's brainless. Somehow, that makes her charming."

"I see," Harley said miserably.

"No, you don't. I like her and, yet, I don't want her as my girl. She isn't you."

"But who *is* me?" she blurted. She no longer knew.

He stared at her for long moments before he turned and leaned his arms against the railing. "I can't tell you who you are, bae. That isn't my place. Only you can figure that out."

"I don't know how to and you know me—"

"You know me, too, Harley, but I sure as hell don't want you to tell me who the fuck I am. Do I know myself? Not really. Everything's changing so fast, I can barely keep up. However, it's up to me to figure myself out."

"I feel like I'm losing you."

He glanced over his shoulder. "I feel the same about you."

"If I could go back to your birthday, I would accept the ring."

"It wouldn't do any good." He looked ahead again, where the bridge lights did little to dent the nighttime abyss. "You still wouldn't be ready. You aren't now. We're here because of some stupid picture."

"We're here because I wanted to kiss you again," she confessed. "That's why I wanted us to be alone. You don't think about our kiss?" she asked at his silence.

"Yeah, but what do you want me to say? I've lied to my dad and yours. That can get me fucking killed. And for what? For you to tell me I'm betraying you if I go to the Homecoming Dance? To hear you want to kiss me? Eventually, it won't be enough. You aren't ready to be my girl so you damn sure aren't ready for sex."

"And you are?" she demanded, already knowing the answer. She'd *felt* the answer during their kiss. However, she'd ignored his erection, pretending if she didn't acknowledge it, it didn't exist.

CJ straightened and faced her again. "What do you want me to say, Harley?" he shouted, throwing his hands up in the air. "Yes, I want sex with you. Again, I ask you, *what now*? The truth is out. Are you shutting me out a little more? Run to Willard and buddy up to him! I don't give a fuck."

"What?" Harley snarled, shocked at the question. "What does he have to do with anything?"

Stalking to her, he thrust his face into herself. "A fucking lot. It's still hard for me to believe you *asked* to partner with that feral hog."

"I asked to partner with him to tell him to leave you alone, CJ," she bit out.

"Say what?" he asked, his eyes widening.

"You heard me. I figured if he backed off, Lumbly would. Instead, the jackass failed you."

CJ considered her for a moment. "And both you and Willard missed the last two weeks of school."

Uh-oh.

Narrowing his eyes, he took her face between his cold hands and searched her every contour. His features veered from thoughtful to recognition to livid in the blink of an eye.

"I'm fucking killing him. He raised his fucking hands to you." Then: "And you fucking *lied* to me."

Harley heaved in a breath, on the verge of telling the truth just to clear the air and have things as they once had been. "I didn't lie to you, so don't use me as an excuse to fight him.

"Fuck off," he spat, releasing her so quickly she stumbled back. "I don't fucking appreciate your gaslighting me, Harley. I know that motherfucker and I know you."

"Not really, according to *you*."

Huffing, CJ scraped his fingers through his hair. "Protect that motherfucker. I don't care anymore." He shoved his hands into his pockets and nodded. "Let's get back to the mall."

Not waiting for her answer, he wrapped an arm around her shoulder and guided her down into the darkness. He was taut and tense, yet he never let her go, aware of her fear and not allowing his anger to ignore her well-being. She wanted to tell him to have fun at Homecoming but didn't know if she'd greenlight his dating other girls.

For their entire lives, their twenty-month age difference was never an issue. High school changed everything, especially if he was determined to participate.

Tension hung between them. She couldn't think of anything to say to lighten the mood. She trudged forward in miserable silence.

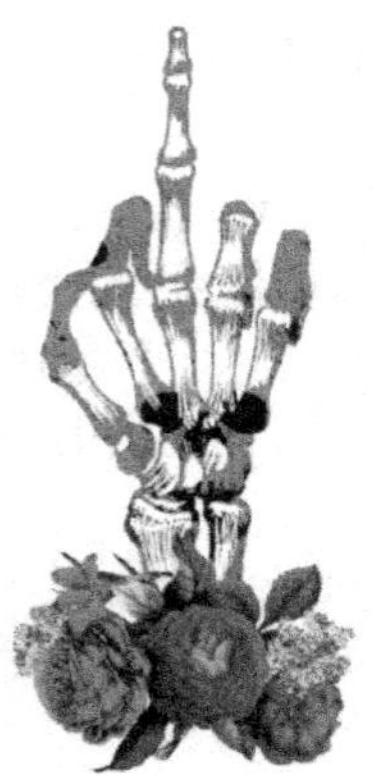

Chapter Thirty Three

RORY

Uninterested in seeing a stupid movie, Rory trekked through the mall, searching for gifts for his mother's birthday and trying to work off his lingering anger and resentment at his parents' latest stunt. The Mattie bullshit was bad enough. Acting ladylike had its place, but not when a bitch was on a warpath.

In Dad's world, Rebel could've beat Mattie to a pulp as long as Mattie remained a lady. In Mom's world, it was perfectly fucking reasonable for a grown ass man and woman to parade naked in front of their kids.

Sometimes, Rory hated both of them.

But he loved them too and he wanted them happy. He wanted his mother happy. No one ever fucking discussed her suicide attempt. Yet it hung in the back of his mind like a bad fucking omen. He'd been staying with Uncle Christopher and Aunt Meggie because his parents didn't know how to be husband and wife and they didn't fucking know how to be parents. Especially during times of trouble. As long as shit went smooth, they were fine. One ripple sent them into a tale spin.

When his mother overdosed, he hadn't known what happened at the time and didn't remember exactly when he'd discovered the truth. It was probably akin to Mattie overhearing Aunt Meggie killed a stupid motherfucker.

For years, Rory lived with the knowledge of how close he came to losing his mother. He'd watched his parents struggle to put their marriage back together. He'd *seen* them fall in love, really, truly fall in love. Then, around the time he began hearing rumors of a feud between the Dwellers and the Gnomes Rory noticed small tears in the fabric of his family.

Dad demanding perfection from Mattie. Mom's cooking going from paleo to poison. Dad turning against Aunt Meggie in slow degrees. In turn, Mom began manipulating situations to pretend she followed Dad's orders, while, in truth, she thumbed her nose at him. Dad obsessed over Rory's future rank in the club. Mom withdrew from reality.

It was all so much for Rory to cope with. CJ, Harley, Lolly, Aunt Meggie, and Uncle Christopher had been his only refuge. Yet, he too was withdrawing from his support system, afraid he'd let slip about his forays into the meatshack. Afraid too of leaving his little sister because her coping mechanism consisted of drugs, sex, and manipulating their dumb fucking father.

Sometimes, Rory wanted to die.

Or kill.

Earlier, when Harley had been trying to talk to him, he'd been so eaten up with rage, he could barely hold a civil conversation. She'd just been trying to help him because she was sweet and kind and his friend. She hadn't changed. *He* had.

Sadness crept into him and he sighed.

CJ needed him, and that gave Rory focus. So far, his anger still percolated, but what was required was sweet and innocent compared to the blood and death living in his head.

Sticking to CJ's plan, Rory headed to the shop with the most luxury items. Whatever other issues his mother faced, lack of good taste wasn't one.

His gift was a Baccarat vase. CJ's was also Baccarat, a water pitcher with two glasses. Harley's gift to his mother would be a candle in a hand painted covered jar. Dad had given Rory his American Express Black with instructions to have the shop manager call him except he was pretty sure that wouldn't be necessary when he saw Gypsy at the register.

He sat his items on the counter. She was several years younger than his mom but looked so much older. She'd gained weight. Her hair was fried and frizzy and her neck was wrinkled. Maybe, this was true misery and his parents were insane motherfuckers who loved drama.

"Rory!" Years of hard partying deepened her voice.

No, not hard partying. *Hard living*. His mother drank and partied, but she had Dad's devotion and protection. Derby was a fucking asshole.

"I didn't recognize you, boy," she said with a smile. She looked exhausted. "You're looking more like John Boy each time I see you."

Rory grinned. "Everyone says that. What are you doing here?"

"I have to make a living," she said quietly. "To support me and my youngest girl." She nodded at the counter. "These are some pretty expensive things."

"Mom's birthday is in a couple weeks." He dug in his jacket and pulled out his father's credit card. "Dad said to have the store call him for his approval, but you know me so do we have to disturb him?"

"You're a cutie pie," she said with a girlish giggle. "Tell him to bring his ass in here."

"He's at home," Rory said absently, a display case behind the counter catching his eye. Specifically, a midnight blue butterfly. Aunt Meggie's birthday was at the beginning of October. That would make a perfect gift for her. He pointed to it. "I want that butterfly, too."

Gypsy glanced over her shoulder, then back at him. "You're here alone? What do you mean Johnnie's home? Kendall isn't with you?"

Fuck.

All Gypsy had to do was call Aunt Meggie and tell her CJ and Harley wasn't with Rory and they were all busted.

Fuck.

"Dweller kids have tighter security than the president of the United States. If you aren't with your parents, you have a detail, so what's going on?"

Fuck, fuck, and double fuck.

"CJ and Harley are at the movie theater, waiting for me. We have a curfew and trailers bore me, so while they're doing the grunt work, I'm shopping." He glanced around, then leaned forward. "But you're right. Mom and Dad, and my aunts and uncles are expecting us to be together. If you tell on us, we're in deep trouble."

"Do you swear—"

He dug in his pocket and got the money CJ had given him. Rory had yet to count it, but he knew it was at least a couple hundred. He handed Gypsy the cash.

Amusement danced over her face. "Are you bribing me?"

He nodded. "Yep."

"I like a man who don't bullshit," she said, laughing.

She stuffed the bills in the valley of her tits, drawing his attention to the two ivory mounds. Red blood would be stark against such white skin. His mouth watered and he swallowed. *Focused* on Gypsy. A living, breathing woman. A manipulator but still fragile and delicate with a warm body to enjoy.

Over the summer, one of the club girls sucked his cock, but he'd never stuck his dick in pussy before.

"What do you want from the case, Rory?" she asked, and he wondered if he'd imagined her flirtation.

"Uh, the butterfly." He pointed. "The midnight blue one."

After setting the delicate crystal on the counter, Gypsy gave him a sly look. "For Meggie?"

"How'd you know?"

"She likes butterflies. When I saw them, I thought of her too. The blue and gold are called Lucky Butterflies. This one is Midnight Diamant."

"Oh. Well, give me all three." It wasn't his fucking money. Besides, his father said to buy whatever he wanted. "We can each give her one."

"You, Harley, and CJ?"

"Yeah. That's why I have three gifts for my mom. One from each of us."

"Gotcha. Let's check you out so you won't miss the opening."

Rory not only missed the beginning of the movie but the first half hour. Luckily, they'd purchased tickets online. Even luckier, he'd seen the stupid movie last weekend with JJ while Mom, Dad, Mattie, and Blade shopped and ate.

However, the GPS would show his and Harley's phone at the theater, so whatever. If motherfuckers didn't steal so much, Rory would've left their devices somewhere and save his eyes the indignity of rewatching bullshit.

Finally, the theater lights blinked on and the end credits rolled. Grabbing his packages with his mother and Aunt Meggie's gifts, he headed outside for a smoke. Once he settled the bags between his feet and lit his cigarette, he looked at his watch. It was almost ten.

Goddamn, but time was crawling. Maybe, he'd go to Macy's and find a few more things for his mother and Aunt Meggie. He didn't want to eat alone and he had more than an hour before CJ and Harley met him in the food court.

"Beta boy, your mommy let you out of your playpen?" Willard Byrd taunted, suddenly in front of Rory.

"Don't you mean that melanin lover?" Wallace laughed, beside Rory, while two other motherfuckers helped to enclose him in their circle.

"Hey, yo, motherfucker," Rory started. "Stay the fuck away from my sister."

So far, Ryder was still conducting recon and couldn't decide one way or the other if Wallace was harassing Mattie. Rory no longer cared. Wallace could be his first live body in the meatshack.

"Or what? If she wants me around, you can't do anything, bitch."

"Where *is* CJ and that half-breed?" The question came from behind Rory.

He dragged on his cigarette and blew smoke in Willard's face. His coughing and sputtering made Rory smile. "I'm telling you one time, Willard, get the fuck away from me and if you can't talk about Harley with respect, don't say a motherfucking word."

"What is it with you Dweller boys?" Willard demanded. "*I'm* in control, cuck. You're outnumbered.

If we want to skin you alive, there's no one around to save you."

Rory should've been afraid, but he wasn't. He didn't give a fuck. Life meant nothing. One moment, everything was fine and happy, and the next, it was all over. Or parents were parading around with no clothes and forcing their kids to do the same. Or stupid fuckheads were in pieces in the fucking meatshack. He blew more smoke in Willard's face. Dweller boys had Dweller fathers. The sooner those dickheads understood that the fucking better. "Suck my fucking cock, motherfucker. I heard you won first place in the Suck Boy Awards, so get on your knees and show your skills."

Predictably, the motherfucker swung; Rory ducked, leaving the fuckhead behind him as the recipient of Willard's punch. Rory threw himself into Wallace, knocking him off his feet.

Taking his cigarette, Rory pressed it into Wallace's cheek, his cock throbbing at the motherfucker's scream and the scent of ash and burning flesh.

Someone grabbed Rory's collar and dragged him away from Wallace. Unfortunately, he lost his cigarette.

Willard slammed his fist into Rory's face and threw him to the ground. Kicks and punches rained over his body.

"*Motherfucker*!" CJ snarled a moment before Willard bounced on the ground.

Harley screamed, and Rory's heart nearly stopped. She toppled onto him.

He dug in his pocket for his phone and held it out, ignoring her red cheek and teary eyes. "Take my phone and call—"

Wallace yanked her by her hair and shoved her away, his eyes wild. Rory scrambled to his feet, fury roaring through him. He wanted their intestines oozing from their navels. Growling, he swung on Wallace. And swung. And swung, not stopping until he was physically dragged away.

And promptly handcuffed.

Mom, Dad, Diesel, Uncle Christopher, Aunt Meggie, Uncle Mort, and Aunt Bailey descended on the police station where Harley, Rory, and CJ waited in a holding cell.

Every inch of Rory ached. He'd been in fights before, but nothing so brutal. Willard had intended to kill him.

The cell door opened, and Mom rushed in, jerking Rory into her arms and sobbing. "What happened, son?" she sobbed, hysterical. "I've never been so worried in my life! You got into a fight at the mall? You're such a good child. I can't imagine—"

Rory froze at his mother's trembles. In the heat of the moment, he hadn't cared what happened to him or what became of his opponents. He'd wanted to kill them. Yet Mom needed her world to be perfect for her to function properly.

No wonder Mattie hid her behavior.

Regret washed through Rory, and he wished he could undo the fight. He was in so much trouble and, because of it, his mom would suffer.

"Rory didn't get into the fight, Aunt Kendall," CJ said quietly. "I did because a random asshole started heckling Harley."

"Stop talking, CJ," Diesel ordered.

Aunt Meggie hurried to CJ, while Rory stood frozen, his arms around his heartbroken mother.

"Sit," Aunt Meggie instructed, guiding CJ back to the longest metal bench in the cell. Once he complied, she studied him. "That isn't what bystanders said, son. From what I understand, you and Harley walked up on the fight."

CJ glanced at Rory and set his jaw. "Check the security footage, Mom."

Mattie. She must've been in on the evening and CJ had already instructed her on what needed doing. For whatever reason she'd taken a liking to Uncle Val and Uncle Stretch's hacking skills from a very young age.

"You sure you not takin' the fuckin' fall for Rory cuz Kendall ain't shuttin' the fuck up?" Uncle Christopher demanded.

Backing away, Mom rubbed her red eyes and sniffled. "CJ, honey, if Rory got into the fight, tell us."

When Dad placed a hand on Rory's shoulder, Rory remembered the gifts he'd purchased for Mom and Aunt Meggie.

"CJ, Harley say she don't know who attacked her," Uncle Mort called from outside the cell while Aunt Bailey still had her arms wrapped around Harley. "Do you?"

CJ folded his arms, his eyes burning with anger. "I don't, Uncle Mort. There were four of them. Harley was walking slightly ahead because we argued over Homecoming. I guess they thought she was alone and called her...*things*. Just as I reached her..." He blinked and glanced away. "Just as I reached her, she was hit," he said thickly, "and I didn't give a fuck. I wanted their fucking blood. As a matter of fucking fact, if I ever see those motherfuckers again, they're fucking de—"

Aunt Meggie slapped her hand over CJ's mouth and shook her head. Her baby bump seemed twice as big as when she'd come to school at the beginning of the week.

CJ shoved her hand away and got to his feet, forcing her back. He glared at her. "They fucking hit Harley, Mom!"

"And Ima fuckin' hit you if you don't back the fuck up off your ma, boy," Uncle Christopher growled. "Megan, Bailey, Kendall, Harley, go the fuck outside. Mutt?" he called.

"What, Outlaw?" one of the cops called.

"Lemme talk to my kid and nephew. Get the fuck out."

"This is *my* station."

"Made fit for modern times with *my* fuckin' money," Uncle Christopher snapped.

"Club money, Christopher," Dad corrected.

"Yeah, son, we supplement your piss poor salary," Uncle Mort added.

"You got five minutes," Mutt grumbled.

"Let's talk," Diesel told the police officer after Harley, Mom, Aunt Bailey and Aunt Meggie walked outside. He steered Mutt into the cold night, too.

Uncle Christopher lit two cigarettes and passed one to CJ, so Dad followed suit and did the same, while Uncle Mort lit his own.

Uncle Chris nodded to CJ, indicating he sit again. For a few minutes, the five of them smoked in silence.

"When the assfucks heard the sirens, they fucking scattered," Uncle Chris finally started, sitting next to CJ. "I can make this go the fuck away, but I gotta know the truth."

Dragging on his cigarette, CJ eyed Rory, then shrugged. "It is the truth, Dad."

No, Rory refused to let CJ take the fall for his actions. He opened his mouth to speak up.

"Christopher, why are you so determined CJ change his story?" Dad demanded.

"Because it ain't fuckin' addin' up. Rory got...fuck his entire face fucked up. CJ got a black eye, busted knuckles and a swollen jaw."

"If CJ walked up on the fight, that shit make sense, Johnnie. That's all Prez saying."

"No, my son doesn't pick fights."

"I don't pick fights either, Uncle Johnnie," CJ snapped. "The motherfucker picked me when they fucked with Harley." He glared at his dad. "Harley fell on Ro. One of them..." His nostrils flared and he shook his head. "One of them yanked her by her hair and the other two started wailing on Rory. I was so busy fighting this massive motherfucker I couldn't help her, Dad." His hand shook. "I've never...I was so scared for her. And all I wanted to do was *kill* those motherfuckers," he snarled. "I wanted to chop their fucking fingers off and shove them up their miserable cocks. Those fucking fuckbags. They need their spinal cords ripped out the fucking assholes because they're fucking cowards."

Uncle Chris and Uncle Mort exchanged grins.

"My ass so fuckin' proud of you, boy," Uncle Chris said, his voice filled with emotion. He gave him a bear hug.

Uncle Mort hi-fived CJ. "Yeah, little dude, you do us proud." He turned to Rory and hi-fived him, too. "Thank you, neph. You helped protect my baby girl."

"Wait a minute. Giving CJ most of the accolades isn't fair."

"Dad, that ship's sailed," Rory said tiredly, stomping his cigarette out.

"But—"

"No fuckin' buts, Johnnie," Uncle Christopher warned, finishing his cigarette like everyone else. "CJ furious cuz of Harley, but that don't mean it started the way he said. I think *my* boy takin' the fall to protect Kendall."

"By turning my son into a fucking wimp?"

"Johnnie, shut the fuck up," Uncle Mort said. "Rory not a goddamn wimp, but he can't be *your* killer and Red saint. Since she his momma and was falling apart, her feeling trump yours, so sit the fuck down."

At Dad's ice-cold glower, Uncle Mort lifted a brow. Flushing, Dad stormed away. "I'll check on Kendall," he threw over his shoulder.

"I think the presents were destroyed," Rory admitted after his father's departure.

"Ain't nothin' but a thing, Rory," Uncle Christopher said. "You all safe and that matters the most."

Chapter Thirty Four

Eight days later, CJ rang the doorbell of a small house with a cracked driveway and a crooked foundation in an older section of Hortensia, untouched by the development of the Medical District and other boom areas.

Even the jailhouse was more modern than this place. CJ still couldn't believe he'd ended up in *jail*. After Harley told him she wanted to go on a date with him, he'd jumped into action. As fucking usual, his plans fell apart.

Scowling, CJ punched the doorbell again. First, Uncle Mort had fucking flipped when he saw Harley. Then, *Harley* dropped her bomb and demanded CJ not go to Homecoming. Fucking *then*, motherfucking Willard struck.

Neither him or Wallace showed their ugly mugs at school this past week. They fucking knew CJ was gunning for them. Unfortunately, he didn't know the other two fuckbags who'd been with them.

And because his life fucking sucked, Mattie had forgotten to tell Rory to send her his location and the store he'd purchased the gifts. Uncle Stretch tracked Rory *alone*. CJ's saving grace *was* Mattie interfering with the feed around the theater and the path he'd taken to reach the bridge.

There'd been questions and suspicions, but CJ, Harley, and Rory stuck to the story that Rory went shopping while CJ and Harley purchased the snacks and watched the trailers for upcoming movies.

All in all, it had been a fucking nightmare week, and CJ wanted to chill with a beer, a bud, and his PlayStation. Instead, he had to deal with Molly.

He pressed the doorbell again.

"Is anyone home?" Mom asked, glancing around the quiet neighborhood. Slipper, Orange, and Fuse waited for her on their idling bikes.

"I hope so," CJ answered. "Molly invited me over to work on our project." Such as it was. She was driving him fucking crazy, but he kept that to himself. He didn't want his mother to worry.

"Call her..." Mom's voice trailed off as the door swung open, revealing a tall man with hard blue eyes and the same color hair as Molly's. He was bare-chested but wore law enforcement trousers.

He gave Mom the once over. "May I help you?"

Mom smiled and a breeze fluttered her golden hair. CJ gritted his teeth at the motherfucker's leer, barely stopping himself from shoving her out of view. She held out her hand. "I'm Megan Caldwell," she said as the man took her hand in his big paw and shook it. "This is my son, CJ. He has a study date with Molly."

The man flicked a glance at CJ before looking at Mom again. "I'm Tom Harris," he said. "Molly's my daughter."

"Nice to meet you," Mom said politely. She hesitated. "You're a sheriff's deputy?"

"For the past twenty years," he told her.

"That is commendable." CJ couldn't read his mother's tone and he couldn't see her face to judge her expression. "You weren't expecting my son, so we're intruding."

"Molly's quite forgetful," Tom said mildly. "But your boy's welcome." He glanced toward the street where Mom had parked her SUV, although CJ suspected he was studying her guards.

She dug in her coat pocket, got a business card, and held it out to him. "My cell phone number's there if he overstays his welcome before I can come back for him."

"He's welcome to study with her as long as he needs to," Tom said as courteous as Mom, but reeking of phony motherfuckery.

"Thank you, Tom." She turned to CJ and offered her cheek.

Obligingly, he leaned down and kissed her.

"If I need to pick you up before four, call me, potato," she instructed.

"I will," CJ swore.

She hugged him. "I love you."

"I love you too." CJ waited until she drove off with Slipper, Orange and Fuse surrounding her SUV before going into the Harris house.

Inside, he found the furniture and décor in as bad shape as the building itself.

"Molly's in her room," Tom said, nodding to a door on the opposite side of the room.

"Uh, does she have a laptop by any chance?"

Tom's smile didn't reach his eyes. "Nope."

CJ gnashed his teeth together. "She said she did! I told her I'd bring mine and she said...Never mind," he finished in frustration.

Instead of commenting, Tom turned away, walked to the opened door on the side opposite Molly's and disappeared into the room.

Cursing to high heaven, CJ stomped to Molly's door and knocked.

"Come in."

At the sound of her voice, he drew in a deep breath. They needed to settle on a science project. Their lack of a laptop was unimportant and if he broached that first, then they'd part ways *without* knowing what the fuck they were working on.

He opened the door and walked into her bedroom. Like the rest of the house, it was small and ramshackle. A mattress with threadbare sheets and comforter served as her bed where she was laying. Plastic bins were stuffed with clothes. Three school uniforms hung on pegs on the back wall, pin neat and clean.

A broken blind hung on the lone window, allowing light to stream in, beaming off cracked walls and dirty floors. CJ couldn't ever remember being surrounded by such poverty and filth. How could she attend Ridge Moore?

She sat and pushed against the wall. Her hair tangled around her, and her breasts pushed against her thin tank top.

"You came," she said quietly, drawing her knees up. She looked so sad.

Stuffing his hands in his pockets, he nodded. "I said I would. I want an 'A'."

She lowered her lashes. Thought for a moment. Cocked her head to the side. "I think excellent is misspelled. At one time, students received 'E's, then it became 'A's. But the spelling people didn't keep up. It should be axcellent. Aycellent. Or—"

"Let's not get off-track, bae," he said with a grin. "We need to decide on our project once and for all."

"I'm hungry. Mama left with her boyfriend and Daddy got angry, so he locked the refrigerator." She clutched the sheet. "I'll suck you off if you buy me a small fry from McDonald's."

Her words stunned him into silence. Since his date with Harley, his cock was impossible. Three days ago during Phys. Ed., he'd recalled how gorgeous she'd been in her outfit and he'd popped a boner.

Molly hopped to her feet and pulled her tank top over her head, baring her heavy tits before she dropped her panties and stepped out of them, revealing her clean-shaven pussy. When she started toward him, he came to his senses and raised his hands. She halted immediately.

"Your dad is in the next room and he's a fucking sheriff's deputy. No way am I allowing my cock to get me killed."

"But I'm hungry. It's *carpe quid diem quo pro*."

"It's *quid pro quo* meaning something for something or *carpe diem*. Seize the day." He turned his back to her. "Get dressed, Molly." Because, truly, his cock was hurting. *It* wanted her...

CJ rubbed his head. Fuck, *he* wanted her, too. As insane as it was, he liked Molly and he felt so bad for her. She was uncomplicated. Unlike Harley who kept him on pins and needles. He wanted to do the right thing by her, but he didn't know what that was.

He could no longer talk to her as his friend. One, Molly was in his life for the next few months. She was his science partner, but Harley was insecure about everything, even her place in his life, so she wouldn't want to hear anything about Molly.

He would have to censor each word, so she wouldn't flip.

CJ had wanted Harley to be his girlfriend, then she'd rejected him and now she seemed to change her mind. That left their age difference. It had never been a problem before and he hadn't ever thought it would be one at any time. Homecoming and Prom never came up, but he wouldn't have believed Harley would demand he not participate.

Her displeasure dimmed his enthusiasm for both events. He wanted to be fair and considerate of her, but he expected the same in return. Was that too much to ask? Was he being an unfair fuckhead?

He could only ask Diesel or Grant, but something was off about one and the other was knee deep in college.

"I'm dressed," Molly said. "Now what?"

Peeping over his shoulder, he saw she wore jeans, a button-down shirt, and a cable sweater, all new. Thrift store tags still hung from them.

"That's a very nice outfit."

"Ryan took me shopping," she admitted.

CJ couldn't imagine the motherfucker buying her or any other girl clothes. Fuck, not even a fucking candy bar. "Ryan Taylor? My cousin?"

"Yeah, silly," she giggled.

"He took you to the fucking thrift shop for clothes?" Cheap motherfucker.

"He lives in a log cabin, CJ," Molly said in exasperation. "He only gets a dollar a day for helping to look after his brainless brother. He told me Devon was born without a brain. Ryan also shared with me that every year, he has to help his Mom and Dad rebuild their house because the wood is used for the fire to keep them warm."

"Are you shitting me? That motherfucker! He's lying to you, Molly."

"Ryan told me himself," she said gravely. "I told him about a lab that grows new brains. It's really expensive though, but he has no patience with Devon when I think he should feel really sorry for him. It must be tough living without a brain."

"Molly!" CJ snarled, glaring at her. "You're not that fucking stupid. I demand you talk with fucking sense and cut the bullshit."

She blinked. "Where do I find bullshit to cut?"

"Shut up," CJ roared, out of patience. He patted his back pocket to check for his wallet. "Where the fuck is McDonald's?"

She poked out her lower lip, on the verge of tears.

Goddamn, all the girls he knew had gone fucking crazy. He heaved in a breath and pulled her into his arms. She sniffled. "I'm sorry, Molly. I didn't mean to yell at you."

"Did Daddy tell you to be mean to me?" she said around tears. "He tells everybody to make fun of me. I used to be smart."

"I barely spoke to your dad." Frankly, CJ didn't like that motherfucker. He was a disrespectful assbag for checking out his pregnant mom who proudly wore her wedding ring. "C'mon, tell him we're going for a hamburger."

She wiped her eyes. "Okay."

Five minutes later, they were walking down the street toward the main thoroughfare. Molly kept up a steady chatter about the days when fucking fish ruled the skies and goddamn birds lived in the oceans. He refused to interrupt her. It would only encourage her fucking stupidity.

"Order whatever you want," he said once they were at the restaurant.

She ordered a basket of fries, a Big Mac, a Dr. Pepper with a chocolate shake and an apple pie.

"Does Ridge Moore have financial aid?" CJ asked, halfway through her meal. Mom and Bunny cooked a huge breakfast like usual, so he bought himself only a shake.

Molly stuffed the last of her burger into her mouth. "I don't know," she said around half-chewed food. "Why?"

"Just asking," he lied, sipping his shake.

"Because we're poor and Ridge Moore is rich?" she asked in that way she had of reasoning some things out while still managing brainlessness.

He nodded.

"My dad's good friends with the Barts. Bash and Cleaner are his best friends. They pay for me. He's helping them with something."

"I don't know any of these people."

"You shouldn't. They are really mean." Her eyes rounded. "They'll kill me. They said they'd know if I mentioned them and shoot me." She paled. "I don't want to die!"

"You won't die, Molly. Don't say anything. They'll never know you told me their names."

"But Bash said I didn't have to tell him. He'd automatically know because my brain sends signals to everyone and allow people to read my mind."

"That's bullshit and—" *Stupid* died on his lips.

CJ suspected she really wasn't stupid. Maybe, she was afraid and used her outlandish theories as a coping mechanism. However, she needed a friend. Judging her or calling her names wouldn't help her.

Reaching across the table, he grabbed her hands. "Look at me, Molly."

Fear tightened her face and turned her eyes into liquid pools.

"Mind reading is overrated." He felt like a jackass for speaking the words, but he had her attention. "You don't trust me so whatever's in your head is completely blocked from me."

"I don't trust you?"

He was pretty sure she did, yet he had to make her believe the opposite so when these Bash and Cleaner and Bart motherfuckers came at her, she could try to defend herself.

Bash?

Cleaner?

Bart? No, not *one*. She'd said Barts.

"Are Bash and Cleaner bikers?"

"How'd you know? They're from Utah. They don't visit too often."

"Right," CJ said, dismissing the explanation and releasing her palm-roughened hands. Utah was hours away, so he doubted this club was a threat to the Dwellers. "As long as you never trust them, they won't be able to read your mind."

"Are you sure?"

"Positive."

She glanced at her forgotten fries. "Can I get a to-go bag? I'll eat them later."

"Don't microwave them," he advised. "Mom taught me a trick. She puts them in the oven to crisp them up. Same with pizza."

"We don't have an oven because we don't have a stove or a microwave. Last year, Mama sold them while Daddy was at work and I was at school."

CJ didn't know how to respond to that. Molly's parents were even more trifling than Aunt Kendall and Uncle Johnnie. "Uh, yeah, okay. Uh, how about I order a pizza before I leave later on?"

"Daddy won't let you if he can't have any."

"It'll be your pizza. You can do whatever you'd like with it." Including shoving it up her father's ass. "You told me you had a laptop—"

"I had it at the time." She shrugged. "Mama took it yesterday."

All righty then. "So we can choose our project. Billson *must* know by Monday. If we don't give him an answer, he's taking fifteen points away, so we'll start with an eighty-five."

"I still think putting flowers within bubbles is a cool idea."

"It is, but we can't do it with solution bought from a fucking store. There's no way it's possible."

"It is if you catch the bubbles and freeze them."

Fuck his fucking life. "We can make papyrus and compare it to common pulp paper. Or—"

"We can study if birth order affects grade point average. I'm an only child. That's why I'm brilliant."

CJ glowered at her. "We can build a robot with LEGO Mindstorms."

"I wouldn't want a robot that has a mind and causes storms."

"We can study maggot mass temperature."

"Aren't those shriveled flies?"

"How about growing vegan Kombucha leather?"

"We can see if we can get a potato to charge our cell phones," she said after a moment, considering his idea then dismissing it.

This was going nowhere. Getting to his feet, CJ went to the counter and asked for a bag so they could take her fries and pie. She threw away the Dr. Pepper but took the milkshake.

"Molly, I'm choosing the project," CJ decided on the walk back to her house. "I'll work on the these tonight and call you tomorrow so we can be on the same page for class."

"Okay," she said glumly.

"What's wrong *now*?"

"You sound like you're leaving." She sighed. "That means no pizza for me."

"My mom won't be able to pick me up for another couple hours, so I'll order the pizza, Molly. Trust me, I'll get hungry soon."

She stopped abruptly and grabbed his hand. "You'll make me have sex with you then?"

"Of course not, Molly!" CJ said, snatching his hand from her grip. "What is it with you and sex? Goddamn. Stop offering your body like it's a free-for-all."

"Giving it away is easy."

Her vulnerable words punched CJ in the gut. "As opposed to what?"

Licking her lips, she lowered her lashes and marched away.

CJ caught up to her. "If bad things are happening to you, you have to report it."

"Nothing bad is happening to me, CJ," she said breezily. "You really blow everything out of proportion. There's probably medicine for that."

He followed her up the rickety steps onto the creaky porch, where she unlocked the front door. CJ had just closed it behind him when Deputy Harris walked into the living room with a towel around his waist and his hair damp. Behind him, the partially ajar door showed a bathroom vanity and a fogged mirror.

"CJ's ordering pizza later, Daddy," Molly greeted.

"Save me a couple of slices," Deputy Harris grunted. "I'll be hungry when I get off duty."

"You've only been home for a few hours. I thought you were off the rest of the weekend."

His gaze flickered to CJ then to his daughter. "I was called in."

"Mama...you won't look for her."

"She's fine, Molly Jean. Mind your own fucking business. Pitching pussy to rich boys don't make you superior. It just makes you a fucking slut."

CJ stiffened. As much as he wanted to say something, he shut the fuck up. Being thrown in jail last week was sobering. Not only was Tom Harris a sheriff's deputy, he had access to a gun. At the very least his service weapon.

He fucked around with bikers and only God knew what else.

Molly's sniffles did something to him, though. Her father's meanness was so unwarranted.

"CJ is my friend, Daddy," Molly said, her voice small and pitiful. "He's Ryan's cousin."

Something dawned on Harris and his eyes widened. "You're Outlaw's kid."

A fuckton wasn't right about the situation; CJ couldn't figure out what, though alarms were clanging through him and the hairs at his nape and on his arms were standing on end. If Molly's father knew of *his* father just by CJ's association to Ryan, then there was some next level shit going on.

"And?" CJ refused to show how shook he was. He took his new cell phone from his pocket and held it up. "You need to talk to him? Let me pull up his number right now." Instead of pulling up the number, he sent his father a quick text. *Call me now.* "I'm shocked he hasn't called me since he tracks my every move and I didn't tell him I would be leaving to go—"

Keep Their Heads Ringin' by Dr. Dre blasted through the small house, CJ's ringtone for his dad. CJ pressed the speakerphone.

"Dad, hey, uh, you don't have to worry. You saw my location on your tracker but Molly and me are back at her parents' house."

At the silence, CJ's palm grew sweaty.

Deputy Harris lifted his brow.

"Yeah, boy," Dad said after an uncomfortable pause. "My ass was wonderin' why you was beamin' afuckinway from where your Ma left you."

"Your ass is really special, Mr. Caldwell," Molly said, frowning. "It spoke at Ryan's birthday party and now it's wondering."

Dad sighed. "Later, son."

The moment the line disconnected, Deputy Harris pointed to CJ's phone. "Let me see that."

"No, sir. I just got my phone back after my uncle broke my old one."

"I said—"

A ringing phone resounded from the bathroom. Glaring at CJ, Molly's dad turned and stomped away, returning a moment later with his phone.

"Outlaw isn't tracking you. You're wasting my time with some type of game when I need to get to work. Give me—"

The phone started ringing again.

"Who the fuck is this and what the fuck do you want?" He listened and his eyes widened before he fumbled with his phone. "Speakerphone's on."

"CJ, you fuckin' hear me?"

"Dad?"

"Listen up, deputy motherfucker. Ain't knowin' why the fuck my boy thinkin' *in his smallest fuckin' mind*, I ain't knowin' exactly where the fuck he at, but I ain't likin' the sound of his fuckin' voice when I called. You was checkin' my woman out. Your first fuckin' mistake. You was studyin' her detail. Your second fuckin' mistake. Whatever the fuck she saw, she ain't likin'. If she unfuckinhappy, my ass fuckin boohooey miserable and that's the last fuckin' thing you want. Underfuckinstand?"

"Are you threatening me?"

"Ain't you gotta go on fuckin' duty, motherfucker?" Dad demanded just as the sound of Harley pipes rose outside. "My ass in Portland at a fuckin' meetin'. Megan ain't able to get to CJ right now. Four of my motherfuckers outside your door and *several* more in the fuckin' area. I ain't too sure what the fuck goin' on—"

“Nothing’s going on, Outlaw,” Harris snapped. “This is all a misunderstanding.”

“But we’ll fail if we don’t do the project,” Molly said. “And if CJ leaves early, I can’t get a pizza.” She turned to her father. “Tell Mr. Caldwell and his ass that CJ is fine.” She looked at the floor. “Just please don’t tell Ryan CJ was here. I’m his date to Homecoming and he’s giving me twenty dollars for a dress.”

“Made from toilet paper?” CJ asked.

She smiled brightly. “It’s cotton, so it might be from toilet paper. If we’re still friends for Prom, he’s giving me twenty-five dollars.”

Her announcement stunned even her father’s assholery away.

“Dad, can Mom take Molly shopping for Homecoming and Prom?”

“Fuck, boy, your Ma like shopping so, yeah, if she wanna. I gotta get the fuck, but Ima wait ‘til Zephyr or Bishop scoop you up.”

“Daddy, please!” Molly cried. “Mr. Billson will drop our grade to eighty-five if we don’t turn in our essay.”

“Thesis statement,” CJ supplied.

“No, a thesis is for science. We’re doing chemistry.”

CJ scowled. “Chemistry *is* science.”

“No, Ryan said biology is about life, chemistry is about the periodic table and science is about the earth and space.”

“Molly! This is why we can’t start the fucking project with an eighty-five. Before it’s done, we’ll have a minus eighty-five.”

“You don’t have to be so mean,” she yelled. “Just because *I* know chemistry isn’t science and you don’t. I say our project should be testing foil in the microwave.”

“That goes against basic physics,” CJ countered. “We’ll burn this motherfucker to the ground.”

"What's physics? Not science, stupid. *Physics.* Physical. It's all about physical education."

"CJ—"

"What's wrong with you, girl?" CJ snarled, ignoring his dad.

"Molly—"

"What's wrong with *me*?" she spat, ignoring her father. "I've been giving you ideas. *You've* turned them down."

"A fucking two-year-old can put a bar of Ivory soap in the fucking microwave and watch it grow. We need a project that takes place over several months. Not three or four minutes."

"I told you we could study your death date. Mine is February thirty—"

"Don't you fucking say it," CJ warned, dizzy with anger. He kicked at the air. "There aren't thirty-two fucking days in February or any fucking month! And there's no fucking way you can live to 2199. It's fucking impossible."

"It is too! My momma told me."

"Then your momma's a dumb bitch," CJ said before he caught himself. "She should be ashamed of herself, telling you that lie. You know what? Forget it! I'm asking Billson to partner you with Willard, so me and Jaleena can work together. You're fucking impossible."

Bursting into tears, Molly barreled to CJ and threw her arms around his waist. "Please, don't! Willard is so mean to me," she sobbed. "Please, I'll do anything."

If he requested to switch with Ryan, then he'd be with a shy girl, who mumbled when she talked. Maybe, uh...her searched his brain for her name. Except he couldn't remember it. She was so unassuming and kind of blended into the furniture. However, the girls in his life were spoiled, loud, and chaotic. A quiet chick wouldn't drive him crazy *and* he'd get the 'A' he sought.

Yet Molly wouldn't stop crying, even when her father reassured Dad that CJ was in no danger and went to his bedroom to dress. She wouldn't shut up, even after her father left and Bishop came in for a brief word with CJ.

When he promised they'd remain partners and Ryan wouldn't find out CJ went to her house, her tears dried up and peace returned.

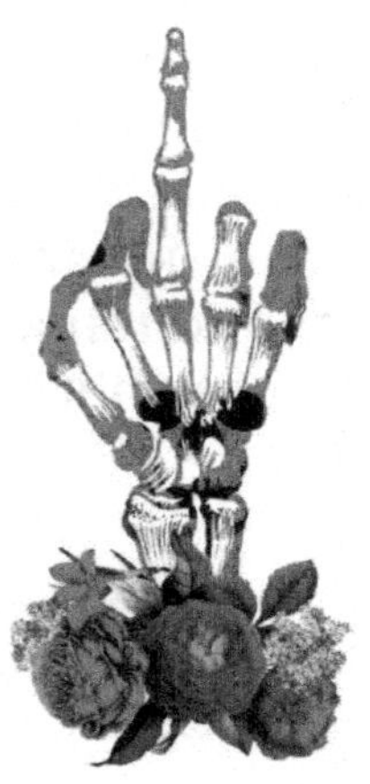

Chapter Thirty Five

Ryan

"Ryan!"

Hearing his father's voice, Ryan's eyes popped open. An hour ago, he'd been lost in bliss, pleased with his and Molly's nudity. Now, not so much since beating Val's ass would ruin his bliss. The motherfucker had warned Ryan about bringing his girlfriend home if they intended to do anything other than hang out in the den.

"Ryan!" Val called again, banging on the door. "Open this fucking door, boy. I have to talk to you."

"Who—?"

Ryan clapped his hand over Molly's mouth. "Shhhh," he warned. "Val's home. Get in my closet until I can sneak you out."

Keys jingled on the other side. Before Molly had a chance to move, the door opened. Panicking, Ryan shoved Molly out of the bed. The sound of a body slapping the floor met his ears and he winced.

"Asshole," she hissed as Ryan mumbled, "Sorry."

A turquoise gaze, almost a mirror to Ryan's, searched every corner, homing in on the rumpled bed and his bare chest.

Offering an exaggerated yawn, Ryan pulled the covers to his shoulders. "Hey, Val."

At his father's glare, Ryan smirked.

"What's up?"

"Molly, if you in Ryan's room, raise your fucking hand. I'm not interested in seeing your bare fuckin' ass."

"If I raise my hand, will Ryan get in trouble, Mr. Taylor?" she asked.

Groaning, Ryan flopped onto his back and stared at the ceiling.

"Get her out of here and you and me talking before me and your momma talk to you."

"Matthew!"

Jesus Christ, this day was getting shittier by the minute.

Val grinned at Zoann's call.

"Don't—"

Ignoring him, Val stared beyond Ryan.

"Fuuuuccckkk," he groaned, knowing Molly had revealed herself even before she said, "hey, Mr. Taylor. You sounded just like your wife."

Ryan scowled at the ceiling, then glanced at Molly, glad she'd managed to wiggle into her dress.

"You heard Ryan's momma, Molly." Val glowered between Ryan and Molly.

"Right," she squeaked.

Disgust swept over Val's face. "I'm going downstairs before Zoann come up."

"That would be a total bummer," Molly agreed with a nod.

"Ryan, come with me, so she can clean up in privacy. Wrap that fucking sheet around your waist."

"Fuck off, old man."

Molly's eyes rounded, while Val opened and closed his mouth, a stupid fish gasping for air.

"Matthew!" Zoann screeched, her footsteps clopping against the wooden floor. "What's going on? Do I hear Molly?"

The question wreaked of Zoann's bitchery.

Ryan tensed. "Don't let her come to my room, Val," he ordered. "I'll come with you if you let me put jeans on first."

"Fuck, fine. Hold on, Puff. I'm coming. I have everything handled, but I'd sure love a beer."

Silence, and then, "Okay. I'll meet you in the den."

As Zoann's steps faded away, Val backed into the hallway. "You got two minutes, boy."

"You think?" Ryan loosened the sheet but before he allowed it to fall to the ground, his father's glare stopped him. "Molly has seen my cock before

"He's right, Mr. Taylor. I have. I wouldn't have let him put it in me if I hadn't."

Goddamn.

"Ohhhhh, Mr. Taylor," Molly chirped. "You look sad but you look like angry too."

"Tell your chick not to analyze me."

"Molly is not my chick!" In his head, she was, but he didn't appreciate such a weak motherfucker labeling his relationship.

"You said I was," Molly complained. "Remember? When you talked me into giving you head? We were at the movies and..."

Drawing in a deep breath, Val folded his arms and stared at both of them, effectively shutting Molly up. "How old are you again?"

"Who?" she asked, blinking.

"Myself," his father snapped. "Who the fuck you think?"

"Um, Ryan?" she asked.

"He's turning seventeen in eight months, Mr. Taylor," Molly said with disapproval.

"MOLLY!" his father gritted, his face reddening. "I meant *you*. How old are you?"

She brightened. "I'll be sixteen in February."

"So you're not legal either?"

She started to nod, then her eyes widened. "I'm going to jail, aren't I? CJ is still a minor. Oh, please, Mr. Taylor, don't have me arrested. I swear I won't be with him again until after his birthday. It'll be the hardest six months of my life. It'll be like...like the moon and the stars collided and exploded and the world is without heat and light and we're all dying of heat and light deprivation and—"

"Shut. The. Fuck. UP!"

Molly released a frightened cry at his father's roar.

"I don't know what the fuck you're talking about, Molly."

"Molly, it's the sun that gives us light and heat."

"Noooo, Ryan," she protested, forgetting her fear. "I'm pretty sure it's the moon. Duh. We can see the moon. We can't see the sun."

Humiliation burned through Ryan.

She twisted her brown hair around a finger. "I'm passing science, so my facts are correct."

"If I try to explain shit to you, I'll lose my goddamn brain cells, so believe what the fuck you wish, Molly."

"Do you mind if I take a shower, Ryan?" she asked, not responding to his father. She cocked her head. "We *are* a couple, aren't we? I told Tresa who told Dina and—"

"No, fuck!" Ryan shouted, losing his patience at her stupidity. Sometimes, she seemed so fucking smart. Other times, she acted like a frightened child. Mostly, though, she was a dumb bitch. "We're fuck buddies. I'm single."

Staring at him, she processed that, her expression blank. “If you say so.”

Stomping to her, Ryan pointed to his private bathroom. “Go take a shower and then leave.”

“You’re so demanding. It’ll be at least two days before I give you head again.” Grabbing the rest of her clothes off the floor, she marched past him, paused to flip the bird, then went to his bathroom and slammed the door shut behind her.

Ryan sat on his bed, the sound of the shower starting loud and intrusive.

“Son?”

Clearing his throat, Ryan sidled a glance at his father, regretting his outburst with Molly. He really liked her, but fuck, she frustrated him. “Yeah, Dad?” he asked absently, allowing a modicum of respect to slip through his distraction.

“You not scared sticking your cock in her might make you as stupid as her?”

“Stupidity isn’t contagious,” Ryan protested, fighting off chuckles at his father’s light tone.

“I beg to differ. Stupidity’s very contagious. If her ass was ignorant, I might agree. I don’t give a fuck if you fuck,” his father continued. “What if your cock start itching or leaking shit other than piss or cum? Speaking of cum, you didn’t do it in her, did you?”

“I used a condom. I’ve only gone without three times.”

“Three times too many, boy. Three times you could’ve been having little yous running the fuck around. Three times you could’ve got a disease that disfigured your cock for the rest of your life.”

“What does a disfigured cock even look like?”

Val shrugged. “Fuck if I know. You think I go the fuck around searching for sick dicks?”

“Jesus, I hope not!”

“Get Molly out, then come to the den.”

The shower stopped and Ryan glanced toward the bathroom door, hopping up, the sheet still wrapped around him.

"No fucking way I'm talking to her again," Val said, rushing to the door and walking out.

"Can I say hi to your mom?" Molly asked, five minutes later as Ryan ushered her to the back door so Zoann wouldn't catch sight of her.

"Lower your fucking voice," Ryan snapped. "And, no. If I wanted you to see that bitch, I would've brought you to the den."

Breathing a sigh of relief as he reached the back door and opened it, he pushed Molly into the cold evening. Her short-sleeved mini dress revealed too much skin for such chilly air.

"Hold on—" he started, intending to get a jacket for her.

"You're really disrespectful to your mom and your dad, Ryan," Molly chastised. "I've met them both, although you probably forgot, and they are so nice."

Shame slid into Ryan, but before he had a chance to comment another voice rose up.

"You taking guff from this femoid cunt?" Willard demanded, limping into view.

Three weeks ago, CJ had beaten the fuck out of Willard, shocking the dumb fuckhead as much as it had Ryan. Other than the occasional fights with fist thrown, he'd thought CJ full of hot fucking air, but he'd broken Willard's nose and arm and fractured three ribs. Only by a miracle, Ryan hadn't been out with the Byrds...*Barts*...and their friends.

"What the fuck are you doing back here?" Ryan asked. Neither him or Wallace had been at school since the fight.

Willard shrugged. “Waiting for an opportune moment to call you outside and checking out your breaker boxes.”

Ryan frowned.

“Why?” Molly asked before he could.

“Shut your fucking mouth, slut, before I punch you.”

Tears rushing to her eyes, Molly shrank back and hung her head.

“Maybe, I’ll bring you to Bash and Cleaner. They’d know what to do with you.”

“Excuse me?” Bash was older than Uncle Chris! Yet, Ryan heard Willard’s insinuation... Fuck, he’d taken Bash for a lot of fucking things but not a child abuser. “Are you out of your fucking mind, Willard? No, fuck, is *Bash*?”

Molly edged behind Ryan, but Willard clamped his fat fingers around her wrist and yanked her to him.

Anger buzzing through him, Ryan shoved Willard’s hand around and inserted himself between Molly and Willard. “Don’t ever put your fucking hands on her. *Ever*.”

A heartbeat passed. Willard would concede at any—

Pig motherfucker punched the fuck out of Ryan and slammed him into the door.

Molly screamed.

Stumbling, Ryan fought to regain his balance. Willard took advantage and landed a blow to Ryan's gut. Pain and fury spreading across his body, he gasped for air. Willard backed away, triumph on his face. Ignoring his discomfort, Ryan tackled Willard to the ground. They rolled around, exchanging punches and grunts. Molly was crying now, begging them to stop.

Finally, Ryan got the upper hand. Breathing heavily, he pinned the motherfucker to the ground.

"You think you're tough, huh?" Willard spat, blood dripping from his nose.

"I don't think, bitch. I *know*."

Willard struggled against Ryan's strong grip. "Let me go!"

"Do you understand Molly is off-limits, motherfucker?" Ryan demanded.

"Fine! Whatever," Willard grumbled.

Ryan nodded and released him. Willard stumbled back, rubbing his sore arm.

Molly rushed to Ryan and hugged him. "Thank you so much," she whispered. “No one ever stood up for me the way you did.”

Smiling, Ryan wrapped his arms around her waist, pain slicing through him. He didn’t want to admit just how much he cared about her. “No problem. Just doing my job as your knight in shining armor,” he joked.

“I need to talk to you,” Willard said, coughing and sputtering.

“You haven’t come to school because CJ wants to kill you, so you sneak onto the property? We have a lot of land to bury you.”

“My old man is working out a deal. I’ll return to school in time for Homecoming. But I wanted to let you know Operation Pillar is going to the next stage.”

“You swear you won’t hurt Harley?” Molly said, on the verge of tears, hanging her head. “She’s always been really nice to me.”

“She hasn’t,” Willard said. “Remember? She stopped you and CJ from being friends.”

“She did?” Molly squeaked.

Grinning, Willard winked at Ryan. “She did. That’s why you’ve been sending her texts telling her how you’re sucking CJ’s cock and you and that man-bitch will fuck him during Homecoming.”

“But I don’t and we aren’t. CJ’s my chemistry partner. I only suck Ryan’s cock.”

"What the fuck are you involving Molly in?" Ryan demanded.

He wasn't sure if he was more outraged on her behalf or Harley's. It pissed him the fuck off how she fawned over CJ, but revenge for that bullshit was up to Ryan. Whatever Bash was cooking up was meant to destroy their lives. He could only imagine how crushed Harley was thinking CJ was fucking Molly. If Ryan wasn't in on all the scheming and he was led to believe that shit, he'd be fucking insane with anger.

The back door suddenly swung open and Zoann stood, glaring between the three of them.

"What are you doing here, Molly?" she demanded as Val joined her.

His comical shock would've been funny if Ryan liked the motherfucker.

"Hi, Mrs. Ryan's Mom," Molly said. "Ryan was sneaking me out so you wouldn't see me and Mr. Ryan's Dad wouldn't get in trouble."

"You knew she was here, Val?" his cunt of a mother hollered.

"Calm down, Puff," Val said, scowling at Molly and finally noticing Willard. "What are you doing here, boy?"

"Willy Byrd is my friend, old man. He can be wherever I want him to be."

"Yeah, bitch, take your cunt and get the fuck—"

Val snapped his brows together, shouldered his way between Ryan and Molly, and punched Willard, achieving with one hit what Ryan hadn't been able to do over several minutes—knocked that motherfucker out cold.

He grabbed a handful of Willard's hair and dragged him to a sitting position, then threw him over his shoulder.

"Next time, I'm shooting this motherfucker, Ryan. He *just* turned eighteen, so this is his one warning. If he disrespect my woman again, he's fucking dead." Barely exerting himself, he looked at Molly. "Get your shit so I can bring you home."

Without looking back, he stomped off, Willard dangling like a sack of trash.

"I'll bring her home, Val," Zoann called. "I have to pick up Devon from his friend's house."

"Whatever, babe," he grunted. "I love you."

"I love you too, Matthew."

"Where's he taking Willard?" Molly asked as his father disappeared around the side of the house.

"Motherfucker should be thrown in the dumpster," Zoann said. "But I think he's just tossing him outside the club gates."

Although Willard deserved it for disrespecting another man's woman, Ryan hoped the incident didn't get back to Bash.

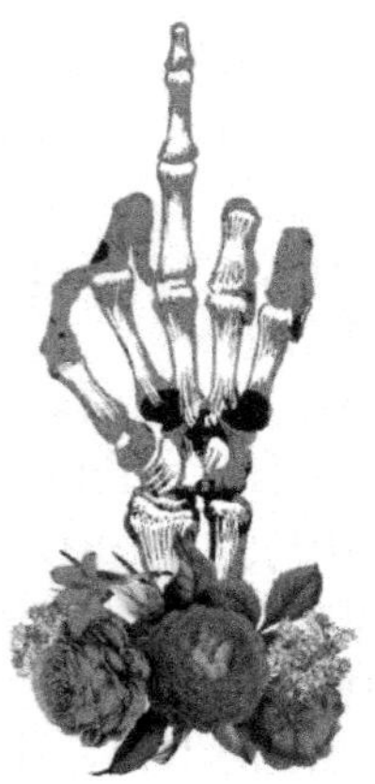

Chapter Thirty Six

September ushered in fall, the air grew cooler, and the leaves began to change colors. Excitement buzzed for two of the year's biggest events. The family and the club prepared for Mom's 35th birthday party which would happen the first weekend in October. At school, Homecoming fever grew, scheduled for the Friday after MegAnn's birthday.

CJ immersed himself with his grades and football practice. Rebel was a miserable beast, and the closer time came for the dance the more distant Harley grew.

CJ searched for ways to appease her. It seemed as if the days of their easy camaraderie would never return. Each time she demanded he skip the Homecoming dance and he declined her, the further apart they became.

He bought her flowers, took her to the skating rink, and wrote her a poem. He invited her on his study dates with Molly and barred Molly from hanging around him outside of their classes or if it didn't relate to their project.

Short of CJ not attending the dance, Harley wasn't interested in any of his efforts. She began hanging out with Nardo Grevenberg, her costar in *Romeo and Juliet*, even when they didn't have rehearsals.

The week before his mother's party, Harley skipped out on the weekly family get together. Uncle Mort and Aunt Bailey allowed her a movie date with Nardo.

"Lucas and me thought it was best, honey," Aunt Bailey said after breaking the news to CJ.

Everyone was in the kitchen, awaiting the dinner rolls, Every time someone walked in, he expected Harley. Finally, he'd asked her whereabouts. Tonight's crowd was small, consisting only of CJ, his mom and Dad, Aunt Bailey, Uncle Mort, Aunt Bunny, Uncle Digger, Aunt Zoann, Uncle Val, and Ryan. Lolly and Knox were in Portland at a business function. Uncle Cash, Uncle Stretch, Aunt Fee, and their kids were in Denver, visiting Sloane and Aunt Georgie.

Rebel boycotted the family. Diesel was with that bitch he married. For once, Rule wasn't using this time during the dinners to meditate. He was babysitting Blade and Gunner.

However, CJ felt sorriest for Rory, Mattie and JJ. They were missing the dinner because they were at the opera with their parents.

Mom sat a tray of piping hot, golden-brown rolls on the island.

"All things considered," Aunt Bailey added.

Uncle Digger snatched one of the rolls, then immediately dropped it and blew on his fingers. "Fuck, they hot!"

Dad swigged from a bottle of beer. "They just came out the fuckin' oven, assfuck. What do your greedy ass expect?"

"What do you mean, 'all things considered', Bailey?" Mom asked, stepping aside so Aunt Bunny could butter the rolls.

Aunt Bailey shrugged. "CJ's focus is elsewhere, Meggie. As it should be since he's older than Harley."

Pressing her hand against her round belly, Mom plastered a smile on her face, unperturbed by the sudden silence, broken only by Uncle Digger's loud chewing.

"CJ's focus is exactly where it should be, Bailey. On school and impressing his coaches."

"And on Molly Harris," Aunt Bailey said coolly.

Uncle Mort stepped next to her and put an arm around her shoulder.

"She's his chemistry partner," Mom said. "He has to think about her to pass the class."

Aunt Bailey drew herself up. "He's your son, Meggie, so of course you see nothing wrong with all the time he spends at Molly's house. Excuse me, you took her shopping as well."

"*What*?" Ryan blared, joining the crowd around the island. "You can't throw Caldwell money around to buy Beta Boy a girl—"

Aunt Zoann twisted Ryan's ear. "Shut your mouth, son," she warned, ignoring the tears in his eyes and twisting a little more. "I'm sick of your attitude. It's bad enough you have it with me. You're not disrespecting your aunts. Am I clear?"

"Val!" Ryan wailed. "Help me."

"You're a fucking man, boy," Uncle Val growled. "Help your fucking self."

Aunt Zoann shoved him away with such force, he slammed into the counter. Hurt gleamed in her eyes and CJ suspected she'd run afoul of Ryan's temper.

"If you hadn't been such a cheap little motherfucker, Meggie wouldn't have taken Molly shopping for her

Homecoming gown," Uncle Val said with disgust, pulling Aunt Zoann into his arms an hugging her. "Your momma went, too. Before you run off at the fucking mouth that might get you killed, ask questions."

"Molly's not your bitch, old man," Ryan snapped. "You don't give a fuck if this motherfucker is fucking her. You don't even like her."

"Molly's a fucking airhead, son," Uncle Val barked. "It would be a fucking crime to dislike her because she won't understand why."

"This is why I hate you."

Aunt Zoann jerked out of Uncle Val's arms. If he hadn't caught her and dragged her against him, Ryan would've been fucked.

Mom sat in the stool Dad dragged to the island, drawing everyone's attention. "Bailey, I understand you're upset on Harley's behalf, but did she mention her unfair demands that CJ not attend Homecoming?"

"What are you talking about, Meggie girl?" Uncle Mort asked, cocking his head to the side.

"Just what Meggie said, Mort," Aunt Bunny said on a sigh. "She's heartbroken and she's been trying to change his mind. I told her to talk to you, Bailey. Or even Roxanne, but she's been putting demands on CJ and me and Meggie. I've never seen her like this."

"What type of demands?" Aunt Bailey asked.

"She asked me to cancel the entire Homecoming dance or rewrite the rules," Mom said.

"We ain't even in that bullshit," Dad said into the stunned silence. "We got a fucking board in place with supervisors and managers. We got a process in place. That shit was Megan idea cuz I ain't givin' a fuck. My fuckin' money. My fuckin' rules, but what the fuck ever. And we ain't changin' shit for our own lil' motherfuckers. As much as we love Harley, we ain't changin' the rules even if we could."

"You should've told us," Uncle Mort said with remorse.

Arms stretched out in front of her, Mom clasped her hands. "Harley doesn't want you to stop her from seeing CJ, so she begged Bunny and me not to say anything."

"I told her little ass she was wrong," Uncle Digger said flatly. "That's why she isn't here and went out with Nardo. Stuck-up little motherfucker. My niece mad at me."

"Meggie and Bunny get a pass for not calling, but *you* don't, son," Uncle Mort snapped.

"The fuck I don't, Mort. Harley and Rebel all gone fucking crazy around this motherfucker. The sanest one of those baby bitches is Molly and goddamn *Mattie*. Harley want CJ to miss one of the most important fucking days of his life 'cause *she* too fucking young. What kind of shit is that? And, frankly, I wouldn't respect the little motherfucker if he backed the fuck out for spoiled bullshit."

Aunt Bailey shook her head. "I...Harley doesn't lie."

"Harley don't throw tantrums either, but I was here when she pitched a major one."

Mom stood up. "I forgot my phone upstairs, so I have to check on Rebel. She might be hungry."

"Let her fuckin' starve," Dad said. "Ain't no motherfucker stoppin' her from comin' to eat with us. Fuck your phone and fuck her."

"But—"

"Ain't listenin', Megan. She followin' our rules or she sufferin' the consequences."

"Once the baby's born—"

"I saw the fuckin' video from earlier, baby," Dad interrupted, glaring between Aunt Bailey and Uncle Mort. "Where she said she prayin' for you and the baby to die."

"Oh, Meggie," Aunt Zoann said, rushing to her and hugging her.

Tears rushed to Mom's eyes and her lips trembled. "She doesn't mean it."

Rebel should've been ashamed of herself. Somebody needed to shake the fuck out of that cow. How dare she spout that same bullshit again.

"It's fine. Really." Mom forced a smile and took Dad's hand into her own. "She's still our daughter." She looked at Aunt Bailey. "And Harley is yours, Bailey, so I understand why you were annoyed with CJ. It's been a long day. I shouldn't have gotten irritated with you."

Aunt Bailey rushed to Mom and hugged her. "You had every right to be upset. CJ is your son and you were defending him. I had no idea about Harley's..." Her voice trailed off and she looked at Uncle Mort.

"Let me talk to my baby girl, Bailey," Uncle Mort said sadly. "Something not right."

Once again, guilt pressed into CJ. Harley was upset because of Homecoming. He wanted to talk to her. Really talk to her as they once had. Somehow, he had to make her understand if he sat out Homecoming, he *would* go to Prom. She would have longer to get used to the idea.

"What the fuck a beta boy?" Dad demanded into the silence.

"A man, or boy, who lacks masculine energy," Mom said, glaring at Ryan.

"No bitch worth insultin' your fuckin' family over, Ryan," Dad said with disapproval. "Ain't none of you boys beta motherfuckers."

Uncle Digger grabbed another roll. "That's some next level shit, lil' bro. Where you picking up on that type of fucking language?"

"Willard, no doubt," CJ grumbled, hating that motherfucker, though word on the curb was he'd be at school Monday, along with his little brother.

"Don't bring up Willard," Ryan ordered. "He's my friend."

"He's a fucking asshole," CJ countered. "He put his fucking hands on Harley. And you know what? She met that pig motherfucker at the end of last school year while I was at practice. I think he raised his hands to her then but she won't tell me." He kicked the island. Thankfully, his steel-toed boot took the brunt of the hit. "I don't give a fuck. He hit her in front of me, so he's fucking dead anyway."

"Shut your whiny ass up, CJ," Rebel snapped, stomping into the deathly quiet kitchen. "Instead of complaining about Harley, tell your father how Lumbly's been fucking with you. He fucking failed you for no fucking reason, dickhead."

"Come fuckin' again?"

Wincing at Dad's question, CJ glanced at his father, wishing he could shake his little sister until the glitch in her brain unwound. "Rebel, shut the fuck up. Better yet, go back to your room."

"I'm hungry. I'm a minor, so your mother is required to feed me."

"She's your mother too, dumbass," CJ snarled, anger surging through him at Mom's sniffle. "And she isn't required to do shit for your ungrateful ass."

He was grateful for Rebel's bitchery switching Dad's focus from Lumbly to her behavior.

"Take your lil' ass back to your room, girl," Dad barked, losing patience with her just as fast as CJ was.

Rebel glowered at their father, though her expression couldn't compare to the death stare Dad aimed at her. Anyone with a functional brain would backtrack at his look, but unfortunately for everyone, Rebel's brain had been taken over by an evil entity without a lick of intelligence.

"You'll go to jail for child abuse if you keep starving me."

Mom, ever the diplomat, inserted herself next to Rebel. "Why don't we go upstairs and, my love—"

"No! I want to eat here with you and my family."

In her dramatics, Rebel forgot the cardinal rule. Their father was keen to remind her, though.

"Don't fuckin' talk to your Ma like that," Dad snapped, his self-control visibly slipping.

"She isn't my momma. She merely gave birth to me. I don't claim her anymore," Rebel sniffed, her stupid ass words not helping CJ's ire.

Nor did it stop the hurt plastering Mom's face.

Seeing her expression set Dad off. "Keep this shit up, and Ima beat your fuckin' ass again," he roared, getting to his feet.

In an instant, Mom was in front of him, grasping his forearms as he and Rebel locked in a glaring contest. Mom whispered to him. His sights were still set on Rebel, but whatever Mom said calmed him.

His aunts and uncles watched the scene unfold with frowns etched on their faces, a contrast to Ryan's amusement. CJ made a mental note to beat his ass if word of Rebel's behavior leaked beyond the family.

"Rebel, I ain't tellin' your lil' ass again. Go to your motherfuckin' room, or I'm fuckin' dragging you."

Okay, maybe Dad hadn't calmed down.

Luckily, Rebel's survival instincts kicked in. She swiped one of the remaining dinner rolls, much to Uncle Digger's chagrin, and stomped out of the kitchen.

Even when Mom and CJ's aunts began setting out the food so everyone could finally eat, tension remained.

Girls! Namely, Harley and Rebel.

Thanks to those two, CJ felt like tearing his goddamn hair out of his motherfucking head.

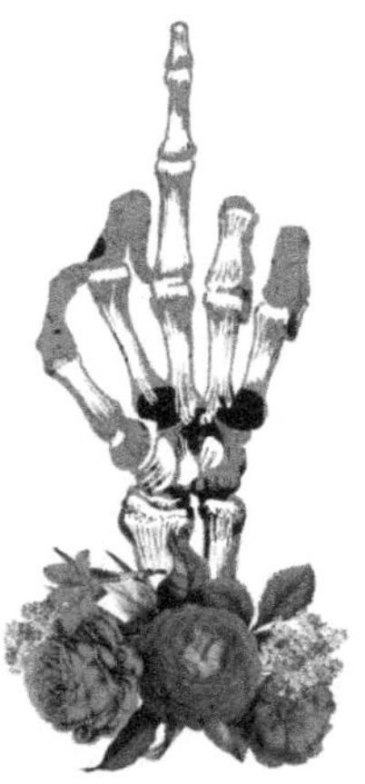

Chapter Thirty Seven

Long before CJ joined the middle school football team, he'd study the upperclassmen and found the boys to be some of the most dedicated and hardworking athletes in high school sports. When he made the JV team in his freshman year and his parents told him attending college was the only way they'd agree to him patching in, CJ was determined to become a starter. Some weeks, he practiced more than he rode.

His football goals were the reason Harley first tried out for the cheer team. By his sophomore year, the star quarterback had graduated, and CJ won the position after a hard-fought battle between him, Willard, and Ryan.

During his team's ten-week regular season, CJ displayed his physical abilities, mental toughness, strategy, and leadership abilities. It was why he fought to remain on the team when Lumbly did everything in his power to see him kicked off.

On the field during the game, they displayed not only their physical abilities but also their mental toughness, strategy, and teamwork. The one game that mattered as much for social standing as it did sportsmanship was Homecoming. CJ hadn't realized how important it was to participate in every aspect of the game until Harley turned into a motherfucking monster.

Instead of helping, the revelations about Harley's behavior at the family get together severed CJ's ties with her completely. First, Aunt Bailey and Uncle Mort grounded her for the lies. Then, at his mother's birthday party, Harley gave CJ an ultimatum—either he back out of Homecoming or never talk to her again.

It didn't help that she did it in front of *everyone*. Their parents, their siblings, their cousins, their aunts and uncles, and extended family. Diesel was there, but he'd left Tabitha at their house. Derby, Gypsy, Aunt Georgie, Sloane, and his band members were in attendance, too. *Grant*. The party had moved from the clubhouse to his parents' home and they'd just finished toasting his mom.

Molly mentioned they should've studied the egg to ice cream batter ratio in a thirty-five-pound cake for their chemistry project and Harley went ballistic. While CJ was grateful Rebel had boycotted the birthday party because she wouldn't have been amused at the comment, he didn't appreciate Harley's bullshit dampening his mom's party any more than Rebel's stupidity already had.

Any ideas CJ had to appease Harley died on the hill of her demands. He threw his all into Homecoming Week, campaigning to become king, fucking thrilled Ridge Moore allowed the crowning of juniors. He couldn't run in his senior year. Likewise, he couldn't run for Prom King if he won the title for Homecoming.

He didn't fucking care. He had a point to make. Petty? Maybe. Oh, fucking well. Bitchery begot motherfuckery.

However, the joke was on him.

The stadium was packed with fans of both teams. It was loud and bright and colorful. Shouts and chants rose in waves. The cheer and dance teams sparkled in glittery costumes, displaying their moves and ability, adding to the excitement. Rebel, Mattie, Molly, Harley, and Jaleena were amongst them.

Yet his insistence on attending the dance had driven a wedge between him and Harley. She hated him, and on such an important night, it was fucking with him more than it had all week. Here, under the bright lights with coaches and scouts watching, it was difficult to focus. By halftime, when the bands took centerstage for their competition, CJ had been sacked twice and his team was down by ten.

Harley hated him.

They'd had arguments. Best friends argued and made up. This time was different though. The rejection of his best bro...

Oh, who the fuck was he kidding? It was a long time since they'd only been 'bros.' Their new title far murkier and more complicated.

Maybe it would've been better if CJ had never confessed his feelings for her last summer. If they'd simply remained as friends and he hadn't told Harley about his deeper feelings, there wouldn't be so much bullshit clouding his mind.

But what was done was done and he couldn't go back to undo it. He had to live with Harley's rejection. It was a bitter pill to swallow, though.

He stood alone in the shadows of the tunnel. Coach Yancy knew the Homecoming Court would be announced as soon as the bands finished, so he didn't order CJ to the locker room. Finally, the bands were filing away and Dr. Marvey, along with other Ridge Moore administrators, were walking onto the field.

Sighing, CJ trekked to where the other candidates were. All the aches and pains that adrenaline blocked plagued him now. He searched the bright field for a glimpse of Harley. Finally, he saw her on the sidelines. Her blue uniform with the big yellow 'R' revealed her figure. Each time they stayed away from each other and CJ saw her again, her body changed.

She had hella fucking curves.

Seeing Harley prancing around in her cheerleader uniform, with Nardo fucking Grevenberg chatting her up almost made him lose his shit. Barely composed, it took every ounce of his strength not to stomp over swing on that motherfucker.

"Attention ladies and gentlemen." Dr. Marvey's call came just in time to prevent CJ from fucking up Nardo, allowing the excited crowd a few moments to quiet down. "The results for our Homecoming Court are in!"

"Hey CJ!" Jaleena said, rushing up to him and grabbing his hand. "Are you excited?"

"I am!" Molly announced, appearing at his other side.

Ryan stepped next to her. He was the kicker and he'd done his job. Without his strong leg, the Titans wouldn't have nine points.

The light haloed Dr. Marvey, gleaming off his white hair. Because life sucked lately, Lumbly was amongst the school officials as the dean took his time announcing the Homecoming court. Jaleena, Molly, and a girl named Scarlet were the nominees for Queen. Once all three girls were present, Marvey switched shit. Instead of announcing the winner, he named the boys in the running.

"Candidates for king are CJ Caldwell."

CJ grinned at the cheers rising around him and waved, wondering where his parents were, wishing Harley was at his side.

"Ryan Taylor," Dr. Marvey continued.

Strutting forward with cocky confidence, Ryan glared at CJ.

"And Oliver Garcia," Dr. Marvey finished after what seemed like forever.

Oliver, who CJ only recognized as the captain of the debate team, was far more civil to his competition, offering them both small smiles.

With less excitement than any of the girls showed, CJ and his rivals smiled.

Jaleena beamed at CJ and gave him a thumbs up.

CJ smiled at her excitement.

"We're so gonna win," Jaleena stage whispered to CJ, the wide smile on her face enhancing her beauty.

"As if," Scarlet snarked, though her tone held no real malice.

"All of you shut up, because we're going to crush you," Ryan boasted, slinging an arm around Molly's waist, and pressing a kiss to her temple.

Molly giggled at the attention. CJ knew they weren't official, but it was obvious that the two cared about each other. More often than not, Ryan was a big fucking asshole, and Molly sometimes seemed like the dumbest bitch alive, but their happiness made him happy.

His cousin caring about becoming Homecoming King surprised CJ, but Ryan's excitement pleased him. If Ryan won, he'd go to the dance in a show of support and stay thirty minutes tops, before making his excuses to Jaleena and heading home. If Oliver won... Well, fuck him. CJ wouldn't even bother with the dance. He'd go home and...fuck! No. It didn't matter how much he wanted to appease Harley, she was being so unfair.

If she hated him for simply not getting her way, then she'd never loved him in the first place.

A part of him hoped Ryan would win. Less bullshit all around, but CJ's competitive side wanted Ryan to eat his fucking words.

"And now, our Queen is..." Dr. Marvey made a production of opening the thick envelope Lumbly handed to him. "Jaleena Davis!"

Squealing, Jaleena gasped and clapped, bouncing up and down. "Oh my god!" she screamed. "Oh my god!"

"The Homecoming King is..." Dr. Marvey snatched the envelope from Lumbly. "CJ Caldwell!"

"You're fucking kidding me?" Ryan snarled, his words nearly drowned out by screams and applause.

As he held on to Jaleena's waist, CJ regretted she wasn't the one he liked. She was a beautiful girl with a bright future ahead of her. And unlike Harley, Jaleena was his age. Under two years separated him and Harley. It wasn't a huge difference, but big enough to cause issues as he reached milestones before her, and their life branched out in different directions. He felt it was momentary, but Harley didn't agree.

Jaleena squealed again and planted a kiss on CJ's cheeks. His cock surged at the feel of her lips on his skin.

Damn that motherfucker. Never staying down.

As the other students cheered for them, he wrapped an arm around Jaleena's waist. She sagged against him, pressing another kiss to his cheek. The crowd roared in approval at their display of affection.

When his cheeks began to hurt from smiling so much, he glanced at his cousin. Ryan still looked pissed, though Molly was trying her best to calm him down. Surprisingly, it seemed to be working, and he actually nodded to CJ.

Jaleena tugged on his arm to regain his attention, and he went back to basking in the cheers. It was almost too perfect, bordering on cliché. The quarterback and his pretty cheerleader date win Homecoming king and queen, who would've expected that? But though it may be a cliché, it was one that CJ was glad to bring to life.

As the crowd's attention dragged on, CJ's mind wandered back to Harley. No matter how hard he tried, she refused to leave his mind.

The Homecoming dance was a perfect example of their lives branching out. His very attendance made Harley cast him aside and run into the arms of another guy, crushing and angering him. However, even if her feelings were fickle enough to move on so easily, CJ's weren't. Even now, he was convinced they were meant to be, and refused to allow another girl to complicate things further.

It would be unfair to Harley to get involved with someone else, and especially unfair to Jaleena to be with her when his heart pined after another.

"Congratulations, CJ," Molly said happily, then took off behind Ryan as he headed toward the tunnel.

"We won!" Jaleena screamed.

"Yeah, bae!" CJ yelled, getting caught back up in the excitement. "Now, we have a fucking game to win."

Bouncing up and down, she hugged him. Before the game resumed, the court gathered together and allowed the band to pay homage to them while the spotlight was shown on CJ, Jaleena, and the other ten students.

At the end of halftime, CJ took position on the field.

For the first half of the game, the visiting team had kept the lead, but winning the title of Homecoming King filled CJ with new determination. He focused on beating the opponents on *his* turf.

With the score tied at twenty-four, with seconds left on the clock, Ryan's field goal saw The Ridge Moore Titans victorious.

After the game, CJ went home to change. Homecoming theme was *A Night at the Casino*, therefore he had a tux. His parents would be chaperones. While Mom dressed up in a pretty gown, Dad wore full leathers.

Hours later and still riding a victory high, CJ left home in a rented limo to pick up Jaleena in Portland. They talked and laughed the entire way to Ridge Moore about everything and nothing.

There was camaraderie between them, but not the deep connection he felt with Harley. As much as he liked Molly, something was missing with her too. Given the past few weeks and how Harley so easily pushed him away, he wondered if he was just more comfortable with her because he'd known her for so many years.

Outside the entrance to the school's athletic center, a long red carpet led the way up the three steps and was laid between gold-clipped black velvet ropes attached to shiny stanchions. A working fountain styled after a roulette wheel centered the walkway that led to the buildings entrance. A recreation of the *Welcome to Las Vegas* sign greeted them when they entered the building. The hallway was a beehive of activity with students queued to have their photos taken under the *Lucky Aces* archway.

Once their tickets were scanned and CJ guided Jaleena into the gym, he paused. Oversized black, red, and white dice hung from the ceiling and sat in strategic places amidst balloons and oversized playing cards. Lit columns decorated with the four card suits indicated the food and drink stations. The DJ was set up on the same Roaring 20s bandstand CJ would later be crowned on.

For the next hour, CJ and Jaleena stayed on the makeshift dance floor, tangled in each other's arms as they laughed, talked, and moved to the beat of the music.

Every now and then, he thought about checking on Harley, but she was either angry with him or spending time with Nardo, and CJ didn't want either discovery to ruin his night. With effort, he pushed her out of his mind and focused on Jaleena, who was a sight to behold in her one shoulder dress. It clung to her curves and stopped at her knees, showing off a lot of her silky skin. The sparkling red fabric complemented her color nicely, and somehow, she perfectly matched her lipstick to the dress. She'd grown her hair out since last school year. Tonight, her short hair was styled in finger waves accentuated by art deco earrings.

She was so fucking gorgeous. Not to mention, she was a lot of fun, easy to talk to, and an excellent dance partner. If he wasn't so hung up on Harley, he'd ask Jaleena to be his girlfriend in an instant.

No Hands by Waka Flocka Flame and a bunch of other motherfuckers were blasting through the speakers, heightening the party atmosphere.

"This is my shit!" Jaleena exclaimed as she followed the song's instructions, grinding against him without the use of her hands.

Fuck him. If she kept moving like that, he'd have to deal with a hard dick in the middle of Homecoming.

"Mine too," he managed, giving himself props for his composure.

At some point, his parents had arrived and now congregated with the other chaperones, teachers, and administrators. Luckily, the adults were deep in their own conversations. It helped how the crowd of motherfuckers on the dance floor swallowed them up and hid him and Jaleena from view. Otherwise, they would've gotten shit for dancing so suggestively.

Especially because motherfucking Lumbly was among the teachers. The little fucking troll was everywhere.

His mother was talking to Aunt Zoann and Aunt Bunny, looking worse for wear. Mom was too pale for his liking. But perhaps, the dark lighting played tricks on him.

Technically, only Aunt Zoann and his mother should've been chaperones since Mark JB wasn't in the upper school yet, but Aunt Bunny offered to help. Being part of the Dweller circuit, they skirted the rules without worry. His mother and Aunt Zoann were expected additions, and CJ barely batted an eye at Aunt Bunny's presence. The same couldn't be said when Uncle Digger volunteered, shocking the ever-loving shit out of him and Dad.

Jaleena maneuvered her body to where her back was flush against his chest and her ass pressed against his cock. His dick jumped at the movement of her hips, and he tightened his grip on her waist. She turned in his arms and stared into his eyes. Her heels closed the height difference between them and allowed their faces – their lips – close proximity. He homed in on her full lips and he licked his at the idea of kissing her.

Then, an image of Harley's face flickered through his mind, and he snapped his gaze forward. He caught Ryan and Molly making out in a corner, where they'd been holed up since the dance started, and diverted his gaze. He didn't want to see his cousin shoving his tongue down the pretty airhead's throat. She was too sweet for that dickhead.

Jaleena bent her knees and leaned forward as the song ordered a girl to drop it to the floor. Though his wandering mind slowed his steps, her movements never faltered. She moved so fluidly to the beat, it was easy to fall in sync with her. Soon, impure thoughts were cleansed from his mind as he became lost in dancing, though the little devil on his shoulder wouldn't let him ignore their intimate position.

No Hands soon faded into *Yeah!* by *Usher, Lil Jon,* and *Ludacris.* As the tempo grew faster, so did his and Jaleena's movements, and his hands gradually returned to her hips.

You love Harley! You love Harley! You love Harley! You love Harley...

He chanted his affection for Harley to remind himself why he couldn't take things further with Jaleena. His friendship with Harley was shaky at best, so anything more between them seemed improbable. Yet, in his head, the status of their relationship wasn't resolved, and he'd promised to give her as much time as she needed.

Jaleena settled her arms around his neck and pressed her soft lips against his. CJ's hand roamed over her curves, even as his chant echoed through his head. Jaleena didn't protest his wandering hands. In fact, she seemed to encourage it, and she gave him a flirty smile. His fingers brushed over her ass.

CJ immediately dropped his arms to his side. "I'm sorry, bae," he murmured. "I shouldn't—"

"You can touch it," she breathed.

His stupid dick twitched in celebration of her words. She pushed further into him, and if he was a weaker motherfucker, he might've whimpered at the friction.

Instead, he grabbed her hand and weaved through the crowd. If he could have, he would've left her on the dance floor. But he didn't want to hurt her feelings and he didn't want a crowd of people to deal with. It wouldn't be long before the Homecoming Court would be crowned and he definitely couldn't walk on stage with a hard cock.

And with Mom there, too.

Fuck.

CJ guided Jaleena through one of the side exits and breathed in the crisp night air, happy it was virtually deserted. When he tried to let her hand go, she tightened her grip.

"I know you want to feel my ass, CJ. I want you to feel it."

His heart pounded and suddenly all he could think of *was* Jaleena's ass. It was round and pretty and perfect.

She drew in a deep breath. "I-I was wondering...I-I mean...I like you a lot and...and..." She released his hand and stepped back. "I like you so much and...and...and..." She bit her lush lip and her face fell. "N-never mind. I'm stupid...just because you seem so cool doesn't mean you want to go steady with me." Her eyes widening, she squeaked and slapped a hand over her mouth.

Protecting girls was what he did, so seeing her distress took his mind off her body and how he'd love to not only feel her ass but see it too.

He wrapped her in his arms. "You're not stupid, Jaleena. You're beautiful and smart."

She relaxed against him. "So do you want to go steady with me?" Tipping her head back, she smiled at him.

Strands of music suddenly floated to them, and they started moving to the beat, grinding against each other.

You love Harley! You love Harley! You love Harley! You love Harley!

You love—

"Mr. Caldwell!"

The squeaky little voice interrupted CJ's internal mantra, while Jaleena jumped out of his arms.

"That is highly inappropriate."

Fuckface Lumbly materialized in front of them like a pissed off imp. Although Rebel mentioned Lumbly's treatment of CJ to Dad a little over two weeks ago, nothing ever came of it. Dad hadn't even brought it up again.

The corners of Jaleena's lips turned down. "We were just dancing," she protested.

"You were moving like a stripper, girl, and Mr. Caldwell's hands were on your nether regions," he barked, eliciting an offended gasp from Jaleena.

"They were not!" she screeched.

Not out here, at least.

"I'm sure you don't know any better, but don't practice your trade in front of innocent children, Jaleena."

"There's no one out here," Jaleena cried, anger and embarrassment crumpling her pretty face.

"Don't talk to her like that," CJ snapped. "*Miss Davis* was having fun and not hurting anyone."

"*Jaleena* had no business grinding like a slut around *children.*"

CJ drew his brows together. The fuckhead wasn't making sense. Until Lumbly's appearance, they'd been alone. When they were on the dance floor...

That dirty motherfucker!

Jaleena narrowed her eyes, apparently reaching the same conclusion as CJ. "Tell me, Mr. Lumbly," she began in a saccharine tone, batting her lashes in an exaggerated manner. "How long were we dancing like that?"

CJ looked at her questioningly, but she just shot him a grin.

"All night, and I've let it go on long enough."

"So, you've watched me dance 'inappropriately' with CJ for hours, and you're just now doing something about it? You are aware how creepy it is to watch two minors grind against each other for so long, right?"

Lumbly's skin flushed, but a triumphant smile spread across his face. "So, you admit to grind—"

"We were following the songs instructions," CJ interrupted, before the little weasel redirected the conversation and tried to frame it to his narrative. "And

Jaleena has a point. Suppose her father were to catch wind of your actions. Or, better yet, mine?"

"They wouldn't appreciate a grown man watching us for so long, CJ," Jaleena chirped, her smile growing as Lumbly's skin grew redder. "Not to mention, he greatly insulted me."

"I cannot believe what you're insinuating, Jaleena! I'm highly offended that you're calling my character into question, an—"

"So, why were you watching us for so long? I can't think of a single reason that doesn't equal you being a creep." Jaleena sniffed, not keen on backing down. She held up a manicured hand as he opened his mouth to say something else, making both Lumbly and CJ gape at her boldness. "You know, my family may not contribute as much as the Donovans or the Caldwells, but we still pay enough to see you removed. You've had it out for CJ the entire year, and I won't let you ruin my Homecoming because you're a bitter little man."

CJ bit back his chuckle at Lumbly's expression. With zero effort, she was eating up the fuckhead; CJ *loved* it.

However, if he'd stayed inside, Lumbly wouldn't have accosted them. They would've been within view of his mother and father, not giving Lumbly free range to harass CJ. Motherfucker was the worst kind of opportunist.

"CJ has done nothing to you, sir," Jaleena insisted.

"Mr. Lumbly—" CJ started as the door closest to him opened.

"All this ruckus for a no-good thug," Lumbly snarled, not bothering to see who'd come outside. "You're as disgraceful as he is, girl."

Lumbly gave short men everywhere a bad reputation. He did nothing to challenge their stereotypical Napoleon complex.

"You're not only dreadful but a fool if you think he's worthy of defense. He'll just use you, then toss you away like trash. He's a biker's spawn, and those criminals only know—"

The door slammed with a thud, drawing their attention. Dad and Uncle Digger thundered toward them. Each time Dad's spurs jingled, the air thickened with anticipation.

"What we know, assfuck? Since you a fuckin' expert on us motherfuckers, tell my ass what the fuck we know," Dad growled, stopping next to CJ.

Stumbling back, Lumbly paled.

"Cat got your tongue, motherfucker?" Uncle Digger barked at Lumbly's silence.

Mom, Aunt Zoann, and Aunt Bunny rushed outside. Aunt Zoann beelined to Jaleena and whispered to her, before taking her hand and ushering her away.

Whatever was about to occur wouldn't be good, evident by Jaleena's removal. Maybe he should follow Aunt Zoann and Jaleena. Possibly, guard the door. Just as quickly, he changed his mind. Dad might think he was running away with his tail tucked between his legs. Definitely not a Dweller's style. Whatever happened, he had to stay at his father's side. He refused to look so weak, no matter how nervous he was.

"What are you doing out here, potato?" Mom asked.

"Jaleena and young Mr. Caldwell were being inappropriate..." Lumbly sputtered, his voice trailing off at Dad's glower.

"The fuck that gotta do with you insultin' my boy? Ain't I told your fuckin' ass to leave him the fuck alone?"

"Mr. Caldwell, I meant—"

"Not to get caught," Uncle Digger finished.

"Go the fuck back inside, Megan," Dad ordered, his gaze not leaving Lumbly's.

"Go with Meggie, Bunny," Uncle Digger said. "Fuck, I'm glad I didn't wear no tux. Always ruining those bitches with blood."

"*What!*" Lumbly cried, trembling so violently CJ thought his legs wouldn't hold him up much longer.

"Come with me and Bunny, CJ," Mom instructed. "We have to check on Jaleena."

"I'll be inside in a moment, Mom," CJ promised.

"CJ—"

He bent and kissed her cheek. "I promise."

"Ima send his lil' ass in befuckinfore, baby."

"Before what?" Lumbly sobbed.

The moment the door closed behind Mom and Aunt Bunny Uncle Digger snatched Lumbly off his feet. The dangling little asshole stammered out pleas and apologies as he was carried into the darkness. Though he was screaming for help, no one came running to aid him.

"Val waitin' with the van," Dad explained.

"You predicted bullshit?"

"Nope. I intended fuckin' the fuck up. I heard every fuckin' word Rebel said the other day, CJ. I warned that motherfucker. He ain't listened. Oh-fuckin-well."

CJ's eyes widened. "What's going to happen to him?"

"Ain't gotta worry about that, boy. Be a kid and enjoy the rest of your fuckin' night." He turned in the direction Uncle Digger had gone with Lumbly. "Your Ma ain't feelin' good. Keep watch. Ain't gonna be long. Ima fuck Lumbly the fuck up and dump him off Turn Creek Bridge. I just hope assfuck ain't hauntin' your lil' ass when you fuckin' cut."

Busted! "I can explain."

"Ain't asked you to, boy. Just know that the fuckhead ain't gonna bother you anymore."

With that, Dad walked away, leaving CJ alone as intense relief swamped him.

Kathryn C. Kelly

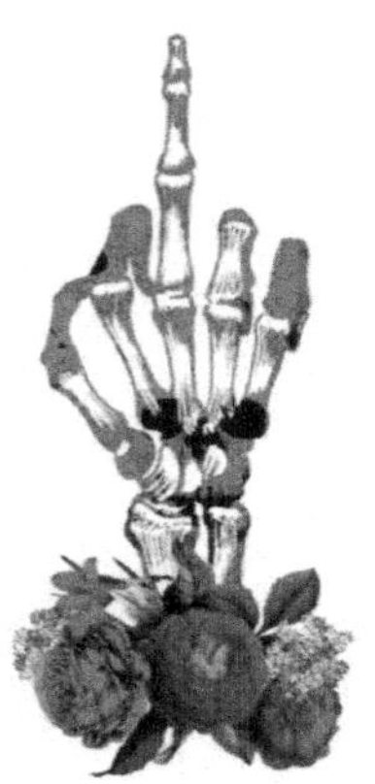

Chapter Thirty Eight

REBEL

Hating the holiday season was a new experience for Rebel, but she supposed there was a first for everything. Instead of appreciating all the Christmas decorations, she saw them as dorky. But *Megan* wanted them, so the house resembled the North fucking Pole. Even the basement, built as the children's sanctuary, couldn't escape her stupidity.

What could Rebel expect though? Once, she loved the basement with a 50s styled diner, a theater, a game room, a bowling alley, a dance club, a unisex sitting room and private ones for boys and another for girls. There was also a kitchen, several bathrooms, and a couple of other rooms because her mother was spoiled and ridiculous, either trying to live out a misplaced childhood fantasy or seeking to control her children.

Rebel bet on the former. Otherwise, Daddy wouldn't have herded everyone down here after they returned from Thanksgiving dinner at the club. The moment they walked into the house, Momma batted her lashes.

Simpering bitch.

Living with Megan Caldwell for almost fifteen years gave Rebel an insider's view on what to expect. The Sunday before Thanksgiving, club brothers began decorating outside and in some of the rooms inside. Thanksgiving eve and morning, Megan and the aunts cooked while Daddy and the uncles drank. Black Friday, Megan and Daddy shopped. Saturday afternoon, the tree for the central hall arrived and they decorated it as a family. Sometimes, their weekly get-togethers fell on that date, so it turned into a fucking free-for-all. Sunday, the club hosted a party to decorate their tree. Cyber Monday, Megan *allowed* her children to shop. Only this year, Rebel wouldn't. She didn't have her debit card and Megan bowed to Daddy's wishes that Rebel hadn't earned the right to spend thousands of dollars.

"Reb, c'mon!" CJ called, ignoring Rebel's shitty mood. "We're going to the disco and dance."

Unlike her, he was in a fucking great mood. Ever since Homecoming, he'd been so fucking...*happy*. He'd won one of the biggest games of the year and was crowned King. Lumbly hadn't returned to school and rumors swirled he was no longer employed at Ridge Moore. Then, tonight, CJ and Harley made up. Rebel wasn't sure what was said, but by the time they headed home, they were giggling quietly amongst themselves.

All was right in CJ's world, while hers was falling apart. Now, he wanted her to fucking dance?

Fuck him.

"Not interested," Rebel retorted. She was perfectly happy, sitting alone in the Cadillac booth, although she wanted to swipe the Christmas bouquet to the black-and-white tiled floor and stomp it. As a matter of fact, she'd go down the line of booths and destroy the bouquets if she could, then she'd do the same to the three on the L-shaped counter, especially the one in front of her parents.

"It's okay, CJ," Megan said, swiveling on the stool and smiling at Rebel. "Your sister isn't in the mood."

Daddy leaned against the soda dispenser behind the counter and glared at Rebel.

Poking out her lip, she glanced at the replicated menu board with offerings of milkshakes, banana floats, apple pie, ice cream, burgers, and fries. They'd come to the diner for their Thanksgiving dessert of warm pie and ice cream.

Gunner tugged Rebel's jacket. "Webel, um on! MegAnn dance."

Rebel snatched away from his grubby little fingers. She didn't have much to say to her family anymore. Not even her twin, which was why she ignored Rule's woeful gaze from where he sat at the counter. But Rebel most *especially* disregarded Megan.

If it wasn't for her stupid baby, she would've spent more time with Rebel. *Listened* to her. If not for that girl child who'd enter the world in late spring and complete the ruin of Rebel's life, Megan would've seen she was a hypocrite and a traitor. Daddy had been like a son to Big Joe, yet Megan married him. There was an even bigger age gap between Daddy and Megan than Diesel and Rebel.

"You comin' to the disco and dancin' with your Ma and brothers or you goin' to your fuckin' room," Daddy told her, forever on Megan's side.

Rebel sidled her father a glower.

At his growl, her heart sped up. Before he'd spanked her, she would've dismissed the anger in his eyes. Now, she knew the truth. It wasn't about *her*. It was about following his stupid rules and keeping Megan happy.

"It's all right, Christopher. Leave Rebel alone. She's hurt and confused. Once Jo arrives, she'll see no one will ever take her place."

"Really?" Rebel demanded, still outraged at the baby's name. "You named me *Rebel*, but somehow I'm special? If that was the case, you would've named *me* Josephine after Big Joe."

"Rebel—"

"Shut the fuck up, Megan," Daddy ordered. "You ain't explainin' yourself to no lil' kid, *especially* one of our lil' motherfuckers. Get to your fuckin' room, Rebel."

She jumped to her feet, forgetting Gunner hovered near her and knocking him over. "I hate you and your stupid baby, Mother. I want you *and* her to fucking die. Today! Now! The world would be a better place without you and her. *Die!* I hate all of you!" she screamed, fed up. "How can you be happy when my life is destroyed and I'm so emotional?"

Gunner wailed bloody murder.

"Fuck your motherfuckin' emotions," Daddy said, stalking toward her.

Yelping in fear, Rebel dodged him.

"Christopher!" Momma called in her stupid sad voice. Fucking weak cunt. "L-leave her alone," she said, on the verge of tears.

Throwing her a look that promised murder, Daddy picked up Gunner and kissed his cheek. "S'okay, boy," he said gruffly, ruffling his fingers through Gunner's dark hair.

Rebel burst into tears, wanting comfort and understanding. "No one cares what seeing Tabitha and Diesel at the club did to me."

"We don't," Ryder agreed with a nod. "We just think you're fucking stupid."

"And a weirdo," Ransom added.

Axel stood between Ryder and Ransom, nodding in agreement. He was on the quiet side. Unlike Rule, an introvert at his core, *Axel* was a sneaky little motherfucker who listened to gather information for his own miserable use.

"Enough, boys," Megan said sternly, her skin red and splotchy in some places but chalk white in others.

Rule rushed to Rebel and tried to take her into his arms.

She pushed him. "Fuck off!"

Megan took Rule's place. Rebel had just enough self-preservation to not shove her away.

"Rebel," Megan said softly, taking Rebel's face between her hands.

Rebel recoiled. "I'm not listening to you."

"It's okay, love," she soothed. "You're hurting and emotional, but it doesn't last. One day, you'll look back on this time and realize it wasn't the end of the world. When you meet Jo, you'll love her and appreciate the infusion of estrogen."

"*Never*!" Rebel sobbed. "She's already taking you away. You already love her more."

Ignoring Rebel's anger, Megan embraced her. The feel of the baby bump made Rebel cry harder.

"When I was carrying you, there was so much going on, Rebel," Megan explained. "Naming you Josephine didn't seem a possibility. It didn't cross my mind," she amended. "There was a lot of animosity for Big Joe." Stepping back, she thumbed away Rebel's tears. "Now, there isn't."

Sniffling, Rebel swiped at her cheeks with the backs of her hands. For the first time in weeks, she appreciated Momma's mothering.

"Tabitha told me she's been off her birth control and might be pregnant with Diesel's baby," she cried miserably, her thoughts all jumbled.

Momma scowled and hugged Rebel again. This time, she returned her mother's embrace, leaned down, and rested her head on her shoulder.

"God, I wish she would shut up sometimes," Momma snapped.

"Ima talk to Diesel and tell him to shut his bitch the fuck up, baby. Ain't no reason for her to constantly fuck with my girl."

"Do it as soon as possible," Momma said, sounding suddenly so tired. She tightened her hold on Rebel.

Then, without warning, she went limp.

Rebel had never seen so much blood or her mother so pale. She'd never heard CJ and Daddy scream and yell in distress, or the rest of her brothers cry in fear.

Daddy had shoved Gunner to Rule and rushed to Momma, taking her lifeless body from Rebel's grasp. He turned and ran, not thinking just acting.

The trail of blood had horrified Rebel and she hollered, allowing CJ to jerk her behind their parents. She stumbled, her hate and anger burning away like mist in the sun.

"Go, CJ," she said, jerking away from him so she wouldn't slow him down. "C-Call Aunt Zoann. She'll know what to do."

"Webel!" Gunner wailed, blocking her with his small body and wrapping his arms around her legs.

"Rebel, is Mom okay?" Ryder asked, blond and blue-eyed in a sea of black-haired, green-eyed mini-Outlaws.

As she lifted Gunner, Rule, Ryder, and Ransom looked at her for guidance. She only wanted her mother.

"What if Mom dies?" Ransom asked, his voice trembling.

Tightening her hold on Gunner, Rebel shook, not protesting when her twin plucked the baby out of her arms.

"She won't," Rule reassured, his confident words contrasting against his shaky voice. "God won't let that happen."

Even in a time like this, he was able to hold onto his faith. Right now, Rebel envied his trust in the divine.

"I'll call Lolly," she said around tears. Her treatment of her mother over the past few weeks suddenly shamed her and she stumbled forward.

What if she did die? Rebel had been so awful to her mother, and she'd pass away thinking her only daughter despised her for something she couldn't control.

Now, hours later, Rebel sat apart from everyone else. They were in a private waiting room at Hortensia General. All her aunts and uncles, Diesel, other club members and their old ladies were there, as well as Lolly and Pop were. She and her brothers were the only kids there. Rule looked after Gunner, not far from her, while the other boys huddled around CJ and Diesel near Daddy.

Since Diesel's rejection and discovering Momma's pregnancy, Rebel had alienated almost everyone either through word or deed. She was *persona non grata*. Her actions warranted the treatment. As long as Momma was okay, Rebel no longer cared about the gender of the new baby. To atone for her actions, she'd spoil her baby sister, she as her family had down with her.

"Reb?" Rule called in a harsh whisper, looming above her. Gunner slept on his shoulder. "The doctor's here."

Nodding, Rebel stood and trudged closer to where everyone else gathered, listening as they got the update.

"Mrs. Caldwell's lost a lot of blood, Mr. Caldwell," the ER doctor said. "Her blood pressure is dangerously low, but for the moment she's stable. *If* she lives through the next critical twenty-four hours, we'll count it as a miracle."

The doctor started to turn, yet Rebel wanted to know about Jo, since he hadn't mentioned her. "What about my little sister?" she cried.

"Oh, baby," Lolly said tearfully, hurrying to her and wrapping her arms around her.

"Jo ain't survivin', Rebel." At Daddy's cold voice, Rebel's heart dropped, and a new bout of tears formed. "You got your motherfuckin' wish."

She regretted every mean word and each sneer whenever Momma tried to bridge their split. Rebel couldn't make it up to her little sister and might never get the chance to correct her bad behavior toward her, *their*, mother. "I'm sorry, Daddy," she sobbed. "I'm so sorry. I didn't mean—"

Her father, the man who'd protected her and spoiled her and loved her, looked at her with hatred. "Shut your motherfuckin' mouth. Too fuckin' late for fuckin' apologies. If your Ma was still home, tryna appease you, you woulda been still actin' like a fuckin' cunt. Now, Jo gone and I might lose my Megan..." His voice cracked and Rebel almost fell to her knees at the stark pain in his watering eyes. He shoved his hands in his pockets. "I got busy with club shit and was rushin' out for a week or so. She fuckin' *swore* she'd remember her birth control. She swore to me, Rebel," he said softly, tears sliding down his cheeks.

She started toward him, and he snapped back to the present.

His wintry glare returned, and he held his hand up. "You a child. *My* child, but you ain't fuckin' stupid. You knew what the fuck you was sayin' and doin' to your Ma. And you fuckin' did it anyfuckinway, refusin' to listen. Your Aunt Kendall tried talkin' sense into you. Roxanne. Your Uncle Mort. CJ. *Me.*"

"Daddy, please—"

"No! *SHUT THE FUCK UP!*" he screamed, wildness creeping into his eyes. "You fuckin' sorry now cuz we ain't gettin' Jo back. She fuckin' gone, Rebel. And, maybe, she so pissed at you for stressin' out her Ma, she takin' Megan with her so you can't have her no more."

Her shoulders shaking, Rebel fell to her knees, wailing out her grief and misery. Lolly rushed to her and dropped next to Rebel, drawing her into her arms and hugging her tightly.

"Tell him, Lolly! Tell him I love him and Momma. Tell him I'm sorry. Please." She felt as hysterical as she sounded. "Please," she wept. "Please tell him not to hate me."

"Ain't hatin' on you, Rebel," Daddy said in a tired, devastated tone that compounded her heartache. "I just ain't feelin' fuck-all for you."

Lolly threaded her fingers through Rebel's hair as her father stomped away. "Your daddy's in pain right now," she whispered.

They all were. Because of Rebel's selfish stupidity, everyone near and dear to her was hurting.

"I'm sorry," she blubbered, the force of her sobs making her entire body tremble.

"I know, sugar," Lolly murmured, kissing her temple. "But that might not be enough."

Rebel cried so hard, she hiccupped. Lolly never pulled punches, but the truth was too painful for Rebel to bear right now.

Lolly's arms stayed wrapped around Rebel as she cried, but she might as well be alone. She felt numb, her father's rejection crushing her soul.

Death had claimed her little sister and was knocking on her mother's door. Daddy blamed her. If Momma somehow survived, she'd probably hold her responsible too.

And if Momma died…?

Rebel shivered. She would forever be without the love of her father. If only she could go back in time and fix her mistakes, take back all the ugly words she said to her parents.

They'd given her the world, and in return, she caused them nothing but pain. Now, this. The unthinkable. She didn't know how to make it right.

Regrets overwhelming her, she was once again overtaken by wrenching sobs and all-consuming grief.

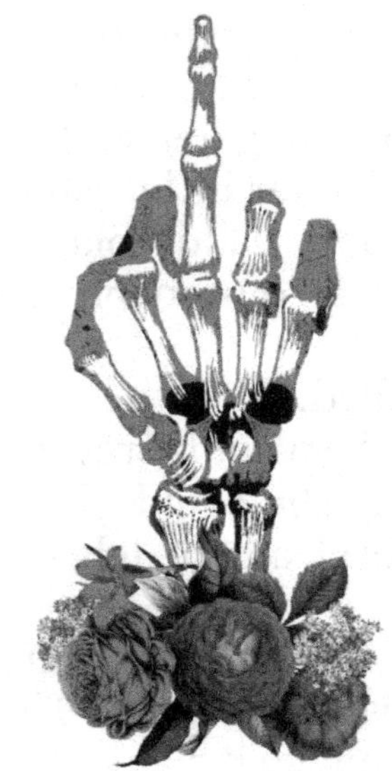

Author s Note

Reckless has been a long time coming. Months. *Years*.

Perhaps, that it why it grew to nearly 260,000 words.

As soon as I realized I would indeed continue the Death Dwellers with a Legacy Generation, I began working on the bridge book. It was 2016 and Misfit had recently been released. As is usual with the Dweller Boys, other stories came about, so I began to push aside CJ's story and that of the other kids as they navigated being the children of notorious bikers and high school students.

In the original series, Logan Donovan was a cruel man who hated everyone and everything. There wasn't much to love about him. I wanted to build upon that hallmark because the origins of the club and the men involved in its beginnings. However, the world changed so drastically, I stepped back from the first storyline for

Reckless between Ryan and Willard. There are seeds sprinkled here and there but I pulled back from the hardcore philosophies that Ryan was developing thanks to Willard, which initially was fostered by men like Logan and Rack.

Over the course of writing Reckless, it became apparent that this was a story that embodied *the sins of the father*. The club was the physical legacy left by Logan, Sharper, Cee Cee, Rack, Big Joe, and K-P, but the lies, cover-ups, and darkness permeated throughout the generations and reverberated from father to son to grandson and great-grandson.

To tell the complete story and move into the next generation, it became increasingly apparent that I had to break the bridge book into two books. Thus, Ruthless was born.

Luckily, it is almost completed and will be available soon.

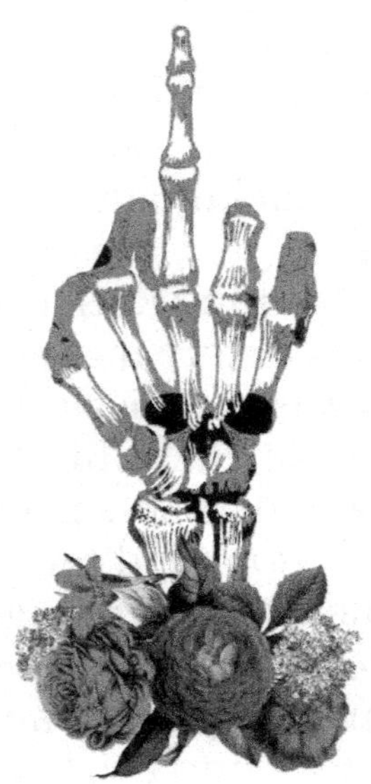

Playlist

O.PP. by Naughty by Nature
Ain't Trippin' by Too Short
Mo City Don by Z-RO
Tipsy by J-Kwon
Mind Playing Tricks on Me by Geto Boys
Where The Hood At by DMX
Chain by Jibbs
Nuthin' But a G-Thing by Dr. Dre (featuring Snoop Dog)
Mama Said Knock You Out by LL Cool J
Juicy by The Notorious BIG
It Was a Good Day by Ice Cube
Ms. Jackson by Outkast
Ambitionz of a Rider by Tupac
California Love by Tupac
Dear Momma by Tupac
All Eyez on Me by Tupac
Player's Anthem by Notorious BIG

Il Na Na by Foxy Brown
Doowap That Thing by Lauryn Hill
Monster by Kanye West
Hard Knock Life by Jay-Z
Can I Get A... by Jay-Z
Drag Rap by the Show Boys
Boom Boom by John Lee Hooker
Gangsta's Paradise by Coolio
Mary Jane by Rick James
In da Club by 50 Cent
Pony by Ginuwine
Let's Get It On by Marvin Gaye
Heard It Through the Grapevine by Marvin Gaye
I Wanna Be Your Man by Roger
Lean on Me by Bill Withers
Tops Drop by Fat Pat
Insane in the Brain by Cypress Hill
No Hands by Waka Flocka Flame
My Blicky by Fresh X Reckless
Who Want Smoke by Nardo Wick
WAP by Cardi B featuring Megan Thee Stallion
Boss Ass Bitch by Nikki Minaj
Gentleman by Psy
Hot Boyz by Missy Elliot
Back in Blood by Pooh Shiesty

Dance Now by J.I.D. & Kenny Mason
Anxiety by Megan Thee Stallion
Automobooty by NLE Chopper, Lola Brooks
Not Nice by Megan Thee Stallion
Love The Way You Lie by Eminem featuring Rihanna
Beating Down The Block by Monaleo
Players by Coi Leray
Rage by Rico Nasty

RECKLESS The Legacy Begins

Wobble by V.I.C.
Pussy Control by Prince
Sad Girls Love Money by Amaarae
Princess Diana by Ice Spice
Hot Shit by Cardi B
Thique by Beyonce
Betty by Yung Gravy
Pressurelicious by Megan Thee Stallion
Can't Stop Jigging by HD4President
Meet Me at Our Spot by The Anxiety, Willow and Tyler Cole

REBEL

Kill For Your Love by Labrinth
Mount Everest by Labrinth
River by Bishop Briggs
Never Tear Us Apart by Bishop Briggs
Chokehold by Sleep Token
Dream on by Aerosmith
Sugar by Sleep Token
Crazy by Gnarls Barkley
I Love Rock & Roll by Joan Jett and the Blackhearts
Hotel California by the Eagles
Teenagers by My Chemical Romance
Sex Metal Barnie by In This Moment
Not Strong Enough by Apocalyptica
Transparency by Willow
One by U2

MATILDA

Winter from Four Seasons by Vivaldi
Unaccompanied Cello Suite #1 in B Major Prelude by Bach
Air on a G String by Johann Sebastian Bach
Raindrop Prelude Op 28 by Frederic Chopin
Prelude a l'apres midi d'un faune by Claude deBussy
Hornpipe From Water Music Suite by Handel
Flight of the Bumblebee by Rimsky
William Tell, Overture by Rossini
Danse Macabre by Saint-Saens
The Trout by Franz Schubert
Marche Militaire by Franz Schubert
By the Beautiful Danube by Johann Strauss II
Aida, Grand March by Verdi
Trumpet Concerto by Joseph Haydn
O Eucharist by Hildegard Von Bingen
Opus 19 by Mendelssohn
Helundes Overture by Mendelssohn
Clarinet Concerto in A Major
Eine Kleine Nachtmusik by Mozart
Horn Concerto No 4 in E Flat Major by Linder
Canon in D by Johann Pachelbel
Clair de Lune by deBussy
Madama Butterfly by Puccini
Ava Maria by Schubert
The Prayer by Andrea Bocelli and Celine Dion
Hungarian Dances by Johannes Brahms

RORY

Little Bitty by Alan Jackson

Your Man by Josh Turner
Honkytonk Badonkadonk by Trace Adkins
Firecracker by Josh Turner
Why Don't We Just Dance by Josh Turner
A Boy Named Sue by Johnnie Cash
Ol' Red by Blake Shelton
God's Country by Blake Shelton
Crazy by Patsy Cline
Behind Closed Doors by Charlie Rich
Take Me Home Country Road by John Denver
Mercury Blues by Alan Jackson
Forever and Ever Amen by Randy Travis
Ode to Billy Joe by Bobbie Gentry
(Ghost) Riders in the Sky by Johnnie Cash
Convoy by C.W. McCall
Rhinestone Cowboy by Glen Campbell
I Hope You Dance by Lee Ann Womack
Stand By Your Man by Tammy Wynette
I Fall to Pieces by Patsy Cline
East Bound and Down by Jerry Reed
Love Will Turn You Around by Kenny Rogers
Highwayman by The Highwaymen
Elvira by the Oak Ridge Boys
Folsom Prison Blues by Johnnie Cash
Coward of the County by Kenny Rogers
The Gambler by Kenny Rogers
Mommas Don't Let Your Babies Grow Up to be Cowboys by Waylon Jennings and Willie Nelson
Bye Bye Love by the Everly Brothers
Coal Miner's Daughter by Loretta Lynn
Your Cheatin Heart by Hank Williams
Crazy Arms by Ray Price
Before He Cheats by Carrie Underwood
Harper Valley, PTA by Jeannie C. Riley
Kiss An Angel Good Morning by Charley Pride
Good Woman, Good Man by Bonnie Raitt
Honey, I'm Home by Shania Twain
Don't Come Home A-drinkin (With Lovin' on your Mind) by Loretta Lynn
You Don't Know Me by Ray Charles
Black Betty by Ram Jam
Sweet Home Alabama

Devil by Shinedown
Back in Black by AC/DC
Pour Some Sugar on Me by Def Leppard
Sweet Child of Mine by Guns N' Roses
Smells Like Teen Spirit by Nirvana
Creep by Radiohead
Knockin' On Heaven's Door by Guns N' Roses
Outcast by Shinedown
The Summoning by Sleep Token
Closer by Nine Inch Nails
Dragula by Rob Zombie
:iving Dead Girl by Rob Zombie
Molly by Mindless Self Indulgence
Pornstar Dancing by My Darkest Days

Connect with Kathryn C Kelly

Thank you for reading Reckless.
If you enjoyed it, please consider leaving a review at your point of purchase and on Goodreads. It means a lot to me to hear what you think.

Email: katkelwriter@outlook.com

Snail mail: 24200 Southwest Freeway, Suite 402, Box #353, Rosenberg, TX 77471

Death Dwellers MC

Kat C. Kelly

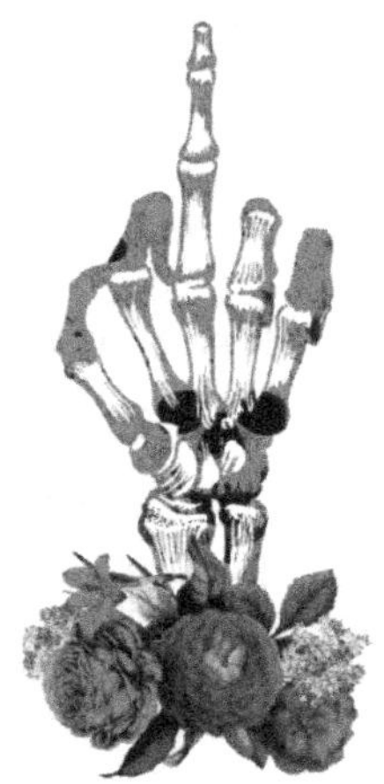

Bibliography

Cocky Hero Club
Savage Suit

Death Dwellers MC Legacy
Reckless
Ruthless

Death Dwellers MC
Misled
Misappropriate
Misunderstood
Misdeeds
Misbehavior
Misjudged
Misguided
Misalliance
Misconduct
A Very Christopher Christmas
Misfit
Mistrust
Misgivings
An Outlaw Valentine
Misrule
Death Dwellers: The Complete Set
Outlaw's Dictionary

Phoenix Rising Rock Band

Inferno
Incendiary
Scorched
Inflame

Dirty Boy Studios

Dirty Boy

Single Titles

Captivated
All My Tomorrows
The Enforcers' Revenge co-written with Emma James
Sexy Santa

Anthologies

Pink: Hot 'N Sexy for a cure: The Books for Boobies 2015 Anthology
When Clubs Collide
Desire Me
The Marriage Monologues – Forever A Dark Obsession Anthology
Sexy Santa – All I Want For Christmas Anthology
Red Stiletto – Call My Bluff Anthology Hazel & Grayson – Brothers
Grimm Fairytales: An Erotic Anthology
Barebacked – Game Player Anthology
Breakfast & Bedlam – Happily Ever After Anthology
Drifter's Vow: Red Rum MC – Vow of Protection Anthology
How Innocent My Love – Secrets of Me Anthology
Misconstrued - Forever His Ride Or Die Anthology
My One and Only – Goodbye Doesn't Mean Forever Anthology
Gods & Goddesses – Wicked Realms Anthology
Ignite - My Perfect Pleasure Anthology
Last Chance To Call You Mine
House of Secrets

Writing as Leslie Ferdinand

Wicked Allure
Picture Perfect
Forty Minutes to Disaster - Down In The Dirt Magazine

Writing as Christine Holden (Mother-Daughter Team Shirley Ferdinand and Leslie Ferdinand)
A Time For Us
Patterns of Love
Bedazzled

Kathryn C. Kelly

A Hitch In Time
Dearest Beloved
Een toegewijde dienaar - Dearest Beloved - Audax Publishing Amsterdam

Kindle Vella

Urchin of the Court
Ace of Spades - Red Rum MC

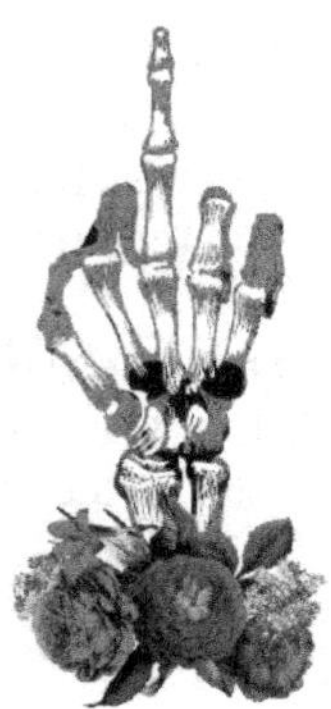

About Kathryn C Kelly

Kathryn C. Kelly is a New Orleans native who has called southeast Texas home since 2005. She had intended to travel the world but always return to her beloved New Orleans. Hurricane Katrina had other plans. She is the mother of three beautiful daughters and the daughter of one gorgeous mother whose footsteps she followed in by becoming a writer.

Kathryn is the former owner and editor of Inside Rose Rich Magazine. She and her mother have been published by Jove Books as Christine Holden. The books have long been out of print but they got the rights back to the five novels and have plans to re-release them soon.

Kathryn is a cancer survivor. In 2010, she felt a small lump in her breast. In 2015, at the urging of her mother, she went in for her bi-yearly mammogram and was diagnosed with Stage 2b/3a HER2 positive breast cancer. On November 30, 2016, she rang the bell. During her treatment, she was also diagnosed with Li-Fraumeni Syndrome.

In 2013, Christopher "Outlaw" Caldwell introduced himself to Kat in the most cliché way *ever*. He came to her in a dream. After the inauspicious meeting, he planted himself in her mind and the motherf...*the gentleman* hasn't left yet. In what was only supposed to be one book about the fictitious Death Dwellers MC, Outlaw has become a source of amusement, a well of frustration, and a bone of contention between Kat and one of her daughters.

She is hard at work on Reckless, the book that will bridge the OGs with a new generation of Death Dwellers. Her work has been included in several anthologies and she is looking forward to other upcoming single title releases, including Savage Suit from the Cocky Hero Club World created by Vi Keeland and Penelope Ward. She is a former RWA member. She also served as Vice President for the SOLA chapter of RWA.

She is a New Orleans Saints fan, but roots for the Texans, the Rockets, and the Coogs (U of H) as long as they aren't playing any Louisiana teams. She loves champagne and sparkling wine. One day, she will try Snoop's brand. She still loves Chivas Regal but had a chance to taste Sassenach Scotch. A #lifegoal is to one day buy herself an entire bottle and keep it all for herself.

In her head, she is a biker babe with a Harley in her garage, waiting for her to hit the road. In reality, she has yet to hop on a bike and ride. She loves Cards Against Humanity, has very strong opinions that she keeps to herself, has to take her time to talk in public so nothing untoward pops out, and always strives to see the best in people and in life.

Made in the USA
Middletown, DE
25 September 2023